Howard O.A. Jones

EDAFOS
DIVINE WIND

EDAFOS

Divine Wind

Howard O.A. Jones

ARPress
ILLUMINATING IDEAS
EMPOWERING VOICES

ARPress
45 Dan Road Suite 36
Canton MA 02021
Hotline: 1(800) 220-7660
Fax: 1(855) 752-6001

Ordering Information:
Quantity sales. Special discounts are available on quantity purchases by corporations, associations, and others. For details, contact the publisher at the address above.

Printed in the United States of America.

Library of Congress Control Number
ISBN-13:   Paperback   979-8-89389-051-8
                eBook   979-8-89389-052-5

Rev. date: 4/3/2019

Edafos was a land divided into many continents, much like our own, filled with many different people, cultures and races. But just as our world was formed by war, so is that of Edafos. The Divines, god-like beings, forged the continents and oceans by their sheer destructive powers called soul, and the few who could create life made sentient beings to aid them in their war, giving them the capacity for just as much power. It was after this war had ended that civilizations truly began to rise. Balheim was the Kingdom of the Nords. Deneaux was the Kingdom of the Deneauxmen, previously slaves who had broken free of the Nords. Den Hall was created by the peaceful beastmen, and Keels by the Elves.

The creation of Deneaux began and ended with the 300 Year War. With this, Deneaux's power was solidified through the realm of Cardia, its continent, and peace was made all throughout its Northern half.

This peace would soon be shattered though. The Nords were not so complacent as to let their slaves go. Their Divines saw it fit that they should continue to conquer, and it was so. The Divines have once again began to move their hands across the realm. To them, it is but a game of chess, but to those living as pawns, life had just become a new hell.

Strangely enough, one pawn no longer decided to play by the rules. He was a young Nord, or Raider, as they were commonly called, growing up in Raider territory. He was to be a soldier to lead the charge and burn to Deneauxic banners like any other respectable Raider. But he was different. His path would be to challenge the Divines, amassing allies to stand with him, for he was not bound by the laws of the people or higher powers. He would act on instinct and faith, for that made a true hero...

A Shattered Home

The city of Denhoec was little more than a large port town. The houses just about ringed around the harbour and went back from there all about the shoreline. They were little more than wooden buildings one to three stories high and were capped with snow.

Jorigsveer rushed over to the upstairs window of the wooden cabin he resided in at the sound of commotion.

"You will never amount to anything woman! You hear me? Nothing!" roared a deep voice.

It was Jor's father, a thick, bearded man with a bad temper.

Jor's mother was curled into a ball near a chair in tears, hoping he wouldn't come inside—and this time, Jor wouldn't take it.

"Then prove it you beast!" he shouted as he threw the door open. The crowd nearby grew larger as they waited greedily for a challenge to be issued.

"How dare you raise your voice at me boy!"

"How dare *you* raise your voice at me, *boy*!" repeated Jor in a more insulting manner.

"Do not play with me, I am the father and you are the son! Now move so I can get back at that...that...dog you call a mother."

The blow made his father's ears ring, and he felt something going down the side of his face. He understood well the situation, and struggled with his sense of direction as another blow sent him into a stack of barrels.

He quickly hopped to his feet. Some of his friends shouted for him to get up and fight instead of being defeated by his own child.

Jor came in for another hit, but his father's arms were longer, and his fists blasted Jor back to his doorstep.

His mother franticly ran outside and urged him to stop. She attempted to wipe away the blood on his head.

"Mother, t-this man has been insulting you for years now, I cannot take it anymore!"

"It's okay Jor, I'm accustomed to it," she pleaded.

He got back on his feet and the exchange of blows continued brutally. Almost ten minutes passed and the men stood their ground.

Jor's father made a swing that was too heavy and lost his balance, and seizing the opportunity, Jor sent punishing heavy blows.

Someone from the crowd threw in a whip for the father, most likely one of his tavern gang.

He picked it up, and cracked it in the air, echoing the sound across the town. It slashed at Jor's body, and the sting was weakening in his wounded state.

"You won't win," Jor managed to say as he struggled to stay on his feet.

Something began to steal away his breath, and laughter came from his father and the crowd. The whip was wrapped around his neck to the amusement of many—including his brothers.

A broadsword was next to fall into the ring.

His father smiled as he saw this, and moved for it greedily.

It was Jor's only chance.

He grabbed it first and cut the whip, and with the same clean swing he slashed his father's clothes.

They stood at odds, covered in blood that dripped and mixed into the snow. Now that Jor felt he had better power over the situation, his senses were back and the world was beginning to become clear. "Don't come back," he said in a low, menacing growl.

"If you strike me, I will never come back," his father replied with a smirk, taunting his son with the prospect of murder.

"I shall not strike down and unarmed man—no matter how vile."

His Father turned to the crowd. "See, he can't stop me. He knows that wench he calls a mother cannot support him, and neither will his brothers! Now watch!"

He turned for Jor with his armed raised, and then slapped him across his cheek. "See, he did nothing to…"

The sharp rod of iron shredded through his shoulder and he fell into the snow, crying out in pain.

"You should be happy I spared your life! I've stayed awake for nights trying to fight the thoughts of murdering you in your sleep or poisoning your morning meals! I didn't kill you because I am better than you," he snapped. "I let you live because you don't deserve to grace Fenalph's Hall. Now get your bloody hide to the nearest healers before I really change my mind!"

"Guards!" Cried his father. "This boy used a weapon in a barehanded duel with me!"

A guard looked greatly annoyed with him, and after putting on some gauntlets, he helped the poor man up. "Don't think for one damned second that I didn't see that whip in your hands Joral! I am no fool to your antics!"

"But that was a whip! He had a broadsword!"

"You used the whip to try to choke him to death; he used the broadsword to maim you, even though he could have killed you instead," he explained. "I personally would have killed you."

"This is not fair!"

"You're right Joral, which is why I'm banishing you from town for a month or two, just so you can get away from the boy's life,"

"Y-you can't do this!"

"I'm head guard," he said sternly. "And I could add a few more months to your banishment if you continue to question my authority."

Joral turned to the house and heaved out a mouthful of spit. "Curse you boy, I want you all to die!"

"I'm not the one who was defeated by his son," said Jor with a smirk as the crowd laughed along. "Now back to the forests where you belong, I-I have a new life to live." With that, he collapsed into the snow with a somewhat comfortable darkness surrounding him.

CHAPTER 2

A Warrior's World

Several weeks after the fight, Jor was back to his normal life in the city of Denhoec—which was once part of the city of Deneaux, but was lost during the worst parts of the 300 Year War. Living with his mother made things easier, but his brothers would sometimes pass and attempt to cause uproar. With help from his mother though, he was able to get away from their constant challenges.

One particular day, something changed.

There was a loud and somewhat rude knock on the door, but the two in the house ignored it. The knock was there again, but Jor's mother was cleaning.

"Son, could you get that?" she asked from upstairs as she swept.

He ran to the door, and opened it to what he hoped was another realm that would disappear if he slammed it and reopened it.

"Hello brother, we need a place to stay and we thought 'Why not at Mother's house?'" said Lok, the oldest brother. He had messy brown hair like Jor did, but had a sharper face and more of a sadistic air about him. He was dressed in furry clothes and had a round shield and spear at his back, as did the rest of the brothers.

"Hell. No." The door was slammed in their faces at that instant.

A spear pierced the strong timber used for the door and almost skewered Jor as he walked away. The rest of the door as pushed down as the fully armed warriors barged in.

"Hell no? You can't disrespect soldiers, it's against the law to not give us free housing," Lok said.

Jor felt surprisingly small against four of his older brothers. "S-Sorry, I had no idea you were—in the military," he amended.

"Hm, Horrin, should we punish our little brother here?" asked Lok.

Horrin was biggest in size out of all the brothers, and his hunger and gluttony is what forced him to leave the house.

"I say we leave him for now, wouldn't want him to die in his house," Horrin said with a nasty laugh.

"What he should do is fix us something to eat!" said Joralkar, the second oldest. He was the most muscular of the group, but still took orders easily from Lok, who was about the skinniest out of all the family.

Horrin slammed his short sword into the table; the same act any raider would put on to look tough, and who wouldn't fall for it considering his size. "Where is our food lady?" he growled.

"We seem to be out of spice weed," she replied quickly.

"Then get some!" ordered Skall, the smallest of the brothers, only able to beat Jor by height.

Jor's face was red with anger and his arm strayed to the knife rack.

"Jor please, I don't want you to be in prison," said his mother. "Or worse."

"Sorry mother, it is just not fair that they can go about ordering you around," he replied.

"I will live, now go get some spice weed before we both have to go to battle with these pigs," she said with a bit of humour.

"Hey, what you two talking about over there?" asked Horrin, annoyed.

"Just getting your spice," Jor replied. "Big fat pig," he remarked under his breath.

He ran up to his room and tied on his cloak, and then he threw his quiver and short bow over his shoulder. He carefully lifted his great sword and slung it across his free shoulder.

Going into the countryside required you to look like someone who would not be preyed on easily, and he knew the soldiers that stalked the countryside would think twice about a cloaked figure that looked like he could swing and slice and oak.

After a few minutes of walking along the coast and looking through the grasses, he figured something was wrong. *Why haven't I been forced to run away and hide from any of the sea raiders?* That would mean they would be occupied, but with what? Either way, he continued on his quest for his spice weed. He hopped through the bushes on the coast, but those horrible moments you look for something rare and won't find it and you look for something common and find the rare objects was occurring far too much for him.

"Damned spice!" he shouted out loud. "Where are you?"

"Help" someone yelled over the next ridge.

Jor ran further down the path to see two raiders standing in a charred ring on the ground, and by some horrible contradiction, there were pieces of sharp ice on the ground.

"What is this?" Jor said as he watched this strange scene.

"Help us!" the two raiders snapped, worn out from fighting.

Jor turned his attention to their adversary. It was a Perialite, a being that had the qualities of a human but the tail of a large lizard. This one was wearing a black, pointy hat like those of fairy-tale wizards. They were also dressed in dark blue robes and there was a bit of fire in their hands.

"Pyro Katastrofi," they said with a surprisingly high pitched voice.

The raiders cowered behind their shields as a burst of flames licked at them.

Seeing that they weren't in any real danger, Jor ventured to ask questions.

"How'd you end up like this?"

"We—thought that they would have some valuable things on them... you know how those divine users have valuable things," one Raider said. "Now help us!"

"Pyro Ekriksi!" said the perialite again in the strange language. A fireball flew towards one of the raiders and threw him into the dust. His burning shield rolled next to him and fell to the side.

"So you were robbing them?" asked Jor, his voice rising.

"So what, we do what we want boy!" the sea raider snapped back. "If you help us take her own, you'll get half of whatever we get," he said quickly.

The perialite's hat seemed to rise a bit as they seemed to look up. From the corner of their eye, a raider charged with his shield ready and sword high.

Jor almost dropped his bow as he pulled it off his shoulder. His hand reached by his back for and arrow, but as the other raider got up and came towards him, his hand moved to his other shoulder and effortlessly drew the great sword he carried after dropping the bow.

The raider stopped cold, but then returned to his charge. *How hard could it be to stop this boy and his heavy sword?*

The raider readied an overhand slash, but Jor held his sword over his head horizontally and crashed into the large raider's unbalanced body.

As the other raider rushed to the perialite, they held their hand above their head to imitate Jor's horizontal block.

"Makhaira!" they said as a white blade formed and fitted to their grip.

The raider's strike weakened as he saw this spectacle, but the perialite wasn't done yet.

"Pyro Ekriksi!" they shouted with a slight echo. A jet of flames came from their mouth as if they were a dragon, burning away at the raider.

Jor held his sword with the point facing the raider's neck for a killing blow when he heard the horrible shriek.

The raider who was attacking the perialite was grabbing on to his face and screaming in a horrifying way. He tripped and fell back on the ground and squirmed around in pain.

The perialite hardly gave any emotion as they lifted their open palm to the raider.

"Pyras Ekriksi!"

The ball of fire, now certainly bigger, struck the raider and his shrieks came to an end as the burnt corpse lay crumpled over.

Jor watched in horror as the man was incinerated. This was a mistake.

The raider grabbed Jor's leg and tripped him, raising his blade for a killing blow.

"Pagos!"

Blood fell on Jor's face as an icicle came through the man's chest. He fell back in the sand and dust and glanced angrily at the perialite's face, then fell back fully, his eyes on the sky.

"Are you okay?" asked Jor cautiously.

The perialite fell to the ground out of what could look like fatigue.

Jor ran over and turned them over. "Sir?"

He couldn't believe what he saw next. This warrior, only using divine power, was in fact a girl, almost around his age.

He sheathed his great sword and slung his bow over his shoulder. He then proceeded to lift the girl in his arms. "Forget the spice weed; we need to get you to safety."

"Mother, Lok! Open the door!" he shouted from outside.

"Have you the spice weed?" asked Horrin.

"Something far more important!" he snapped back.

"Can't be more important than my food," Horrin replied, steadfast.

"Open the damn door!"

"You can't talk to your brothers like that!" Lok said with amusement.

"Sorry," Jor said, trying to sound meek. "You know well I wouldn't talk to you like that. Please open the door, it's an emergency."

Joralkar opened the door and was surprised by the blood on his face, and even more by the humanoid in his arms.

"So what happened boy?" asked Lok angrily.

Jor had known this question would come, so he decided to say that he would replace the raiders with highwaymen and tell the story exactly. He knew well what would happen if he said he killed his brother's comrades.

"It seemed that she helped me fight off some robbers, she used too much of her divine powers, I assume, and fainted from fatigue."

"And how can you prove she isn't a witch?" asked Skall.

"When she wakes up we will deal with it."

"When she wakes up she will probably kill us," said Joralkar.

Jor learned that compliments on his brothers' strength always got him out of situations. "You could easily deal with her; I mean she only let off two attacks before fainting, what could she do in this state now?"

"Okay then, we'll let this go until she awakes," said Lok with his hand on his head, annoyed. "If anything goes wrong, I'm having you two hanged."

The brothers went up to their respective rooms and left Jor and his mother alone in the kitchen downstairs.

"Do you think she can speak our language? Jor asked.

"Maybe. Didn't you hear her say anything back there?" his mother questioned

"Only those strange words she said before an attack."

"Then we have our prayers to look to," she said as she put her hand on Jor's shoulder. "She better be able to thank you for your help though," she joked. Jor didn't share her jolly mood.

"I suppose," he said, unsure of the near future.

CHAPTER 3

The Souls and Divines

The room was too bright for her as she opened her eyes. She sat in the bed and looked about as she tried to get a grasp of her surroundings. She almost screamed as she saw the nearby figure move a bit.

Jor sat on a chair sleeping upright. "How long was this guy here for?" she thought.

She realized he had awakened and he almost fell to the ground as he saw her staring dead at him.

"Up I see," he said, rubbing his head and yawning.

"Who are you?" she asked quickly.

"I am Jorigsveer Great-Blade," he replied proudly, if not a bit lazily. "Who are you?"

She hesitated, and seeing no danger, she spoke. "Jane Pagos."

"Those kinds of names are strange around here."

"I know. What I want to know is why you are asking so many questions?" She looked down. "I don't mean to be so rude, it's just getting uncomfortable."

"Sorry, I'm just curious as to your powers and how you are...different. Not every day I see a person who isn't a human."

She turned her head to hide her glowing cheeks. "You think I'm different?"

"I do," he replied, once again yawning. "But you should get out of bed; my mother is getting food ready."

As Jor and Jane, still dressed in her robes, went downstairs, every one of his brothers' hands went to his blade.

"Ah, your awake milady," said Jor's mother, stirring a steaming pot.

Now that Jane was on the ground standing level with the others, she was quite small in size, to be exact, she was below Jor's shoulder.

"I guess I am." She smelled the stew that was being made for breakfast, and opened the pouch on her robes. "Spice weed would make this much better."

"So you had all of the spice weeds the whole time?!" exclaimed Jor and the others."

"I'm sorry, you needed any?" she replied with a questioning look.

Horrin slammed his dagger in the table. "So it's your fault I had tasteless stew yesterday!" he shouted, enraged.

"Lok, do something!" Jor pleaded.

"Don't give me orders boy. People need to live with consequences," Lok replied as calmly as ever.

Horrin raised his fist and aimed low to make sure he could hit the undersized target.

"Apsis!" shouted Jane with the familiar echo as a full white shield stopped Horrin's attack. Jane easily showed that she was running out of energy fast. She was already panting.

Jor grabbed her hand and they ran outside. They dashed across the street and between alleys until they made their way to the docks.

"Jorigsveer," she said out of breath. "Did we really have to go all the way out here?"

"Seeing that Horrin is mad about his lunch, we may have to stay away from the house for the day," he replied, also panting.

Jane took off her hat and used it to fan herself. Jor realized how good she actually looked. She had black hair that was braided down her back to where her tail started. Apparently her race might not believe in cutting hair. She had bright blue eyes that Jor wouldn't mind stealing looks into. Her skin was clearer compared to many of the women in Denhoec. She probably lived in the warmer parts of the world.

"Now what are you looking at?" she asked boldly.

"N-Nothing, I'm not looking at anything," he replied quickly.

"Are you insulting me now?"

"No, no. I'm just..." he stopped himself, looking around.

Several sailors turned to look back at the strange girl in the middle of the dock. She paid them no mind and put back on her hat.

"Now why would you do that for?" Jor asked, his face turning red.

"Do what now?"

"Hide all that beautiful hair," he said quickly.

"I don't care how much people look. I won't be here for long anyways. My mind is on getting away from that accursed tower and living life in a new city."

"Well Denhoec is halfway across the continent. I don't know if you can go any further than that," Jor began before he was cut off.

"Yes!" she shouted. "Free at last!"

Several people stared at her for her outburst, but frankly, she didn't care.

"Jorigsveer, where do you go to relax or have fun?" she asked in a completely different mood.

He noticed how much prettier she looked when she was happy, and almost blushed when he saw her holding both his hands. He noted that perialites must have a seriously one-track mind.

"I usually go home for that, but if not, I sometimes go to the coves," he said, shaking himself out of his enthralled state.

"Then let's go there!" she commanded as he followed.

The beach had had bit of the Northern gloom to it; dark, cold and depressing.

"You have fun here?" Jane asked dully. "I've honestly never seen grey water and that is something I can go without."

Jor pointed to some large piled rocks in the distance. "I failed to mention that the cove is a bit more of an underground spring. I discovered it some years back and no one seems to know of it."

Jane's eyes brightened as she saw the large pool of underground water.

"How could you be the only one to know about this place?" she asked, starry eyed.

"Well you know about it don't you?" he said, a bit confused at her statement.

Jane began to disrobe, but Jor looked away.

"What strange perialite custom is it that you are doing?" he asked, putting up his hands.

"What? I can't go in with my robes, they'll obviously get wet."

"Don't you have spells for that?"

"I don't use spells, I use soul energy," she replied forcefully.

"So you plan to go in naked?"

"Are you Nord people simple? I'm wearing a damned bathing suit!"

Jor looked at her blankly.

"The people in Crill thought up of them. They're clothes women wear to go in the water," she explained

Jor continued to watch her with a blank expression, and she shook her head and continued.

"How did I end up in this country?" she asked under her breath.

Jor turned away for a while, and his mind began to ponder on how his mother was doing. *No way am I going back to that building while that hog Horrin is about. I hope mother is alright though.*

Jane tapped him on the back and startled him. As he turned, he was amazed.

"I suppose perialites like walking about in their underwear?" he asked, blushing all over.

Jor took off his shirt and pants then dove in in his shorts. Jane followed.

"Have you ever been outside of Denhoec?" Jane asked him.

"Nope. I've been on trips with my father up and down the coast for raiding, but that's it."

"So you plan to stay here your entire life?" Jane asked in surprise.

"I don't know much about the outside world really. Maybe I could go with you if you plan on leaving. Me, you and my mother."

"You seem to be catching the bad side of hell in your house. Don't you have any friends?" Jane questioned now with a bit of concern.

"My brothers and father drove them away," Jor replied blankly. "All I have are you and my mother."

"I know how you feel. I left a lot of friends back at the tower," Jane said with apparent sadness in her voice.

"Which tower?"

"From the 300 year war, when Wintella and her followers destroyed 5,000 raiders," she said. "You know, from the stories."

Jor laid back and looked up, though his eyes seemed to be looking at something farther away than the ceiling.

"I'm glad I met you Jorigsveer," she said with a smile.

"Yeah, I'm glad I met you too," he replied equally.

Chapter 4

Palace Shatter

Jor rolled out his bed the next day to help prepare for the "Kings" of the house. Before he left the room, Jane stopped him.

"I suppose you don't brush your hair then," she said with her hands on her hips.

"I don't plan on leaving the house today so it doesn't matter much," Jor replied groggily.

Jane grabbed his head, and with surprising strength, pulled him down and began brushing.

"You just want to touch my hair don't you?" joked Jor, though he cringed with each brush.

"If you don't plan on cutting it, you may want it to look good at least."

She let go and let him get up. "Now you're ready for the morning," Jane said with her usual bright smile.

Jor smiled along. *At least she cares, though it would be better if she cared a little less.*

As the two went downstairs, the brothers and a few others had their weapons drawn.

"Hello brother, it seemed that you left out some detail about your little spice weed hunt," said Lok, testing the grip on his blade.

"I assure you, all you heard was true, except for my glory in battle, that was exaggerated," Jor replied.

"You can't trick me today; I know what the little lizard girl did."

"Then what did she do? No, what did we do?" Jor asked, confronting him.

"You murdered two men of your country, and therefore, you must be punished as an enemy to the Jarl."

Several guards grabbed Jor and Jane and forced them into a wagon outside.

Their mother came outside in a mess of tears. "Please don't take him away; he still has a life to live!"

One of the soldiers turned to Lok and nodded, then picked up his heavy axe from the snow.

"Mother, you are to be executed for housing an enemy force," said Lok with a dead, emotionless stare.

The man raised his axe, but then bits of blood dripped into the snow.

Their mother had had a dagger in her dress, and knew well she couldn't go down without a fight. It went through a space in his chainmail and into his chest. She turned to Jor.

"You should have had a better life, and I believe you helping the girl was a noble thing to do. If you are truly to be executed, make sure you die the warrior way. Like a Great-Blade," she said, holding the bloody knife. "No matter what, I'll be proud..."

Three more axes curved down from the air, and it was over. She took a step forward, the axes in her back, and fell.

"Finally rid of that weak woman," said Skall, though in a more depressed tone.

"You bastard Lok, I will kill you!" Jor shrieked fanatically. "You are no Great-Sword! You are nothing! You hear me? Nothing!"

Lok drew his blade and stepped forward to Jor, but Skall and Horrin held him back.

"We can't kill him! The Jarl will have your head if you do!" Joralkar warned.

As the wagon left town, the realization was beginning to set in to Jor that his mother was in fact dead. Along to coast, he saw once again the grey skies and seas, and he knew he couldn't die like this.

He wept silently but bitterly as they went. Jane could only put her hand on his shoulder.

Alda Breach-Breaker was a girl you could consider beautiful whether or not you were a raider. She had slightly dark skin and somewhat shiny long black hair. Her brown eyes stared blankly in the distance as she stood guard in the Palace Shatter main hall. She was outfitted with a large, round raider shield on her back, and crudely made plated chainmail. The owner of the castle thought it unfit for her to wear the open helmet that the raiders wore for it would hide her hair.

He disturbed her.

Whenever he would pass through, he would try to flirt, but she abused the one great power she had as a castle guard to keep him away. "I'm on guard duty my Jarl; I'm not allowed to speak." And when he left, she would laugh inwardly at him.

Today though, he would be in the main hall for some kind of trial. She could care less though, as she assumed it would be some deserters or bandits, or anyone else who the Jarl doesn't find favour in.

"Bring in the prisoners!" exclaimed a guard.

Jor and Jane were pushed, rather fiercely, into the main hall, then they were forced to their knees before Jarl Akneel River-Rush.

"Now what have these children done?" asked the Jarl as his eyes widened. "Is this a joke?"

The Jarl's advisor took in a deep breath for the charges. "We have the acts of murder, and treason. We also have evading arrest, robbery, illegal use of weapons, illegal ownership of weapons, illegal hunting, use of divine power; mostly known as soul, for illegal purposes, the use of divine powers for murder and the refusal to house the land's raiders."

Jor's tears were spent on the way here, now there was only seething rage. "Lok you bastard! Show your sorry hide so I can shoot it like the worthless pig you are!" He shrieked.

"Look my Jarl, he slanders me and my unit," said Lok. "Isn't that an additional charge?"

"Slander? You dare speak of slander?! Who was it that laughed when that animal I was forced to call a father slandered my mother? Who hated everything mother tried to do to help and slandered her for it as well? Answer me then?!"

"He is obviously speaking from his fear of being caught like any adolescence."

"Why Lok? Why kill your own mother?" Jor said, his rage spent.

"Silence child! Lok is a trusted soldier and you refuse him? Your only brother? "Why" I ask you in turn," said the Jarl.

Jor's rage was now beginning to turn to the Jarl.

"Jor no, just stop for me at least," begged Jane.

He hung his head and waited for punishment.

This doesn't seem like the ordinary case, they should at least put some investigation to this. Alda let the thought linger, but knowing she had no power, she did as always and remained silent.

The Jarl took the giant, double-sided axe from the wall. "With the severity from the crimes and the act of murdering two of my soldiers, I sentence you to dea-"

"My Jarl, we are under attack!" interrupted a guard.

"What?! Who dares to attempt to take my throne?"

"I don't think they want you crown, money is the last thing they may want."

"Money makes the world go around. What else could they possibly want?"

"Our lives."

The door broke open, and a blood-crawling shriek gave way. A skeletal monster stood at the doorway, but there were no weapons in its hands.

"Keravnos Katastrofi!" it shouted with an echo.

Jane's eyes glowed with a white colour. "Jor, we have the cover of chaos, let's go," she said quickly.

Several guards rushed forward, but then a string of furious lightning shot out from the skeleton's bony hands, killing everyone who neared it.

"Pyro," said Jane with a quiet echo as she burned away the rope on her hands. She burned away those on Jor's hands also.

"Oh no you don't!" exclaimed the Jarl as he stood with the axe still in his hands.

"Soul technique: Pagos cloud!" shrieked the monster with a dry voice.

"I'll deal with you two later, the bag of bones is mines," growled the Jarl. He rushed forward with the heavy weapon in hand, only to be killed and covered by dead frost.

"This is where my skills come in handy," said Alda to herself. She pulled her shield off her back and strapped it on her left arm, then charged for the skeleton.

"Hydro Pagos Ekriksi!" it shouted. The small but deadly sharp icicle flew towards Alda, but it shattered against her half iron, half wood shield.

She dropped the ground, and with a swift swipe with her leg, she tripped the skeleton. She quickly rose up and turned her sword upside down in her hands to slam it down for the killing blow. "Remember, between the third and fifth rib," she said to herself. She stopped.

There was nothing between those ribs!

"Katastrofi!" the skeleton commanded.

Alda put up the shield in time for the blast to only knock her away. She smiled as she got back up. "I was always waiting for an enemy that would spike my bloodlust! Come at me skeleton!" she shouted with the smile of a hungry wolf.

"Makhaira, Apsis!" shouted the skeleton as a sword and shield formed in its hands.

Alda took a heavy overhand chop that staggered to skeleton, then she banged the pommel of her short sword on its skull, slightly shattering it.

The skeleton in turn took quick swings, but they didn't even nick her chainmail. It swung high and cut across her face, but in her state, it barely fazed her.

She banged her shield in its face once more and ran over by the body of the Jarl. She tore the axe from his dead, frozen hands and the horrible smile crept across her face once again. "Time to rest in peace!"

The skeleton put up its shield out of what could have been fear, bravery, or intense stupidity. The axe shattered it and split its skull as the rest of the bones fell to the main hall's bloody floor. Alda seemed to regain her correct state of thought as her eyes stopped shining and returned to its normal red.

Jane and Jor began to attempt to sneak away, but Alda slammed the axe into the stone floor. "You two shouldn't try escaping, it is against the rules."

"It was against the rules for my brothers to falsely charge me with crimes I didn't commit, but did that stop them?" Jor said, standing to face her.

The main hall shook from what could have sounded like an explosion.

"Where is the way out?" asked Jane.

"This way," Alda pointed with the axe.

The guards ran across the walls to either defend or escape the Castle Shatter. They fired bows and crossbows from the walls but to no success. The undead army kept their menacingly slow march to the castle.

"Katastrofi!" shouted one as the blast hit the outside of the main wall.

"Erebus Katastrofi!" shouted another. The part of the wall that held a mass of archers went up in a destructive blast. Dark energy still surged about the area after it hit.

The three ran through the halls of the castle until they felt another violent shake.

"Be careful," said Jane, her eyes glowing white once again. "That was a dark destruction attack that just hit; we could quite easily die from it."

"I don't care, I just want to get another fight underway," said Alda calmly.

"So docile for another raider beast," said Jor.

"How could you say something like that to me!" exclaimed Alda. She sounded as if her feelings were hurt.

"Oh, so now you're sensitive?" Jor snapped at her.

"Apsis!" shouted Jane as she held the soul shield high.

Several bricks fell from to ceiling of the halls.

"Let's stop arguing and go!" she said.

The group continued on their way with Jane putting up soul shields for the skeletal attacks.

CHAPTER 5

Legend of the Deadlands

The group made their way out to castle's back doors and ran into the hills for a better view. The results of the attack were devastating. The walls were crushed and left as rubble on the ground. The outside of the keep and main hall were filled with holes from the soul attacks. This scene meant that whoever wanted the country will not stop until every raider is dead.

"How do the dead walk?" asked Jor.

"Anyone who works in the arts of necromancy can easily bring up a few skeletons or zombies, but skeletons that can use soul and magic? This is totally uncalled for!" Jane replied.

"Okay, but when do we get to break more skulls?" Alda complained

"When we get around to killing the necromancer in question," Jor replied.

"Okay. But where do we find a necromancer?"

"If there was one around, I would have sensed them especially. This one is so powerful that they must be making them act from away," Jane replied.

"Then couldn't that be from anywhere?" asked Alda.

"Well, are there any large mass burial sites nearby?"

"The Deadlands to the North, but it is only known to me in stories, not in reality as far as I know," Jor replied.

"Then we shall head to the North," Jane said as she took point.

"No. I'm not going to a cemetery country," Alda said sternly.

"But weren't you the one who was itching for a fight?" Jor asked.

"I like fights that are somewhere near fair, going in there would most definitely *not* be fair."

"Well it's your country, I could just as easily leave for Deneaux and live there, but I want to help be a hero for once," said Jane. "But I guess if you have no honour, you have no honour."

"To the North then Perialite! I shall crush every minion of the undead for this land!"

Jor looked at Jane and smiled. "You westerners are something else."

The sun seemed to shine far more than it did in the hills than in Dawn Harbour. The sunlight, however, began to disseminate as they neared the Deadlands. The trees seemed scorched and there were old shattered weapons and armor on the ground. Siege machines also littered the landscape and almost complemented the ashy, pitch black soil.

As they walked further in, they saw the many stones and old swords used as quick grave markers in the heat of battle those days in the 300 Year War.

"When do we get to break things?" moaned Alda.

"When will you stop complaining about wanting to fight?" Jor replied, annoyed.

"When I get to fight!"

"Just walk ahead and keep quiet, we will reach whatever it is we are looking for."

They remained quiet for a few more steps, then Jane started up a new conversation.

"Who started the 300 Year War? I missed the lesson on it back home."

"The raiders, when they came off their boats in South Deneaux, or Ykoric Denhoec as you know it now. They basically made siege to our port, Dawn Harbour, and moved up and made siege to Palisade Castle, or Palace Shatter. From there they fought for 50 years to hold the border they created. They did the same up in Seaxfallen, and the great knights of the Pantheon wouldn't stand for it. They just went to war after that," said Jor. "I know at least that half of the story. It was really long."

"But what happened here? I mean there is a gap between two countries that were at one point together."

"This place was called Harmony or something. They say that the raiders pushed on to the peaceful people here, and when the people couldn't take it, they unleashed their soul energies with the help of a great Divine."

"You really believe in Divines and super powered mystics?" asked Alda mockingly.

"Jane is proof of the Divine power," Jor replied.

"Well, I believe in Soul, I'm still unsure though on the existence of any immortal all powerful beings," said Jane.

"So you believe that mortals could obliterate an entire country?" asked Jor.

"You did say they fought with soul, and that is very, very destructive," said Jane.

"Then we probably would have seen the great walls, castles, forts and hills that covered this area," Jor replied.

"Bah, how do you know that there were hills and castles here, were you there before the war?" asked Alda.

"I'm pretty sure there are books on the subject...if you can read them," Jane said.

Alda turned her head and pouted, defeated at the hands of illiteracy.

There was a giant, black gate ahead, with several thousand graves on the other side as far as the eye could see.

"Jor, this is as far as I go," Jane said, taking a step back.

"What, scared?" Alda taunted.

"Yes."

"You are the most powerful person here, why would you be scared of dead bones?" Jor asked.

"Soul is very dependent on courage and mental strength, I lose both near grave yards," Jane replied.

Jor tugged on her hand. "Just come on. We'll be fine."

"Besides, your boyfriend is right next to you," teased Alda.

Jane grumbled something and went on through the gate.

As they walked, Jane stayed close to Jor while Alda was a few feet behind.

"I bet you're going to hold hands next," she said.

A few stones fell out of place and something thin a white fell to the ground.

Jane inhaled sharply and latched onto Jor. He and Alda reached for their blades.

"Kill me! End this nightmare!" shrieked the skeleton.

"I was just about to do that," said Alda.

"Wait!" Jor exclaimed as he put up his hand. "What good would killing you do?"

"I was a warrior here in the Harmony," it said. When my wife, kids and brother were killed fighting the raiders, I swore I would kill them all. I don't know when I died, but I felt like I woke from a dream and I found myself as nothing more than bones. Please, if you kill me now, I may pass on!"

"Shouldn't have told me that story, now it is far harder to kill you," Jor said, pitying the poor soul.

"Then think about it as freeing me from this prison of bones."

"Oh just move Jor!" said Alda. She pushed him out the way and smashed the skeleton's skull.

A glowing, distorted image of a person floated above the bones and did what looked like a smile. "I suppose I can tell that you are a raider, the boy on the other hand is calmer, like those of Deneaux. Either way, I thank you for your help, may the great one smile upon you."

He faded.

Jor turned to Jane, who was pale with fright. "I suppose you won't let go of my arm?"

"N-n-n-not anytime soon," she replied.

As they walked, there was a thick fog; thicker than previously at least.

"It's the fog of war," said Alda quietly to herself.

"It's scary; that's what it is," Jane said. Her eyes flashed white, and Jor and Alda tensed when they saw this.

"Jane, your eyes!" Jor exclaimed.

"Yes, I wish I could close them," she replied.

Alda drew her blade with a half spin follow up. Sparks flew from inside the thick fog.

"Jorigsveer, we seem to have fallen for an ambush!"

"I know that, who is ambushing us?!"

Several skeletons in heavy armor stepped out of the fog. Each on had a rusty, decomposing long sword.

"Heh, they don't have helms, just swing for their heads!" said Alda, ready for the battle she long awaited.

She made and overhead slash, but the skeleton avoided it—almost as if the sword faded through it. Jor drew his great sword and parried several attacks one-handed.

"Jane, off my hand! I can't swing this thing with one arm!" shouted Jor.

She seemed to be paralyzed by fear and didn't hear.

Jor jerked his hand free and blocked several more attacks.

Alda jabbed at the skeleton, but it dodged again and again. She changed her attack pattern and started to jab and slash, but the skeleton continued to nimbly dodge. From there she lost her temper.

"Feel the blood lust of a Breach-Breaker!" she roared as her eyes turned red. She began a lightning quick hack and slash motion with the Jarl's axe. The skeleton struggled to dodge, and now it began to parry and block also.

"Tachista!" exclaimed the bones. It began to move smoothly away from the axe swings, ducking and bobbing left to right.

One skeleton walked towards Jane, who stood as the only one not fighting. She turned to it and stumbled as she tried to run away. It held its blade to her neck and whispered in a strange language.

"Pagos Katastrofi!" she shrieked.

Everyone stopped fighting and turned to see an icy block with is spikes facing away from Jane. A perfect example of an ice destruction attack.

"Apo Pano Tachista!" she shouted next as she appeared before another skeleton within the blink of an eye. "Pagos Ekriksi!"

An ice spike shredded through the one's armor, then another, then another, until there were only lifeless bones about.

There was a light blue aura about Jane, and the ground around her was freezing over.

"I haven't gotten to the point of realising my ice Soul since my escape. Jor, let's get what needs to be done here finished so we can leave."

Alda and Jor's mouths were wide open and hanging.

"All that power and you're scared of grave yards?! You shouldn't even be scared if death walked up to you!" said Alda.

"I'm going to have to be careful with my energy now; I once started a small snow storm because I never held back," Jane said with a strange serenity.

"A small snow storm would give this place a nice new theme actually," Jor joked.

"Yeah, you'll have a nice view as an ice cube."

They continued the long walk through the ravaged country. Houses began to appear; skeletons also littered the streets. There was an especially small one before them.

"I guess everyone gets killed in these kinds of wars," remarked Jane as she pulled her hat over her eyes.

"Yes, I was quite sad when I figured out I died," said a voice of a child.

Jor looked up, not surprised to see another ghost. "I suppose you want us to help you pass on again?"

"I can't, everyone who died here is forever bound as energy, but I'm unable to cry, so that is good—right?"

"Energy? Why?" asked Jane, obviously intrigued on the subject of energy.

"Lady Mortha feeds on us to retain her immortality, and there are so many of us that there is a designated day for us to let her feed and to regain our energies."

"Why can't you just stop giving her energy?" asked Jor.

"Then we may be drained to the point of becoming a will-o'-the-wisp, but that hasn't happened to anyone yet."

A familiar being began to approach.

"Look, it's the soldier from before," Alda said.

"Seems my son was right, I am bound here," he said, rubbing the back of his head.

"Then we'll force that Mortha hag to free you!" Alda exclaimed. "Where is she?"

"A Divine cannot be slain, can she?" asked the boy.

"If she feels pain then we may have a chance at beating her," Jane said.

"Then let's hope she can bleed," Jor added.

"So where is this lady? I'm anxious for an opponent," Alda said as she cracked her knuckles.

"She resides in the Peace Hill manor," said the soldier.

"And take this," added the boy as he pulled a pitch black staff from the spinal cord of his skeleton. "Make sure Mortha remembers the name of Adele Alan."

The walk to peace hill strangely corresponded with its name, despite the fact that they were heading towards a hard fought battle.

The gate was also open.

"This is a trap in the making," Jane said.

"So, we are well good at falling for traps," Jor replied.

"I knew I should have stayed in Deneaux, much better guys, and it's safer," said Jane under her breath.

The inside of the building glowed with ectoplasm, and there were webs in every possible corner as if they were hand placed. Across the bottom of the hall were neatly placed skulls.

"Nice interior, I can almost feel the impending doom," Alda said sarcastically.

"Quiet, we don't want to attract any unnecessary attention," Jor said.

A faded green light was before them in the halls. It bounced about several times and went down another corridor.

Jane smiled. "Follow the light!" she said as she ran off.

"Stop Jane, you'll just lead us into another ambush!" exclaimed Jor as he ran to get her. Alda quietly followed.

They went through what seemed like endless halls and rooms until the entered a large dining room. The light went before the door at the other end and faded.

"This is it Jor," Jane said with a determined look.

"So what is the plan?" he asked.

"To rush in and smash everything?" Alda asked.

"We will ask her first, and then if push comes to shove, we will fight."

The group gasped as they opened the door to the throne room of the Divine Mortha. The ground had a blue glow to it, and ectoplasm dripped from the walls.

There at the throne was a woman with grey skin and black hair. She looked only slightly aged despite the fact that she was around before men walked Edafos.

"Oh Mortha the great Divine, as...pilgrims from other lands, we wish you to free the souls of the Men of Harmony," said Jane, attempting to sound more like a worshipper than an enemy.

"I should kill you where you stand girl. I am a deity, therefore I know everything that occurs in my realm, and now you wish to come here and insult my intelligence?!" she snapped at them.

"I did not know Lady Mortha," Jane replied quickly, putting up her hands.

"Just stop it! I already sense that you three are ready for a battle, and you'll get one! Soul Technique: Dead Flame!" she commanded.

An inferno of green fire blew towards them hotter than a live flame.

"Fos Hydro Hoplon!" Jane commanded in return. A wall of bright water rose before them and negated the effects of the attack.

There was a green spark around Mortha's body, and she stumbled.

It was the last thing she expected to feel. It was a feeling she had not felt since her last great battles.

Fear.

"Erebus Pyro Katastrofi!" she shrieked angrily. "Erebus Barrage!" "Sel Katastrofi!"

Jane's icy aura began to show. "Pagos Hoplon!" she shouted as a wall of thick ice rose before them. She swung around and held one hand out. "Sel Pagos Katastrofi!" "Fos Barrage!"

Mortha's dark spheres of energy were torn apart by the spheres of light thrown by Jane. A burst of pressure came as the two Katastrofi attacks clashed. Jane ducked behind the ice wall as the green flames hit it.

"Heh, I'm feeling a chill," Jor said with a smile at the corner of his mouth.

"That means I'm fighting with near full power," Jane said as the frost around her kicked up.

"Then let it snow," Alda shouted in encouragement.

"Come my skeletal horde, protect your queen!"

The door behind them swung open, and armed skeletons poured through.

"We'll take these Jane, focus on fighting Mortha!" Jor said as he drew his great sword.

"Now this is a battle!" Alda shouted as she wielded her axe and her eyes glowed red.

Jane and Mortha eyed each other; then a smile broke on Jane's face.

"Pagos Ekriksi!" she shouted as an ice spike flew towards Mortha.

She knocked it away with her hands, the raised hers. "Erebus Pyro Katastrofi!"

"Pagos Hoplon!"

"Erebus Katastrofi!"

"Fos Katastrofi!

The hall lit up one again. But this time, Mortha seemed to get tired.

"Mortha, you are not as young as you used to be!" Jane taunted.

"Don't play with me!" she shrieked back. "Erebus Katastrofi!"

Jane knocked away the dark ball of energy. It flew into the crowd of skeletons and took out a few.

"Aduro Pertusus!" shouted Jane. A bright, thin line of energy pierced Mortha's heart.

Something strange dripped from her Mortha's mouth that instant; then she coughed up more and more of it.

Alda and Jor hacked away at enough skeletons that they were reconsidering the idea of attacking the two teens and held their position at the doorway.

"Even you should know what that is," said Jane as she pointed.

"No, this can't be!" she cried out. On the ground before her throne was thick, black blood.

Jane spun the black staff in her hands and hefted it back. "Unlucky for you, I was a skilled javelin thrower. Oh, and this is from Adele Alan!"

The spear flew silently through the air, and fell right into Mortha's chest. The light that guided them earlier floated near Mortha. It then glowed brightly before revealing itself to be Adele.

He held the spear as Mortha's green aura flowed into it. Adele began to yell uncontrollably, but held the staff despite his anguish.

The soldiers at Denhoec fought fiercely against the skeleton invasion. But then one after the other just simply fell apart. The Raiders could only watch in surprise as the entire offense ended.

The skeletons near the door fell apart also before Jor and Alda.

Bones made of hardened obsidian fell to the ground before Adele. They were what was left of Mortha. He still held the staff firmly—something only a mortal being could do.

"Adele, you're—alive!" Jane exclaimed, a little surprised.

"I-I am, I suppose the power of a Divine can revive a person, even one who has been dead for 500 years I guess," he said, still in awe.

He walked down from the throne and the group realized he was still a boy.

"So what does it mean if you're a 500 year old 11 year old?" Jor questioned.

"It means I have the liberty to grow and age again," Adele replied happily. He held some of the bones in his hand. "This should fetch a good price at a jeweller."

The warriors, now triumphant in their defeat of a Divine, left the manor for their next adventure with a new ally.

CHAPTER 6

The Zeran and Ayan Saudi

Zen Zeran was a rider of the steppes and next in line as king. Despite his father's many wives, he still claimed to be next in line to rule.

That didn't stop the other nobles from laughing him out the halls though.

Now he had the burning desire to truly be king so he could laugh in *their* faces. But now, he worked as a soldier in the wars that out lasted the 300 Year's War between Zeran and Ayan Saudi. His hope is to continue to gain ranks until he had the army in his hands, then he would take Zeran by force and prove his legitimacy.

He snapped out of the trance he was in and focused on the commander.

"Today we are staging a simple skirmish on the men of Ayan Saudi; all I require you to do is to move swiftly across the sands and kill them as they charge. We must use the gift granted to us that proves our superiority here in the steppes and deserts—our horses." He turned and drew his shining sabre from its scabbard. "We move now!"

The warriors quickly followed as they came down on the Ayan camp in a thundering charge.

The Ayan quickly rose to their feet—too quickly. Spears were picked up from where they were buried in the sands, and the horsemen, unable to slow down, were skewered along with their horses.

Zen carried a bronze tipped spear himself and cut it through several of the Ayan warriors. He then heard the cries of several horses in the distance. Up on the hill were the silhouettes of several hundred cavalry men, their spears up in the air and their flag waving.

"Commander, those are not our cavalry!" shouted Zen from across the camp.

"Damn those Ayan bastards; retreat!" he called. The surviving men turned on their mounts and hurried for the high dunes.

The enemy cavalry were on the dunes opposite to them a few minutes ago, but now they were charging and skewering any fallen riders in the camp.

"Commander, the Ayan are catching up to us!" shouted Zil, a friend of Zen.

An arrow grazed Zen's cheek and struck one of his comrades in the back. He fell and caused the rider behind him to fall.

"First they are spearmen, and then they are lancers, now they are archers! What next, they get artillery?!" ranted the commander.

There was a loud thud and sand flew into the air, joined by the chorus of screams from several men and horses. The Ayan had catapults set up, along with several smaller ballistae.

Zen wiped the blood that dotted his light brown skin. He spun the spear so that the tip was facing behind, then he took out his sabre and began carving the end.

"What are you doing Zen, the Ayan are right behind you!" Zil shouted.

He almost dropped the sabre when he turned to see a spear tip a few inches from his face. "Kenta; faster!" he commanded his horse.

Its legs cut across the sand and left the Ayan behind. The spear in Zen's hand now had two sharp edges. "You Ayan should really learn to keep your distances!" he taunted. He threw the spear into the sand to the side of him. The Ayan couldn't turn in time and his horse was skewered. The other riders were close behind and tumbled down, created what could look like a domino effect.

The Zeran riders cheered as they continued their retreat and soon disappeared back into the desert sands.

Zen retied his hair into what those in the eastern cities would call a "ponytail". Not a good hairstyle for people who spent their lives on horses. They had set up camp near a small oasis for the night.

Zil whacked him on the back and he lurched forward. "Nice work Zen, you should have looked back though, just to see the look on those Ayan warrior's faces," he said with a laugh.

"I did it to survive Zil, not to kill all those people," Zen replied.

"The Ayan well deserved it and you know it, now hand me your sabre."

Zil pulled the slightly curved blade from its scabbard and began to streak it with several marks. "That is how many of those Ayan pigs you slaughtered today."

Zen took a long look at the sabre then turned to Zil. "Why are we at war with them?"

"Because our fathers fought them, and then their fathers, and their fathers before them," Zil replied proudly.

"But what caused it all to begin?"

"They say the Divine Emir Sahra'a was bored one day and told some of the Ayan warriors that they were free to take all the Zerani princesses to be wives, but then he told the Zeran that Ayan warriors would arrive in the steppes to take their kingdom, and they wouldn't stop unless all their land was taken. Long story short, the Ayan warriors were intercepted and a horrible battle took place. Each swore they would avenge their fallen and here we are today."

"But that is trickery!" Zen protested.

"If it is the wish of the Divines to see us capture the city of Sahra' Ayana, then so be it."

"Hm, if I had my chance at that Divine, I would give him a piece of my mind!"

"Be quiet Zen, Divines do horrible things to those who speak ill of them!"

"Attack me from away? Then that proves that that Divine is a coward!"

"They could kill you right now if they wanted to!"

"Well they haven't, so that says something more!"

Zil stormed away from the pond that Zen was nearby and walked back into camp.

"Sahra'a, if you are harbinger of chaos and death, then face a true man of Zeran, and test your so-called power!" he said to the moon.

The small troop of wounded and battered cavalry made their way across the desert sands once again. Zil rode with the commander and gave occasional angry glances at Zen, who was riding alone.

"Zen may bring us misfortune on our journey commander," said Zil

"Sahra'a smiles upon great warriors like him," the commander replied.

"Yet he curses his name."

"Zen would never do such a thing."

"Well he did last night, quite boldly at that."

"Then we simply pray that the Emir forgives him."

The scout fell in next to the commander, his telescope in hand. "There is an unmarked cave before us commander."

"We passed this way to get here, how can there be a cave now and not when we were coming?" asked the commander.

Zil looked again to Zen and back to the commander. "We should just ignore it."

A second scout was riding hard for the commander, considerably faster than the other, and as he passed, the warriors drew their sabres. An arrow tip protruded from his chest and blood flowed endlessly from it. "More Ayan cavalry are about," he coughed and struggled to take in the next breath of air. "We are surrounded."

At that point, he fell to the ground and silently lay there.

"Everyone ready you weapons, we are under attack!" called the commander.

The now infamous Ayan riders were now seen somewhere off in the distance in every direction riding hard to encircle and annihilate their enemy before they pulled together another slick strategy.

Zen and several other warriors rode alongside the commander for what could be the slick strategy in creation.

"We find a weak point in their line and charge through it like hell," he said.

"That is our strategy sir?! I thought we would find some position or let a small group ride around to take their siege equipment or something!" exclaimed a soldier.

"Tell me, where do you see an opening on this closing circle?"

"The commander's right, we either die fighting here or breach a weak spot in their lines," said Zen.

"We may just about die here because of your regard for the Emir!" shouted Zil.

Zen put his hand over his face and released a heavy sigh. "If Sahra'a really was this great person, then we would not be fighting this war, we would not be under attack, and we wouldn't be having this conversation."

"See commander, he blasphemes our Emir in the open deserts for all to hear!" said Zil.

"Look, why would he send this big an army just to kill me?"

Zil's sabre slowly escaped its scabbard as the steel shined brightly in the mid-day sun. "He probably cursed our force because we refused to solve the problem at its root!"

"Zil, you are my brother, you would not dare enter combat with me," said Zen as calmly as he could.

"If the Emir wishes it, then let it be so!"

"Zil! Listen to sense; our enemy is out there, not here!"

A soldier grabbed Zil's hand. "If this boy is cursed, he will surely fall in battle."

He put away the sabre and frowned. "I never wished for you to turn, my brother, but if the Emir sees you an enemy, he will surely dismiss you from our realm."

"The Ayan are soon upon us!" shouted a forward scout. Nearly fifty blades gleamed brightly as they were drawn; soon to be crimson in the sands of the desert.

CHAPTER 7

The Battle of Emir's Rift

There was a vicious roar from the Ayan riders as they came within earshot, and now, backed into a corner, the warriors of Zeran howled an inhuman war cry that sent a few enemy riders to fall back several ranks. The men of Zeran now wheeled about their horses and began to charge in return, still screaming the horrible war cry.

Zen, his sabre drawn, rode with the charging force. He turned to see Zil riding next him.

"Zil, I was proud to be your spirit brother," said Zen.

"And I was proud to be yours," he replied in all sincerity.

The lines crashed into each other and instantly men were on the ground bleeding from wounds by lances.

"This isn't gonna work!" shouted Zil as his blade cut cleanly through an Ayan's neck.

"That's why we have a plan B!" shouted Zen. He pointed his sabre for the nearby cave.

"You have to be kidding me! I'm not going in there!" said the commander as he barely dodged a couched lance.

"We have only a few minutes before the Ayan behind us close the gap! We do it now or become the unknown and forgotten soldiers of this war's history!" shouted Zen again.

The commander reluctantly rose his sabre in the air, and at the top of his lungs screamed "Retreat! The Ayan will not return us to the sands!"

The riders wheeled their horses back to the cave, and in a mad frenzy, they drew their bow and rained arrows on the pursuing Ayan. The arrows were rocketing the helms of those who it had not pierced their skull. The arrows seemed to be following some magic path as they killed many an Ayan rider.

They were only a few inches away from the cave. Zen turned to see the commander straggling behind and becoming gradually closer to the pursuing Ayan.

"Commander, we must hurry if we wish to escape through gap!" he said.

"Zest here is a bit in his years," laughed the commander grimly. "He is wounded too, and he is my best horse."

The Ayan were slowly catching up to him from behind, and the gap of escape to the cave was slowly closing. Zen had to think quickly.

"Grab my hand and try jumping onto my horse!" he said hastily.

An Ayan neared the commander, but in a practiced motion, he whipped out his recurve bow and slammed and arrow in his chest.

"My hand commander! More Ayan will soon be behind you!" screamed Zen, his voice cracking.

The commander's hand reached out, but seemed farther away as Zest slowed.

"Charge man, charge!" shouted Zen.

The Ayan were only a few feet away now.

"Hurry!"

The commander drew back his bowstring on the horses behind, and Zest leaped forward to Zen and Kenta.

"Yes commander, now grab my hand!"

The Ayan were closing in, and the gap was also closing before them. The commander reached out and made a firm grip to Zen.

But then the commander's grip loosened.

Blood. Zen realized that horrible but all true part of life was all over him—but even more on the commander. He saw that a large wooden stake had shredded through him from the Ayan ballistae...

He turned to see the gap and it was just about to close. They would have to cut their way through by force. He took the commander's sabre and held the two, giving a cry that seemed to echo across every dune, every grain of sand.

"For Zeran!"

The other riders, eyes bloodshot from anger, resounded that cry and charged in the next line of Ayan soldiers. They swung wildly with no regard to parrying or blocking. Blood flew high into the air and accompanied by the screams of the Ayan.

It was open. The gap was forced open.

"Now charge like hell!" exclaimed Zil, pointing his bloody sabre at the cave.

The small army charged towards the mysterious cave, hoping that this was truly a blessing.

Sahra'aThe Bane of the Deserts

Zen threw himself from Kenta's saddle and lay sprawled out of the sandy cave floor, the sabres still in his hands.

"Commander!" he cried bitterly. He could not expect the same brave man that led him these few months to answer.

"What of him?" asked Zil.

"The Ayan killed him with their siege machines," he replied.

Zil fell on the cave floor, and breathed heavy as he leaned on a wall. "He must have faked it, like when he got caught scouting that one Ayan camp those months ago," he contemplated frantically.

Zen wiped the blood from his face and held out the hand. "This is his blood, the bolt went straight through him; no mortal man would survive it!"

Zil grabbed Zen's bloody hand and wept bitterly for all the soldiers to hear. If they were not crying on neither the inside or outside, they were not human.

The cave was quiet, like a dead silence filled it to a deafening extent. As they went deeper in, they could feel something dark about the place. It truly was quiet, but no one spoke. They only continued to walk.

It was when they were navigating across a strip of stone over a dark pit that they heard the noises. If you listened closely, you could almost make out screams of fear and pain. It seemed that the shouts of the Ayan warriors were echoing within the pit also. There were several bright red flashes, then somewhat visible fire, but they vanished as quickly as they came. The soldiers hesitated, but crossed, knowing the Ayan would follow them far past here. They made it to a large space in the cave and looked fearfully at the camp that was set up inside. With sabres drawn, they searched the many tents and found only one bit of evidence that people were there—blood.

The soldiers turned to Zil and Zen for options.

"We could stay here for a while," said Zen.

"And let the Ayan catch us? No chance," Zil replied.

"I don't think the units will go deeper once those moans are in earshot."

"Well they won't accept the idea of the Ayan rushing us in here."

"Then I have an idea."

Zen held up an arrow to make sure he had everyone's attention. "So, how many of you are good shots?"

The Zerani warriors took up positions behind the boulders and stalagmites that seemed to conveniently fill the dark parts of the cave. The left an arrow slightly notched and waited for the pursuing Ayan.

They sat for fifteen minutes in wait for the Ayan. Something came down the winding path they followed earlier over the pit. It had a smile on its face, but yet it had no face. It had hands, but no fingers.

It was a body, but yet not one.

Zen gave the signal shot and it made a direct hit on the being. A volley of many more arrows made their way and crashed into the being. It raised its hand to where the arrows flew. "Khthon Katastrofi!"

The stalagmites grew and twisted like the swaying branches of a long dead tree. They rose to the roof, then turned to the Zeranian warriors.

Zen heard several agonized screams and turned to aid them, but there were only bloody, shredded bodies spitted up the stone. He made another effort to hit the thing, but the arrows had no effect. He decided that his sabre may be best here.

He ran up the winding path with his two sabres in hand. The being turned and gave the same smiling crease. "Geo Katastrofi!"

Zen danced about trying to escape the rising spikes in the stone, all the while wondering if this was real. He charged once again as the cave floor settled. His first sabre broke through the figure, but it grabbed the second one before it hit an area that looked like something was inserted. Zen looked up at it, but in horror, he realized. "You're made of sand!"

Zil and several other soldiers who were ranged challenged stayed back at the camp in hope of finding who set it up.

Something white was in view from a dark tunnel. Zil gave the command to lower their weapons but keep them nearby.

It was a little Ayan girl in simple white robes.

"Maybe she is from the camp," said Zil as he got up.

The girl walked to the middle of the camp and smiled. Then she began to chuckle, then laugh, then it was a maniacal laugh. Not the kind of laugh a little girl carries. She spoke in a strange tongue right after.

"Excuse me?" asked Zil, not at all afraid.

"It seems you all only speak the new Zerani tongue. I said 'You Zerani soldiers are so foolish. It may be a shame to kill such fine men!'".

"Look, I wish for no games. Now tell us, where are the owners of the camp?"

The men looked down at the girl's feet to see a pool of blood gathering. She looked up and smiled. "Here they are, courtesy of Ema, the embodiment of blood."

"What trickery is this?!" asked one man, terrified.

"Not trickery, Divinity."

Zen quickly pulled is sabre out of the sand beast and began swinging wildly in panic at it. It made no effort to stop him; it only did what looked like staring. The sabre in Zen's left hand neared the area with the depression in the sand being's body and it appeared to feel pain. Zen quickly noticed the spark that flew as the sabre cut across the depression.

"Geo!" it commanded. Zen jumped and spread his legs apart, then pointed his sabre blades to the ground as he balanced with them on the rising pillar of stone. He jumped down and spun sideways down at the figure with his sabres. There was no giving up here today.

"Ema Metallos!" she shouted after one of the soldiers. He stepped back, but then his chest began to bloat. This horrified the other soldiers as they froze, staring helplessly. A large iron spike broke through the man's skin, but there was no blood as he dropped to the cave floor. The iron slowly oozed away and flowed into the bloody puddle below Ema. She dropped her gaze on yet another soldier.

He glared back angrily and notched an arrow, pulled the recurve bow back at full draw and released. It thudded right into Ema's forehead. It was silent for a moment, but laughter soon broke it.

Ema jerked her head back up and forward, her neck cracking a little too loud for comfort, and ripped the arrow straight out and melted away the tip. "Keep it up toys! You may actually entertain me after so long a time of sitting in this cave!"

Zen dropped unto the sand man with his blades continually spinning and hacking about its body. It was too slow and only stood and made attempts to block. It would flinch every time Zen got a chance to strike its weak point, and he could sense it beginning to weaken. The beast used its sandy hands in a last ditch effort to protect its body. Zen saw the weakness, and with both sabres, he jabbed through its crossed arms and shattered its stone heart.

The sand slowly fell as the red light in its eyes dimmed. Zen noticed then, that as more sand melted away, it had the form of a human.

Then horror found its way back to his soul.

The last of the sand melted away to reveal a mummified corpse, its mouth opened wider than any human could manage, and even though it had no eyes and limited facial features, he could see that whoever it was when it was alive was in horror themselves at their time of death. It fell into the pile of sand and lay unmoving.

Zen turned again to look on his share of troops, but they were all spit upon the violent stones that ripped out the ground or killed by the other sand men that appeared in the room. The only option now was to make it to Zil and his units and warn them of the imminent danger. But he would have to fight his way through many of these powerful beings to get to the camp. Zen knew that dying in here was impossible for him. He had to survive.

"Dance monkey, dance!" laughed Ema as she controlled one of the Zeranian soldiers to dance. She could simply do this by controlling his blood as she always did.

Many of the others lay torn apart literally limb from limb or with holes shredded through them from her blood to iron transmutations. Zil frowned as he saw this and ordered his remaining men to use their recurves. "Wait until she finishes with Ash'kan, then we strike."

Ema frowned and clenched her fists. Ash'kan's face instantly turned pale. "I'm bored with you now, die." Blood pooled under the man and flowed into the hole left by the arrow in Ema's head, healing it. "Now who else wants to play?"

"Now!" exclaimed Zil. The other archers jumped up from behind the cover of the tents and fired. The arrows shattered against the stone wall that appeared; Ema was nowhere to be found. "Where the hell did she go?" asked Zil as he looked around. A man screamed from behind the group and they quickly turned around.

Ema's hand had shredded through the chest of one of the soldiers.

In her hand was his beating heart.

"Stop this madness girl, we wish you no harm!" begged Zil.

"You shot after a little girl, doesn't that demand retribution?" asked Ema in return. There was a flash of light and movement then three more soldiers went down.

"Please, I have family in Zeran that want to see me come home. So do many of these soldiers!" begged Zil again.

"Then I will lay waste to Zeran; it must have lots of blood there."

That was the breaking point for Zil, no hope to survive here. No hope period. He was backed into a corner, and now was the time to ascend to glory.

"Attack!" he commanded as the rest of the men drew their sabres.

"Hephaestus Katastrofi!" Ema echoed.

Zen arrived to the camp and watched in horror as the giant ball of fire blew away the last of the Zeranian soldiers. Ema turned to him and smiled. "You're Zen Zeran aren't you?"

"W-What do you want with me?" he asked.

"The Emir wishes to see you."

Zen rushed down and fell in the ashes of his fallen comrades. "Where is Zil?"

"The defiant one?" she said. "You're on top of him."

Zen couldn't do anything but stare at the ashes.

"Come, the Emir wants to see you." Ema put her hands on his shoulder and they soon found themselves within a room of golden walls, embezzled with gems of all kinds. Coins, weapons, crowns and other valuables were also stacked up in piles nearby a giant, gilded throne. Upon a golden throne sat Sahra'a, the Emir of the Desert. He wore a mask of pure gold; the left half crying and the right side laughing. He had three hands on his right and left sides of hid body and had a belt with six golden scabbards. He spoke with an echo.

"Welcome, Zen Zeran, to the hall of glory!"

"W-Who are you?" asked Zen, still traumatized from the current events.

"Do you not know? I am the man you said you wanted to speak with, the one who caused this so-called great bloodshed across the endless sands."

Zen's fear quickly turned to rage as the bane of his existence faced him. "Why Sahra'a? What kind of Divine destroys his own people?"

"The more people die, the more blood my brothers and sisters have to either absorb or use to defend the sands from the other Divines," he explained.

"There are others like you in this world? Is there no safety?" A dagger grazed his arm and he fell on his knees, grasping the wound.

Haima, sister of Sahra'a, stood with her arm outstretched next to his throne. She had to look of a Zeranian female in at least her twenties. She wore a cloth that covered her nose and mouth and seemed to not be afraid to show off her body, as she was dressed as an Ayanese belly dancer.

"You do not speak of the other Divines or damage the name of the Emir in his hall!" she commanded.

"Or what, you kill me? I'm already dead!" Zen replied.

"And that you shall remain; Zen Zeran, I hereby banish you from the deserts!" commanded the Emir.

"Wait! I have questions!"

Haima held up another throwing knife, but the Emir halted her. "What do you wish to know?"

"If you are the lord of the desert, why didn't you take my life instead of allowing the other warriors to die?"

"It was much more fitting to have everything you love destroyed before you, besides, your friends are in my spire, fighting for fun for an eternity."

The Emir waved his hand and the images of several Zeranian spirit filled the room. One turned and smile at Zen.

"Zen, you finally made it to the land of the Divines!" exclaimed Zil mightily.

"No Zil, I am still on the mortal plane," Zen said, holding back tears.

"So you defeated the sister of Sahra'a? You are mightier a warrior than I previously thought."

"I'm in the Emir's hall."

Zil side stepped and swung his sabre several times. "Then ask him to bring you to the realm of the divines so you may fight the eternal battle!"

"Zil, this is not you! You love fine women and a drink whenever it comes!"

"And a fine battle also."

"Zil, this cannot be you."

"Zen, you must learn that one's spirit is the embodiment of one's emotions and true feelings. My true self loves to fight and I cannot deny it. Now, battle calls my name, and she is too fair a maiden to resist!"

He slowly faded along with the rest of the warriors, and Zen stood once again before the Emir. "Now are you ready for the next punishment?"

"Do your worst Sahra'a, nothing you can do will hurt me further," Zen replied with a hard but heavy heart.

Flames rose around Zen as the Emir waved his hand. "You are now to be banished to the lands to the North, where there is no true warmth!" The fire overtook Zen and he faded, never to be allowed into the deserts again...

CHAPTER 9

The Den Revolution

Den was the proud home of many of the beast men, people with the personalities of men but the bodies of animals. Within Den were the provinces of Fel, Fox and Den as the capital.

The men of Den were usually mistaken for werewolves due to their size and extreme resemblance to wolves. They stood upright and were classed into two main groups: the nobility were called High Fen, and the commoners were low Fen. They had little difference except the quality of living and dress.

Next were the Fox, who were considerably smaller than the Fen, but they made far better merchants due to their non-threatening appearance. They also had more agility and dexterity than most Fen.

Lastly, there were the Fel. They slightly resembled cats, and their appearance did not heavily resemble one. They were smaller in number than the Fen, but they made up for it with their archery, agility and other warrior skills. And when the time came, there women could get any attacker to think twice about destroying a place where such beauty could exist.

All together they could live peacefully and defend their Kingdom when the time came...until the head chief was murdered by a Fox and Fel assassins. This started a revolution that divided the country and brought about its current war.

Akina Akin was considered the prize Fel Hall. Most of her people were furry, and required little clothes, which actually made people think of them as savages. She had only a fur wrap to cover her chest, but wore a colourful robe to her knees. She had to show her royalty after all.

She was the kin-in-line of the Akin house of the Hall of Fel, the new capital that was created after the revolution started. Her father had three other illegitimate daughters, one of which was the second commander of the rebel units. All Akina had to do was sit in the halls and wait for her turn to rule.

Her waiting finally came to an abrupt end.

A unit of ten men stormed into the keep with a stretcher. Akina and the other servants and nobles in the keep went to see the commotion. It was Akin, her father, who was on the stretcher, hovering over life and death.

They brought him to his quarters and lay him on his bed. He groaned as he attempted to get up, but his soldiers stopped him. "You must relax and let the shaman come," said one.

"No kind of mortal healer can save me, only a Divine has the strength!" he struggled to reply.

Akina rushed through the door and dropped on her knees on the side of his bed. "Father, what has happened to you?"

He pointed to an arrow lodged in the left side of his chest. "This is an obsidian hooked assassin arrow in my chest, it's also poisoned with something otherworldly."

"Kinigos, touch our Chief, let him live!" screamed one the servants as they began to pray.

Akin coughed up black blood from his mouth and his eyes stared blankly. "Akina, strike first and kill first. Always look for the way of peace. Do not let those among you claim the throne because of your age—and don't die—Kinigos sees a light in y-you." His eyes seemed to lose the bright liveliness it always showed, and for once, Akina was alone.

It was now a year after the event and she was now fifteen. She had already gained the throne and left the matters of war to her sisters and commanders, even though she was to be on the battle field herself by custom. Akina had now adopted a melancholy outlook on life and had none of the colours she previously had in her own eyes. She just frowned at everything that was of the Kingdom, and sat on the throne, brooding.

Her current issue now was to live up to her father's last words and bring peace to the Kingdom, and her sister Illeth began to arrange for the strongest of the Fel, or the strongest of the anybody, to attempt to win Akina's heart.

Everyone failed.

It was then that her sister Kullskash, the still second commander, gave her the idea to unleash her vengeance on the enemy on the battlefield to get the Fen and Fox to surrender. She at first declined, but remembered her father said to strike first, and went along with it. *How hard could stabbing big clumsy wolves be?*

C H A P T E R 10

Yellow-Mark Blunt-Claw

Yellow-Mark Blunt-Claw was given his name due to the fact that he lived in an Orphanage that had a human in charge. He grew up alongside them until he was drafted into the military of the Fen. He himself was a Fen, but when it came to battle, he was the first to retreat. He was named Mark by the owners of the Orphanage, and was later called Yellow-Mark because of a yellow streak painted on the right side of his face and the fact that he was a coward. He was also called Blunt-Claw because of his failures in the arts of war, and everyone knew a blunt sword dealt no damage.

Nowadays though, he worked as an assistant accountant for some Fox merchants. What he lacked in strength, he easily made up for in smarts, and that surprised the Fox that took him up.

Today was a regular day of traveling with the wagons and carts and Yellow-Mark was with Will, the master accountant, counting their profits.

"I tell you Mark, those Deneaux merchants can be damn well stubborn when they have to admit they lost a deal," laughed Will. Most Fox were dressed like humans and many of them enjoyed living the rich life as merchants and other high profit jobs.

"It's amazing how you got all those weapons for such little gold," Yellow-Mark replied. Despite being a weaker than ordinary Fen, he was still quite big and only wore a fur Kilt and sandals.

Will flipped a coin and caught it with ease. "It's all about looking inferior, the dumber you look, the less willing they are to buy for a high price. And when they are reluctant, you bring up the big deals, and when they still refuse, you walk off. They'll feel sorry and pay even more in hope that you reconsider. In the end, you will end up with more coin then you wanted to gain."

"And a vacation with pay for a job well done," added Yellow-Mark as he stretched.

"Yes, yes. I also heard that the beaches of Dicidi in Zeran are home to women that arouse the imagination."

"Life is good Will, life is good."

The horses outside began to get noisy as several men shouted in anguish.

"What the hell is going on out there?" asked Will.

The door of the wagon was thrown open and a combination of crossbows, spears, bows and sabres were pointed in their direction—all in the hands of the Fel.

The merchants shuffled uncomfortably in the ropes they were tied up in. Kullskash smiled as she saw this and stood before them. "A caravan of the Fox carrying weapons to aid in killing our people; how shall we deal with them Chief? Execution?"

"It's up to you sister, this raid was your idea," Akina replied.

"Hmm, then let's kill the Fen first, then the rest of the caravan. Let us see now, how can we kill you? Poison, archer line; the choices are endless!"

"How about you take me and leave the rest of them to return to their families?" blurted out Yellow-Mark.

"Now the Fen is a hero, how wonderful," said Kullskash sarcastically. "No one here lives, no matter the sacrifice." She held a crossbow up to his chest. "It would have been a noble deed though."

"Kullskash, let him live," commanded Akina.

In a huff, Kullskash dropped the weapon a folded her arms. "Whatever you say, chief."

"We will depart with them to the Hall, and imprison them there until I can come up with something."

They used the wagons and horses of the caravan to burden the prisoners, and for a faster arrival. Akina was in the main wagon with some of the higher priority prisoners.

"Will, what do we do now?" asked Yellow-Mark.

"I really don't know. I'm just glad they are letting us live, I mean I have a niece and nephew to feed," Will replied.

"Tell me Fox, do these relatives care for you?" asked Akina.

"T-They always jump into my arms once I ever get the chance to go home."

"And you Fen, do you have family?"

"I have no one except the caravan, which is why I chose the let the Fel kill me to save the rest of the caravan, I have nothing to lose, except a few coins, but even that does not amount to one's life."

"That is what makes you different to most men then. I usually get requests from nobles, but I always declined. One thing you learn as Chief is that noble men are never noble. You only see that quality in the people that are overlooked in society, the ones who will especially take a spear in the front-line instead of hiding behind his army."

Will and Yellow-Mark were amazed by how much the leader of the Fel were revealing to them.

"Why are you telling us prisoners this?" Will asked.

"You have something—family. All I have are my sisters. My father was struck by an arrow in the heat of battle and died in the halls not too long after. She wiped something from her face and her voice cracked every so often. "I am the Chief of the Fel, yet I have nothing."

"Then I could be your friend, at least until we reach the Hall," said Yellow-Mark.

Akina looked at him in awe. *This Fen who knows nothing of me extends his friendship towards me. Why has no one else taken the time to do this?*

"I may work my power to ensure that you may be my friend for as long as possible Fen, I-I cannot forget this."

She smiled.

Chapter 11

The Eye of the Storm

The men that worked with the caravan rode off into the forests to return home, while Will and Yellow-Mark stayed. Akina had pardoned them, seeing no reason to execute or imprison them.

She gave the usual small but true smile to Yellow-Mark. "Now what do we do Mark?"

"How about a look at the town?"

"I would love that."

The first place she showed Will and Mark was the Hall. Many bows and spears were hanged up on the walls, and could tell the story of the battle in which each turned the tide. She next brought them to the Hall of statues, which housed the monuments to the fallen leaders of the Fel. In was situated further behind the Hall, and usually only to those higher up in society could enter, though many normal citizens could enter if they had a hero ancestor.

"This is my father Akin, one of the liveliest Chiefs we had," Akina said. She forced her eyes to remain dry, but a few tears still escaped.

Mark put his arm on her shoulder. "Remember people like that, you may one day be like him you know." He lifted her head. "Be happy you had a father to follow, I have to forge my own destiny."

"I still miss him Mark, he was the only friend I had."

"And now the Divines gave you us," added Will. "I think that's how it works at least."

"Then I will thank Kinigos for his blessing."

"And Kinigos thanks thee," boomed a voice.

The group turned to see a Fen with a large bow made from vines and mossy logs. He wore a strange plate skirt made of unknown metals and smiled at them. "Your father truly was a cheerful man. He easily gets the night going in my Great Hall of eternal rest."

"K-K-Kinigos?!" gasped Will and Mark together.

"The one and only; you three act as if you've seen a ghost."

"A Divine stands in our presence and you expect us to stay relaxed?" Akina asked, surprised but still with a hint of gloom in her voice.

"I'm only here for a short while, I have a message from your father."

Life began to show in her eyes again. "What does he say?!"

Kinigos whispered in her ear. "The Fen is quite taken by you, if you wish for any love, he is where it stays."

Akina's face lit up bright red and she looked down. "Does he really say that?"

"Quite right, he went to war with the Fen, and he finds something good in this one. You should follow his guidance."

Will and Mark were still looking fearfully at the godlike being before them, but Kinigos smiled in reply. "You two have a war ahead of you," he said seriously, the smile instantly fading. "Give it all you've got and you may survive."

"But I can't fight!" protested Mark.

"That's why Akina will teach you."

"I seriously can't fight. I mean, have you ever seen me around weapons, particularly bows and crossbows?"

"I see all; you just need someone friendlier to teach you." Kinigos patted Akina on the back. "Isn't that what friends are for?"

Akina's smile was slowly returning, but in the back of her mind was the thought of Kinigos' words.

C H A P T E R 12

The Archer

"Alright Mark, this is what we call a spear," said Akina as she passed the rod to Mark.

He fumbled with it and dropped it, then picked it up, all the while struggling under its weight.

"How about we give you a sword then?"

Mark held the blade and made a few experimental swings, and on the fourth swing, it slipped out his hand and nearly impaled a passing servant.

"I wouldn't possibly think of giving you a dagger now, you would probably lose it," Akina said with her hands of her hips.

Will was poking at a sack and hay target in the training room with a strange, thin blade.

"What's that you have there Will?" asked Akina.

"It's a rapier, a blade that I believe was tailor made, or in this case black smith made, for stabbing," he replied. It tore through the targets with ease, and he looked a bit fancy dealing with the weapon.

"That doesn't look like a weapon for war," Akina replied.

"On the contrary; I can easily down the biggest Fen you could throw at me with this thing."

"And what happens when you have to parry?"

"Just dodge."

"What if you can't dodge?"

"Then I'll parry."

"With such a thin bit of metal?"

"It is made of many different light-weight materials that also happen to be strong, so I can stop a sword lunge with ease."

"Ok, you win Mr Finesse," said Akina, casually accepting defeat.

Mark was where the two left him with a short bow. He marvelled at the lack of sharp edges and threatening points.

"That is what you call a short bow Mark. It fires arrows of many kinds and is a bit of a favourite of mines," said Akina.

"They never had this when I was in the Fen military," Mark replied.

"I could give it to you—as a friendly gift I mean."

"Don't think I didn't hear what Kinigos said Akina, just be cool about it," said Will, still poking at the targets.

Akina kept herself from blushing and took the bow from Mark rather fiercely. She took up some practice arrows and aimed for a target at the far end of the room. She pulled back and released, and the arrow slammed into the target's torso. She took several other shots that hit the arms and torso again; then gave the weapon to Mark. "Try it."

Mark quickly put the arrow on the string, and when he released, the bow string smacked at his arm and the arrow dropped a few inches ahead. He held his arm in pain and wondered how it could have penetrated his fur.

"I forgot you don't have braces," Akina said. She found a large pair taken from one of the few units of Fen archers that were killed near the beginning of the revolution and slid them unto Mark's arms.

He took aim again and released, only for the arrow to fall.

"You have to notch the arrow on the string, and release not too soon but not too late." She held the bow and his arm and showed him the proper technique. Will smiled and made signals to Mark.

"Shut up Will!" he snapped at him.

"Hey, hey. I didn't say anything, you're the one blushing."

Akina realised she was right on Will's big body as she showed him how to fire. She realized how soft Fen fur was. "Um, I think I've shown you enough, fire away."

Mark shook his head at Will and aimed for the target. He made sure the arrow was in place, and released.

"Damn Mark, you should go hunting with me," exclaimed Will as the arrow hit the center of the target's head.

"That was probably a fluke shot," Mark replied as he notched another arrow and fired. Another lethal hit to the head, this time though, the target shook from the force.

"I could appreciate your modesty, but even I could not make a shot like that at your level of skill," said Akina.

"Thank you then Akina, means a lot coming from a warrior such as yourself..."

Hiss! Thud!

The black shafted arrow smashed through the head of the target and slammed into the stone wall behind it.

"Toxon Katastrofi!" commanded a voice. The arrow's tip glowed, and exploded violently.

The other Fel warriors rushed down to training room with their weapons drawn, plunging into the smoke.

"I'm fine, but Will and Mark..."

"Our priority is to protect you first Chief, we shall go about helping the others once your safety is ensured," a guard said.

Mark limped out of the smoke with Will over his shoulder. "I'm fine, you need to go!"

The guards nodded and took her upstairs. Will regained his consciousness and looked around. "Mark, get my foil, that assassin is probably still around!"

"You aren't in any condition to be picking up a sword," Mark replied.

"You aren't in any condition to be firing a bow, but yet you still have it," said Will.

Mark looked down to see a quiver with strange arrows to his side and a red-stringed bow. "These aren't my arrows or my bow!"

Will felt something to his side and jumped from Mark's grip. He realized that there was a pitch black foil to his side, and his wounds were fully healed; same with Mark.

"The hell is all this?" Will said, confused.

"Kapnizo!" commanded the voice again as the smoke in the room dispersed.

Before them stood a man, most likely human, dressed in all black.

"You are not the Chief!" he exclaimed, his eyes widening.

"Neither are you, so what?" Will replied smartly.

"Don't toy with me Fox; I have far more power than any mere mortal!"

"Oh, so you expect us to believe that you are Divine?" Mark asked sceptically.

"I am Zekalien, Divine from the school of the Dark, and assassin for the many greater Divines."

"Then prove you are what you say you are!" Will snarled as he drew the black shiny blade.

There was a small spark about Zekalien and he stumbled. "Ekriksi!"

Will side stepped the blast and charged for him.

"Pyras Ekriksi!" Zekalien commanded once again.

Mark notched an arrow and fired. It slammed into the fire ball and it exploded on Zekalien.

He rolled back; then jumped to his feet. He drew two black daggers and met Will's charge. The two exchanged swings that let large, visible sparks fly.

Mark took aim again and fired. Zekalien side stepped it but Will's foil pierced his left shoulder. Again were the bolts of dark lighting around the blade. He hopped back against a wall and raised his hands.

Mark notched yet another arrow; this one though, looked hooked and shined with what little light was in the room.

"Teresa Katastrofi!"

"Will, get down now!" shouted Mark as the arrow was released. He ducked down but kept his foil drawn.

The arrow flew and appeared to literally cut the air as it went. It broke through the dark sphere of energy that came from the assassin's hands, and it imploded from the hit. The hall shook violently and stones fell from the roof.

Zekalien screamed in terror as the arrow came towards him. He raised his hand as a final defence and the missile pierced his palm and went out through his shoulder.

The energy began to flow into the arrow and his cries were silent. His skin began to burn away piece by piece. He reached for his daggers, but Will picked them up. "Not this time."

His body finally wasted away and dark bones fell to the ground. They shined just like the last arrow that ended him.

Mark frowned as he tugged the arrow from the wall. He turned to see it landed next to the first arrow the assassin fired. He pulled that one out to and was horrified.

They were the same kind of arrow.

Akina and the other warriors were coming down. Akina looked fearfully at the arrows, and horrible memories began to creep back into her mind. They were the same arrows that killed her father.

"M-Mark, where did you get those?" she asked.

"The first was from the assassin, the second was in this quiver I got somehow," Mark replied.

"These are not metals formally of Edafos, those are made of obsidian," said a familiar voice.

Kinigos walked up to the group, his face more serious than when he spoke of the coming battles. "Those are arrows I made myself to aid in the war against the school of the Dark in the realm of the Divines. They would always give a near instant killing blow to beings like me, but they would give an agonizing death to those of mortal kind."

"Like spitting black blood?" Akina asked.

"That would be the effect of the special poison placed on the arrows of my closest mortal servants. But as with many Divines, their hearts were corrupted and they soon took off to end their own enemies."

"Then it's your fault that father fell that day!" exclaimed Akina as she charged furiously for Kinigos. She made and overhead strike with her spear, but Kinigos simply raised his longbow and stopped it.

Akina looked fearfully at him and slumped to the ground in tears. "Why can't father return!"

"He is happy in my realm, is that not enough for you?"

Akina ripped her dagger from its scabbard and aimed for her neck. "Then I wish to join him!"

"No Akina!" yelled Kinigos.

The dagger was knocked right out of her hand. Mark lowered his bow and shook his head at Akina. She immediately ran to him and cried into his chest bitterly.

"If you were to die, your people would have no leader," he said.

"I'm a horrible chief Mark; I don't even attend to the matters of the kingdom. My sisters would be far better than me at it!"

"I don't believe that," Mark replied.

"I refuse to believe it also," added Will.

She continued to cry either way.

Kinigos waved to Mark. "Make sure she lives, and try to keep her distracted from my matters. I shall get my loyalists to help dispel these beings. Oh, and you can keep the obsidian weapons."

"Then take care," Mark replied.

Kinigos opened a strange, bright portal and walked in. "Remember Akina, your father is watching you!" His last words echoed.

CHAPTER 13

Dasimay the Damned

The last few Deneaux soldiers fell into the dust. A figure with a longbow in hand smiled sinisterly as their blood stained the forest floor. "I have offered the blood of the fallen to you master," she said.

"Then you have proven yourself," boomed a voice in the forests.

Dasimay was the sister of Akina, Illeth and Kullskash. She smiled confidently at her reflection in a pond nearby. It was her curves and natural beauty that made killing soldiers an easy task. She just had to lure them into the forests and finish the job. She would seem tall to most, but without her longbow, she stood only a few inches above Akina.

Her longbow was another story.

It was made of obsidian and appeared to be layered by overlapping obsidian scales. The bowstring itself was made out of a silk found only in the realm of the Divines. The entire bow was taller than her. It was a gift to her by Toxotes, the Divine of the hunt.

"Now Dasimay, it is time for the end of your sister's rule—and the beginning of mines."

"I shall make sure to keep this country together during the battles. Wouldn't want to rule over rubble," she said.

"Yes, now go Dasimay, take what is mines."

Illeth was briefing Akina on the matters of the war and of the kingdom. Will and Mark were ordered outside at the time and Akina was now day dreaming about them, mainly of Mark.

"Are you even paying attention Akina?" she asked.

She snapped out of her trance and smiled shyly at Illeth. "Sorry, but you have to remember I'm not an adult. I'm going to zone out from time to time."

"I suppose it's ok, I mean when I was being thought to do the work of a scribe and advisor, I would always fall asleep out of nothing."

Akina managed a small laugh. "Imagine what boys you would dream of."

"Chen the guardsman was almost like an idol, but I'm sure he wouldn't have time for me," Illeth replied. "And who do you dream of?" she added smartly in an attempt to shift the question.

Akina was back to day dreaming and smiled. "Maybe one day Mark," she said softly.

"A Fel and a Fen during the revolution? The irony of it all." Illeth joked. "Sounds like the work of a famous playwright."

"Y-You didn't hear that!" said Akina.

"No, I didn't," agreed Illeth.

"Please don't tell him!"

"He could already know."

"Illeth, stop playing with me!"

"I'm not playing with you. I'm toying with your emotions."

The two burst into laughter, Akina ending first of course. "Why didn't Kullskash end up like you?"

"She actually is; you just have to catch her when she is not on the battlefield."

"Is that even possible? I mean Kullskash is hard to imagine without her bow and daggers."

"She is nicer than you think; we're lucky to have her as a sister."

"As I think of you," said Akina as she put her arms around Illeth.

"Ok, now back to the problem of the bodies of the Deneaux soldiers found in a grotto."

"Why are these deaths a problem? Don't the bodies of those nosy Northerners pop up all over every so often?"

"Well yes, but the problem is that they were killed by obsidian arrows, something we all know too well about."

"Just get the sentries to go on armed lookout for anyone nearing the Hall with bows. That should be enough...I hope..."

"Yes my Chief," Illeth replied as she left the room.

Akina looked at the shiny amulet Mark had got her a few weeks ago and held it near her heart. "One day Mark, one day."

Night had fallen and the best of Fel Hall's sentries stood in the lookout towers with bows, crossbows and javelins, as well as any other long range device they could get hold of.

Dasimay had hidden her bow in the forests and approached the gates. She waved up at the sentry and smiled. "Would it be too much trouble to let a little Fel into the city, I just got back from helping a friend in Deneaux and brigands could take me this night."

"Sorry, but you were exiled. I am not as stupid as you would believe," the sentry replied.

"What if I did you a favour?"

"What could you give me that I would possibly want?"

"A bit of enjoyment for the night as all, maybe some for your friends too."

A rope fell from the tower and Dasimay happily climbed.

"So what about your friends, soldier, wouldn't want you comrades to miss a piece of me," said Dasimay as she kicked off her boots.

His hand slowly moved up her leg. "I plan to have you for myself; then we will see about the other guys."

"I'll assure you, they won't get tired of me, and neither will you."

Mark awoke that night and found himself sweating. It was another one of those horrible dreams where arrows made of obsidian would fall around him, destroying everything. He would then see the entire land burn in fire and lava; tears of sorrow falling from the eyes of Kinigos and many other Divines. He would then see each fall to the power of the mighty volcanic stone and the world would turn permanently dark. These dreams had begun to be an annual occurrence, but he would try his best to pay them no mind.

Will was beside his bed with Akina. "You look like you've been having constant heart attacks," said Will, concern in his voice.

"It's just dreams Will, they have never killed anyone," Mark replied.

"They are causing you trouble, and that means they are causing me trouble," said Akina.

"Just go to sleep."

"Will, you can go; I'll stay here with Mark."

"You sure?"

"Yes, yes. Just go to bed."

As soon as Will left, she pulled out the amulet. "You remember this, right?"

Mark sat up and smiled. "I didn't really buy it though, I just found it and no one wanted to claim it."

"It means a lot to me you know. I always got piles of gifts from men— but this one means something."

"You're welcome I guess. After so long you really do seem more as a friend to me than a superior."

"That is why it was hard for me to have real friends. My title—and maybe my emotions after my father died."

"You did seem a bit depressed when I met you."

"And you were the one who brought my joy back. You are just a likable person."

"I guess I am, but you are just sometimes fun to be around. You ever take the time to listen to your own laugh?"

"No, why?"

"You have a beautiful laugh, and a beautiful smile. It makes me smile in turn just seeing it for even quarter of a second."

Akina smiled and tried to hide he face in the dark of the room. Mark patted her back.

"Why don't we go about this in the morning?" He yawned. "I would much like to go about and smash these hidden antagonists in my dreams."

She got and made for the door, but looked back. "Goodnight Mark."

"Night Akina," he replied, half sleeping.

The Ants, a sort of race of dark sprites that would hardly be able to meet a man's waist, were obedient creatures that were chosen by Toxotes as lesser servants. So far they had smuggled in Dasimay's longbow into the hall while she distracted the guards.

Dasimay kissed one of the guards on the forehead as she held a bottle of Fox wine that the guards had given her. The group had come over for the "Entertainment" she said she would provide, and so far, they have gotten that and more. They were drunk and enchanted, and Dasimay made sure to keep them that way until the signal came. She turned to her left and looked into the darkness of the streets below.

There it was; a red spark.

"Sorry boys, but I seemed to have left something in the streets, would you mind if I got it?"

"S'long as you come back and all, we'll all be waitin'," said one of them in a drunken daze.

She climbed down the ladder to meet the awaiting ants. They handed her that large, black, threatening weapon that seldom left her side and she took aim, though she didn't have an arrow nocked.

"Toxotes Katastrofi!"

The tower went up in a large explosion that lit up the city, but no sentry meant no alarm. That probably made no difference due to the fact that there was a large, bright explosion in a city at night.

"Tonight shall be night that the glorious Toxotes moves the hearts of his loyal followers!"

Will was on the verge of sleep as he heard the blast and was already strapping on his belt, which he usually placed his foil. Mark followed his example and took up his bow.

"Now what the hell is going this time?" asked Will, his annoyance clear in his voice.

"Maybe some fireworks," he said sarcastically. "Let's check on Akina."

"Khthon Katastrofi!" commanded Dasimay as stones shot up in the air and toppled the wooded houses in the city. She smiled at her work and turned to the wall. "What horrible features; I should probably redecorate. Hephaestus Ekriksi!" A large section in the wall went down as a fireball as tall as a house crashed into it. "Sagittarius Barrage!" Dasimay let many arrows of pure energy fly into the city, giving brief shines of light as the hit.

Already, the more aware guards or other sentries that she had not enchanted were charging down the streets.

"Please, it would have been better if you all stayed in your houses to die peacefully. Keravnos!" A stream of lightning poured out from her fingers and struck the warriors. The charred body of each fell to the ground.

Soldiers pushed and shoved Will and Mark aside as they rushed to get their weapons and armours. As they realized that this really was an attack, they ran to Akina's quarters.

She was already taking up her bow and spear, and turned in her version of dead surprise as the two came in. "Do you two know what's going on? Because if I have to wake up before the sun is up, something is really wrong."

"We are as much in the dark as you are with this Akina," said Will. Mark nodded.

"Then let's go kill whoever is causing this racket so we can go back to sleep," she said.

Dasimay laughed as she walked down towards the Hall. Warriors began to pour from every alley and road that crossed the main road to the Hall. She frowned. "You people really have no sense in any way, do you?" She lifted the large bow and drew it back. "Exochos Pyras Toxotes Ekriksi!"

The three ran out of the hall and looked down at the destroyed building.

"What the hell?! Are we under siege or something?" exclaimed Akina.

A great inferno rose into the sky and obscured the view of the street below in flames.

"Even the men of Deneaux could not cause this much destruction with their siege engines!" said Will.

"Then it probably isn't a siege engine causing this," said Mark.

"And it's not."

The group turned and saw Kinigos with his three Fen loyalists. They were all armed with his distinct natural longbow. The loyalists were also armed though with horrible looking great swords that had many hooks and sharp curves. "This is the work of that damned girl Dasimay! Toxotes is just waiting in the background like a coward!" He howled into the sky, and many of the nearby warriors growled angrily at this new enemy.

Dasimay frowned and looked up at the hall. "Come then you big, hairy scamp! "I'm well up and ready for a challenge!"

Kinigos and his men charged down on all fours at an incredible speed, jumping over and dodging the rubble left by her attacks with ease.

"Toxotes Barrage!" she shouted as she released a hail of arrows.

Again they kept running, dodging whenever they needed.

Dasimay went to her side and picked and arrow. She drew and released quickly, fumbling every other arrow and dropping it.

Kinigos and his men were just about in range and Dasimay was already dashing backwards.

"Khthon!" one shouted. Vines shot up from the ground and tied around her ankle.

"Pyro!" she countered as a fireball burned away the plant.

"Soul Technique: Mouth Cannon!" commanded Kinigos. There was a shockwave near his mouth as he said it, and the invisible energy flew towards Dasimay.

It was too fast for her to dodge and made a direct hit to her left side, charring her fur and turning it black. She struggled to her feet and made for her bow, but a loyalist was already coming down with a downward thrust with his great sword. She rolled away as it brought up the stones nearby.

The same loyalist was charging for her again, and she raised her hand to him. "Hades Ekriksi!"

The Fen hardly dodged the surprise attack and felt a horrible pain on his right side. He stumbled and reached for his arm. It was not there.

He struggled to put up his other hand for a counter attack, but Dasimay was too fast. "Pertusus!" The small beam tore easily through his flesh and pierced his heart, killing him on the spot. She watched as he was crumpled on the ground.

"Geo!" commanded the second loyalist as vines began to rise around Dasimay. She rolled away and held both hands in the air.

"What the hell is she doing?" asked Kinigos to himself.

Dasimay spread her feet to form a stable stance, and raised her hands. "Ishis Teresa Katastrofi!"

The loyalist stopped in his tracks as he saw the blast and attempted to cancel it out. "Fos Ekriksi!" The ball of light that he sent was no match for the mass of dark energy and it was overtaken. As was he as the attack hit him.

The third loyalist saw that this was no mere Fel, considering the fact that she was killing immortal men. But yet she was no Divine.

"Nirimos; watch out!" cried Kinigos from away.

He turned to see a large mass of neutral energy coming towards him and attempted to stop it with his own hands. He held it in place with all his strength, and was actually beginning to push it away.

"Pertusus Katastrofi!" she commanded as the beam went through his chest.

The blast shook the ground where Nirimos stood and the neutral energy sphere soon followed, crashing down as his strength gave way leaving a crater where he previously was.

Mark grabbed Akina's hand. "We need to get you out of here."

"I shall not leave my country in its time of need Mark. I will weather out the storm."

"You don't weather a hurricane. We need to get you away!" said Will.

"My people would never forgive me if I ran to save my own life."

"Then let's evacuate your people. That way you wouldn't leave their side," said Mark.

"Or you could just let me kill you," said a voice.

The three looked down in horror as Dasimay walked up the stairs to the Hall. She smiled sinisterly at Akina, but then turned her back and raised her hands to the sky. "Arise, master of the Hunt and of the predators of Third Earth! Arise Toxotes; Bane of Kinigos!"

Kinigos' eyes widened as he heard the name Toxotes. During the 300 year war, he and Toxotes had fought bitterly for many years at the battles of Fang, Claw and eventually Rage, where he eventually got his followers to weaken him. He then sealed Toxotes into the earth and built Fel Hall over it to make sure anyone of his clan would have trouble finding him.

The large Fen rose from a crack in the earth, and released a mighty howl that sent anyone nearby into the rest of the city to hide. He was as big as Kinigos, but seemed a bit thinner. His fur was jet-black and his eyes were red, with grey lines extending from the end of each and then down his face.

"My true love, Toxotes!" exclaimed Dasimay as she vanished from nearby the keep and appeared by his side.

"Yes Dasimay my dear, I have awoken to wreak revenge on Kinigos!" he began. "Where is he anyway?"

"Right here Toxotes," he replied calmly as he appeared before them.

"Still just a big, fuzzy idiot. Good old Kinigos," Toxotes spoke, looking down on his old enemy.

"Just quit your horrible jokes and get back into your seal, or head back to the realm of the Divines."

"After all you have done for me? I would be such a horrible person if I didn't repay the favour." His fist had already slammed into Kinigos' stomach, and he coughed from the speed of the blow, lurching forward to ease the pain. "Not yet Kinigos, we still have much to do."

"Why yes we do. Gaia!" the vines were about the reach out the ground, but Toxotes countered.

"Ishis Exochos Hephaestus Katastrofi!" the city was surrounded by a ring of fire, and the heat was slowly beginning to become unbearable. The plants began to wither, the required earth energy slowly beginning to be choked out.

"Toxotes please. You can kill me but not my followers!" he begged.

Toxotes shrugged in return and looked at the Fel warriors. "They are just a bunch of extra hairy humans, and this world has enough of those."

He waved his hand and the ring began to close in, turning the wood wall to ash without it even burning.

Kinigos drew several strange markings into the ground and smiled. "Take care, my followers." He rose to his feet and howled at the moon. "Men of Fel Hall, retreat to Fang!"

A smaller ring formed around the city, and every citizen's found themself glowing. They slowly began to levitate, and then they vanished in a bright light.

"Now we can continue our little skirmish," said Kinigos to Toxotes.

"Oh I can only wait."

The tribe found themselves on the forest ground in the middle of the night among old broken ruins. Akina looked about at the confused, panicked and grieving citizens. Apparently, the dead Fel were also transported to the clearing.

"What do we do now Chief?" asked a citizen fearfully.

She scratched her head thoughtfully. "I-I don't know, but I'll think of something," she replied.

"Think of something?! We have wounded here!" another snapped.

"Are you raising your voice at me?"

"Most people here are ready to do so until you get things going."

"I need to think, I am not Kinigos."

"We can clearly see that you are not!"

Kullskash, Illeth, Mark and Will came to her side.

"Give me some time and I will put something together."

Several citizens began to grumble in protest. They soon became shouts and many were raising their fists in the air.

Mark looked side long at the horse drawn cart that had seemingly appeared. "Akina, you may want to step back a bit," he advised.

She followed and took a step back, only to escape the wide arc of a sabre. Kullskash side stepped a spear thrust and lunged out with her sword. There was a short cry of pain and her sword returned to her, covered in blood. This enraged the people further, and Akina was pulled back from the battle.

Mark had taken her to the cart and threw her in, firing several shots with his bow as he let her go. Kullskash and Will were slowly backing away from the mob in an attempt to run into the cart and not get stabbed while they turned their backs.

"Crouch!" commanded Mark. The two bended their knees but kept on deflecting and dodging any strikes coming their way. He held three arrows in the gaps between his fingers and fired one after that other rapidly. The mob fell back as four of their number went down. "Now hurry up!"

The two of them ran over and jumped onto the back of the cart. Mark jumped onto the front and whipped the reins. The horses neighed loudly and charged down the forest road, leaving the rabble alone to think of their own way out of this.

This was a new age, Akina thought. The age of the Divines.

Chapter 14

Deneaux

Jor frowned at the map he held in his hands. Adele had been no help so far in directions due to the fact that he only had knowledge of the roads that existed 500 years ago. Alda had never left Denhoec a day in her life.

"Jane, which way?" he asked finally. He had told her that he could lead them easily to this huge empire of Deneaux with just the map, and refused any help that Jane offered.

"Giving up I see. Give it to me." Her eyes looked over it carefully and she pointed to one of the dirt roads nearby. "That should do it."

"A dirt road? Really?" asked Jor.

"I took this same road when I left here. It leads straight to Deneaux."

"They sound very sophisticated to have dirt roads," Alda added. Jor smiled.

"Yes, the High Chief would never leave the roads in this kind of state," said Adele. The proper term would be King, but that word was rarely used all those years ago.

Jane smiled and shook her head at Adele's comment. "Only because you're cute Adele." She began walking. "You guys can take the roads paved with gold; I'll take the dirt road to our intended location."

Jor, Alda and Adele looked at each other.

"Let's go with her then," Jor said finally.

Jane was ahead of them with her eyes glued on the map. Jor frowned again and took up pace to get next to her.

"So you know maps well?" he asked.

"Enough to get me around. Where I used to live, I got training with these kinds of things."

"I guess I can't argue whether or not you know where you're going," Jor replied.

"Please; I always know where I'm going..." She rammed head on into and oak and fell on her backside. Alda struggled to smother her laughter and turned away.

"Then I guess you would rather enjoy reading the map yourself raider!" she shouted towards Alda.

"Sorry, but I bash trees, they don't bash me!" she said, bursting into laughter.

Jane cursed under her breath and continued on her way, making sure to stay in the middle of the road.

After about half an hour of walking, they were beginning to see the towers of Deneaux.

"I told you we could get there," Jane said as she ran forward happily. She crashed into something again and fell on her behind. "Not another damned tree!" she exclaimed. She looked up and saw something that definitely was not a tree.

It was a Deneauxic guard.

"Who are you to be going around and bumping into things?" he asked. She tried to answer, but was taken aback by this handsome soldier before her. He had relatively clear skin, but had a scar or two. His hair was blonde and went down to his neck. He had striking blue eyes that enthralled her despite the fact that they stared angrily at her. "Well, state your name citizen."

"O-Oh, I'm Jane Pagos, and these are my friends."

Jor and Alda nodded, but Adele extended his arm to him. "I always wanted a chance to see a modern day Deneaux guardian. How goes your duty?"

The soldier shook his hand firmly and smiled. "Now I'm doing fine since I met up with two beautiful young ladies and a young admirer," he replied.

Alda shrugged the comment aside and looked the other way.

Jor felt somewhat hurt as he realized he was left out, but shrugged it aside as well.

The soldier helped Jane up from the ground, and kissed her hand once she was up. "My name is Turner Gales, militia man of this fine country."

Jane giggled and blushed at him. "Would you have time to give us a tour?" she asked.

"It's a good way down the next hill to get to Deneaux; we could talk on the way."

"I would love that," Jane said as she kept hold of his hand.

Jor cringed at the sight and followed with Alda and Adele.

"So Jane, what brings you to this side of the Cardia?" Turner asked.

"I had some trouble up at the tower of Divines, but nothing too big." She was too busy staring into his eyes to even recall the troubles she met at her home.

"Trouble? How about I get the rest of the army together and rough them up a little?" he joked.

Jor cringed again as she laughed along with his terrible joke. Adele walked up beside him.

"You seem disturbed," he said simply.

"Well I'm not," Jor replied in an even simpler reply.

"Why don't you walk up there and join in on the fun?"

"I'll live."

"Then why not talk with Alda?"

"Alda does not want to talk to me. More simply she doesn't talk unless it concerns smashing and hacking."

"Smashing and hacking what?" asked Alda as she suddenly appeared right behind them.

"See, that's all that she pays attention to."

"Hacking and smashing? That's all I'm ever interested in." Alda patted Jor on the back. "For a small raider you can swing that sword."

"I doubt that would be what my mother wants."

"That's crazy talk, any raider would be proud to have their son in the heat of battle and giving blows."

"My mother is dead Alda," Jor replied.

"Then she is probably smiling at you."

"It almost felt like you cared for something other than fighting just now."

"You're welcome too Jorigsveer," Alda said sarcastically.

"We're here," said Turner.

Alda and Jor were astonished by the size of the walls that defended the city. This was no ordinary town. This was Deneaux.

"Those are some high walls!" Alda exclaimed.

"Yes, but they seem quite old," Adele said.

"It's been five hundred hundred years Adele, the walls will probably look old," Jane said.

Turner regarded them strangely; then took them past the gate guards and into the city.

Deneaux truly was a sight to behold. The buildings were arranged in rows that went far down the streets and formed probably hundreds of alleys. The streets were covered by cobblestone that stretched for miles around, and people were busy with their daily lives. It was also surprisingly warm, and Jor and Alda both realized that they were sweating in the thick clothes they were wearing.

"Turner, do you think you could get us something else to wear?" asked Jor.

"Probably I could get something for you, raider girl, we in Deneaux have beautiful dresses and skirts," he replied, ignoring Jor.

"You apparently can't see me then?" Jor asked, a little aggravated.

"Oh yeah, I could probably get the tailor to throw something together for you." He turned to Jane again. "And for you Lady Pagos, I will try to get you something with class. It won't be the best since I'm paid generously, but it will be something to fit you perfectly."

"Pfft, Lady Pagos my foot," mocked Jor silently.

"I think I can sense a worm of jealousy in you," said Adele.

"I'm not exactly for relationships, but I can see it too," said Alda.

"I am not jealous!" Jor protested.

Several people looked at him. He glared back and they soon got back to their own business.

"It is causing an imbalance in your energies. I can see it and sense it," said Adele.

"We will continue this argument when there are fewer ears about."

They made their way to an inn and bought several rooms. Adele and Jor sat in a room that they shared with Turner. Turner however, was off with Jane to the tailors. Alda soon came in with them.

"So I heard you like Jane," said Alda with a small, slick smile.

"Damn you Alda," Jor replied.

"I can sense your energy spike a bit when you're near her," said Adele.

"And what do you know about energy?" Jor challenged.

"You may not believe it, but my powers are up to par with Jane, though I'm a bit weaker due to not using my powers over the span of two hundred years."

"Then let's see a demonstration," said Alda.

"Pyro!" commanded Adele with the echo that accompanied soul commands. A fire burned brightly in his hands. He soon extinguished it. "That is nothing compared to the amount of energy I used fighting Mortha those years ago, she only defeated me because of a piercing attack to my throat."

"But we are off the topic of Eros and Jor," said Alda, alluding to the Divine of Love.

"You are hell bent on ruining me, aren't you?" Jor asked.

"I want to see how much you can take."

"How lovely."

Adele put his hand on Jor's shoulder. "You have a brother and sister to support you Jor, talk to us about any problem."

"Well, I don't trust Turner as much," Jor said finally. "He's just about been ignoring me since we met him. Not to mention spending every waking moment with Jane."

"So you do like her," said Alda.

"It's not that! We're just good friends and she just hasn't been hanging out with me as much."

Adele didn't want to be on Alda's side of the argument, but he didn't want to throw away his own questions and thoughts. "So she is a good friend?"

"I suppose my only friend when she was staying in Denhoec. I really could tell her anything."

"And that's why you liked her...er...as a friend," said Adele.

Jor nodded uncertainly; then feeling that this may disclose certain information, he focused his attention on the sound of the door being ripped open, and the angry shouts of the innkeeper. They ran downstairs to see a boy around their age, if not older, dressed in a sand coloured shirt and same colour hide kilt with leathery pants. They soon saw the sabres at his side.

"Who the hell do you think you are to be breaking down the damn door to the inn?! Apparently you must think that you are the only person who goes through it!" ranted the inn keeper.

The boy dropped to his knees. He looked exhausted to the point of dying on the spot. The innkeeper was a pitiless man and took no care to his situation. "Now you're going to die? Do it on the streets so I don't have to clean you up!" As he got closer to throw the boy out, he felt something cold on the flesh of his large belly.

"You better show some quality service before I have to clean you up," he said hoarsely, not removing his sabre from the man's body.

"Don't worry, we'll pay for his stay," said Alda.

Jor and Adele looked at her, puzzled as to why she was offering to help this stranger.

"A-Alright, just keep him away!" the innkeeper replied.

The boy lay quietly on the third bed that was in Jor and Adele's room. Alda frowned at how quiet he was, despite the fact that he was awake.

"You going to play mute?" she asked.

"My words only know to talk of my never ending sadness," he replied, shifting away from her on the bed.

She saw that the sabres at his side were still bloody. "What happened?"

"They cursed us. We were surrounded, and hardly survived. We fell to the rift that brought the downfall of my spirit brothers and the death of my joy."

"Who are 'they'?"

"The dreaded Divines: Ema, Haima and Sahra'a, their big brother. They will destroy everything!"

Alda wasn't the best at conversations, but she could tell this subject was ripping him apart.

"So what's your name?" she asked quickly.

"Zen Zeran," he said with a great amount of effort.

"Well, a warrior needs a rest after every great battle. You probably deserve one now."

Zen was already sleeping.

Jor smiled as he walked into the room. "You really seem to like him."

"Shut up Jor!" she exclaimed. She turned back to check on Zen, but he was too far off to hear anything.

"I always knew you would find someone eventually," Jor remarked, glad for revenge.

C H A P T E R 15

Rough Affairs

Jane spun around as she showed off the dress Turner had gotten her. It was a basic red dress, but the shimmering objects and its material made it look otherwise. It was made for humans, but she simply let her tail drag slightly on the ground. Turner offered Alda a dress, but she quickly declined.

Jor had been tempted to look up, as he had kept his eyes focused on his feet to not make any eye contact with either Turner or Jane.

"Not bad Jane," said Adele. "You could pass off as a noble any day."

Turner held out a dark robe and held it near Adele. "Yep, perfect size for a soul guardian as yourself."

Adele's face lit up as he took the garment. "How did you know I was a soul?"

"I can sense a bit of soul energy here and there. I'm not exactly a pro at it though."

A horribly made jerkin landed on the table near Jor. He looked up and saw Turner wasn't even looking in his direction.

"Turner, take your jerkin, I don't need it," Jor said.

"What? You rather stay in the walrus skin of yours or switch to something that normal people wear?" asked Turner.

Alda and Jor looked slightly hurt by the comment, but Jor kept back a modest amount of his seething rage. "My mother made this."

"Well she didn't do too good a job. You should really make your own clothes then if you don't want to end up in that horrible rabble of cloth."

80

Jor slammed a dagger down into the hard wood of the table, and he knocked his chair over as he got up. "My mother died for me and the selfish dogs I'm forced to call brothers by right of birth. She made this and every other rabble of cloth I wore since day one with love and compassion. Now you pass it off as walrus skin?!"

Turner's hand dropped to his hilt and he smiled.

Adele noted the action.

"In the kingdom of Deneaux, every citizen is entitled to his own opinion," he replied.

"Perhaps it would be best if you two could get along," said Jane, an air of authority around the simple comment, making it sound like a command.

They stared in each other's eyes, neither man backing down.

Jor turned and pulled his dagger from the table and sheathed it. He glared at Turner one last time and stormed back upstairs.

Adele, already dressed with the black robes over his regular clothes, ran up the stairs behind him.

"Jor, are you ok?" he asked to the form that was wrapped up in sheets on the bed.

"I was so close to fighting him. Almost too close," he replied, as if Adele wasn't there.

Adele took a seat on the bed beside him. "I suppose now you have a reason to dislike Turner."

"I might try to get things straight with him tomorrow, peacefully mind you."

Adele patted his back and smiled. "I'm going back downstairs then. See you tomorrow."

"Yes. Yes. Now let me sleep."

The group ate breakfast that day at the inn. Most of them didn't want to bring up the confrontation that occurred last night before another one began. They turned as they heard the wooden stairs creaking.

"Zen, you're awake," Alda said.

"I thank you for your service to me, I will not forget it," he replied. "Do you have space for another friend?"

"To friends, yes. Are you a friend?" asked Jor.

"I am in debt to you all, if you wish me to be a friend, then a friend I will be."

Jor smiled and pushed out a seat for him. He took a seat and smiled at Alda.

"Aren't you a raider? It is most unusual to find your people outside of Zeran," he said.

"There are raiders in the deserts?" asked Adele.

"After the 300 Hundred Year War, they sailed to the deserts because of insufficient sailors and soldiers to survive the crossing of Hell's Sea," Zen explained.

"I'm from the east in raider land," said Alda.

"Then there is one thing that is true," said Zen. "Raiders of the east are far prettier."

Alda choked as she heard his comment. Jor and Jane burst into laughter at her reaction. She turned to him angrily.

"Just keep those comments to yourself, or you'll see how ugly I can get!"

Turner looked side long at Jor and smiled sneakily. "So Lorkeri, how you feeling?"

Jor frowned as he looked about for another person in the room; then he finally realized that Turner was insulting his name, but tried his best to not take it. "My name is Jorigsveer of Clan Great-Blade."

"Great-Blade? I haven't heard of this great clan 'Great-Blade'," Turner replied.

"There were only eight of us before—things happened."

"No shame in being disowned Jorigsveer; it's only natural for someone with such cowardice to be kicked out of your clan." He made sure to make another comment that would hurt him further. "You really couldn't call yourself a Raider."

"And I thought the men of Deneaux had class, I guess I was wrong. You just seem like another bandit or brigand to me," Jor replied calmly.

"What did you just call me?"

"Did I hit a nerve, or is it just me?"

"You really don't want a tavern brawl this early in the morning. Hitting a guardsman is a chief offense."

"And that is why I won't hit you."

"Are you sure?"

Jor sighed. "Why don't we stop this and get along?" He extended his hand.

"Get along with the guy that could have stabbed me last night?"

"I'm sorry okay, I just got mad," he replied, trying to sound as calm as he could.

"Then don't get mad around me if you plan on breathing," said Turner. He stormed out of the inn and slammed the door behind him. The innkeeper cringed.

"I'll see if I can talk to him," said Jane as she left the room.

Jor put his hands over his face and slumped in his seat. "How could I have messed that up!" he exclaimed

Adele put his hand on his shoulder, a movement Jor was starting to get used to. "You two just need time away from each other."

"And how do you suppose we do that?"

"Why not take a tour of the city? It seems like a good idea to me."

<h1 style="text-align:center">Chapter 16</h1>

The Eros AffairsPart 1

Jor and Adele were out on the city, taking up the beauty of the many gardens and high statues. It was surprising though; that everyone kept a strange marking that resembled a heart, only that it was drawn using only straight lines instead of curves.

"Adele, you know those symbols?" asked Jor.

"They seem familiar. They're probably something to ward off witches and ghosts and supernatural things of that nature," he replied.

"In a city with so many guards? I don't think so."

"People have strange beliefs, but this one baffles me."

There were loud shouts coming from the resident district square nearby.

"Now what's happening?" asked Jor as he ran ahead. Adele followed.

"Get back! Alice is mine!" shouted one townsman.

"You'll get her over my dead body!" another replied.

The two men soon began fighting, and as they fought, more and more joined in to the full force street brawl.

"What the hell?" said Jor, astounded at the size of the battle. Even fights in Denhoec, Raider territory, never got this bad.

"What are they fighting for?" asked a townsman.

"Apparently they are fighting for a girl named Alice," Adele answered.

"What?! That's my girl, get away you rats!" shouted the townsman as he attempted to enter the brawl, only to have a spiked club crash against his face.

Jor noticed someone from the corner of his eye run into an alley, and a street fight was not something people stopped watching. "Adele, you try to stop the fighting, I'll go check on someone."

Adele nodded and Jor ran off down the alley. He spun his obsidian staff in his hand and then held it in front of him. The tip glowed faintly as he gave the command. "Pyras Aerio Katastrofi!"

The sky lit up in a fiery explosion that almost instantly stopped the fighting. As they saw the boy with the pitch black staff and robes, they ran in fear of provoking this "wizard's" wrath.

Jor vaulted over old crumbled blocks and crates as he made chase to the person. They soon realized they were being followed and picked up pace.

"I only want to talk to you!" shouted Jor in a futile effort to stop them.

"You wanna talk? Pyro Ekriksi!" they commanded in return. The small fireball flew down the thin alleyway and struck Jor in his chest. It burned away easily at the fur material and struck his chest. He staggered, but kept on going.

"I'm not in the mood for a fight!" he said through clenched teeth. "But if you plan on shooting me like that again I *will* reconsider!"

"Aerio Ekriksi!"

Jor forced himself unto the walls to his left side and drew his bow. It selected an arrow but it was blown away by the attack. He took another one and nocked it, then fired.

"Apsis!" she commanded as a small white shield made fully of energy formed on her hand. It successfully blocked the arrow, but Jor had already followed up on the attack and pinned her on the wall.

"What's your problem?!" he asked.

"I thought you were another one of those assassins coming to kill me!" she replied. Jor realized she was a Fel, he immediately realized also why so many men were fighting over her. She was most likely the cutest girl he'd ever seen, or would ever see.

He let her go. "I'm sorry, I just thought you may have known about the street fight, assuming you were the reason for it."

She looked away. "I'm Alice, the..." she stopped, as if she would say too much. "I'm just someone you should stay away from."

"You have a problem? If so, I could deal with it."

"Stay by me any longer and you may join a battle you can't deal with!"

"I survived that little fire you set on me, how hard could more battles be?"

"And who the hell are you?" shouted another voice. A townsman stood before them, but what set him apart from the rest was that he had a Deneauxic hand-bow.

A Deneauxic hand-bow was a small crossbow you could strap to your wrist. It was standard for soldiers and guards to have them, and many criminals and enemies to the kingdom knew why. At close range it could kill a man by sending a small, sharp bolt into soft spots like the neck and eye. The bolts were usually poisoned with simple substances that weren't meant for the human body, or with tainted blood.

"Well, talk, or else we could get down to business," he said again.

"What do you want?" asked Jor, putting up his hands.

"I want to know why you are messing with my girl."

"I'm not messing with your girlfriend," said Jor in a joking tone.

"Yes you are," the man replied in an opposite tone.

"No I'm not."

"Don't play with me damn it!"

"But I'm not playing with you—I'm toying with your mind."

"Why you little..." The man's words faded as he crashed on the ground.

Adele slung his staff back over his shoulder and frowned at Jor. "I thought you liked Jane?"

"I do, I mean I don't, I mean—you know what I mean!" Jor replied quickly.

"I quite frankly don't," Adele replied.

Alice's face lit up. "A love problem? Erosian Vigil can help you!"

"An Erosian Vigil?" Jor and Adele asked, both confused.

"We are—people who help in the issues of love," Alice replied, as if she did again not want to reveal too much.

"Now I remember!" exclaimed Adele. "You work for the Divine Eros!"

"Shut up boy! Do you want the Meso and his men to hear you?" asked Alice as she looked around.

"Meso?" asked Jor.

"The sworn enemy of Eros. He is slowly gaining numbers to go to war with her. For now though, our battles are always in secret."

"But you still haven't explained the street brawl," Jor said as he folded his arms.

Alice coughed. "Oh yes, well you see I wanted some loyalists for Eros, and by doing that I befriended many big, strong, attractive..." She was drooling for some time until Adele snapped his fingers. "Oh, sorry about that. But I got several men to be my friends in hope of them becoming loyalists."

"And you got too friendly," Jor said flatly.

"Yep, and now the whole district is fighting tooth and nail over me," she said, proud of herself.

"Then you could come with us to stay at the outcast inn," said Adele.

"Alice, are you down there?" asked a voice not too far off.

"That would be a wonderful idea, let's go," she said quickly.

CHAPTER 17

The Eros Affairs Part 2

"You're bringing an agent to a Divine in the same building as us? What were you thinking?!" shouted Jane angrily. "I especially thought you would go against something like that Adele."

"It was either that or blow up the entire Resident District to stop those crazed citizens," Adele replied.

"And we all know whose fault it really is," Jor said.

"Look, I'm only following the orders of Eros," said Alice.

"And getting yourself in trouble," said Adele under his breath. Alice heard the remark but paid no mind to it.

"Hey, be happy we get the company of another fine woman," said Turner as he tickled her chin.

"And who might you be? A big, strong guardsman come to my rescue?"

"Adele, Jor, she has to go," Jane said sternly.

"You sound quite jealous," Zen pointed out.

Jane's face lit up bright red, fully out of anger though. "Be quiet Zen, why don't you go build a sand castle somewhere?"

Zen smiled at her attempt at an insult. "No sand here, only a mad perialite girl. Right Alda?"

Alda was sitting in the corner of the room laughing at the whole situation. Now she frowned as she realized Zen was trying to bring her into the conversation.

"Yeah whatever," she replied. "Does in here feel hot to you?"

The innkeeper wiped his head with a cloth. "Sure has been."

Turner, Jane, Alice and Adele cringed.

"Something wrong?" asked Jor.

"Ekriksi!" shouted Adele. The door was flung open, but as the intruder took a step in, the blast of soul energy crashed into him.

The rest of the warriors drew their weapons and ran for the door.

"Geo!" shouted a voice. A large stone pillar shot out the ground in front of the door.

"Katastrofi!" commanded Alice. The stone erupted from the energy of the attack, but another larger stone took its place.

Jor took out his bow and got everyone's attention by standing on the counter. "Alice and Jane will keep attacking the stones that form up by the door. Me, Adele and Turner will go up and see what we can do from upstairs."

They simply nodded and followed the orders. Jor and the others rushed up the stairs and ran down the narrow hallway that led to the different rooms. As Jor was about the pass by a window, a fireball flew through and burnt the wall.

"That would not have been fun," he said.

"Neither will this," said Adele. "Thinami Hydro Ekriksi!"

"Apsis," commanded several of the attackers outside as they blocked the wall of water thrown at them with their tiny energy shields.

"Pagos!" Adele followed up. The water on the ground and in the attackers' clothes began to freeze up.

Jor took up the vantage point from the window and fired into the dark, aiming only at the sudden movements made. "I can hardly see them!"

"I'll handle that," Adele said. "Fos!" The area lit up as the ball of light came down.

"Turner, let's go!" said Jor as he brought his bow to full draw. Turner came with his hand-bow and opened fire with him. The two fired volleys after the attackers that were dressed in black below.

"Soul Technique: Burning Meso!" A large fireball broke through the wall, and as it faded, it revealed a horrible, jet-black figure with overly long arms. A smile broke on his face as fire caught around the hallway. "Bring me Alice and I *might* leave you with your mind intact."

"I'm not taking that chance," Jor said as he drew his great sword. Turner followed with his standard soldier's short sword and aided in the charge.

As they got halfway to him, he lunged with his long arms, knocking the two away.

"Anemos Ekriksi!" commanded Adele. The sharp blast of wind hacked away at Meso's side, leaving gaps.

They simply resealed themselves. "You are going to have to do a better job than that if you want to even cause pain."

"W-What are you?" asked Adele as his shoulders slumped.

"I am Meso, the embodiment of hate, servant to the hordes of the Erebus Isles and enemy to that wench Eros." He raised his hands. "Teresa Pyro Ekriksi!"

Adele hardly dodged the black flames that blazed past him. He smiled as he felt an increase in the amount of dark energy. "Teresa Ekriksi!" he commanded in return.

"Teresa Hoplon!" commanded Meso as a dark shield formed up on his arm. Adele's attack collided with it, but was not powerful enough to pierce the shield.

"Now I really want to know what you are," Adele said.

"I am a Divine my boy, nothing more and nothing less."

The candles were instantly blown out, and the hall way was shrouded in darkness.

"Damn it," said Jor as he tried to get back to his feet. He stumbled, but was able to make it up. "Adele, where are you?"

"Shut up Jor, we don't want him knowing our location!" Adele snapped at him.

"You forget that I'm a daimon. Our people are invisible in the darkness, and it makes our vision clear."

Turner rose to his feet and held out his hand. "Fos!" he commanded. There was a small flash in his hand, then a bright light illuminated the area.

Adele smiled and raised his left hand. "Aduro!" he commanded, and an even brighter light filled the room.

There was a silent hiss from Meso as he was thrown aback by the great lights. It was burning him. Eating slowly away at his being—destroying him. "Hephaestus Katastrofi!" he commanded in a desperate attempt at escape.

Adele watched in horror as there was a red spark in his hand. He slammed his own hand onto the wooden floors. "Gaia!" he commanded. The floors moved away board by board and the three dropped back down on the inn's ground floor, hardly escaping the flames that flew above them.

"Adele? What the heck are you doing down here?" asked Alice, a steady stream of standard white neutral energy flowing from her hands and smashing into the large boulder before them.

"Meso is up there giving us a new kind of hell, and I'm not the one to take it," Adele replied. "How long does it take to destroy one simple stone?"

"An extremely long time," said Jane. She was releasing a steady stream of frost on the boulder, focused right where Alice was aiming.

Adele raised his hand, but cringed and lowered it. "That last command took a lot out of me."

Alice and Jane lowered their hands and let out a sigh of relief.

"We aren't going to break through at the rate we're going," said Jane.

The building began to shake, and as soon as it did, the roof and upstairs lit up in an extreme burst of fire.

"Ishis Aqua Aegis!" commanded Jane at that moment.

Many of the attackers retreated when the guard arrived, though they could have put up a good fight against them, but such was not part of Meso's commands. The guards now looked at the burning tavern, searching between the flames for any sign of life.

The building exploded from the roof and many of the guardsmen fell or stumbled as it shook the area. Right before the explosion though, you could hear an echoing shout.

"Get the citizens and militia to bring buckets to put out the flames, and hurry!" exclaimed the head guardsman to another.

Jane fell to her knees, the large shield made entirely out of water surrounding the group. Alda held her axe ready and pointed into the flames. "I see someone!"

Alice stumbled as she saw the figure.

Meso.

"Now I've finally got you my dear," he said, a ball of dark energy animating between his two large palms.

"Meso, please," she begged.

He smiled as he saw Jane struggling to keep up the shield. She was going to run out of energy soon, and once this shield was down, there would be nothing stopping Meso from destroying them. "No."

"Meso, if anything you should be begging," said a voice.

Meso turned his head to see another Fel, this one was smaller than Alice by a head, and wore a white dress.

"Kilan? How the hell did you find us?!" asked Meso in surprise.

"I just sensed a heap of fire and dark soul energy around this point, far more than would be found in nature. All that was left to do was follow it." She pulled a black and silver dagger from the sleeves of the gown. Meso cringed at the sight.

"Don't think that little knife is going to hurt me!" he yelled, his voice cracking as he did. He aimed the energy in his hands at Kilan, and released.

She simply jumped away from the attack, and in mid-air she clasped her hands together. "Aduro Ekriksi!"

Shining balls of light cut into Meso's side, tearing away once again at his sides. It reformed, but he seemed tired.

She landed on a burning platform and pointed her index finger at Meso. "Fos Pertusus!" A bright, thin beam shot out of her hand and shredded through Meso. He recoiled and raised his hand.

"Pyras!" he commanded as the flames engulfed Kilan.

"Tahitita!" she commanded in reply.

The flames surrounded the platform, then came together in a small ball, then it burst and exploded in all directions.

"Meso's distracted," said Alice. "Let's try getting out of here."

Jor sheathed his great sword and took up Jane, who had just about passed out from holding up the shield. Now that it was gone, he realized how hot the room was.

A wall of dark energy shot out of the ground before them. "Don't think you kids are getting out of this one!" Meso yelled.

"Fos Makhaira Barrage!" commanded Kilan as she suddenly reappeared.

Meso still had his attention on Jor and the others.

And his back turned on Kilan.

The knives made fully of light stabbed into his back. He screamed in agony as he felt himself slowly burning away once again.

"You thought you could get away from me huh?" taunted Kilan.

"I did, the question is though," he paused and raised his hands slowly. "Do you think *you* will get away?"

Kilan turned in horror as the night engulfed her. The shadow was thin and twisted like a snake.

Meso turned back to the group. "Now you're finished."

"Not yet!" shouted Adele. "Astrape Barrage!" "Fos Ekriksi!"

A pink aura pulsated around Alice as she smiled at Meso. She winked. "Soul Technique: Snake's kiss!" she commanded.

"Khthon!" commanded Meso as a boulder shot out of the ground and stopped the string of lightning. He side-stepped the burst of light and his eyes grew wider as he saw Alice's follow up attack.

She was instantly upon jabbed at him with hand. It instantly began to burn and he stepped back.

"I can't see straight! What did you do to me?!" he asked franticly.

"You're captivated. I could have tried the move earlier, but you would have had the energy to dodge it."

His vision was blurred and he was having trouble breathing. He had to do something to save his skin, but his options were limited. Then he remembered.

"Get me back to normal or I'll kill the girl!"

Alice's mood quickly turned from confident to frantic. "Please Meso, don't do this!"

"Then get me back to normal!"

"The effects will eventually wear off, I can't do it manually!"
"Then Kilan dies!"

"Tachista!"

Adele charged into Meso, his fists taking away pieces of Meso's dark body with each lightning fast strike. It was nothing like Meso or Alice had seen before. Adele's staff slashed across his neck and sent him sliding into the flames and rubble.

His aura burst out from within him, a black flame-like energy that represented his major element. "Aduro," Meso's eyes widened as he felt a surge of the opposite energy. "Ekriksi!" Adele screamed as the large sphere of light slammed into the night serpent.

The sky lit up as if it was day for a second and the district shook violently once again, this time though, it was a much stronger shaking.

The citizens dropped their buckets and ceased in putting out the flames. They immediately ran for their lives, along with the guards.

The area was silent. Only the sounds of the cracking fire could be heard.

"Adele, Kilan!" shouted Alice as she searched between the flames for any signs of life.

There was no reply.

"Damn it Adele, where are you?" asked Alda, her battle axe still in hand.

In between the flames, a figure was walking forward. As they got closer, it could be seen that they were holding someone in their hands.

"Please do not tell me that it is Meso approaching," said Zen, a good amount of anger in his voice. Alda noted that he firmly held his sabres ready.

Alice's face lit up as, out of the flames, Adele appeared, holding Kilan in his arms.

CHAPTER 18

The Eros Affairs Part 3

Adele flinched as Alice dabbed the strange liquids she kept on his skin. She told him that is was to clean the cuts that he had attained in the battle and help them to heal faster. Jor and Turner went through the same procedure, flinching with each touch of the foul liquid. Kilan had simply gone through it quietly.

Meso had escaped that night, and the group had no problem doing the same. The guard had arrived later that night with Paladins and Mystics from the Pantheon Castle. They investigated the dead and the damages done to the building, and promised the innkeeper compensation for the building.

"All done Adele," said Alice as she put away the chemicals.

"Thank the Divines that's over," he said. Alice looked side-long at him but said nothing.

Adele smiled at Kilan, but she frowned at him in return.

"What do you want?" she asked in a completely different voice to that of when they were fighting Meso. She at first spoke loudly and challenged Meso whenever possible. Now this voice sounded quiet and shy. She realized Adele was about to speak and she regretted her own words.

"I just wanted to know if you were ok."

"Do I look ok?" she asked, sounded a little more aggressive than she intended.

"So you're a fighter eh?"

"So are you," she said blankly. "Maybe we should be friends," she remarked sarcastically.

Adele put his arm around her. "Why not?" he said equally.

Her energy spiked for a moment and a powerful backhand flew across Adele's face. "Who do you think you're messing with?!"

"I'm not messing with anyone. I'm just trying to talk to my civilized friend Kilan!" he replied angrily.

"I'm not your friend!"

"And you apparently aren't civilized either!"

She grabbed him by his collar and hoisted him up.

"We could take this outside if you want!" shouted Adele. His voice cracked, but his point carried through.

"I thought the men of Deneaux never harmed women?" she mocked

"Well this one blew up a few Raider women when their longboats landed on the beaches of Harmony!"

Kilan dropped him. "Harmony? That place has been gone for centuries."

"I know. I was killed at the battle there by the Divine Mortha. I had put up a good fight, but that hag was three seconds faster and caught me with an obsidian spear."

"That's and interesting story," said Kilan. "But how are you here if you were killed?"

"Mortha used the energy of many souls on other worlds to gain strength. It would not be impossible to drain her energy with an obsidian weapon, as spirits can make contact with it. If Adele here were to get all of Mortha's energy, he would be able to revert back to mortal form," Alice explained as she put her supplies in the shelves.

Kilan frowned in thought at what was just said. "So you were struck down by a Divine at the battle for Harmony?"

Adele nodded. Alice snickered.

"Then that would make you the Dark Champion wouldn't it?" asked Kilan, her cheeks turning rosy.

"The what?" asked Adele, totally puzzled by this new title.

"When you died that day and Harmony was taken over in the years after, people began to see you as a Martyr, and thus the men of Deneaux charged head on into the Raider threat and held the border for all those years." Alice patted Kilan's back. "You even have a week dedicated to you, with plays and games and everything. Not to mention that it is Kilan's favourite holiday..."

"Oh no, please don't say more," she pleaded.

"As long as I knew Kilan, she would always watch the mural of the robed figure on a black mare doing battle with the Divine of the Dead, sighing at the idea of being able to meet her childhood hero."

"I never thought I would be so famous," he said. He paused and realized something else. "I never thought I would be famous to girls either. Can I go see this mural?" he asked.

"Alice will take you," Kilan replied quickly.

"You forget I have guests here at the Star-Crossed Inn," said Alice.

"Then I'll take you," she said, defeated.

Adele extended his arm to her.

"I'm being very generous to walk you there. Holding your hand will be too far."

"You seem to forget that I'm your favourite champion."

Kilan smiled. "You'll have to be more than a little lover boy to prove to be the Dark Champion."

The streets of the Chapel district were unusually empty today, Kilan noted. Something strange would have to be going on for priests and the sick to not be heading to the temples, but she dismissed the idea. It was a little foggy out after all.

"Is that the mural?" Adele asked.

On the wall of one of the temples was a large painting that was bordered by silver stars and large round shields. Upon it was a green land, and at the edge of it was the sea. Many longboats were painted there, and many Raiders with axes, swords and spears were in them. In the middle of the painting was a figure in black robes and a pointed hat. The black horse he rode was reared up on its hind legs. The Champion's right hand was extended towards a painting of Mortha. From his hand came black streaks of lightning. In the other was a silver broadsword with a blue hilt.

Mortha was another story. She had a long, hooked nose and red beady eyes. Her hair was made up of horrible strands of black moss, an ingredient in many poisons. Her teeth were sharp and pointed, not to mention green and mossy. In her left hand was the black staff that had struck Adele down those many years ago.

Adele frowned in thought at the image, then a grin widened on his face. "And to think I could hardly lift one of those damned broadswords."

"So you fought Mortha with your soul energy alone?" asked Kilan in awe.

"Almost had her too." He studied his staff carefully. "But she had better aim—and immortality for that matter."

"It was a great battle though?" asked Kilan.

"We both stood our ground and were blasting away at each other for less than half an hour."

"And what about leading the men of Harmony into battle?"

"You really need a lesson in history don't you." He extended his hand again, and this time Kilan took it. He brought her to a bench nearby and sat down.

"You don't look happy."

"I am in a way, but all this raising my sword high into battle with the 'who knows how many soldiers that I apparently led-'"

"Ten thousand," Kilan interrupted.

Adele shook his head. "All of that is fabricated. You know who the Dark Champion really was?"

Kilan scooted over closer to listen.

"Adele Alan was page to Sir Leonardo George of the Knights of Harmony. He sat in an office all day signing papers and writing out all kinds of documents. Yes Darkness was my chosen branch of soul, but I only got to practice in my spare time—in secret. We were supposed to be studying Light Soul, but that was far too bright for me."

Kilan smiled at the idea of him hating light just as much as Meso, and gestured him to go on.

"I never owned a horse, I walked to where I wanted to go. As I said, I could hardly lift a sword, and I wore regular old chainmail. I only recently got these robes."

"So all what they said, the battle that almost destroyed the coast, the thousands of dead Raiders—all of that is just over exaggerated?"

"Over exaggerated is an understatement. I'm a complete opposite to this Champion. You can continue to celebrate him, because he is surely another person."

Kilan put her arm around him. "You know, I think I like this Adele Alan character, he sounds cool."

"Cool? That is another over exaggeration."

"Then what about cute?"

Adele's eyes widened at her compliment.

"I'm sure that fits you fine."

The Eros Affairs Part 4

Adele and Kilan were walking hand in hand back to the inn.

"Have you ever had a first kiss Adele?" asked Kilan.

Adele blushed. "Why do you ask?" he replied nervously.

"You seem like a—I can't say the word, but you seem like you could have had a few girls following you around and laughing at everything you say," Kilan replied.

"I was locked in a tower all day with a ton of paperwork. If anything, I wouldn't know what a girl was," he said flatly.

As they entered the inn, a few eyebrows rose.

"Adele and Kilan? Weren't you fighting this morning?" asked Alice in mock surprise.

Kilan quickly pulled her arm away from Adele. "We still are, we're just—making sure we didn't get lost in the fog."

"You two looked like you wanted to get lost in the fog," said Jor.

Kilan blushed and headed for the stairs. "I'm going to bed," she said in her soft voice.

"Adele, aren't you going with her?" asked Alda. Zen raised an eyebrow at the joke and looked for Adele's reply.

He simply ignored her and turned to Kilan. "Have a good rest then."

"Ok then, my champion." She said with a small smile.

"What did you two do while you were out?" asked Jane.

Adele smiled slyly. "I learned about the Dark Champion of Harmony."

The ground shook violently in the land of the Divines, cracking the ground. The area was a large forest, much like those of Den, but beneath the thick canopies were horrible beasts that Toxotes had let run free in his realm to do as they liked. They were the ants again, but these were considerably larger, and far more dangerous.

"Damn you Toxotes! Where is my Kinigos you bastard!" screamed a woman as several trees went down.

It was Eros, the Divine of love and marriage. She herself was another Fel like Alice and Kilan. She was far more beautiful and stood taller than both of them.

"Ishis Exochos Hades Hephaestus Katastrofi!" she screamed. The area was silent. Then the forest erupted in an enormous fiery blast that decimated several kilometres of it. "Toxotes, get out here or I will personally obliterate your realm with my own two hands damn it!"

Several ants hopped out from behind the trees, but Eros snapped her finger. "Soul Technique: Lux Lucis Flash!"

The Ants were torn apart as rays of light shredded through their bodies. Eros aimed again for the forests.

"Soul Technique: Red Lament!" A black and red circle marked with strange runes was projected over the ground. "You're going to regret this Toxotes!" She raised both her hands. "Red Lament invoked! Lament of Lux Lucis Hephaestus!"

The forests within the circle were burnt away by the inferno created by Eros.

"Is that wench serious?" asked Dasimay. She sat with both her legs on Toxotes' laps and her arms around his neck.

"She wants her husband Kinigos back, and who would I be to deny her?" said Toxotes.

"Oh hush with the modesty," she replied as she kissed him on the cheek.

"Dasimay, do you think you could take care of her?"

"Fighting a Divine like Eros alone? Are you sure I could handle that?"

"Why couldn't you my dear? If it helps, I'll send you with the Damned: Keevaal, Norik'sai, and Kos-Kin-Kai."

The three Fen immortals appeared before Toxotes at his call. "What do you wish of us master?" they asked in the same rough, grizzled voice.

"Make sure no harm comes to Dasimay as she does battle with Eros. Aid her in battle." Toxotes frowned, then smiled as an idea came to mind. "And bring her head on a platter."

"Toxotes you coward, stop hiding behind your little monsters and..." Out of the corner of her eye, she saw a glistening light. She instantly disappeared and reappeared in the air.

"Pertusus!" commanded a voice.

Eros simply moved to the side as the thin, piercing beam flew past. "Where's the follow up Dasimay?" she taunted.

A flurry of fists came towards Eros. She dodged them, dancing in the wind as she did. Dasimay's elegance and beauty only was rivalled by Eros, and seeing her like this enraged her even more. The speed of her attack increased, but Eros simply disappeared again.

"Where the hell did you go now?" asked Dasimay as she scanned the area.

"Exochos Pertusus!" she commanded. A large beam of soul energy surged forward Dasimay. Smoke filled the sky as the attack hit.

Kos fell on one knee as he felt the pain from taking the hit. He snarled and rose to his feet. "Hermes!" he commanded as he disappeared.

"Hermes!" commanded Eros as she did the same.

The other two Fen followed. Dasimay struggled to find the combatants energy as they sped around the area, kicking up dust and sending surges of energy into the sky.

"Now I'm mad, let me in the battle!" shouted Dasimay as her longbow animated from nothing into her hand. She felt something wrap around her neck, then felt darkness come over her as she realized she was sent flying by a powerful blow from Eros. She regained her consciousness and slid on her feet. "Damn Divines."

The ground shook as a low whimpering was heard, and both Kos and Norik came rolling through the ash and dust on the ground.

"Where is Keevaal?" Dasimay asked.

The bloodied Fen dropped to the ground, totally unmoving. The only sign of life from him were the groans of pain.

"Sagittarius!" commanded Dasimay as she released a shining, white arrow.

Eros grabbed it a few centimeters from the bow. "You're going to have to fire more than arrows to keep me away from my Kinigos."

"Ok then, Sagittarius Pertusus Katastrofi!" Dasimay commanded. The two Fen got up and immediately and dashed away from the impact zone. Destruction and Piercing were seldom used together, and the Fen knew that sitting there and gawking would not be the best idea.

The area lit up in a pure white blast as small, thin beams came surging out of it from every direction.

Toxotes looked out and the impact zone from his throne room built high on a stone pyramid. "Yes Dasimay and my loyalists, rid the world of Eros so that I may get through to Meso and Sahra'a. Our grand plan is almost complete." He smiled once again. "Edafos will be ours."

Eros lay in the center of a large crater, her body bloody and broken.

"Eros, are you all right down there? You seem to have a few holes through your major organs," Dasimay laughed.

"Just you wait half-born, Efiia will put you *and* that ugly tramp Toxotes into your places," Eros replied.

Half-Born was a term for beings born with Divine and mortal blood. Dasimay was one of the few half-born that existed in the realm of Edafos.

"Efiia is a pure, full on, tried and tested idiot Eros, you of all people should know that," said Toxotes, who had just appeared.

"There you are. Why did you send your guard dogs after me?" Eros attempted to lift her head up, but wasn't strong enough. "You should have come out and fought me like a man."

"And risk losing? No thank you."

Eros coughed up a mouthful of blood. "You really are a dog, aren't you Toxotes?"

Dasimay pulled out an obsidian arrow and nocked it. "It's high time you shut your dirty little mouth."

"Or maybe it's high time you shut yours! Soul Technique: Maxim Beam!" the voice commanded.

Toxotes jumped out of the way just in time, but Dasimay took a direct hit and was lost in the large beam of blue energy surrounded by white and yellow glowing runes.

"Efiia?! What are you doing here?" asked Toxotes, clearly panicked.

"I sensed that a fellow senior Divine was in trouble and made haste to rescue her," he replied.

Efiia was the Divine of Intelligence and was part of the a higher ring of Divines in the school of Divines. He was regarded as a sort of leader in the senior ring, despite the fact that they were all equals. He was good at giving advice in many situations, and was a very unique fellow.

He was also insane.

"G-Get back you old fart!" shouted Toxotes desperately as a black longbow animated into his hands.

"What? I believe you stuttered."

"Toxotes Barrage!" he commanded as a rain of arrows came towards Efiia.

He waved his hand in a dismissive gesture, and as he did, a league of spiritual knights broke through the ground, stopping every arrow with their large shields and armor.

"That was your soul technique: Call of the Kings, wasn't it," said Toxotes.

"How did you know? I didn't say anything, or did I?"

"Stop toying with me old man!"

"I'm not toying with you, I'm messing with your..."

"Shut the hell up you smart—stop no!"

The knights were already upon him and they began to hack and slash at him over and over again. The first couple slashes had cut him badly, and now he was dodging for his life, only relying on their continuous use of the same strokes.

Efiia leisurely walked down to the crater and picked up Eros. He smiled brightly at her and turned to his knights. "Dandy job men!" he called to them before disappearing in a large blue sphere of energy.

Alice almost dropped the kegs of cider she held as she neared Turner and Jane's table in the inn. Kilan was already downstairs and frowned at Alice.

"Eros has arrived Alice."

Right then and there was a knock on the door, and Alice hurriedly opened it. She turned pale just as she did.

"Eros, my guardian and protector, what has happened to you!" she cried as she saw the bloody body of Eros in Efiia's hands.

"Alice you imbecile, I am fine," Eros replied hoarsely.

"You must feel fine, because you certainly do not look fine," Efiia said.

"Shut...up Efiia," grumbled Eros as she passed out.

"I think you should take her up from here, I have to attend to these... problems," said Efiia as he laid Eros onto the ground and disappeared into the fog.

"The men of Meso will be on us now," Jane said.

"And that is what I want," said Kilan. "The second Meso shows his ugly face again, I will put my dagger through his head."

"That is fine for you soul power users, or whatever you are called. Me, Zen, Jor and Turner aren't ready for your level of fighting with these fireballs and ice walls," said Alda.

"We could teach you all," offered Alice, but Zen was already shaking his head.

"I watched a Divine use those same powers to murder my spirit brothers; what makes you think I will want to use those same powers?"

"You could use them for good like those at the Pantheon Castle," said Kilan.

"I think I will trust in the strength of my sword arm and the purity of my steel for now," Zen replied.

"Well, I'll be happy to learn, once I find a good teacher," said Jor with a smile.

Jane opened her mouth to speak, but Alice took up the chance before her. "I'd be glad to teach you!"

"Can you take more than one student?" asked Alda.

"I suppose I could help you," said Adele.

"Well, if Alda will do it, so will I," said Zen.

Turner frowned at it all and turned to Jane. He noticed a change in her facial features as Alice had offered to train Jor, almost like she winced.

He threw the thought aside and put his arm around her shoulder while stretching. "Guess this'll mean we'll be alone for a while."

"Alright Jor, let's get started," said Alice.

"In the fog? That does not seem like a good idea," Jor replied.

The small group stood in the square near the same mural with the Dark Champion.

"Ok, your soul is your life force, the only part of a mortal that is in truth immortal. Soul relies heavily on your level of willpower and courage, not by your physical strengths. But just like your physical strength, soul diminishes the more you use it, eventually killing you if you use up more than what is necessary to keep it bound to your body."

"So any special ways that I can begin using it? I mean I have loads of willpower and courage," Jor boasted

"That's good then," said Alice. "Now all you have to do is learn about the natural soul energy around you and how they can strengthen, or weaken your soul in turn."

"Now I'm starting to get lost."

"As you use your energy, it adds to your environment, meaning that if you can get off enough attacks of one element, you'll be using the rest of them without much energy. The problem is running out beforehand."

"Can you explain when Adele and Jane get that strange glow around then?"

"That's a matter of personal skill really. Jane is one of those 'special' gifted people who can 'grow grass with each step' or 'kick up a hurricane with each step'. Even Divines don't get to that level."

"And what happens when you use too much soul energy?"

"You're asking a lot of questions," said Alice with one of her sly smiles. "I like a smart man," she said under her breath.

"Excuse me?" asked Jor.

"Oh nothing; now what was your question?"

"About using too much energy..." he let it tail off.

"Oh yes, you die."

"Say what?!"

"I'm joking, I'm joking. You only die if you use too much of your own energy," she returned to the subject, "As I said, when you use a lot of elemental energy, you gain an aura related to it."

"I don't mean to sound like Alda, but when do we get to smashing things?"

Alice giggled. "If it makes you happy..." She kept her hand low and out of Jor's attention. "Ekriksi!"

Jor heaved himself to the side as the attack neared him. Alice's giggles soon turned to laughter.

"That wasn't nice!" he replied rapidly. He couldn't find anything else to say in his panicked state of mind.

"Soul is for fighting, it's not supposed to be nice."

C H A P T E R 20

Battle at Bearded Run

Twelve steel tipped spears lined up on a small sand ridge on the beachhead of Bearded Run, the landing used by the Raiders during the closing months of the war.

"Ifadeel, what do you see out there?" asked one of the elven captains, Gailo.

"Soul Sight!" commanded Ifadeel as his eyes began to glow white.

Several more units of twelve to fifteen men came down into the ditch.

"Captain Gailo, more units on the way," said one of the commanders to him.

"Good, if what was seen by those farmers is correct, we'll need far more than a hundred men."

Several hours had passed when they heard the sound that chilled their ancestors' blood those many years ago.

The chanting and beating of drums.

They heard it from out at sea, the deep thumping noise made by the drums, then the chant that came with it, and the sound of lapping waves against another object.

"Damn, just when I thought it was just simple peasant rumours," said a soldier as he tightened the grip he had on his halberd.

Ifadeel ceased his soul sight and winced as he tried to return to normal vision. "We have a ton of ships coming in!"

"How many Ifadeel?" asked the captain impatiently.

"Around..." he paused, unsure of himself, "Around two hundred. Each can hold about more men than we have here alone."

The small army looked uncertainly at their captain, and he gave the outward appearance of confident planning, but on the inside felt a deep fear welling up.

With this many ships came so many men, and considering again the amount of men on the ships, he might not be able to get enough men, even if he mustered every soldier of Keels.

"Ifadeel, hurry back to Rein-Keel and alert them to the possibility of a siege."

"Yes captain," Ifadeel replied as he climbed out from behind the ridge and ran for the cover of the trees.

Upon the flagship, which was more of a large galleon instead of the smaller longboats about it, was the Nordic commander and Jarl, Gulnar. He was large and muscular, wearing thick furs and an average iron medium helmet that exposed most of his face. Some of his blondish, stringy hair was hanging down from the sides of the helm. His eyes were bright like a child getting a sweet as he laughed heartily.

"Aren't I great Faen?" he asked one of his commanders. Gulnar was famous for his overconfidence.

"Why yes my Jarl, you will prove it once again when we take Keels and force our way into Crill," Faen replied blankly. He was used to the bragging for so many years, so he adapted and praised Gulnar to make his head considerably larger.

"And when we take the turn for Crill, we'll be able to watch a splendid light show."

"Yes, yes. Fenalph will probably break down that tower and take apart all those Perialites that like to study there."

Gulnar stretched and yawned, then his hand reached down to the hilt of his broadsword. "Great Cardia, you will soon be mine."

"Muster the entire army?!" exclaimed Sen'del, one of the elder councilmen. He wore his regular black robe and let his long, grey hair hang down.

"It will be that or we fight a superior enemy that also outnumbers us," Ifadeel said, folding his arms.

"We don't know if they are still superior."

"Well we need more men either way, and soon at that."

Sen'del frowned as he took a seat, deep in thought. He made a dismissive gesture to Ifadeel. "You can go back to the line; your comrades need you."

"Yes Councilman," he replied as he stood at attention and saluted.

"That's it!" exclaimed the Sen'del as he rose from his seat.

Ifadeel was startled by his sudden outburst and turned to the councilman. "What's it?"

"We'll use the pact we have with Deneaux! Once we get word to them we'll have thousands of men and who knows how many Divine Knights from the Pantheon Castle!"

"But we'll need one of our best riders to get to Deneaux in time to get units into Keels before the Raiders get too deep into the country."

"And I do have one in my mind," Sen'del replied slyly.

"Please, don't tell me," said Ifadeel as he put his hand over his face.

Lyradel, called "Lyra" by her family could have been considered the prize of her family, if she wasn't such a rough character. She wasn't exactly a tomboy, but wasn't exactly a girl either.

Just wild, reckless, crazy Lyra.

"Don't play around with this Lyra, you are on a royal mission and the fate of the country lies in your hands," advised Ifadeel.

She shrugged it aside. "Yes, whatever, just tell me where to go and I'll be off."

Ifadeel shook his head. "Just go to Deneaux and try your best to get your way to military officials. I packed the royal seal for emergencies and..."

"So which way is Deneaux?"

"Uh, just hit east hard until you make it to high stone walls. Because of the treaty, we have a big road between our countries, so *follow* the path," he said, putting emphasis on the word "follow", hoping it would counter her reply. No luck though.

"Roads are so boring, can't I go through the forests at least once?"

"No."

"Ok, but if I get taken by highwaymen, don't come to my funeral." She pulled on the reigns and soon was off before Ifadeel could reply.

"If it weren't for the Raiders, I would enjoy the idea of you being taken."

"Damn Raiders," cursed Gailo quietly as he studied each man as they disembarked the vessels.

"It's even more than we thought captain," said a soldier looking through a telescope.

The soldiers nearby let out a small, startled cry as they heard someone drop in.

"Quiet you schoolgirls, it's me!" exclaimed Ifadeel quietly as he pushed away a broadsword near his neck.

"Have they sent help?" asked Gailo.

"The men of Deneaux will soon come to our aid—as long as our messenger doesn't screw up."

"Screw up, what kind of person could fail a mission of that magnitude without dying?"

"Lyradel."

The captain stared blankly for a few moments, then let out an involuntary cry. "They sent out Lyra!?"

"Quiet captain!" exclaimed several of the men nearby.

Gailo realised his mistake and spoke more quietly. "They sent someone with her?"

"The only other person with her would be her horse," Ifadeel replied. "I'm hoping the horse is competent enough."

"Then I shall start writing my will."

"Don't fret captain, those Raiders will need several hours alone to get everyone off those ships and set up a command post."

"Excuse me? A Raider army on the shores of Keels?" asked the grey haired man as he paced around in his tent. He was the commander of the border patrols that watched over the border of Keels and Deneaux.

"Why else would they send me here?" Lyra said as she sat on his desk.

"You're lucky you have a royal seal with you; I'll send one of my men to the King with your message."

"Thank you, now I'll need a new horse to get back home, mines went lame a few hours back."

Two firm hands clenched her arms and the commander smiled. "My men need entertainment after all these weeks of standing watch, I believe a pretty little thing like you may be good at giving that."

"Let me go, please?" she said, begging slightly.

Jor focused on the area between his two palms as if there was something actually there.

Alice smiled and patted him on the back. "You're going to need to relax to get anything to form without a command."

"Well sitting here quietly produced nothing," Jor replied, clearly frustrated.

Alice went behind Jor and put her hands on his. "Some people can only unlock their true potential when their emotions are a certain way."

"And what emotion do you want me to show?" asked Jor as he looked into her eyes.

"I'm not sure, Jane may give you one," Alice replied as she nodded in Jane's direction.

Jor noticed that every once in a while Jane would turn and frown at he and Alice, then quickly turn back to Turner and turn back again.

"Jealousy is a powerful weapon Jor. In this case though, it's a means of entertainment," she said in his ear.

"Alice, do you genuinely have any feeling for me. Or am I just one out of the hundred guys you're with?"

"I don't know if I told you this, but I'm a love oracle."

Jor recoiled a bit. "Please don't tell me you're one of those damned gypsies."

"No, no, I'm just a simple teller of Eros' word," She nodded at the table. "That card proves it."

Jor recoiled again as the burgundy card happened to be on the table.

"Go on, open it."

He picked up the strange card and turned it over. "You are bound by faith to save a hero. A soldier is only the humblest to save her?" he read.

"You're lucky then, the rest usually say 'A warrior you shall be in the battle for the elusive black cat'."

"So this means what?" he asked, puzzled.

"It means you have a girlfriend," teased Alice as she pointed to his hands.

Jor's face lit up a he saw the faint mass of white light in his hands. "So where do I find this so called 'hero?'"

"She is at the border," a voice replied.

Jor looked up to see Eros, who had suddenly appeared, still in bandages and wraps.

"Eros!" exclaimed Alice happily, "You're feeling better I hope?"

"I could be better, but I heard your prediction, and came to help you out."

"So you'll explain this card?"

"Exactly." She lifted Jor's arms and studied them, then looked down at the patched up part of his clothes, which was burned off when he was trying to get to Alice. "I guess you could make a good warrior in the Deneaux army, considering that they need more men, you'll be easily accepted."

"Joining the army?!" Jor exclaimed.

"To get the girl you have to get into the army," she said simply.

"I think I'll try my luck with some of the girls here, or better yet, stay single."

"You forget, Jorigsveer Great-Blade; I am Eros, Divine of love and marriage. Telling me you're staying single is like telling the King you won't pay his taxes. And you know well what happens if you do that."

"But being in the military means I'll be working in an occupation where I could die."

"Simply living gives the possibility of death, and you mortals will eventually die. You all can be very squishy sometimes."

"Yeah, but I'm young!" Jor protested. "I still have years ahead of me."

"Yes, years with the girl you'll soon find."

"You're lucky you're a Divine," said Jor as he took up his short bow by the wall. "Alright then, I'll join the Deneaux military, but if I die, don't attend my funeral."

"I'll look you up in heaven and give you a pat on the back for trying," Eros replied, waving him away.

The recruiter frowned in thought as he looked at Jor. Half Raider and half kinsman wasn't exactly the kind of person to fit in with the rest of the men, but he was strong looking, and somewhat bright at least.

"I'll take you, but why is it you want to join the army?"

Jor opened his mouth to speak, but searched for the right answer. He found it.

"A Divine calls me to join the forces of the good men of Deneaux, who am I to challenge them?"

"Ok, you'll be on border patrol then. Take these papers and head west to the Keels-Deneaux border post to begin active duty. And remember to address your superiors with 'sir'."

"And a salute?"

"You'll see it when you get to the camp, now hurry; I have more men to sign-up."

It was dark out as Jor walked up the forest path to the border post. He had his weapons sheathed and had a torch in hand.

As he continued on the path, her heard shouting from a lit up tent at the edge of the camp. Common sense and intuition told him to investigate, or was it another type of sense? Either way he had to check it out.

"What's going on in there?" he asked as he neared the tent, a dagger in his right hand.

"Just trying to break in the new wench, she is a feisty one though," a deep voice replied.

"Help me!" screamed another violently.

Jor literally tore open the tent to find an elven girl pinned down by another soldier.

"Who are you?" asked the soldier as he turned quickly. A punch from the girl let a trickle of blood from his lip and he turned angrily to her, then raised his fist.

Jor grabbed his arm and threw him on his back outside. "Who do you think you are to be striking a girl?" he asked angrily.

"Listen," he begged, seeing the long dagger to his side and great sword on his back. "You can have the wench, I was just breaking her in for you!"

"You talk like she is an animal!" Jor shouted.

"She ain't human, is she then?"

A rock hard punch smashed into his jaw, then another to his face.

"Where is that racket coming from?" asked the commander of the border post.

"Jim's tent sir, sounds like a brawl!" a soldier replied as he picked up his halberd.

"Alright," he looked at the five soldiers in his command tent. "You all come with me."

The men rushed over to the tent to find Jor still pummelling the man senselessly and quickly threw him off.

"By the four boy, what in Efiia's name is wrong with you?" asked the commander.

"You have your men raping an elven child!" Jor yelled in reply.

Five halberds swung around to meet his neck and lay only a few centimeters away.

"Keep your mouth shut here boy, or you may regret it," said a soldier.

"Yeah, things get borin' up ere' and we need entertainin'," said another.

"And why are you here anyways?" asked the commander, his own rapier nearing Jor's throat.

Jor took out his papers and shoved them towards the commander. He eyed them carefully.

"Not a good start for a recruit, is it?" he asked humorously.

"Not a good move for a commander and his men messing with little girls," Jor answered equally.

"And not a good move to be beating down your comrades."

"I might do it again if I see you attacking a helpless..."

"Speak a word and you're dead, and now that I have you, you won't get out of this camp alive."

Jor clenched his fist and glared at the commander. "Alright *sir*, not like I have anywhere else I wanted to go."

Gailo frowned as he shifted uncomfortably in his position on a rocky outcrop on the beach. He chose the spot to closer observe the raiders and their numbers. By now, he saw them only unload the ships and set up tents. Now was the time to go, since they looked as if they would be there for a while.

Now he sat in Sen'del's office with Ifadeel and a few other soldiers and scouts.

"Those raiders seem to be taking their sweet time setting up camp," said Gailo.

"And they haven't even started taking off those siege machines they carried," added Ifadeel.

"Siege machines? When did they have siege machines?" asked Sen'del, surprised at this new piece of information.

"The scouts and I had found another fleet down the bay carrying hundreds of catapults, trebuchets and things of that nature," Ifadeel replied.

"Then we need to gather the army. Has your sister arrived yet Ifadeel?" asked Sen'del.

"No sir, she should have been here by now."

"Do you think she made it to Deneaux?" asked Gailo, concern showing in his expression.

"I doubt a small group of bandits could have taken her down, so there could only be some serious happening to keep her from reaching Deneaux," said Ifadeel. "Do you want me to find her?" he asked quickly.

"We may need you here Ifadeel, you're one of my best scouts," said Gailo.

"But sir, who will we send to get her?"

Sen'del smiled and straightened his back from his leaning position over his desk. "Come on, it's Lyra we're speaking of, she's probably hanging around in Deneaux just to irk you."

"I suppose this may not be the first time she do so, I guess I can afford to keep my mind on watching those Raiders."

Gailo patted him on the back. "That's it Ifadeel, she'll probably be back soon enough."

Jor frowned as he looked at himself in the command post mirror. He was dressed as a recruit in the Deneaux army uniform: shiny steel chainmail with a blue and white tabard with a pattern of four square sections over it. He had his dagger at his side and a sharp steel short sword in its scabbard on the other. He wore regular brown pants with steel kneecaps and a kettle hat that had a less than perfect fit.

He noticed someone moving in the mirror and looked behind him. "Who's there?"

No answer.

Jor slid his dagger silently from his belt and took an aggressive stance, his feet wide apart and the dagger held out near his body. "Don't make me look for you."

"Cool it, it's me," said the elven girl.

Jor sheathed the dagger. "Oh, it's you."

They stood in silence for a moment.

"For a moment, I thought you would be on my side, but I guess you're one of them."

Jor noticed the tavern girl dress she wore. It was white with a long slit to the side that would expose her left leg fully if she wasn't careful, and if it were only lower on her chest, it would be exposed. He also noticed how dirty it was and a few tears on the sleeves. Her eyes were green and she had hair that was a sort of faded blonde that almost seemed white. It was short and messy, a style most elves never had.

"You look like you have fallen on bad times," he said, trying to sound the least bit offensive.

"Well, these bastards here took me up as a play thing when I was delivering a message to the King, so yeah, bad times."

"So you haven't tried to escape?"

"I'm almost in the same position as you, run and die, fight back and die, so I just go along with it." She turned away. "It's not fun playing house wife for a day with these grown men."

"Then what if I figured a way to get you out?"

"How do you plan to do that? Get the army of Keels together and storm the border post?"

"I could get Eros to do it for me," he replied.

"So you'll get a Divine to save us? I don't know if you've noticed, but Divines can't step foot in Edafos."

"Eros has," he replied blankly.

"Just quit dreaming and accept your position."

"Jorigsveer of clan Great-Blade does not even comprehend the meaning of 'quit' or 'give up', I'll kill every living thing here to save an innocent soul!" he said heroically.

"If you're going to kill everyone, take me first," she replied dully.

Jor sat silent and noticed the tears welling in her eyes.

"No one dies under my watch. If I made it through the Deadlands, I'll make it through here."

Lyra felt a firm hand grasp hers. "Last time I'll allow someone to give up is when they need to meet their creator, but if it is not yet your time, stare death in the face, spit in his eyes. Stand tall before it, and it may cower and back down. I've gotten through hard times, and this is just another stone in the road," he reconsidered what he just said and spoke again, "Well I suppose this could be a small boulder in the road, but either way we still can get around it. Got that?"

Lyra stared at him, a faint light of hope showing in her eyes.

"Just hang around me, and I'll take out the eyes of anyone who dares to even look at you the wrong way!"

She wiped away her tears and smiled somewhat. "Alright, but by the way, my name is Lyradel, but my family calls me Lyra, sometimes Lee.

"What about friends?"

"You're the first, so I guess you can."

Several hundred longbows lurked over the edge of the ridge. The decision was made to try and harass the raiders as they attempted to set up the camp. Attacking the siege equipment would be too risky, as they found another fifty ships filled with even scarier raiders moving in. Attacking the main force gave them the chance to take out the man in charge and possibly end the siege. The fog that was rolling in was getting deeper by the minute, so action had to be taken quickly.

"Captain, are we seriously doing this?" asked Ifadeel.

"Apparently we are," he replied. He put his hand up. "Archers ready."

The sound of several hundred bows being put under tension gave a somewhat echo.

"Fire!"

The many arrows were sent flying into the sky, then arced down into the tents and ships below.

You could hear the screams of several men and the cries of attack from others; thank goodness, though, as they were still not seen.

"Thank you for this fog," said Gailo. "Our arrows must have had to cut its way through it. Now, second volley! Fire!"

Again, the cries were heard, but then there was the sound of arrows slamming against something heavy.

"They've probably put up their shields sir," said Ifadeel to the commander. He nodded.

"Then let's go back to Keels before they start charging us."

"You long-eared bastards aren't going anywhere!" shouted a voice.

"Everyone, ready your..." Gailo's command was cut off by the sound of steel ripping through flesh. He swung around and quickly ducked as a battle-ax almost beheaded him.

A well-aimed arrow made its way into one of the eye spaces in his helm and quickly put him down, but another soon took his place.

Gailo unsheathed his broadsword and struck a raider through his heart, lifting him slightly before removing the blade from his body and letting him fall. Another battle-ax curved his way, and he deftly fell to the side of the ridge. As he moved, an arrow whizzed past and struck the raider. Another elf made the third follow up and lunged his spear into the floored enemy.

"Captain, they're coming up the beach!" shouted Ifadeel as he nocked an arrow and fired into the oncoming shield wall.

"Everyone, up the ridge!" Gailo commanded as he threw aside a charging raider and side stepped the attack of another. "They can't get us if we're in the forests!"

The small army ran up the sand hill quickly, some slipping as they did.

Ifadeel was almost up when a hand grabbed his leg and threw him down.

"Ifadeel, hurry!" yelled the commander as he came down to meet him.

"You're not going anywhere, elf," said the big raider. He held two broadswords in his hands and lunged down with one.

Ifadeel rolled to his left and avoided the first. The second one came soon after and he rolled to the right. Just as he did, he pulled out two daggers. "Let me see you dodge this!" he shouted as he let one dagger fly. It hit the raider in his neck and he stumbled backwards, gasping for air but choking on his own blood.

Another raider ran in to finish Ifadeel, but the captain had already thrown a spear left by a dead elf, and it put him down. He hauled Ifadeel to his feet and ran back up the dune with him.

"Thanks Captain," he said.

"Thank me if we make it out of this alive."

The shield wall had broken up and was now attempting to go up the dunes. Bad for them though, that Gailo had spotted them.

"Archers, reform and fire unto the ridge!" he commanded. The group began to come together again, but as they lifted their bows, they were dropped by another rain of arrows.

"What the hell?" Ifadeel began, looking around.

A group of raider archers were giving support to the raiders that were attempting to make their way up the ridge, but the fog had slightly concealed them.

"Retreat!" commanded Gailo as he held his broadsword high.

"We can't commander! They are attacking from the forests!" shouted a soldier through the mist.

"Well, we can't go by the sea, our only option is to push the men in the forests until *they* have to retreat!"

Several elves rushed out form the fog to Gailo's side, clearly terrified.

"That couldn't have been a man," said one.

"Neither could it have been a giant!" exclaimed another.

Several blood crawling screams came from deep within the fog, and only weapons and helms fell back from them, rolling to a halt near the captain's feet.

The gigantic being came towards them now. A massive character standing two men high and two men wide. He wore a large gathering of fur and had weapons of many kinds strapped unto his back. He wore a skullcap that had a metal covering for the eyes.

"That's one hell of a monster then," Ifadeel said in awe.

He gripped a large battle-ax, and with a mighty roar, he hefted it for an overhead chop.

Ifadeel drew back his bow and fired, sending an arrow into his chest. He neither recoiled nor showed any sign of pain. It was probably stopped by all his furs.

The elves jumped out of the way as the battle-ax crashed into the ground, kicking up dust as it did.

"I'm not dying here Ifadeel, at least not today!" said Gailo as he came to his feet.

"Neither am I sir," Ifadeel replied as he rose and let another arrow fly. This one hit the giant's neck, but he didn't flinch and continued his steady trod towards them.

"How the hell do we kill it?" asked a soldier.

"You don't," said the behemoth in a deep voice. He stopped suddenly and smiled.

Several round, blank objects with a burning string on top of them landed by the other elven soldiers, and as the fire went down the string, the object exploded, killing them instantly.

"What form of black magic is that?" asked Gailo.

"If it were magic I would have sensed it," said Ifadeel.

Another one landed in between the two, and Gailo quickly tossed it back, breathing heavily and holding his chest as it exploded in the distance.

"This is too much for me Ifadeel," he said.

"Come on captain, you're only thirty eight," Ifadeel replied, a bit of humour in his voice.

Another landed between them and Ifadeel quickly tossed it back.

The giant stood, laughing at the two elves as they panicked each time the bomb was tossed. One landed near his feet and he quickly knocked it away with a kick.

"That's it!" exclaimed Ifadeel.

"Eh?" asked the captain.

"We can use these round things to take down that giant!"

"And how do you suppose we do that?"

Another bomb landed in between them, and instead of tossing it away, Ifadeel threw it towards the large raider. It exploded right before his face and it knocked off his skullcap. He recoiled and grabbed his face, shouting in pain.

"Now we hit him!" said Ifadeel as he charged with his two daggers. Gailo followed close behind.

Ifadeel leaped into the air and held unto his fur covered arm, then began to climb unto his shoulder. He aimed his dagger for the giant's neck, but then...

Thud! Thud! Thud!

Three arrows flew into his back, ignoring the tough leather armor he wore. He slumped down but remained on the giants shoulder.

"Ifadeel!" cried Gailo as he charged. Several raiders came to block his path, but he was far more concerned for Ifadeel and hacked them aside as if it was a reflex.

Ifadeel sat there, unmoving. The commander called out again, but no reply.

Several more raiders began a circular shield wall around the captain, the giant closing the large gap from behind.

"You people make me sick you know," he said. They only smiled eagerly in return. Taking down a captain was a quick way to promotion, and more pay, they knew.

"Gailo, your broadsword!" exclaimed a voice.

He turned to see Ifadeel climbing unto the giant's skullcap and threw his sword. Ifadeel in turn caught it and spun the blade downward, then thrust it straight through his eye. In was a deep enough wound and made for a killing blow as the large being crashed into the ground.

"They took down Faren!" exclaimed one raider.

"No matter, they still can't escape!" reassured another.

Several arrows slammed into the large round shields the raiders carried. Three of them were floored from the unexpected arrow barrage.

Two lines of archers stood behind Gailo and Ifadeel, and soon after the arrows were released, several more elves rushed the raiders, taking them down easily.

"Alright, let's move!" Gailo commanded as the force retreated back into the forests of Keels.

Chapter 21

The Eros Affairs Part 5

Jane paced around the upstairs room of the inn for probably the sixth time for the day.

"You're going to eat away at the floors if you keep doing that," said Turner.

"Sorry, I just feel a bit lost," she replied. It sounded like she would continue, but stopped herself.

"You've been doing that since..." he let it tail off and frowned at Jane.

She sensed what was coming to his mind and went to the door. "I'll just go out for some air then."

As she opened the door and walked out, she hit into a furry obstacle. It was Eros.

"Darling Jane, it's not wise to tackle a Divine," she said smiling.

"Sorry, just had to go do something, somewhere."

"Turner doesn't seem happy about something. Isn't it your duty to cheer him up?" asked Eros.

"Right now wouldn't be a good time."

Eros had clearly ignored her and went on talking. "Ever since that Great-Blade boy left, you and Adele haven't been the same. And it makes Adele feel more uneasy when you're uneasy, and the effect spreads to Kilan and Alice."

"Is that why you've been doing all that pacing? You miss that mountain goat Lorkeri, or whatever his name is?" asked Turner, his anger starting to boil over.

"His name is Jorigsveer," Jane replied, and soon wished she hadn't.

"I had a feeling something was going on between you two!" Turner exclaimed furiously.

"We're just friends Turner!" Jane more or less whimpered in return.

"Then why are you going on so crazy about him leaving?!"

"Because he's leaving for the military, an occupation that could get him well killed!" Her voice was quivering now. "What if he gets killed out there? I don't want his last memories to be of you two and your constant fighting!"

"And what about me? In two more weeks I'll be back on duty!"

"You're just a guard, not a soldier!"

"So, I could be killed in a riot, or what if there is a revolution?"

"What if war breaks out, what then?"

Turner stood furiously, but couldn't find a reply for Jane's statement. "What if I bring your boyfriend back here then? He could probably haul you across the ocean to sit around fires and eat raw venison if that makes you happy."

"Why don't you like Jor, Turner, he never had anything against you but yet you put him down over and over! That's probably why he went off and joined the army!"

Turner slammed his fist into the wall beside him. "And I'm damned glad he did! The blood of another raider kin in the dust is one step to the complete justice their people deserve! I'll be glad as hell if that bear gets his head split out there!"

Soon after he finished, Jane had ran out the room in tears, and then outside of the inn.

Eros frowned sadly. "I thought you two liked each other well."

Turner sat down on the side of his bed and covered his face. "I guess we did, but that's before I realized the truth between she and Jor."

"You mortal males have a strange outlook on relationships."

Turner looked up. "How so?"

"Well, you always assume your female counterparts are with other men, when they are clearly just friends with them."

"So you're telling me nothing is going on between that Jor character and Jane?" Turner asked, a bit of scepticism in his voice.

"My agent Alice has been getting close to Jor…" She paused and frowned a moment. "It may have made Jane a bit jealous."

"Heh, never thought girls got jealous."

Eros took a seat beside him and smiled. "Did I tell you the story of how me and Kinigos got together?"

"Who?"

"Kinigos is the Lord of Den, Divine of Nature. "When we were in the school of Divines, there was this other Fen that would always try to get my Kini."

"Kini? I have to remember to address him as that when I meet him," Turner joked. "So what did you do, blow her up?"

"It's a long story Turner, a very long story."

Jane sat down on a bench back in the same square with the mural of Adele and looked up at the moon. She thought back to when they were teaching, Jor, Alda and Zen how to use soul energy. Her mind soon went on Alice also.

"Why couldn't you have taken Jor faster, just so I wouldn't have to feel these ways."

"So you dislike this 'Alice' girl, don't you?" asked a voice.

A shadow was slowly creeping around the bench.

"Who's there?" she asked quickly.

Two large, familiar arms wrapped around her, and she made no effort in turning.

"Meso, what do you want?"

"Your hate, Jane Pagos, your malice and your anger," Meso replied.

"Too bad, I'm not mad."

"No bother, I can take it from you without your consent."

Jane's eyes flashed black as a dark aura began to form around her. Another shadow began to form from the ground up, and as she fainted from the drain of her energy, the shadow grew into a mirror image of her.

"Greetings Daimos-Jane, are you glad to be finally free of your binds?"

"Yes my lord," she replied. This copy of Jane looked exactly like her, but instead of the black robes and black, pointed hat, she wore a dress that stopped above her knees. Near the ends of it appeared to be ripped, and had orange and red streaks that resembled fire. The dress was sleeveless, and showed off a strange black dragon war painting on her right arm.

"I need you to go back to the inn where Eros and her agents are staying and defeat them," Meso commanded.

"And kill Alice?" she asked.

"You could kill her too."

"Can I take Turner?"

"If it makes you happy, now go before anyone sees us!"

The door to the inn was swung open, and to everyone's surprise, it was Jane, as bright and happy as ever.

"Oh Jane, you're finally back from your walk," said Alda, who was cleaning her sword.

"Why yes I am, now where is Alice?"

Zen, who was sitting on the other end of the table to Alda, looked up. "Why are you asking for Alice? And what's with the suggestive outfit?"

"I just wanna tell her how I feel. The outfit is just to...spice things up."

"But you see her every day."

"So, you never know when someone might...die."

"Miss Pagos, are you feeling well?" asked Zen, somewhat concerned.

"I'll be better once I find Alice."

Alice was leaning on the doorway to the side room in the shadows. "Here I am," she said simply.

"How about you come over here, so I could see you better, you know?"

"Why, Jane Pagos, what a pleasure it is to see the real you, in person," said Eros; she was now coming down the stairs.

"Well of course it is the real me, who else could it be?"

Turner followed behind Eros and looked sadly at Jane.

"Oh Turner my love! How are you today?" Jane exclaimed.

"Jane, are you alright?" Turner asked, surprised by the newly dressed Jane.

"Of course I am, now come down here so I can see you better."

Eros put her hand up to block Turner and turned to Alice. They both gave the same command. "Anemos Ekriksi!"

The blast of wind sent Jane flying out of the inn, taking the door with her.

"Let's go, Adele and Kilan will have to catch up," ordered Eros. Alice nodded and went along.

Alice and Eros stepped outside to meet with Jane, or whoever they could be. She got up and smiled.

"How did you catch on?" she asked.

"I feel insulted that Meso would send me such a horrible excuse of a spy. I would believe Meso to be Jane if he changed into her himself," said Eros.

"I wasn't meant to be a spy, I was meant to be an assassin." She raised her arm and her palm faced them. "Hephaestus Katastrofi!"

"Poseidon Aegis!" commanded Eros.

The two attacks collided, causing steam to envelope the already foggy area from the intense fire and cooling water.

"Eros!" called Alice through the steam.

A heavy fist made a reply and sent her sliding unto the stone road.

"Kilan! Adele! Eros!" she called again, trying to get back up.

Jane appeared again. "No help for you today."

A hand wrapped around her arm. "Then what does that make me?"

She turned around and smiled. "Adele, what are you doing?"

"I'm not stupid; I can tell Jane's energy patterns. She is almost all ice soul, not dark and fire."

"Yeah, so who are you?" added Kilan as she stepped through the mist.

"I'll make a name for myself when I kill the Divine Eros!" she exclaimed in reply. "Psyche Katastrofi!"

Jane awoke to the sound of the blast, and as she tried to get up, she stumbled. Last she could remember was the argument with Turner. He probably feels sorry, she thought. It would a great idea to get up and meet him, but your energy supply was far too low.

Her eyes widened now. She remembered what Meso did, but once again she was too weak to get up. "Damn."

A cold, but gentle hand touched her, a touch that felt like it came from her own mother. She realized how cold it was now, and stood to see who gave her the touch.

No one was there.

"What was that?" she asked herself as she looked around. Another cold wind blew through, and she sensed this time, that it was from her. The ground around her was covered with frost, and she had her light blue aura around her again.

She was full power—no, far better than that.

Jane watched as flashes of light went up into the skies, and knew it was time to join the battle.

Alice wiped the blood that was on her head away and raised her right hand. "Aduro Barrage!"

The daimon girl side-stepped the attack, and it crashed into Adele, who was making an attempt to sneak attack her. Kilan was next in the exchange as she swung her dagger near Daimos-Jane's neck. She in turn grabbed it, then grabbed Kilan's arm.

"You all should know better than to fight me."

"Shut up you wench! Mouth Cannon!"

As Kilan finished the word, the daimon sent a stinging slap that turned her head, sending the blast into one of the nearby building.

"Meso!" someone shouted through the fog and steam.

The daimon dropped Kilan and looked about. "Who calls the name of my master?"

"I do! Exochos Pagos Ekriksi!"

A wave of frost over took Daimos-Jane, and almost froze her on the spot.

"Pagos Khthon!" they commanded again. A sharp, frozen stone rose out of the ground under the daimon, and she only partly managed to dodge.

"Anemos!" the daimon commanded. A blast of wind blew from her and the steam and fog that covered the area was dispelled.

Jane and the daimon now stood only meters away from each other on the stone street; the only thing setting them apart was their clothes and Jane's ice aura that laid frost by her feet.

"Seems you somehow got your power back Jane, good job," the daimon teased. "Now I get to beat you and your friends at full power."

"Ekriksi!" commanded another two voices. Two white masses of energy struck the daimon in the back, but did little damage, except for the slightly large hole in the back of her dress.

She turned to see Alda and Zen with outstretched arms, their palms facing her.

"So even the worthless trash can use their energy," she remarked as she readied for an attack.

"Pagos Hoplite!" Jane commanded from behind.

A large spike shredded through the daimon's back and lodged itself in her torso.

Adele rose slightly and wiped the blood away from his mouth. "That would have to have killed her now."

Laughter came now, from none other than Daimos-Jane. She turned to Jane now, blood almost freely flowing from the sides of her mouth and through her nose.

"It will take far more to kill a daimon. Pyras!" Her body was enveloped in fire, and the frost that covered her and the ice spike were evaporated.

The group watched in awe as the hole still remained in her, bloody but healing slowly.

"Guess I'll freeze you then," said Jane.

"Ugh, I wanted to be just like you, you know? But now that I see how lame you are, I'll have to be someone else."

"Lane isn't that bad of a name for someone who looks just like Jane," Zen remarked. Alda knocked him behind his head and he acknowledged his mistake.

"Why thank you, when I kill the rest of them I'll see if Meso will let you live," she turned to Jane. "Now let's see if Lane can beat Jane. Pyras!" A small inferno began to glow around her arm.

"Aqua Pagos!" commanded Jane as a ball of water formed around her hands, then froze.

The two charge at each other, and as their fists collided, the area was once again cloaked in steam.

Eros strained to see as she peered into the steam. "Everyone alright?" she called out. She watched as two blue lights and two red lights spun and collided.

Zen, his sabre in hand, ran to Eros' side. "The rest of them are staying put, the only ones in that brawl are Jane and Lane."

"Good, I have an attack to wipe her out, but I can't pull it off under pressure." Eros kept her feet apart and stood in a ready position.

Lane punched for Jane's face, but she knocked her hand aside and threw her off balance. She came in for another attack while she was off, but Lane came forward with a tackle. Jane simply hopped back, and then dashed forward. Lane swung high for her head again, but Jane ducked and sent her an icy uppercut that lifted her up in the air slightly.

Lane quickly looked up to see Jane inhaling deeply. "Damn you Pagos."

"Soul Technique: Frost Cannon!" commanded Jane as she exhaled and unleashed a heavy fog of frost on Lane.

There was a short, muffled cry, then silence as the thick fog of frost continued to blow over her.

"Someone, clear up the fog!" shouted Eros as her body began to shine.

Alice stepped forward and held her hands out to her sides. "Anemos!" she commanded as another wind blew through and cleared up the area.

The frozen form of Lane sat in the middle of the street, unmoving.

"Now we end this, Soul Technique: Maxim Beam!" Eros commanded as a beam of light animated from her hand.

A dark form moved in the way and gave the command "Ishis Exochos Teresa Pertusus!" The attack suddenly stopped the Maxim Beam with an identical beam, except it was black with surges of dark purple.

"It's Meso!" exclaimed Alice.

A cry came from behind, and as Alice turned she saw the crumpled body of someone in black robes, and a bloody battle-ax in Alda's hands. "Looks like we have company," she said as she turned to face another man.

Zen fired and arrow from his short bow and it slammed into the enemy's cowl, dropping him instantly.

Turner quickly fired his arm-mounted crossbow and it stuck itself in the arm of another attacker. They hardly realized he was there and before they knew it, Turner's sword was going through their chest. Turner now turned his attention to Eros and Meso. Eros was on her knees, trying her best to force back to mass of energy Meso was sending.

"Fos Ekriksi!" Turner commanded as a ball of light flew from his hand and into Meso's back.

He cursed, cringed and turned angrily to Turner, but quickly directed his attention to Eros, who was now standing tall and winning the exchange. He nodded his head in the direction of Jane when he quickly turned to Turner and smiled.

Jane was hardly beating back the daimons that began to charge after her. In her hands she held a staff made fully out of ice, the tip having a bit of blood on it.

Turner charged to get by her side, but more daimons kept coming his way. He slashed one across the neck, dispelling it, then as another came with a follow up overhead slash, Turner raised his sword horizontally above his head, blocking the attack and then kicking it down.

Another large group began charging him, and he knew this group wouldn't fall as fast as the first few.

"Do not fret Turner Gales, your allies are by your side," said Zen as he appeared suddenly to his side, wielding both his sabers. Alda soon followed and held up her round shield.

The daimons stopped a few feet away from them and slammed their fists on the ground madly. Turner and the others stared and waited.

"Move!" shouted Adele as he suddenly appeared before them. He stabbed forcefully with his staff and Turner had to move his head to one side to avoid being hit.

They turned to see a large, dark, standing shadow behind them, its large arms right above their heads.

"Thanks for the save Adele," said Alda.

"Watch you back next time, I can't keep this kind of speed up," he replied.

"Adele, Eros may need some help," said Turner. He nodded in reply, but as he tried to go over, a mass of dark energy crashed into him. Alice caught him as he went flying, and raised her hand.

"Aduro Ekriksi!" she commanded. Another sphere of light came from her hands and tore apart another shadow. Now, Adele noticed, they were making sure that Meso and Eros would be left alone.

"We need to storm Meso!" he yelled to make sure everyone heard him.

Alda watched closely at the amount of daimons that came charging from Meso's position and smiled. "I like that idea."

"What about Jane?" asked Kilan as she limped forward.

"I'll get her, just focus on rushing Meso!" commanded Turner as he ran off.

Jane inhaled and exhaled frost on the attacking daimons, and as she froze the coming wave, another was right upon her.

One of them fell after the sound of steel thudding into flesh, and three went down from a full swing.

Jane smiled as she saw Turner at her side. He smiled back and raised his hands to the coming wave. "Fos Pagos Ekriksi!"

The shining shards of ice tore through the skin of the daimons, but some were able to weather the storm and continue attacking.

Turner locked swords with one and turned to Jane. "We won' push them back at this rate!"

"Then brace yourself Turner, this release will be at a whole new level," Jane said her body tense. The frost that lay at her feet began to grow and solidify into large icicles, and a chilly wind began to blow through that put frost on the daimon's bodies. The wind soon got faster, and the chill grew colder until the attackers realized they were freezing up.

It was Jane's snowstorm, the result of her excessive use of large amounts of ice energy in one environment.

Turner noticed that he hardly felt cold at all and no frost was growing over him, but yet all the nearby enemies were frozen stiff. "Jane, you're going good!" Turner tried to say through the high winds. Jane simply nodded and smiled.

Alda hacked away at the frozen or half frozen warriors and daimons that barred her way. It now began to be a bit too easy and she let Zen and the others take out every other block of ice you could identify as an enemy.

Adele looked ahead to see Meso, still keeping up the beam. Eros was again back down on her knees, and this time the strain would begin to weaken her until she would have to give up. Just as Adele attempted to join in on the battle, he felt a heavy, blunt force on his cheek, and he slid a few meters through the snow that was now forming up.

"Adele, watch out! It's Lane!" warned Alice.

Adele looked up to see Lane standing over him. He tried his best not to look up that short skirt she wore.

"Getting a little confident, are we little Adele?" she asked mockingly.

"Last I checked, you were supposed to be frozen solid," Adele replied bluntly.

Lane hoisted him up by his collar and smiled at him. "Didn't you notice all the fire energy I had?"

Now that she said it, he realized that he had let his guard down a little when she was frozen, and wouldn't have seen her thaw out. "You are a smart girl Lane, I'll give you that."

Lane kissed him on the cheek. "You know Adele, you aren't that dumb either.

"Get the hell away from him you unholy wench!" screamed Kilan as she slashed at Lane's back with her dagger.

Lane screamed in pain and dropped Adele as she realized her energy was being drained. Kilan took another overhead swing, but Lane barely dodged and her long braid was cut off from near her head. A ball of energy slammed into her torso the second she dodged, and she staggered back.

Alice held out her index finger and aimed for the heart. "Fos Pertusus!"

The small beam went straight through Lane, and she fell silently to the ground, a steady stream of blood flowing from her mouth

"Now Adele!" shouted Alice, who was now tired and low on energy.

"Aduro Ekriksi!" commanded Adele as the sphere of light energy flew from his hand. It crashed into Meso's back, and he shouted in pain, losing focus on his exchange with Eros, and consequently letting his beam get taken over by that of Eros. The stream of light now slammed into him, wasting away at large portions of his body each second. Adele leapt out of the way at the last second before he too could be caught in the blast.

The energy smashed him into one of the nearby buildings. Now, defeated and wounded, he faded back into the shadows. The streets lay frozen with a few bodies of the human followers of Meso. The warriors all stood by Eros, covered in the blood of their own and that of their enemies.

"My inn!" cried Alice as she and the others walked down a road near the northern coasts of Deneaux.

"Be happy you didn't lose your life Alice," Eros replied, but Alice still continued.

"Think of the bright side of this," Alda said. "If Jor hears there was a fight near the inn, he'll be right over to check on you."

Jane glared at her, but she smiled and shrugged.

"Where are we going exactly?" asked Zen. "I got to get my horse Kenta back from the stables and I doubt you all will be here when I come back."

"Just a few more miles and we'll be there," Eros replied.

After what could have been a half an hour walk, they finally neared a small, rocky bay.

"Ok, we'll go right over there," said Eros as she pointed to the side of a high cliff.

"I don't mean to be rude Eros, but what is it we're looking at?" asked Adele.

"Kilan should remember where this is," she said.

Adele turned to her and she looked down thoughtfully. "We've been here before?"

"Remember when Meso's men attacked our temple in the seaside district and you and the other priests were forced to retreat?"

"Oh!" exclaimed Kilan as the memories came back. "The sanctuary!"

They had been walking while they were speaking and now were in front of the face of the cliff that Eros had indicated.

"Alice, give the command," ordered Eros. She glanced to see a quizzical stare from Adele.

"Not to be rude again, but why aren't you giving this 'command'?"

Eros looked around, then spoke softly. "It's an obsidian barrier that I had built to defend against any Divine forces that might try to attack me and my followers."

"Ah, but wouldn't that mean you would be powerless inside?"

"Obsidian is a strange metal Adele, best to tell you once we're inside."

"Eros Edafos," commanded Alice, and a hole opened up on the side of the cliff face.

"Well my guests, welcome to my mansion," Eros said happily.

"But what if Meso's mortal followers come for us? The obsidian won't affect them," said Kilan.

"You talk as if we'll be defending ourselves child," Eros replied.

"Well....won't we?"

"No child, this time we shall take the war to Meso."

CHAPTER 22

The Keels Reinforcements

"And that is an Autumn Sparrow," said Lyra as she pointed out the bird in a nearby tree. "I used to imitate there calls to catch them when I was younger."

"You did a lot of things outdoors when you were younger," Jor replied.

"To be honest, I've always wondered if there were any other girls that could trap a fox or ambush birds like I could."

An orange-red colored oak leaf flew by the tower they were standing in, and Jor caught it.

"Lyra, you ever seen snow before?" he asked.

"No, I live too far up the coast for snow."

"Heh, and to think I would be chest deep in that stuff if I wasn't careful in Denhoec."

"You used to live in Denhoec?" she said in surprise. That's a far way from here. What made you take that journey?"

"I had to help save a friend of mine, and got in trouble for it. So far, the only one who suffered was my mother." Lyra noticed he lowered his gaze as he mentioned his mother.

"What happened to her?"

"My brothers...they killed her."

"What?! What kind of monster kills their own mother?" Lyra asked angered and puzzled at the same time.

137

"My brothers are the monsters you're talking about, and once I'm done here, I'll kill them, my father if we ever cross paths and anyone else who stands in my way," Jor said sternly.

"And here I thought you were another 'honor and chivalry forever' kind of guy," said Lyra as she looked down at some of the higher ranking troops.

"Who said I was any kind of knight?" Jor asked.

Lyra blushed. "Oh nothing, just a card a love oracle gave me several years back, I hardly remember it though."

"Come on, you can tell me," Jor said as he shoved her a little.

"Alright, alright. The card said: 'You are bound by faith to save a hero...'"

"A soldier is only the humblest to save her," Jor finished.

Lyra looked up at him oddly. "You got one of those damned riddle cards too I see."

"Yes, but both of ours speak of a hero that is rescued," Jor ventured.

"T-That means nothing, you just rescued me, and that's it!" Lyra exclaimed.

"I wonder though, what makes up a 'humble soldier?'" Jor asked jokingly.

Lyra blushed even more and punched him on his arm. "Damn well nothing! To be humble soldier you would have to have been a real soldier beforehand, were you a soldier previously?" she asked, getting up in his face.

"Who said that I'm not? Heroes in the stories were always soldiers. They did big things and killed big stuff like killed trolls and dragons."

"Have you ever killed a dragon or troll? I think not," Lyra said as she looked away.

"No, but I have killed someone even more powerful than the two of those combined," Jor bragged loudly with mock pride.

"What did you kill then? A Divine?" Lyra asked mockingly.

Jor looked around before answering. "When I was about to be executed in Denhoec, and undead army attacked the castle. We escaped with the help of a castle guard and we soon were forced to go through the Deadlands, it was there that we did battle with the Divine Mortha Rigortis."

"Let me guess, you defeated her all by yourself?" Lyra said sarcastically.

Jor laughed. "Not I! Mortha would have simply burnt me to a crisp, it was my friends who killed her, I just aided the castle guard in keeping the room clear of her undead minions."

"You almost sounded like you were telling the truth. I hope you know you're not good at impressing girls," Lyra said as she folded her arms.

"Don't believe me, eh? Wait until I show you her obsidian staff. My friend Adele has it."

"You better not be talking about the Adele from the stories."

The bugler let loose one of his long, horrible strings of notes that told the units to get to the middle of the post.

"There are a lot of things you don't know about me Lyra," he said with a smile and a wink as he headed down the ladder.

"Jor I will never like you!" she shouted at him as he waved and ran off.

A man in bright, gold trimmed steel armor was mounted on a white horse in the middle of the camp. He had blonde hair, but it was cut on both sides and made a Mohawk—not a hairstyle you would normally find in Deneaux, or Cardia for that matter.

"Noch?! What are you doing here?" asked the commander as he ran up to the paladin.

"Word has come from Keels that they are being invaded, I need some men from this post to reinforce Keels," he said. "Oh, and I'm also here to question you about the elven messenger you may be keeping."

The commander cringed at the thought of being found out, but then smiled at the glaring Knight. "I see those idle rumours are getting to you people again, best to pay no mind to it I say."

"Well, when we were sent one of your men on the subject of the Keels invasion, we asked him how he got the information, and after a few hours of interrogation, he told us that there was an elf messenger being held in the camp." He smiled slightly at the commander. "And I would've enjoyed being able to reward you both—preferably in money."

The commander looked at him sidelong. "How much are we talking about here?"

"I'm open to negotiate it, as long as this messenger shows up."

"We may need to exclude the elf, she may probably be back in Keels already."

"Manuel my friend, why did you leave out the fact that the messenger was a she? I wouldn't mind meeting such a brave girl."

"Lyradel wouldn't mind negotiating the price," Jor interrupted.

"Get back in line recruit, before I make you drop!" shouted Manuel, but it almost seemed as if Jor had ignored him as he went ahead.

"This man has kept her as a slave for his men's entertainment! And he stopped me from even leaving camp and telling anyone!"

"Manuel, is this boy's accusations against you true?" asked Noch in some surprise.

"Of course not! That boy just isn't up there if you know what I mean. He has a history in my camp of shouting and getting into fights with my men, not that he has won any for a matter of fact," he replied. He called over the man that Jor had fought the night he came to camp. "I mean look, living and breathing evidence of how dangerous that boy is!"

"He almost took her innocence away!" Jor yelled.

Noch recoiled in horror and disgust at the thought that his great countrymen could be into such activities. "Manuel, what..."

"It's true!" Lyradel said as she pushed through the ranks of men.

Noch recoiled again as he saw how torn up and dirty this young lady was.

"It was horrible! All of them were touching me and handling me like some kind of cow!" she cried, the tears streaming down her cheeks. "I felt so dirty and bad!"

Jor was astonished by her sudden move from tomboy to defenceless little girl, and more importantly, by her tears. It was then he noticed, that she was faking it for the sake of extra sympathy from the paladin. He kept his smile inward as she glanced at him.

Lyra hugged him from behind, as a child would grab on and hide behind their mother's dress. "I only managed to survive because of this valiant soul, Jorigsveer Great-Blade. He saved me from those monsters and kept me safe through it all."

Noch's eyes glowed white as he glared at Manuel and his men.

"Please Noch, listen to sense! I am sworn to protect the people of Cardia, even if it would cost me my life! If I took that oath, why would I do such things to the young girl?!" he stammered.

"Soul Technique: Soul Shock!" commanded Noch as white lighting quickly surged around the commander. He flew a few meters and fell into a pile of broken training posts where he slowly forced himself up to remain conscious.

"It seems you've forgotten that I am Noch, the greatest commander in the Pantheon Castle! I can tell a man's moves before he even arms his soldiers, so no, I will not listen to your sense!" He now turned back to Jor.

"You have an odd name for a Deneauxman, and you look a bit more... er, well, you seem like you would do better in sealskins, no offence."

"None taken sir, but you don't seem to have an all too common name either," Jor pointed out.

"That is true, I am from Sepala, a land far over the great oceans. It is just one beautiful, giant forest," he said proudly.

"Be proud of your homeland then; I come from Denhoec, Raider land."

"Well, now you are a man of Deneaux my friend, now come with me, so we can take our friend to court...." He let it trail off but turned in horror.

Time seemed to slow as Jor turned to see the commander hefting up a black crossbow. It was already loaded and ready to fire, and the commander was lining up for a shot.

"Ekriksi!" Jor commanded. The white sphere of compressed energy flew through the air and slammed into the commander's face. Just as it happened though, the bolt was released and came towards Lyra.

Blood splattered on Jor's face after a short cry, and he turned to see Lyra crumpled on the ground.

"Lyra! Are you okay?!" he shouted as he shook her violently.

No response.

He rolled her over the see a long cut across her cheek, he almost relaxed as he saw it was not life threatening, but then he remembered back to the fight with Mortha, when the obsidian staff Adele had sapped Mortha's energy away.

"The bolt, it was obsidian!" Jor shouted as he looked up the Noch, who had already leapt off his horse.

He touched her forehead and exhaled deeply, as if it were a sigh of relief—or one that comes before the telling of bad news.

"That bolt drained most of her energy when it grazed her. If it had stayed in contact with her any longer, she would have lost all the energy needed to continue all normal bodily operations."

The two watched in surprise as she opened her eyes. Jor held her hand, and she gripped his slowly before passing out again.

Jor frowned as he stared at the cliff face near the bay and wondered if that love oracle that claimed to have been sent by Eros herself was pranking him.

"Hello, anyone there?" he called.

"Nope, just a lonely cliff face," someone replied from inside.

Jor was startled and almost fell into the sand. "Okay, you've had your fun, now open the damned door."

The stone slowly came down to reveal an opening. Alda waved to him, giggling at her own practical joke.

"Keep thinking that talking rocks are a joke," Jor warned as he frowned at her and walked past.

He was amazed as he watched the giant stone pillars that held the room together. He also noticed that there were large lamps that kept the room bright, but it didn't seem like the light was from fire.

"It's made from pieces of our very own sun," said Eros. "One of the few things that exist that are more beautiful than me."

"This place is amazing Eros," Jor replied.

"Jor!" exclaimed Alice happily as she ran over and hugged him.

"Come on Alice, it couldn't have been that long a time," he replied.

Jane embraced him next. "Glad to see you're back in one piece."

Jor felt a sharp pain in the back of his head as something hit him. He turned to see Adele smiling at him.

"Leave some of the women for the rest of us Jor," he said before grabbing his hand firmly.

"Well Lorkeri, you finally made it back," said Turner as he came from one of the lower rooms.

"Good to see you too Turner," Jor replied with little emotion.

Tuner extended his hand to Jor, and he quickly looked up in awe. "Why can't we just kiss and make up with all the fighting we've had?"

Jor shook his hand firmly. "Now all we're missing is Kilan."

Kilan was focusing on a small ball of soul energy and sat in the corner with her legs crossed. "Hey," she said blankly before returning to her work.

"Hey guys, we've got a lot of visitors!" said Alda from down the hall.

"Friend or foe?" Eros called.

"They got oracle cards, so friend I guess."

Eros smiled as she saw the small crowd before her.

It was the warriors from Den, accompanied by Noch and Lyra.

"Well, come in, we probably won't bite. But you all may want to carry in that wagon, don't want anyone getting suspicious after seeing it outside alone," she said to Akina and her friends.

Lyra folded her arms and frowned, while blushing, when Jor put his arm around her.

"This is Lyradel from Keels," he said. "She may be a bit aggressive, but she's really cool if you get to know her." Jor told the rest.

"Wait, you think I'm cool?" Lyra asked.

"Yeah girl," Alda said. "I wouldn't ever see myself having the courage to get on a horse!"

Lyra looked at her oddly, but smiled afterwards. This might as well be her only chance to make friends, so why not take it.

"You dress—differently," said Eros as she looked her over. "Most women here wear those long dresses."

Lyra was wearing a loose brown shirt and her pants looked to be made of hard leather.

"I'm different from most girls—like I don't enjoy those frilly dresses."

She looked up to see the black staff, and Jor felt I grip tighter than that of Jane in the Deadlands on his arm.

"Isn't that spear…" she couldn't finish the question.

"Just relax, it's in safe hands. Don't you remember when I told you about defeating Mortha?"

"I thought you were bragging when you said it!" she exclaimed.

"It really was a hard battle, I doubt anyone could even exaggerate it or fabricate it to make it more intense," Jane said.

Noch was grooming his horse in the corner of the large hall when he noticed Alice was not too far behind him.

"Yes Fel?" he asked.

Alice had her hands together behind her back when she walked forward and gave the paladin a big smile. "So I heard you got a love oracle card."

"So I have, why do you ask?"

"Just curious to what it says and all."

He pulled out the paper from a small satchel tied to his horse's saddle and read it aloud for her to hear. "A child of Eros calls for you."

Alice smiled at him again, this time it was a smile that made him shift uncomfortably. He assumed this child of Eros to be a literal blood child of Eros, a being as elegant and beautiful as the goddess herself. He also assumed they would be a human or something near that, not a Fel.

She was pretty though, and not that far off from being a human either.

"Maybe we should hang out some time," he said coolly. Alice almost fainted.

"Ok then, maybe you could teach me how to ride a horse—or handle a real sword, not a soul sword."

Noch turned and stared in awe as he realized how much soul energy this one woman had. She was almost up to his strength, basically she was just about there. And now she wanted to handle a real sword? It was everything he wanted in a girl and more.

"You know, how about we talk here?" he asked, and the horse grunted at the thought of not getting his mane groomed, and Noch smiled. "Don't worry boy, we'll finish soon enough."

"So children, what brings you to the marvellous country of Deneaux?" asked Eros to the Den band.

"The Fel of Fel Hall have forsaken their chief, and we came here for refuge until I can reclaim the throne," Akina replied drearily.

"Added it will be even more troublesome to do that with Toxotes and that other girl rampaging about," Will added.

Eros' eyes widened at the mention of the dark hunter. "You were there when my Kini was captured?"

"Kini?" Mark asked with raised eyebrows.

"Kinigos, were you there when he was captured?" Eros replied hastily.

"We were only about for the battle at Fel Hall, but soon after Kinigos teleported us away to battle Toxotes," Illeth said.

"Then you don't know if he is safe?" asked Eros, he voice now quivering.

"Kinigos is the Lord of Den, it would be impossible for him to not be fine!" exclaimed Kullskash. Illeth knocked her behind her head for raising her voice, but Eros just smiled a bit sadly.

"I love how you mortals have so much faith in us Divines, yet I am the wife of Kinigos and still wonder if he is in terrible danger."

"Kinigos' wife?" asked Akina.

"Oh! Forgive me for not introducing myself. I am Eros, Divine of love and marriage, apprentice to the Lord of Deneaux, Efiia, Divine of Knowledge and Wisdom."

"It is an honour to meet you Lady Eros," Akina said with a bow.

"Now where is your chief, you spoke of them earlier but they have not distinguished themselves yet," said Eros as she looked about.

"I am chief of Fel Hall, Lady Eros," Akina replied.

Eros bowed her head in reply and noticed that Akina gave her a puzzled look.

"Lady Eros, you are a Divine, why do you bow to a mere mortal?"

"I'm acknowledging your position of power, Chief Akina, and by the way, you may call me just Eros, but Lady Eros is fine also. Now come let me show you to your quarters, you must have had a long journey from Den."

CHAPTER 23

Men of Meso

Meso frowned as he sat upon his throne in the dark room of one of the many abandoned houses near the warehouse district of Deneaux. He had problems that needed to be solved, and being low on energy wasn't going to help him resolve any of them. Lane could help him of course, but she was far better suited for breaking or hurting people, not for sneaking around and gathering information.

Now he was going to have to summon his loyalists and allies...people he told he would need no help from. Now he was prepared to take any "in your face" comments they would make.

"Come forward, loyalists." He spat out the last word, and then came silent footsteps in the dark.

"Well Meso, I'm glad to say that you are being serviced by the greatest silent movers in the land," said one man.

"And by some of the most lethal too," said another.

It was a group of three men and three women, each in black robes that stopped at the waist, tied by a crimson sash. They wore loose pants that were worn by people who did a lot of running, jumping or kicking. On their heads were dish shaped straw hats and a few of them wore black masks that covered their face.

"You all be damned if you start up with me. I'm not in the mood," Meso said darkly.

One of the bigger men came to one knee and bowed. "Oh master Meso, we would never do such a thing to you in your current state—we would rather wait until you are better to tease."

"Ugh, now let's get down to business," Meso replied in disgust. "So for the past few years, I have been leading my soldiers against those of Eros, and also whipping up a bit of chaos here and there for the fun of it.

Now I have gotten the aid of Lane, a powerful Daimon who is the opposite of the Soul warrior Jane Pagos. The problem is, she's as dumb as, well, I couldn't think of something that would compare to her, so I need you all to go with her in dangerous reconnaissance missions for support. But you all will be doing the regular missions."

"But sir, why fight the war when you can't kill the opposing leader?" asked one of the women.

Meso raised an eyebrow. "What do you mean 'can't'?"

"Well, if we want to finish her off, we would need and obsidian weapon, which I'm not seeing."

"Are you even thinking this through Meso?" asked another woman in an instant follow up question.

"Yes! I have an obsidian weapon!" Meso burst out.

"Then where is it, dare I ask," said the third woman, who was a bit younger than the other two.

"I...don't...have it," Meso said, defeated. "But I will eventually get one!"

"Do you have any leads on where it could be?" asked the bigger man.

"Don't bombard me with all these questions before I send you back!" Meso yelled, but then regretted as he felt a sharp pain in his side. He raised his hand into the air, and a strange energy flowed around the ground, and then formed into a map of Deneaux and the surrounding areas. Meso pointed at one cave. "There in the damned..."

"Reaper's Dungeon sir," said the younger woman.

"Yes, in the damned Reaper's dungeon you'll find something, and take Lane with you! Now hurry before Eros and her annoying soldiers get to it first!" he commanded, and cringed as he held his side again.

"Yes Sir," the daimons replied in unison. They faded into the shadows soon after, to begin with their mission.

Noch frowned as he opened up a small map of the country side around the group in Eros' Sanctuary.

"I've been getting news of attacks on the smaller villages and farms outside the main city by bandits. It's been years since attacks of this magnitude have been spotted, so I'm deciding to temporarily suspend the mission at Keels."

"I assume we'll take them quickly, I mean bandits can't be that tough, and we have a larger mission afterwards, so they really have to be quick to dispatch," Jor said. He was back in his regular recruit armor and ready for any calls he might get.

"I've seen battles with bandits down in Northspire, and they usually used to be composed of farmers and townsman that fell too far into debt, or people who like to hit others, armed with simple bows, daggers and such, and wearing rags or regular clothes. But once, another Paladin and I were on a scouting mission when we ended up approaching one of their hideouts. I'll tell you, they put up a fight, and in the end, we had to blow the entire outpost to get rid of them."

"Sounds like a lot," Turner said in a bit of awe.

"And they were armed and trained like professional soldiers—some even had a good grasp of soul and didn't hesitate to nearly blow off my friend's head clean off."

"So what you're saying is that we could be facing an enemy far more powerful than us that can also outnumber us?" Jor asked.

"Yes, but the problem is finding their hideout, and not getting ambushed on the way," Noch replied.

"So where do you think the hideout is located?" asked Turner.

Noch pointed at something on the map that resembled a cave. "That is Reaper's Cave."

Eros had entered the room without them noticing and startled Noch as she came up to the table and studied the map.

"Reaper's Cave I see, planning to finally seal it?" Eros asked.

"And why would we seal a normal cave?" Noch asked in return.

"Well, its home to an obsidian weapon."

"What obsidian weapon?" Noch asked.

Eros frowned and folded her arms, then looked down.

"If you're not going to answer, then at least tell me *why* you're hesitant to answer."

"There's a dragon, the mighty Dodecagon of the Polygon Clan."

"And you know him?" Turner asked.

"Ok, so I got Kini to steal me a few of his master's treasures, wasn't it in the name of love?" Eros asked, trying to sound as innocent and sincere as she could.

"Don't worry, the spirit wolves of my land would go about the land at night for hunts, and when they did, I would always steal some of the gold they hoarded," Noch replied. "No one's truly innocent."

"Do spirit wolves breathe soul?" Eros asked. "I think not."

"Breathe soul?" the three asked.

"The men of the Polygon Clan aren't like normal dragons that breathe fire or frost; they'll let loose a barrage of light and shock you with lightning."

"Great," Jor said as he threw his hands in the air. "First we have invading Raiders, marauding bandits and now Soul Dragons that guard obsidian weapons."

"Well, let's get to the problems in our nation first, and that is the issue of that cave and the bandits. We'll handle the bandits first, then I may get others from the Pantheon Castle to check out the Reaper's cave, agreed?" Noch asked.

Jor and Turner nodded.

"Then let's head off."

The daimons kept a straight face as they sprinted through the forest, staying as silent as they could. Together, they were and efficient force that could even stand against large armies.

They were comprised of six warriors with different key roles.

Se'dah was the biggest of the three males, and everyone seemed to have adopted him as leader, and he fit the position. He was born Aridi, a desert nation much like Zeran or Ayan Saudi, but it was further down in the southern deserts. They were at constant war with Svenswell, a nation born after a revolution in the southern territory of Ayan Saudi by several Raiders after the 300 year war.

Se'dah grew up in an environment of constant violence, and held his own due to his daimon abilities, which let him merge with the shadows and having more soul energy than normal people, added he took less damage than normal people in fights.

Gregory was a daimon born in Northspire, and trained as a squire until the war started with Southspire, and soon after, a revolution. The Knight he followed was killed in battle, and in his rage and grief, he defended his master's castle against nearly 500 revolutionaries—by himself.

Kinsei was a man born off in the distant lands of Changquan. He was a simple farmer that had everything stolen from him by his town's corrupt government, and turned to the daimons for help. He was then possessed by one and lost his face, his body forever becoming a shadow in a cloak. But his inner rage made him turn to those who stole from him, and he left the town, leaving nothing but ashes behind.

Keelia was of the Boreas Andras, a race of birdlike people, but in truth, she was a mutt of the race, due to that fact that she had a human body, but kept the wings of her mother. She was also from a long line of Daimons, just like the others except for Kinsei. After massacring travellers for the fun of it, she looked towards a new means of entertainment, and met Meso and his loyalists.

Delta was a Perialite that trained at the school of Divine skill, and when it was found out she was a daimon, she ravaged the instructors and students that attempted to subdue her, leaving only blood in the room.

Dianne was Delta's younger sister, and during the chaos and fighting, ran off with her sister to escape death. She was far more interested in the history of the land and read many tomes, spending most of her time in the libraries at the tower. Out of all the members of the group, she resented violence and hardly took part in the fighting; she also never killed anyone, making her far more pleasant to deal with than her cold brothers and sisters in arms.

"Is the cave close Dianne?" Delta asked.

"A few more paces away and we'll be there, I just thought that we would have been there by now though," she replied.

"Silence!" whispered Se'dah. He nodded off to the left, and the group turned to see several men holding torches heading up the road.

"I hear someone got away at one of the last raids," said one.

"Yep, some of the others think they'll alert the guard, but I doubt anyone will believe them," another replied.

"Banditry is so tricky you hear, I'm glad my job is just to shoot and stab things," said the third man, and the two others laughed along with him.

"Se'dah, are we authorized to terrorize these bandits?" Gregory asked.

"Our mission is to recover an obsidian weapon you fool, not terrorize bandits," Keelia replied.

"On the contrary," said Dianne. "Considering its Meso that gave us the job, there is a high chance that there will be no obsidian weapon."

"Well if we do find an obsidian weapon, why not try it on these fine fellows?" asked Kinsei. "And if not, we take out or fury on them,"

"I wouldn't mind it at all," said Se'dah, and the rest of them nodded, except for Dianne.

"So what was this place called again?" asked another bandit who was coming up the road.

"The Reaper's Cave you idiot, we put a sign just ahead, but you're apparently too dumb to read."

"So we sneaking in Se'dah?" asked Delta.

"It's night is it not? If we do find that weapon, I would enjoy having a host of bandits to test it on," he replied with a slick smile.

They soon faded within the night, and slipped through the small village of tents surrounded by wooden stakes, and into the cave behind it.

Se'dah frowned at the cave's interior. There were a few make shift tables built by the bandits, and the room appeared to be a makeshift tavern.

"I hate alcohol," he said grimly. He turned to a tunnel that seemed to lead deeper within the cave, then frowned again as he spotted a barrier made from simple planks.

"Ekriksi!" Dianne commanded, and the barrier fell apart after it was struck by the white mass of energy.

"Much better," Se'dah amended.

"This is very boring," Keelia said. They had been walking down a path that was exceptionally slimy and slippery for a good time now.

"I can agree," Gregory added.

"Well, what about our bigger problem?" Dianne asked.

"And what is that?" Kinsei asked.

"The fact we forgot Lane."

Se'dah stopped in his tracks and nearly slipped. "Wasn't she right behind us when we left Deneaux?!"

"Well yes, but I guess she ran off," Delta said.

Dianne fell hard on the ground, as if knocked down, and she looked angrily at her comrades. "Alright, who pushed me?"

They looked at each other, puzzled, then Kinsei smiled.

"Get out here Lane before you give the rest of us heart attacks," he said. "You've proven that you aren't as dense as you seem."

The Daimon faded from the wall and smiled at them. "Seems you caught me this time," she said.

"I should have blown up the ground under me, that would have put you in your place," Dianne commented.

"Then I would have blown you up, and *you* would learn," Lane replied.

"Just come along, we have a mission to complete, and your dumb antics aren't getting us anywhere!" Dianne exclaimed.

"Alright, don't get your undies in a bunch, I'm coming."

As they walked, they noticed that the cave itself seemed far more imbued with soul energy, and that meant it was the beginning of either a barrier, or an opponent that was ready for them.

Se'dah noticed that he could see a faint light not too far off, but as he took a step to approach it, the air itself sparked.

"Who dares enter the lair of the Mighty Dodecagon of Polygon?" asked a booming voice.

"Our master Meso has spoken of an obsidian weapon within this cave, and we are here to retrieve it," Se'dah replied.

"What? I mean....there is no such thing here!" the voice boomed again.

"Would you be kind enough to let us look around then?" asked Keelia.

"N-No!" the voice shouted back hesitantly. "If you want the scythe, it's in the next cave over!"

"Ah, so it's an obsidian scythe in here," said Gregory.

"There is nothing in here! Not a d-damn thing!"

"Then why are you sounding so jumpy?" Delta asked.

"B-B-Because I'm....Shy, that's it, I'm shy!"

"Last I checked, our own Dianne liked shy guys," joked Kinsei. Dianne stared daggers in reply.

"Whatever you do, you cannot come in here, there is a big—spider problem!"

"Then we'll fix it like the heroes we are," Gregory replied, and he and the others charged in.

It was a large chamber within the cave, and there were many shining, blue Crystals of varying sizes along the walls. At the Center was a giant, black dragon—Dodecagon Polygon.

"You're a big fellow, aren't you," commented Kinsei. "Dianne only goes out with guys her size."

"What the crap man? Will you leave me alone?" Dianne exclaimed.

"Enough!" Dodecagon exclaimed, and the group fell quiet. "Do you wish to lose your lives for a simple scythe, made of the forbidden stone?"

"We risk our lives in Meso's glorious name, Dodecagon, but no one has to die if you hand over the..."

He quickly cut Se'dah off. "I am sworn to protect the scythe with my life, and I shall give it only to Efiia or his loyalists."

"Do we have to take it then?" asked Lane.

"Apparently so," Delta replied.

"Not if I have anything to say about it!" Dodecagon exclaimed. "Aduro Barrage!"

Out of his mouth came a long burst of shining projectiles, and the daimons moved quickly in response.

"Pertusus Ekriksi!" commanded Delta.

"Erebus Ekriksi!" commanded Kinsei.

The first smaller beam shattered as it hit the dragon's scales, and the second one faded as it got near.

"Aegis!" Dodecagon commanded, and as he did, a wave of white energy went across his body, and disappeared. "Aduro Arena!" he commanded again.

A ring appeared around the cave floor, and it seemed to be comprised of smaller runes at its edge. It stretched all the way to the cave wall, and Se'dah quickly clung to the side of the wall, high above the ground.

Kinsei and Lane began to shout and scream in agony as the ground lit up in a bright light.

"Se'dah, what's going on?" Dianne asked.

"The light is affecting them, as they aren't pure daimons!" he replied.

"Then how do we win?" asked Gregory.

Se'dah looked at the black dragon with disgust. "We have to get that weapon away and retreat while we can."

"Got it," said Gregory as he began his charge. Directly behind Dodecagon was a pedestal, and most people would know that important things are held on pedestals.

Dodecagon took a heavy swing with his tail, and as it impacted Gregory, he felt some of his own energy drain away.

It seemingly seconds, Gregory slammed into the cave wall and hit the ground hard soon after.

"Good grief, Delta, Dianne, it's up to you two!" Se'dah exclaimed. "I'll distract that glorified lizard."

The two sisters nodded, and began their charge.

"Hades Ekriksi!" Se'dah commanded. The large mass of darkness slammed into the barrier around Dodecagon, shattering it, but the remaining energy faded once again as it got near.

"Your attacks are futile daimon," he said blankly. "Zeus Barrage!"

As with all the dragon's attacks, it came from his mouth, and that made the lightning even fiercer. Se'dah shouted in agony as the lighting shot through his veins.

Dianne stopped that moment to turn, but that was her worse mistake of the day, as Dodecagon made another heavy sweep with his tail and sent her deep into a wall.

His tail was coming back to strike Delta, and with all her strength, she caught it with both hands and moved a few meters, but managed to stop it completely.

Dodecagon felt a chill go down his spine, and he turned to see Keelia with the Obsidian Scythe in her hands.

"No, please do not take it!" he begged. Keelia smiled in reply and let her wings unfurl.

She lifted herself up in the air and flew straight past the black dragon, and then through the opening that led to the chamber.

He turned again to Se'dah, who saluted him and ran off. Before he knew it, the chamber was empty.

The daimons looked out at the bandit camp. It was filled with many tents that held sleeping bandits and highwaymen. The only ones that were awake were the sentries that stood guard in the small towers around the redoubt.

Se'dah held the weapon across his shoulder and smiled. "It's a good night for some carnage!" he exclaimed, almost too loudly.

"Damn Se'dah, are you trying to wake the dead? We are not necromancers," complained Dianne. He shrugged the thought aside.

"Hey Lane, wanna be the first to try out this little scythe?" Se'dah asked, holding out the weapon.

Lane's eyes lit up like a schoolgirl about to receive candy and grabbed the scythe away from his grip. "Can I really?!"

"Sure, why not?"

A few bandits were already out of their tents and stared strangely at the intruders, and soon after, the alarm went off.

Lane held the scythe firmly and charged at her new test dummies, smiling all the while as she mercilessly cut the bandits apart.

Blood splatted on Kinsei's face and was accompanied by a horrible scream. "You think Meso will be happy about such a destructive thing in the hands of that menace?"

"Sure he will," Se'dah replied, wiping off some of the splattered blood from his own face.

Noch frowned as he studied the redoubt from his secluded position in the forests.

"That smoke seems too thick to be coming from a simple fire, and no one lights a campfire midday," said Noch.

"It could be a fire," Turner added.

"Possibly, but I believe that there could have been a battle there."

"Well, it could be possible that the bandits turned on each other, I mean they are bandits after all," said one of the Paladins.

"Bandits that are that coordinated won't turn on each other," Noch said

Jor's eyes widened at a thought. "Eros said that there was an obsidian weapon in the cave nearby, correct?" he asked.

Noch nodded.

"Then isn't it possible that someone may have gone after it, and destroyed the bandit camp in the process?"

"It is I suppose," Turner said. "But what normal person is strong enough to do that? Even Jane or Alice might be unable to take on a whole camp worth of armed bandits."

"It could have been a Divine then," Noch said. "Or even worse, Eros may have gotten it herself just to play a trick on us!"

"Divines can't touch obsidian, it will turn them into a pile of bones if they do," Jor added.

"So we do have clues on who it could be," said Turner. "They would have to be powerful, be it in soul or magic, or possibly several other means. The only problems are that there could have been an army involved."

"True, but who do we know now that would want an obsidian weapon?" Jor asked.

"It would have to be someone with a Divine enemy, or a treasure hunter," Noch replied.

"Then we may have a culprit," said Jor.

"And who may that be?" Noch asked.

"Meso and Eros have been fighting for years, and Kilan and Adele already have obsidian weapons and are allies of Eros," said Turner.

"And that would leave Meso with no weapons in his arsenal. Being unable to kill your enemy is a huge disadvantage in a war," Jor continued.

"And since Meso was likely wounded in that last battle in town, he would have to send out some of his best soldiers," Turner added.

"And that could only be one person," Jor finished.

Noch silently vaulted over the redoubt walls, then rolled behind a pile of broken barrels and tables. The rest of his small army was waiting in the edge of the forest near the redoubt's entrance.

Noch tried to move silently through the camp, but his heavy armor jingled and jangled with every step. "Next time I get leave, I'm going back to Sepal and getting myself some furs to wear."

He stopped and frowned at what was at his feet, then fell short of breathe as he looked up and saw the center of the camp.

"This was the biggest group of bandits I have ever seen!" Noch exclaimed.

Jor turned back and saw some of the other soldiers piling up the bodies. "Looks like a small army to me, this Kingdom looking at a revolution?"

"Nope, our King may be old, but he has many years ahead of him," said Noch. "Some say he may even be immortal," he joked.

Two Paladins and a woman in white hooded robes approached.

"Sir, we have studied the energy patterns in this area, and it is dominantly fire and dark soul energies," said the woman.

"You know, I think Adele did mention something about Lane having fire and dark energy, opposite to Jane's Ice," said Turner.

The hooded woman turned to him. "Tell me, did this Jane person happen to be a daimon, or a daimon possessed person?"

"Whatever that is I doubt it, Jane's usually sweet and well mannered, unlike Lane who was wild and aggressive. The two looked alike though," Turner replied.

"Then that would mean that a daimon had to take out her negative emotions and thoughts and imbue them with the daimon created in the process to create a 'Daimos version' of the person," the woman explained. "And there hasn't been a daimon that was confirmed to be that strong."

Turner looked at her blankly in reply, and it was clear he didn't and wouldn't understand.

"If there is a powerful daimon you're looking for, you may need to check with Meso, the Divine of Hate," Jor replied.

"I'm not particularly into the subject of Divines, but I believe that may take some looking into," said the woman, the other Paladins and Noch nodded in agreement. Soon after though, their eyes flashed white, except for Noch.

"We have intruders," said one of the Paladins.

"They're not intruders," Noch sighed. "They're friends."

Jane warmly embraced Turner as the small group walked into the center of the camp. With Jane were Alice, Lyra and Eros.

"What are you doing here?" Jor asked, slightly amused.

"Eros wanted to check on an old friend, and she needed an escort to keep her safe, so that's why we're here," Alice replied.

"And why on Edafos did you bring Lyra?" Jor asked again.

"Just came along to get some fresh air, that's all," she replied.

"You're going to blush Lyra," Jor pointed, keeping his face as serious as he could.

"What do you want then, a kiss on the cheek?" she snapped back.

Jor couldn't help but smile. "If it makes you happy." Lyra turned her back, but couldn't help but look back at Jor a few times when she thought he wasn't looking.

"Alright, I have had enough with this reunion, if you girls plan on staying out here you are free to do so, but I'm going on in," said Eros as she made her way to the cave.

Alice kissed Noch on the cheek, then shouted off to Eros, "Coming!"

"Who is that?" asked the woman in the robes as soon as Alice left.

"What's it to you, Roseanne?" Noch asked, showing hint of humour on his face.

"Nothing, just thought you would rather be with someone more—human," she replied, the robes still casting a shadow over her face.

Noch ignored the comment, and felt relieved as Jor and Turner came up to him.

"Permission to enter Reaper's Cave," they both said, standing at attention.

"Permission granted you losers," he joked. "Not get in before I order you to."

Eros frowned as she neared the main chamber. For the past few minutes of walking, they could hear a faint sound that resembled crying, now that they were here, it was as loud and ear-splitting as ever.

The group beheld the sight of the black dragon, Dodecagon, curled up and crying.

"Dodo!" Eros called as she came with outstretched arms.

"We may need to stick around Eros some more," said Jor. "We'll get to hear all the funny nicknames."

Jane, Turner and Alice nodded and laughed. Lyra remained as straight-faced as ever.

Eros gently rubbed the large dragon's nose, and he seemed to calm a bit. "So Dodo, what seems to be bothering you?" she asked softly.

"T-T-T-The bad people took the scythe!" he cried again.

"Don't worry, they're gone now and won't ever steal from you," Eros replied.

"I don't have anything for them to steal; now Efiia and Alcino are going to be mad!" Dodecagon exclaimed.

"And I am quite disappointed at your work!" exclaimed a voice.

Out of a blue fog came Efiia and Alcino, the Divine of the Strong-Willed. He was a tall man with a rough and stark face. He was very muscular, even down to his muscular facial features.

"Oh come on Alcino, let the boy have some peace!" said Eros.

"After he commits one of history's greatest failures?!"

"It's not his fault, right Dodo?"

"It was seven daimons that attacked me, and one of them had wings!" he explained.

"No, no, no, you have wings too, so no excuse!" said Alcino.

"You see how big he is!" Eros exclaimed. "He can hardly even move in here!"

"And being big should make it difficult in getting the scythe, but apparently he is far too incompetent."

Eros sensed that he would soon go back to crying, and made attempts to calm him.

"You know Alcino, if memory served, didn't you lose a few obsidian items yourself?" asked Efiia.

The big man was instantly stopped. One could quite easily see he was racking his brain.

"That's true actually, like when that team of mortals snuck into your palace and stole an obsidian dagger," said Eros.

"Or when Emma seduced you into giving her that obsidian cane," added Efiia.

"And when my Kini knocked you out and walked off with your longbow—in my honor," Eros said, hugging herself at the thought.

"I didn't lose those, I just let those people have them free of charge."

"You seem to be very generous," Jor said.

"Shut up mortal, you have no say in Divine matters!" Alcino snapped back.

"This guy is a real joke," whispered Lyra to Jor.

"I heard that!"

"Oh really, what did I say then?" she asked.

"That doesn't matter, all that matters is that you stay out of our affairs!" Alcino turned to see that Eros, Efiia and Dodecagon were enjoying this, and he couldn't leave them to it. "What's so funny?!"

"Oh Alcino, the stupid scythe is gone, so instead of going off in here, why not go off on the people who took it?" said Eros.

Alcino was about to protest, but then stopped as he realized she was right, the problem only was that...

"I can't fight a group of daimons wielding obsidian arms," he said finally.

Eros smiled slyly. "What, the Divine of Strong-Will is frightened for his life?"

"NO! I'm just thinking tactically, can't go in blindly and lose...I mean...not have a glorious enough victory."

"Alright, how about you go with some of my followers, they have a few obsidian arms to spare."

"Pfft, I don't need help."

"Suit yourself Alcino, I'll go for the scythe if you don't want it, or better yet, you could let Efiia have it, he's much more responsible."

"I don't believe that will be my wisest choice, Meso's men are able to match my might if they work together, and Lane would be there trump card," he replied.

"Well, I wouldn't mind going one on one with another one of Meso's troops," said Jor.

"Then it's settled, we'll continue our operations against Meso," said Eros brightly. "You can help too Dodo."

"A whole dragon on our side? That's one heck of a handicap to Meso," said Jane.

"I'm a lot weaker than I look, especially in my human form," said Dodecagon.

"Come on, it can't be that bad," Turner said.

The black dragon closed his eyes, and he began to glow white, and when the light vanished, his human form was revealed.

"You're...a lot smaller than I expected," said Lyra.

Dodecagon, in his human form, was a mere child, around the age of five or six wearing dark blue robes.

Eros lifted him up and gave him a tight squeeze. "Come on; let's get out of this dusty old cave."

Noch and Roseanne were outside checking a bandit's body for soul energy when Eros and the others came out of the cave.

"Who's the kid?" Noch asked.

"Are you a Paladin?! I love Paladins!" Dodecagon exclaimed as he ran over to Noch.

"Hey, hey, I'll be open to autographs later, just have to finish some things up over here," he replied. He patted the boy on his head. "Eros, this one yours?"

"Sort of I guess, I'm taking him with me. Meso won't be ready when he starts to burn things down," she replied.

"He can still do all that stuff in human form?" Alice asked.

"Yep I can, it just won't be as powerful though," Dodecagon replied.

Jor and Turner came up to Noch.

"So are we going to turn over dead bodies for the rest of the day?" asked Turner.

"Or are we going to smash some raiders in Keels?" finished Jor.

Noch looked about the camp, seeing where they were setting up the bodies to be burnt, then over to the tents. "Might as well hang out here for the day, let the rest of the men relax, I can see that the way to Keels won't be too safe in the foreseeable future."

CHAPTER 24

Battle at the Square

Back at the Sanctuary, it was a normal day, or at least it seemed normal.

Akina smiled as she turned to Kilan, but only a serious frown was returned, followed by an offensive silence.

"You do not speak much, do you young Fel?" Akina said.

"There isn't much to say," Kilan replied.

"There has to be something; what do you do for fun?"

Kilan raised an eyebrow, and then watched her palm. "I suppose I like practicing my soul."

"Maybe you could teach me sometime."

"I'm not a good teacher, the Perialite and the other Fel, they are good teachers."

"Ok then, what else do you like?" Akina looked over to where Mark was taking aim and firing shots at a target. "Or who do you like?"

"I'm not interested in boys," she snapped back silently and quickly.

"And you work with the Divine of Love and Marriage? You must be joking."

"I must remember to change my alignment one of these days," Kilan said to herself. "And what is it to you if I like someone, I mean, why would I tell you?"

"I just wanted something to talk about," Akina said. She patted Kilan on her back. "I just wanted to make new friends with the ones here, and you are currently the only one here of my race."

"Well, did you ever like someone Akina?" Kilan asked shyly.

"You see the Fen with the bow?"

"Yeah."

"Well, the first time I met him, we were taking over his caravan, and even after that, he was still kind to me. Now, he is one of my best friends, just haven't gotten about telling him."

Mark, had just made a shot in the bull's eye, and turned to see Akina smiling, and did the same. She waved in reply and he went back to shooting.

"Well, have you ever heard the stories of the dark champion?" asked Kilan.

"I faintly remember how the tale goes, but I've heard it."

"Well, the champion is somehow back from the dead, and is once again serving Deneaux," Kilan pointed off in Adele's direction. "I won't hold it against you if you don't believe a word of what I am saying."

"Pfft, the world stopped making sense years ago; it wouldn't be very big if undead heroes began popping up all over the place."

"What should I do though, I mean, does he think about me the same way I think about him, what do I say or do?"

"What is the most memorable thing you two have done together?"

"Hold hands, that's about it."

"Well, I guess you're on the right track, though I should be the one asking for the advice."

"You know Akina, I wouldn't mind hanging out with you."

"Me too," Akina replied.

Now the stage had switch to Zen, Alda and Adele as they went about the market.

Adele was looking for items that could amplify his soul energy, or help it in some kind of way.

Alda was simply browsing what weapons she could get.

But Zen on the other hand was looking for gifts, and they would have to be very eye catching for Alda to like them.

"These earing are guaranteed to raise your soul to an entirely different level, and are used by the Paladins and Soul warriors of lands near and afar," said a salesman to Adele.

"And what is it that makes these earrings so powerful?" he asked.

"They....er, they are made of a special soul energy emitting...rock."

Adele placed his hand on the salesman's stall, and it began to glow white. Soon after, all of the earrings shattered into tiny fragments.

"Now, what caused them to break just now?" Adele asked.

"You see, the reason they broke was..." the man stopped mid-sentence and began to run, but Adele held him by the back of his collar.

"You lying dog! You do not deserve to occupy this Grand Kingdom! Astrape!" Adele commanded.

The surge of lightning ran through Adele's arm, and then began to flow through the con artist. He fell to the ground, hardly conscious

The market soon turned to near panic as they saw the man on the ground, and the guards came quickly in response.

"Boy, what happened here?" one asked.

"I caught this man trying to sell useless stones that he said could amplify soul energy, and I couldn't leave him to steal people's money," Adele replied.

"So, that's no reason to...do whatever you did!" exclaimed another guard.

Adele seemed puzzled. "So you say I can't stop him from doing that? Wasn't there laws in place for that?"

The lead guard sighed, and exhaled deeply as he began a lengthy explanation of Deneaux's current laws.

Zen frowned as he looked at the long line of jewels and rings that sat inside a glass case.

"So you getting something for a girl, young one?" asked the older man that owned the stand. He was clearly Zerani, but he was dressed like a man of Deneaux.

"Well, what do you have that would impress a Raider?" asked Zen.

"You'd be better off buying them a weapon of some kind, like a really large one."

"Do you have anything that a tomboy would like then?"

"I do have some animal theme necklaces and rings, and possibly some bracers," said the man as he searched through a crate behind him. "Would this girl by chance be a Raider of the seas?"

"Maybe. All I know is that she was a castle guard."

"A castle guard you say? What is her name?"

"Alda Breach-Breaker."

"Lovely. I was also a castle guard when I was a young man; how about I make you a custom necklace, one that should be an emblem of her clan. I will tell you when it is ready."

Zen shook the man's hand. "Thank you kinsman."

Alda was leaning against a wall and watching a blacksmith work when Adele approached.

"These guards are idiots, can't even keep thieves off the streets," he said. "And that guy wasn't even a good one."

"Deneaux is nice compared to Denhoec if you like quiet, peaceful, high up living," Alda replied.

"Isn't it still trying to turn into a real nation?"

"I suppose so, but who needs a nation when they have a big enough army to wreck anyone who goes against them?"

"The kind of people who want loyal men."

"Soldiers? Loyal? I've never heard of that."

"And that is why Denhoec will never be a nation worth recognizing."

Alda tossed the comment aside and continued to watch the smith do his job.

It was on the opposite side of the square, that trouble was brewing.

"So Kinsei, you really up for this?" asked Keelia.

"Of course I am, besides, Meso will be ecstatic once we bring the obsidian staff," he replied.

"Then off with you; be back for me, okay?" she said as she patted him on the back.

Adele approached Zen, who was currently watching the jeweller work on Alda's necklace.

"Hey, we'll be heading back to the sanctuary soon, you coming?" Adele asked.

"I will in an hour or so," Zen replied.

As Adele was about to turn, a large man blocked his path.

"Hey kid, I like that staff on your back," he said.

"Oh this, it's just a simple rod," Adele replied.

"Can I at least touch it?"

"I'm pretty sure you shouldn't."

"And I'm pretty sure I should."

Adele sighed. "I'm sorry, but I can't let you touch my staff, for whatever reasons I may never know."

Adele heard steel sliding from a leather scabbard, and he found himself with his staff already in hand.

"What do you want?" Adele asked. "And I mean your real motive."

"That staff doesn't belong to you," Kinsei replied blankly.

"And I assume it doesn't belong to you too."

"It does now."

The sound of clashing metal soon rang out, and the market turned quiet at the sight of the boy with the staff and the man with the scimitar.

Zen had his sabres in hand already, and watched the scene patiently.

"This battle will be far worse than anything you have ever experienced boy," Kinsei warned.

"I've fought far worse before you were born, you should be the one worrying," Adele replied equally.

A black aura lit up around Kinsei, and the same around Adele as they began to exchange attacks, blocking and parrying each strike from the next.

"Do I dare go near that?" Zen asked himself. He shook the thought aside; getting near that would probably mean instant death to him.

The two leapt back from each other, and Adele raised his right hand, holding the staff in the other, and commanded, "Erebus Pertusus!"

"Erebus Hoplon!" Kinsei commanded in reply. A dark shield appeared before him and blocked the thin piercing beam that Adele had sent. "Erebus Katastrofi!"

"Erebus Katastrofi!" Adele commanded in reply.

The area between them exploded and pulsated with dark energy.

"We won't get anywhere with this, darkness won't defeat darkness," said Adele.

"You're right boy, I might as well finish you now," Kinsei replied. He charged forward, and launched himself into the air, performing a no-handed cartwheel and landing before Adele. Before he could think, he was sent crashing into the ground by a powerful kick to the chest.

Adele quickly got up, but Kinsei was ready, and another kick was on its way. Adele was able to hold his leg, but Kinsei soon made him release as he back flipped, then came forward and slammed his knee into is stomach.

Adele lurched forward, but quickly regained himself and made an attempt to make space between them, but Kinsei was already coming in with another kick that sent him crashing into a stall.

"You're one pretty little butterfly, aren't you?" said Adele as he struggled to his feet.

"I can show you the butterfly jump if you want," Kinsei joked.

"I'm pretty sure you won't, Fos Katastrofi!" Adele commanded.

Kinsei leapt into the air, leaving from his left foot and spinning with both his legs in the air, then landed on the same foot, avoiding the attack completely.

"Damn it!" Adele shouted.

"That was the butterfly jump," Kinsei replied.

"Alright, time to pick on someone your own size!" exclaimed Zen.

"And what will you do, Zerani?" Kinsei asked.

"Ekriksi!" Zen commanded before running around him.

Kinsei grabbed the attack and laughed. "Is that all?"

Kinsei felt a sharp pain in his side, and he looked down to see Zen's sabre in his side.

"Not feeling so high and mighty now?" said Zen.

He hardly dodged the kick that Kinsei sent, and grabbed his leg as he did.

Kinsei panicked. "Astrape!" he commanded, sending pulsing lightning around himself.

Zen barely dodged the attack, and leapt away, leaving Kinsei to shock himself with the lightning.

"Ekriksi!" Zen commanded again. The small ball of neutral soul slammed into Kinsei's chest much harder than they had thought it would, and sent him sprawling into the dust. "Makhaira!"

Kinsei regained himself soon after, and he quickly rolled to the side as a soul sword slammed down into the cobblestone where he previously was. He leapt to his feet, and saw Zen readying another attack.

"Erebus Katastrofi!" he commanded angrily.

Zen jumped quickly out of the way, falling by a pile of rocks and cutting himself. The area where he was standing exploded with dark energy.

Zen soon stood up again, the same with Adele, but they were now both in pain and exhausted.

"Tired already? I was looking forward to more sport," Kinsei said.

"You might want to be careful, that wound is bleeding pretty well," said Adele as he pointed to his side.

Kinsei laughed. "This hardly even damages me, someone like you should know that, or did you not see me as a daimon?"

Adele's eyes widened as he realized, and he made a futile attempt to raise his hand.

"Now will you let me finish you?" Kinsei asked.

An axe soon arced over Kinsei's head, and he felt a sharp pain in his shoulder as he moved.

It was Alda who had now come to Zen and Adele's aid, but the question was, would she be enough?

"Who are you?" she asked.

"I was about to ask the same thing," Kinsei replied, holding his bloody shoulder.

"My name is not important."

"And neither is mine."

As Kinsei came forward to give a long barrage of kicks, Alda swung and made a long horizontal arc with her battle-axe.

It was enough to keep him away, but he could fight long and short range.

"Erebus Ekriksi!" he commanded.

The ball of dark energy flew towards Alda, but she held it with her left hand, and redirected it to the sky where it sounded fizzled out.

"So you know how to deflect simple soul eh? Erebus Katastrofi!" Kinsei commanded again.

Alda tossed herself to the side in an effort to dodge the attack. The market stalls behind her went up in the dark explosion soon after.

She quickly got up and went to where she dropped her axe, but a thin beam flew past, and she was hardly able to dodge, falling backwards onto stones.

"You're not getting that toy back," Kinsei taunted.

"I don't need it," Alda replied as she drew a steel long sword.

"I won't let you get close enough to use that."

"We'll see."

Alda charged forward, vaulting over the small craters and shattered stalls created from the battle.

"Erebus Barrage!" Kinsei commanded.

Alda skilfully dodged the incoming masses of dark energy, then slid behind a crate.

"Hydro!" she commanded as she spat out a large mass of water.

As soon as it got to Kinsei's outstretched arms, she raised hers, and commanded, "Pagos!"

Kinsei's eyes widened in alarm as he realized his arms were frozen all around. "What did you just do?!"

"A trick a friend thought me, you're just lucky she isn't here!" Alda replied as she began her charge once again. She was right before Kinsei when he swung his leg high for Alda's head. She managed to duck, but another was on its way as he hopped back. She lunged forward with her blade before being sent into the dust by Kinsei's powerful kicks.

Kinsei coughed up a not to modest amount of blood as he tried frantically to pull the long sword out of his side—the same side where Zen stabbed him with the sabre.

The confidence shown earlier in his face had now disappeared, and he showed only a boiling rage.

He soon shredded the sword out of his side, splattering his own blood across the ground nearby him. He now stood over Alda, and raised the weapon into the air, and swung down heavily.

KLANG!

It was only barely deflected by the daggers held in Alda's hands, and he now raised the blade back up for the true finishing blow when....

"Not yet you monster," said Zen as he only barely raised his left hand. "Emma!" he commanded.

Four lines of blood shot out of the other side of Kinsei, and he soon staggered back, dropping the blade on the ground.

Keelia soon came flying in for the long sword on the ground, but Adele, who was only slightly conscious, managed to notice her, and raised his hand.

"Keravnos!"

The lightning struck her unexpectedly, and she crashed into the ground from a few feet. She quickly turned to see the condition of her wings. They were safe for now, and she soon stood on her own two feet.

Adele stood up shakily, and commanded again, "Fos Keravnos!"

"Damn it! Apsis!" she commanded.

The small soul shield shattered and the bright lightning struck her.

Kinsei managed to turn and raise his hand to Adele. "Erebus Ekriksi!"

The dark energy crashed into Adele and soon fizzled out, but the impact was enough to fully knock him out.

Keelia soon grabbed Kinsei and spread her wings, then took off high into the sky.

Alda soon got back up, and ran over to Adele. "By the Divines Adele, are you alright?"

"Adele is as tough as nails, he'll wake up soon enough," Zen said confidently, though through pain.

She quickly ran to his side now. "Zen you think you can stand up?"

"Probably can, rocks are hard to land on correctly," he replied.

Alda noticed how cut up he was, and touched his cheek, where there was a large bleeding gash. "We need to get help."

Adele soon returned back to consciousness as Zen had said, and he partially lifted his head. "Don't tell me you're getting all romantic, save that for when we're not bleeding please."

Zen, Alda and Adele were able to leave the market area without being seen, and now made their way to the sanctuary.

"Adele, are you okay?!" exclaimed Kilan as she ran up to him.

He raised his hand to stop her. "I'm fine girl, no need to go into a panic."

"But your lip, and eye, and...face...Jeeze, you get mauled or something?" she asked.

"I got kicked," he replied blankly. He lurched forward as he felt a pain in his chest. "I may have a broken rib too."

Zen had decided to bandage his own wounds, as he used to on the battlefield, holding some of the wrappings in his mouth as he wrapped them around his arms.

Alda chuckled from where she was leaning on a wall out of sight, and Zen looked up at her.

"What's so funny?"

"It's just that you're binding yourself up as if there is no one here that knows a thing or two about being a doctor," She motioned to where Illeth was caring for Adele.

"I'm just accustomed to it," he replied. "Don't you remember that I was a soldier?"

"Well you are a different kind of soldier," she said.

Zen went back to tying, but looked back up to Alda. "How do you feel about jewellery?"

"I only see that stuff as something you sell off to the merchants," she replied.

"What if it bared a symbol of your clan?" he asked.

"I-I might keep it, why do you ask?"

Zen tried in vain to hide his blush. "No reason, just wondering what you liked."

Alda smiled and shook her head, then went back to her own thoughts.

Keels

The men had risen early to begin the march to Keels from the redoubt, and were soon on their way.

The march would have taken nearly a week to complete, but they had roads that went directly between Deneaux and Keels, so the march would only take a few days.

It was at the first resting point when Jor noticed her.

Jor, Turner and three other soldiers sat around one of the fires that had been lit in the camp that they had set up. It wasn't too late out, and the troops needed to eat, so they sat around the fire and waited.

"So, what brings you into the military?" asked a soldier. He was bearded and seemed to be in his late thirties.

"It really is a funny and somewhat embarrassing story," Jor replied.

"Alright then; so what brings you to the military, kinsman?"

"I was a guard, but when I heard this guy was joining up, I couldn't leave him alone," Turner replied, indicating Jor. "Oh, and he joined because of a what? A love oracle card was it?"

Jor coughed loudly and blushed. "Well, my friend gave me one, and her friend demanded—commanded me to join the military," Jor replied simply.

One of the other soldiers turned and whistled as a figure approached. "Looks like lunch is coming with a pretty treat."

"Excuse me?" Jor and Turner said, their jaws dropping.

"Oh hi Jor," said Lyra as she set down a tray with bowls of simple vegetable soup to them.

"L-Lyra?! What are you doing here?!" he exclaimed, greatly alarmed.

"Didn't you know? Noch let me join as a quartermaster and medic," she replied casually.

"You know this fine example of elven ladyship?" asked the other soldier.

Lyra pretended not to hear him and smiled at Jor, Jor managed to smile back.

"This is who the love oracle sent me to, and it had to be the one girl I couldn't impress."

Lyra patted Jor on the back. "I'm not into that kind of stuff."

"Then what are you into?" asked Turner.

"Hunting, tracking, sneaking—Jor mostly knows," she replied.

"Hey serving girl, bring us some grub!" shouted a soldier not too far away.

"Alright, time to go for now, see you tomorrow."

It was now the second day of the march, and the area had gotten more wooded and most of the path was covered with shade.

Jor was now walking near the back, where the supply carts were—and where Lyra was.

"Hey Lyra, nice walk isn't it," he said as he approached.

"Yeah, I guess," she replied, her head down.

"Something bothering you?" Jor asked.

"No, now don't you belong in any tight formation?"

"We're walking free for now, no need for formations."

"Then why not go talk with one of your soldier friends?"

"Because my friend is troubled by something, and I don't like leaving friends with problems," Jor replied sternly.

Lyra sighed. Defeated now, she spoke up. "My family, I don't think they are worried that I was gone."

"Wouldn't that mean they think you are capable?"

"No, they think I'm irresponsible, wild, crazy—they don't think I'm a girl, in a sense."

"The fact you survived at that border post shows you to be very capable."

"I only survived because you were with me."

"And when you confront your parents, I'll be there with you."

Lyra looked up at him, and saw that he wasn't joking or making empty promises.

He was serious.

"You would really do that for me?" she asked.

"I've faced down things worse than angry parents; I should come back out with two arms and one leg."

Lyra giggled at the comment, but realized how she sounded and stopped herself.

"I suppose you want me to hang out more with you now or something."

"Just seeing you giggle that one time was good enough," He shoved her a little with his shoulder. "You do have a pretty smile."

"Alright lover boy, say that around my brother and you'll get shot."

"Don't worry, don't worry, I'll just be there as a support, but in the meanwhile, I think I will enjoy the scenery."

Noch smiled as they finally reached the end of the forest path. The walk took three days in total, and it would be nice to find a place to relax while they garrisoned at Keels.

Many of the inns and taverns were filled with adventurers and mercenaries from miles around that would help fight with, or against the raiders, depending on the price.

The soldiers would be garrisoning Fort Letry, a large stone structure that was hid almost perfectly within the forests that made up Keels. For now though, all they had to do was drop off their things and head out on their own endeavours, as the first day was to relax after all the walking.

Lyra shuffled her feet uneasily as she stood before the door to her two-story home.

"You look very, very scared," Jor said comically.

"I'm not!" she protested. "I'm very, very, very, extremely scared." She made an attempt to knock, but she pulled her hand away, the repeated the same sequence of motions roughly five times.

"Just knock the damned door!" Jor said impatiently, then knocked.

Lyra cringed each time he rapped at the door with his fist, and put her hand over her face when she heard the footsteps coming.

A tall elven man with long brown hair and an extremely serious look on his face answered the door, but the expression changed as he lifted Lyra up, laughing, and brought her inside.

"Honey look, our daughter has returned!" Jor heard him exclaim from inside.

"Our Lyra? Our child has returned?" the female voice said with disbelief present.

"M-May I come in?" Jor asked uncertainly.

"Yes you may," the man replied, trying to hold in his excitement.

Jor had to smile as he saw the one bigger elven man one crying and hugging Lyra, or more specifically, choking her.

"Daddy please, you're embarrassing me!" she managed to cough out.

Another elf, this one noticeably younger than the others, entered. The room went quiet as he did, and he almost instantly ran over and embraced Lyra.

"I guess I'll just wait outside then, don't want to screw around with family affairs," Jor said as he started awkwardly for the door.

"Don't go, I haven't introduced you to my parents yet."

Most could see that Lyra and Jor were far from each other in terms of height, Lyra being far shorter, but she managed to get behind Jor and push him forward.

"Jor, these are my parents, and that guy is Ifadeel, my brother. Family, this is Jorigsveer Great-Blade, a friend of mine."

"Good day," he managed to say.

Ifadeel's eyes ran about Jor curiously, then he glared at him. "You look like one of those raiders."

"My father was Raider, and my mother was a mix of Raider and Deneauxman, and both of her parents were mixed," Jor replied.

Ifadeel grabbed Lyra by the arm and led her to a part of the room where no one would here, while Jor and Lyra's parents struck up a conversation.

"Lyra, is this kid for real?" he asked.

"He's cool Ifadeel, no need to suspect anything!" she replied.

"Did he do anything to you while you were in Deneaux—did anyone do anything to you?"

Lyra bowed her head, but Ifadeel lifted it again.

"Are you going to answer me?"

"The other soldiers had me as a—form of entertainment, but Jor saved me from them before things got out of hand, and he protected me through the whole thing."

"How do you know he didn't want you for himself?"

"Will you stop being a prick and listen with your ears? Jor is nice, and yes he may try to flirt with me every once in a while, he is still cool, understand?"

"Pfft, you talk as if nothing is going on between you two, I mean, why don't you call him by his full name, or is that your little nickname for your boyfriend?"

"Everyone calls him Jor."

"Well you shouldn't."

"You don't control me."

"But I'll protect you."

"Well did you protect me when I was captured in Deneaux?"

"I had no control over that!"

"Answer my question."

"No."

"You know who did protect me?"

"That's beside the point."

"That is the point."

"Lyra, I'm trying to help you."

"And being overprotective won't help."

"I just want you to be safe."

"And Jory will keep me that way."

"Oh, so now you have a new nickname for him?"

"See, I can call him what I want."

"Alright, but when you start popping out bastards three at a time, just know I warned you."

"I'll make sure to name one of them after you."

Ifadeel soon began to storm out, but Jor turned to him and Lyra.

"Everything ok?" he asked.

"No! Things won't be ok until you stay away from my sister!" Ifadeel shouted back.

"A pretty quarter master is hard to stay away from," Jor replied jokingly.

Lyra's parents looked at Jor strangely.

"Isn't that a military line of work?" asked her mother.

"I've been serving as a quartermaster in the same troop as Jor, and the job really pays well. And I don't even need to fight."

Her father frowned. "Not what I expected you to work in, but I suppose you could keep the job, as long as you don't get involved in the fighting."

"So you're letting your daughter hang around a bunch of hungry, greedy soldiers?" asked Ifadeel.

"Your sister is an independent soul. A little work around older men and women should teach her a thing or two about responsibility," said Lyra's mother.

"Ugh, let's go Jor!" Lyra exclaimed.

"Go then, get killed with that walrus!"

Jor turned to him now, his look as menacing as ever. "Keep making walrus and seal themed jokes on me, and you'll know how it is to fight an above average Raider." He indicated the Great sword that he carried. "And I hope you know this thing splits materials you'd never think could be shattered, including bronze, iron—and bone." He and Lyra left, and the house fell silent.

Jor so far was now on guard duty, but not on the castle walls or on a stone tower.

He was in a tree.

"I'll never get used to this," he said to himself and he tried not to look down, but instead ahead at the few clearings that were before Bearded Run.

It was a pretty scene at least. Keels was filled with trees. Every direction you turn in, there was a tree not too far off. This gave the place a natural shade and constant greenery, and since many of the trees were larger than the average castle wall, you could place archers and sentries in them to spot the enemy quicker and rain projectiles on them.

The only option when it came to attacks would be to burn down the trees, but many knew of the many soul beings that walked the forests.

And they never took kindly to someone burning down their forest.

"Hey Jor, I think I see something!" exclaimed a soldier in a nearby tree.

"It won't do me any good if you just tell me you saw something, is it in the sky? On the ground? Is it big or small? What?" Jor asked.

"It's in the sky, and it's coming at not too bad a speed," the soldier said.

Jor looked up, but was only able to see a dark speck. He kept straining to see until it came into sight.

A fireball, and a big one too.

"Fireball!" he shouted.

There was a large amount of movement being heard from below, and cries of astonishment from the other sentries in the trees.

"Sentries, we need you down now!" shouted Noch, and they quickly scaled down the large trunks of the trees and ran for the fort.

Turner ducked behind one of the battlements, a loaded crossbow in his hands. For the moment, he could only hear the rabble and confusion as men got together their weapons and armor and got into position.

After it had all ended, Turner could hear the sounds of marching men.

And the area seemed a little too hot.

Lyra and several of the other cooks and medics had gone out to get supplies, and as they began to return to the Fort, they saw a giant fireball as big as the Fort itself crash into the forests around it.

"What was that!" one exclaimed loudly.

"I don't know, but whatever it was, it hit Fort Letry," another replied.

"Jor," Lyra whispered under her breath, here gaze set on the forests around the fort.

Turner now raised his head from behind the battlements to behold that the forest before them was completely annihilated. Not even the tree stumps were visible.

But now, he could clearly see the large army coming towards them.

"Hold positions!" commanded Noch.

The defenders did so, and the Raiders were now within range.

"Just wait," he said, trying to make sure everyone heard but the enemy.

Now they could see ladders being raised up to be put on the walls, and it was then that Noch gave the command.

"Fire!"

The men shot out from behind the battlements to the Raider's surprise and unleashed a hail of crossbow bolts upon them.

They soon began to fall back and hastily pulled together a shield wall. Several raiders also began forming up behind them and raised bows and crossbows.

"They're gonna start shooting!" shouted a soldier as he quickly fired and hid behind the battlement.

"Don't worry, we got this!" Noch shouted, trying to keep a reassuring smile on his face.

Several cut off screams were heard to the eastern wall now, and several of the medics attempted to get over. One slumped down as quickly as he got up as an arrow slammed into his side. The second made it over, and called for two more. They made it across now, but all the movement turned the eastern wall into a target.

"Get the wounded into the keep, and keep low!" Noch commanded.

The medics nodded and began dragging people, whether dead or wounded, into the keep.

"Hey Noch!" called Jor from the wall below. "When do we get our turn to attack?"

"I don't know, for now we need to just hold out until they get within reach, or more simply, until they get on the walls!"

"But isn't that, well, dangerous? I mean they are raiders after all," Turner said.

"We'll see."

Out on the western borders of Keels, there was a fort by the name of West Key, and it stood prior to the battle at Fort Letry.

It was fully garrisoned by Elves, and had never seen action, making the garrison grow lazy and out of shape.

"Hey Leaf, they say there are Raiders up north, on Bearded Run," said one elf to another.

"Probably just rumours Keswick," the other replied, looking lazily out into the trees.

"Yeah, you know the 300 year war ended forever ago. Why would the Raiders come back just to lose again?" said a third

There was a muffled cry off to the side, and the three turned to see what it was.

"Everything okay over there?" asked Leaf.

No reply.

"I'll go check," said the third elf, and he went around the corner.

"What?! Who the hell are you? Wait, stop, no, ahhhh!"

The two elves drew there blades now as they saw the crimson blood of their comrade fly into the air.

Around the corner came a large green man with two red pickaxe shaped weapons in his hands, and soon for them too, the world became red.

The battle was short and bloody, and with the takeover of Fort West Key, the Orcs could move in from Crill and deeper into Northern Keels— from behind.

Now, after several days of walking, they stood atop a hill overlooking Keels, and an evil grin crept across one's face.

"Today, we avenge or fallen forefathers!"

Lyra and the others now turned to see men charging in from the hills.

"Are they reinforcements?" she asked.

"We were the only reinforcements sent," a soldier replied.

Bells began ringing to the south of the capital, then there was shouting.

"Is it possible for the Raiders to attack us from behind?" Lyra asked, her gaze not moving from the south.

"You Elves are impossible to get past in wooded areas, it shouldn't be possible," the soldier replied.

"Then who is down there?" she asked herself. She looked at her belt dagger, then back to the south.

"Let's go."

Fort Letry was now riddled with arrows and bolts to the point that soldiers only needed to pick up fired ammunition and use them themselves.

Bodies were also accumulating, and Noch now realised that they may soon not have enough healthy men to fight.

He now had the options to either call for more reinforcements, or abandon the fort and let them into the town.

He couldn't call either.

"Sir!" said an elf as she saluted. They seemed tired and out of breath.

"What is it?" Noch asked, snapping out of deep thought.

"The capital is under attack sir, by Orcs it appears."

"What?! How did that happen?" Noch asked now.

"Fort West Key was taken over, and now they may be pouring in from Crill, using West Key as a resting spot and stronghold."

"Damn it, is the Keels army fighting?"

"The Orcs sir, t-they have not lost a man yet, while we have lost nearly a hundred!"

Noch put his hand over his head, and looked out at the coming raiders. "Divines save us." He now turned to the elf. "Do you think there could be a way for the Keels army to defend here while we get more reinforcements?"

"I doubt it sir."

"I'm going to have to send a messenger; would you be able to head over to Deneaux?"

"Raiders have also moved to start blocking off the roads, and by the time I would be ready to leave, the Orcs may be in position to block off the entirety of the capital."

"Then I guess we'll have to hold out for now," Noch sighed deeply. An arrow whizzed past and slammed into the wall beside him. "We're going to need a miracle."

Lyra and several other soldiers ducked behind a building as they neared the Southern parts of the capital. Now they could see what was happening was far worse than they previously thought.

Orcs stood, some with arrows in their torso and arms, shredding apart elven soldiers and citizens.

"Impossible!" said one soldier in awe. "Only a Divine can do such things!"

"You're welcome," said a voice from behind.

The group slowly turned their heads, and as they finished, they had to look up, especially Lyra, to fully see the large Orc that stood smiling.

"Now let me show you what I can do."

The Orc took a heavy swing with his Battle pick, and the beheaded body of a Deneaux soldier fell to the ground.

The second soldier lunged with his halberd and made a direct hit, but the Orc only laughed in reply.

"It'll take a lot more than that to bring down Titus himself!" He raised the battle pick and then dropped it, leaving only a short cry from the soldier.

"You're next little one."

Lyra sent a dagger flying, then nimbly hopped to the side. She sent another as she landed, and they both slammed into the Orc's chest. He laughed again.

Now seeing she was fighting the equivalent to a titanium wall fifty inches thick, she turned around and ran for the Fort.

"Tachista," Titus commanded. He appeared before Lyra near instantly and swung, but Lyra managed to dodge again.

"I can't die here," she said to herself, then dodged another attack.

Titus swung again at the same speed while Lyra was mid-jump. She looked to her side to see him ready to swing, and she knew she wouldn't dodge this one.

"Tachista!"

Lyra now realized she was in someone's arms, and as she looked up she realized.

"Ifadeel!"

He looked down at her and smiled, then cringed slightly. "That last move took a lot out of me; we'll need to get out of here as fast as we can." He stood up and commanded again, "Tachista!"

"What?! Stop right there!" shouted Titus.

They soon faded in and out of sight with their quick movements.

"Into the Keep, now!" shouted Noch.

"What does he have in mind here?" Jor asked himself as he scrambled for the Keep, along with many of the other soldiers.

The raiders soon began to move forward too, their ladders being raised high up.

"Yes, that's it, bring your sorry sealskin hides onto my wall, and we'll see how strong you are," Noch said to himself, gripping his blade.

Chapter 26

The Leagues

Efiia frowned as he placed his hand on a large, glowing blue stone inside of the Sanctuary.

"Everything okay?" Eros asked.

"Titus—He's in Keels, along with Fenalph," Efiia replied.

"What are they doing down there?"

For once, Efiia was serious. "He's taking Keels, and he doesn't plan on anyone escaping."

"But what about Jor, Turner, Noch and Lyra?"

"Lyra is attempting to escape from Titus with her brother, but he's running out of energy quick. Jor, Turner and Noch have gone into the Fort Letry Keep."

"How is the battle going then?"

Efiia removed his hand from the stone. "They don't seem to be able to escape Keels, and with the Orcs destroying the capital from the south and the Raiders from the North, it doesn't seem possible that they may survive."

"Noch won't survive?" Alice asked now.

The two hadn't noticed she was there, and realized they could not say anything to change her thoughts.

Eros sighed deeply. "The Raiders are pushing forward with probably ten or twenty times the amount of men Noch has—it's hard to see them win something like that."

"But can't you two go down there and help him?" Alice asked, tears welling up in her eyes.

It was Efiia's turn to sigh. "Fenalph isn't a normal Divine like Eros or Meso. Even I have right to fear him."

"You have to do something!" she cried.

Eros embraced her. "Just have faith; things may turn for the better.

"So are there more of these powerful Divines?" asked Mark as he now entered.

Efiia raised an eyebrow. "How many of you were eavesdropping on us anyways?"

"Most, if not all of us have been listening," said Akina as she peeped from the hallway.

"We must try to keep our talks more private Eros," said Efiia as he shook his head.

"True," she replied simply. "We can't just let them die out there though," she said, quickly changing back to the matter at hand.

"The way you make it sound, their best option would be to surrender," said Adele.

"But then what will the Raiders do to them afterwards?" asked Zen.

"What if more help was sent? Like a rescue party?" asked Alda.

"They would need one huge rescue party," said Will.

"Then why not rush down there ourselves? I haven't hurt anyone in days and now seems like a great time," said Kullskash.

Everyone's eyes now turned to her.

"You know, we still have that wagon," said Illeth.

"But the ride may still take a few days," Will replied. "They may be dead by then."

"Noch's a serious smooth talker; he could find some way through this," said Alice, whipping away the tears."

"But wait, the North League will still try and stop us," Eros considered.

Efiia put his hand over his face. "I'm not going into dealings with them, I said so already."

"What's a North League?" Kilan asked.

"A group of Divines is called a League, and is usually made up of about four or more Divines," Efiia explained.

"Efiia, Alcino, Kinigos and I are a League," said Eros.

"And Fenalph and Titus are apparently a League," Efiia continued.

"But didn't you say that a League is made up of four or more Divines?" Adele asked.

"True, but Titus and Fenalph both count as six Divines," said Eros as she laughed weakly.

"Can't you get anymore Divines to help you?" Zen asked.

"Your realm of Edafos might be extremely strong and able to sustain huge quantities of Soul damage, but if we were to call for more Divines, a war that would destroy Edafos would surely ensue," said Eros.

"What about the Divines that are already here?" Illeth asked.

"We would have to find them, then pick out those who accept our ideals and those who wouldn't," Efiia said.

"So if we were able to make friends with these Divines, would they help us?" asked Akina.

"Maybe, but not every Divine is powerful enough to stand against an enemy, some are peaceful while others prefer to use an army," said Eros.

"Like Mortha?" Alda asked.

"I always forget that you killed her, the wench was one hell of an annoying brat, and was one of the many girls to go after my Kini," said Eros idly. "You know Efiia, did that one country off to the south have a Divine?"

"There are many Kingdoms to the south, like Den, Northspire, Iron Hold, Southspire most importantly, that is truly to the south," rambled Efiia.

"The one with the Boreas Andras people," Eros said.

"Oh, Boreas," Efiia said, returning to the current topic.

"Did or did they not have a Divine?"

"I believe they did—oh wait; they had one Divine."

Eros looked up at the group around her, then smiled to herself. "Figuring out a way to group you all so that some may fight here while others go abroad will be a hellish task."

"May I help Mrs. Eros?" Efiia asked.

"I wouldn't have let you leave me alone for this; stress is for my husband, not me."

CHAPTER 27

The Battle for Keels

The heavy ladders clattered unto the walls, and the raiders soon began their ascent into Fort Letry.

"Noch, what do you have in mind here?" Jor asked him, gripping a crossbow tightly.

"We need more of them on the walls, I want to rack up the carnage," Noch replied.

"Heh, I thought your people were peaceful," a soldier remarked.

"We are, but when war time comes, we are known to lower enemy moral with our...atrocities," Noch said as he made an imitation bird call, signalling for his trap to be sprung.

About now, dozens of Raiders were on the wall, and some even had to wait as they tried to clear the walls up for more men to get on.

Being bunched up did have its downsides.

A line of crossbowmen swung up from behind the upper battlements and rained a volley of bolts onto the raiders, and soon after, another volley was on its way. Many were unable to put up there shields in time due to a lack of space, and dozens perished on the spot.

"Let's go, we charge em' now!" Noch shouted. His men echoed a mighty battle cry and rushed outside of the keep, hacking away at the unsuspecting raiders

Many made attempts to climb down the ladders, but they were pushed back, and many fell to their dooms.

The men now uttered a mighty cry again, raising their weapons high as they did.

Now, a Raider approached, holding a white banner with a grey wolf emblem.

"Why do you fight, men of Deneaux?" he asked, he voice loud and clear as the noise settled.

"We fight to defend our country!" Noch replied, hearing several growls of acknowledgement from his men.

"But you cannot win, for our God is with us, and yours is not!"

"Then prove it! Efiia and Eros guide us!" shouted a Deneaux soldier.

"Our Lord Fenalph, our mighty Fenalph, shatter this fortified hill into gravel, but spare the men upon it!" he called to the skies.

The soldiers on the Fort looked about, but nothing happened.

Until the rumbling started.

It was a low vibration in the ground, but it soon grew until they could feel themselves shaking violently.

"Off the walls! Now!" Noch shouted, and the men followed.

Many threw over ropes and slid down, while others used the left back ladders. As the last of them got off the walls, the Fort was split in two, and crumbled to the ground.

"Where are Efiia and Eros to save you now?" the Raider asked Noch looked back at the crumbled remains of the Fort, horrified at what he had just seen.

"Commander Noch, we have to move," Turner said, snapping him out of the state.

"Yes right." He raised his sword into the air, and it gleamed in the sun, making it easily seen by his men. "Retreat!"

The men easily followed the command, and made their way to Keels desperately, hearing the Raider's cheers and shouts in victory behind them.

Ifadeel now fell to one knee, his face covered with sweat and breathing heavily.

"Lyra, run now!" he shouted.

Lyra moved out of his arms and made an attempt to help him up, but he pushed her away.

"Go now before he kills you!"

Lyra turned and ran, but as she got only a few feet ahead, Titus stood before her, a nasty grin on his face.

"No escape for you elf," he said as he raised his large Battle pick.

"Dynami Ekriksi!"

A large white ball of pure soul energy slammed into Titus' side and sent him sliding through a building nearby.

Noch smiled, his hand glowing white. "That was what was killing all the elves here? This country needs to step it up on the military."

"WHO DARES TO STRIKE THE MIGHTY TITUS!" boomed a voice.

Noch turned to see the Orc coming his way, walking slowly but menacingly.

"Sir Noch dares strike 'The Mighty' Titus," he replied mockingly.

"Do you even realize who I am?"

"Just another big green thing from who knows where."

Just as Noch finished the sentence, a white flame-like aura whipped up around him, and in only a few seconds, Noch fell back into the dust.

He was fighting a Divine.

Titus now raised his Battle pick again, and as it crashed down, it was turned slightly as it slid off the side of Jor's great sword.

"Hurry up Noch! I thought the order was to retreat!" Jor shouted.

Noch soon got up and took off with Jor, but Titus again appeared before them.

"You aren't going anywhere," he said.

"Let us pass or we'll cut you down!" Jor exclaimed.

"No, it is you who shall be cut down," Titus replied coldly. He faded again, and Jor turned to see him right before him.

"Tachista!" Noch commanded. He faded as he said it, and in a fraction of a second, he grabbed Jor and they both escaped from Titus' attack. "That guy is a Divine Jor, he's different than most."

"Divines are still killable," Jor challenged.

"Well this one isn't, now let's move!" Noch began to glow with a blue and white flame aura. "Spirit wolves of Sepal, come to my aid!"

Several ethereal wolves animated out of nothing and charged for Titus.

He swung and dispelled the first, but right after another clenched unto his arm. He reached to attack it, but another bit the other arm, and the next clawed him consecutively on the torso, with another following up to claw his face.

Titus unleashed a blast of compressed soul energy, and the wolves went flying—but not to their expense.

Titus' arms were now crimson with the blood as the wolves tore his flesh away from him.

He cringed.

And the wolves seemed to smile.

The pack charged forward, and as Titus swung, some dodged and others faded, then reappeared above him, latching back unto his body as they got the chance.

"Damn it! Get off!" he shouted.

They did as he said and slid back in the dust, not losing their footing as they did.

"Spirit Cannon," the chanted together, in a deep, grizzled voice.

With the echoing sound of a howl, a blue beam slammed into Titus, burning away at his flesh.

Noch and Jor reappeared a ways away from the battle.

Noch fell to his knees now, and his breathing was short.

"Noch, are you alright?" Jor asked, panic in his voice.

"Those wolves....Those beasts..." he managed to say. "They take a lot from me."

They both heard a shout from where they were previously, and Noch's smile widened.

"Never...mess.....with the men....of.....Sepal," Noch said faintly. He collapsed onto the ground, and Jor reached down for him.

"Noch, Noch answer me!" he shouted.

No response.

Noch was still, and Jor couldn't tell whether he was barely breathing or...

Jor lifted him and held him on his back. "You're not dying on me today, whether you want to or not."

Turner ripped his blade from the body of a recently slain Raider, and turned to hack down another.

"Keep up the defence, we'll have them retreating once Noch gets here!" he shouted.

"Orcs!" shouted a soldier whose voice was quickly cut short.

The large green man charged into the battlefield, bloody axes in both hands and a grim smile upon his face. "Who is ready for carnage?!"

"Think you can insult my legion? Hell no," he growled under his voice.

Steel clashed with steel as the Orc hardly managed to dodge Turner's attack. They both broke away from each other, but Turner stepped forward and swung.

The Orc parried with one axe, but Turner now lunged with a long dagger in his other hand. It hit, but hardly marked the Orc's hardy exterior. The Orc swung with his other axe, but Turner ducked under and got behind him, then lunged the dagger in his upper back. He hauled himself up unto his shoulders and held his sword under the Orc's neck.

"Sleep tight in hell."

The Orc fell into the dust, and Turner stood behind him, his hand and sword drenched in blood.

"Never thought a slit throat would bleed that much," he said, shaking off some of it.

"We have Raiders making a break for it!" shouted a soldier from away.

With the first Orc death in the battle, and that caused by one man, the Raiders began to route.

But Turner Gales wouldn't have that.

He loaded his wrist bow and fired, taking one router down. He ran for a discarded crossbow on the ground and quickly fired that, killing another Raider.

"What are you all waiting for, take them out!" shouted another soldier as they fired a crossbow.

Several more Raiders fell at the hands of the crossbowmen, and the sight of even more dead lowered the moral of the others, making them route in turn.

Jor finally made it up to Turner.

"What happened to Noch?!" he asked, panicked seeing their leader unconscious.

"We met up with a Divine, we were hardly able to escape," Jor replied simply.

Turner looked about, then noted the town hall and several smaller one story buildings around it.

"We'll need a defensive perimeter if we want to survive today. No point in trying to break the line around Keels, they'll just cut us down from there."

"What about our medics?" Jor asked.

"We'll have to hope that they find us."

Ifadeel now attempted to stand up, but Lyra stopped him, and sat him back down on the bed of the ruined house they were hiding in.

"You need to rest Ifadeel," she told him.

"And you need to get out of here," he replied equally.

"I'm not leaving you behind, no matter how pissy you can get!"

"Oh, I'm the pissy one?"

"Just shut up and rest, no one knows we're here and I intend to keep it that way!"

They sat in silence for a moment, and Ifadeel noticed the concerned look on her face.

"What you thinking about?"

"Ways to shut you up without killing you."

"You're thinking about that soldier, aren't you?"

Lyra opened her mouth to protest, but she realized Ifadeel was more concerned than angry. She sighed.

"I've just come to see him as, well, the kind of guy that digs you out of that bad spot."

"He has really helped you before?" Ifadeel asked.

"When I was captured at the border post he did, but I never truly thanked him for it like I should've." She put her hands over her face. "I was hardly ever nice to him it seems, but yet he was always nice to me; smiling with me, joking with me, even trying to flirt with me." She now looked out of the window, which was more accurately a hole in the wall.

"You like him?" Ifadeel asked.

"I wouldn't mind hearing his voice just one more time, no matter what he says."

"Lyra!"

"Now I'm hearing things, see what you caused," she said to Ifadeel.

"Lyra, or anyone for that matter!"

"I hear it too," Ifadeel said.

Lyra looked out the window to see Jor, Turner and a few other soldiers going down the ruined streets.

"Jor!" Lyra called as she came running down the stairs of the building then towards him

"Lyra!" he said, relieved. As she neared him, he embraced her tightly. "I was too worried about you!"

Lyra stood there in Jor's embrace, trying to take in what was happening. She was hardly ever hugged nowadays, but now by a boy she wasn't even related to.

And now he was even worried about her.

Ifadeel now limped outside, and froze entirely at the sight.

Jor looked up at him, then ordered the other soldiers to help him walk. "It's going to be a long walk back to our perimeter, might as well speed it up."

City Hall had been transformed from the local government's luxurious housing to a messy military fort.

Ifadeel and Lyra were soon together again on the ground floor, where most of the wounded were being tended to.

"It seems that the Raider boy is somewhat decent," Ifadeel said.

"Now will you give him some slack?" Lyra asked.

"Maybe—maybe not."

"You know, how is it you boys become instant friends again? Was it fighting alongside each other?"

"No matter what he does or says, I'll never, ever, ever fight alongside him."

"We got charging Raiders!" a soldier shouted.

The combined Deneaux and Elven forces had already gone to the windows and roof with bows and crossbows before the sentence was finished.

"So you plan on forsaking your elven comrades then?" she asked.

"Damn," Ifadeel muttered as he picked up his bow and limped to a window.

The Raiders fell only a few at a time to the projectiles of their enemies, due to their large round shields.

"We aren't going to beat them like this!" Turner shouted.

"Well you have any better ideas?" Jor asked as he fired into the charging attackers.

"I'll give the command once they are in range, and we'll see if they'll come back!"

"What are you planning human?" Ifadeel asked.

Turner held up his hand and didn't answer. The rest of the defenders saw this and held their fire.

The Raiders now interpreted the cease of fire as being due to low ammunition, but still kept their shields up. They began trying to break down the doors of the hall as they reached it, and those inside could see that they were breaking through.

"Oil!" Tuner shouted.

The raiders looked up fearfully after hearing the command, and to their terror, they watched as the hot oil rained down.

The soldiers inside cringed at the sound of their cries of pain and agony, but then watched as the few that weren't burned turn around and run. Many of them were picked off by the defenders now, and they cheered as the last of them disappeared into the forests.

"Turner, I didn't know you were this brutal," Jor joked.

"I didn't either," he replied, wiping the sweat off of his face.

CHAPTER 28

King Carel the Joyful

Efiia strolled through the halls of the Pantheon Castle. He turned and opened the large gilded door to the throne room.

Before him stood and elderly man, probably in his late nineties. Despite this, he sat proudly on the throne, wearing only blue robes and holding an oaken staff.

"Efiia, is that you my friend?" he asked.

The guards around him held their halberds with a tighter grip, but Efiia paid no mind to it.

"It is I," he replied simply.

"Haha, now what brings your sorry hide into my court after all these years?" the King laughed.

"At first, it was just to say hello, but after a few odd events, I had to report to you."

"And what of these 'odd events'?"

Efiia now turned serious, as did the King. "You know of the Sepalese man you sent to reinforce the Elven city of Keels?"

"Yes, the Noch boy, capable man, capable Paladin."

"Well, I've lost the ability to sense his presence on this plane, but I doubt he is dead, and his men have been forced out of Fort Letry and into the capital itself."

"What?! Impossible, Fort Letry is reasonably placed within the trees; it should take weeks to take down something like that, even with a small garrison."

"Well...There is a Divine there, even more powerful than I, the Lord of Deneaux, and he burned down the forests and shattered the Fort."

"A Divine more powerful than you? You jest."

"I don't, he was the cause of the Three Hundred Year War, and now he has chosen to come back, this time though, he wants to win."

"I'm going down there myself then, with all my Paladins!" the King exclaimed.

The men on both sides of him exchanged troubled glances, and then returned back to attention.

"Servants, bring me my weapons and armor, and then call for the Paladins! I shall not be undermined by men nor Divine!"

Eros looked around the sanctuary, noticing how many of the people inside seemed to socialise with each other if different groups.

Jane, Adele, Zen, Alda, Dodecagon, Alice and Kilan seemed to stay together, though Alda seemed somewhat detached from them.

Will, Mark, Akina, Illeth and Kullskash also seemed to be together.

If she wanted some to stay in Deneaux with her, she would need people that could stand up to Meso and his soldiers easily, but Efiia might need some to help out at Keels.

"Hurry up why don't you," she said to herself.

"So you expect an old man like me to run here?"

Eros let out a startled cry as she turned to see Efiia right next to her. "Damn it Efiia, learn to let people know you are coming."

"Sorry, I just came to tell you that...well....the King is going off to Keels himself...with his Paladins of course, but..." he let it trail off.

"But what?" Eros asked.

"His age is a bit...ripe you know, I fear he may hurt himself."

"During the battle?" Eros asked

"Getting down the steps of the Pantheon castle," Efiia replied.

"Why didn't you tell him to stay?"

"He is the King of a mortal Kingdom, I can only advise him, not order him."

"At least that makes things a little easier for me."

"How so?"

"Now I can keep more here to fight Meso, and maybe get a few to find that Divine down south."

"Fel Hall is down south," Akina said sadly.

"You children must learn how to not eavesdrop," Efiia replied.

"Give the girl some slack, she lost an entire Kingdom down there, the name alone puts her on the verge of tears," said Illeth.

"Pfft, then why not take it back?" Eros asked.

"We'd be fighting three wars at once if we went down there again," Will said.

"Then why not try and start up peace talks, you mortals are always up and about with peace treaties."

"Akina is the only one with status here, and you know what happened," said Kullskash.

Eros tossed a necklace over to Akina, who caught it.

"That charm you're holding carries my symbol, anybody tries to harm you will have to go through me. It basically makes you near immortal...at the expense of my own energy, so don't get stabbed with obsidian."

"So you want us to end a three-way war and unite the Kingdom again?" Will asked.

"Deneaux is in debt to Den as Keels is in debt to Deneaux, the countries have helped each other in the past, and are bound to do so as long as a good King lives," Eros said.

"And they would do well in the coming war," Efiia said, almost to himself.

Mark got up, stretched and yawned. "Well what are you all waiting for, let's go."

Roseanne rode alongside the King with several Soul Mystics beside him. Behind them were around fifty mounted Soul Knights and Paladins.

"Are you sure you can get through this my King?" she asked finally. She heard several others behind her sigh in relief as she asked at her expense.

"I may be old, but this body has enough energy to tear apart entire mountains if need be," he replied.

"So is it really true what they say, you know, with the passing down of soul energy itself from Kings?"

"It has to be, or else I wouldn't be this strong."

"Do you believe then that we will be able to break into Keels and then back out?" asked a Soul Mystic.

"If we focus and have faith, we can do anything. Remember that as long as you live, and the mountains will crumble and the seas will part at your word."

C H A P T E R 29

Battle for Keels Part 2

The small unit ran down the streets of the sacked city of Keels. Many of the buildings had fallen, and if they hadn't, they were only crumbled masses of stone and planks, or a wooden frame.

"Those damned Raiders," a soldier said to himself.

"That's why I'm killing the next one I see, and mounting his head somewhere menacing," another soldier replied.

"Down!" shouted a third soldier.

The rest went prone unto the ash covered ground, hardly moving.

A unit of Raiders passed down the street carrying with them several wagons.

"What do you think they have in there?" asked Turner.

One of the wagons stopped abruptly at a command, and the one behind it almost crashed into it.

"Damn it Firjir, we have explosives in there! Are you *trying* to get us killed?" shouted the one who gave the first command.

"Sorry sergeant, didn't know you wanted us to stop," he replied.

"Explosives?" Jor asked.

"I don't know too much on the subject, but they say it's some kind of exploding stick or ball," Turner replied.

"Like Soul?" Jor asked again.

"No, they are made in dwarven factories or something."

"Listen up, we're putting explosives at every square inch of this city; the men of Deneaux won't know what hit them, and I don't plan for them to," shouted the sergeant to his men.

"Ok, any of you here Souls?" Tuner asked the other men.

They shook their heads.

"Alright then, head back to the command post and warn every one of the Raider presence."

"And what will you be doing?" Jor asked.

"Pyro Ekriksi!" Turner commanded quietly. A flame ignited in his hands as he said it. "Now go!"

Jor and the others soon dashed down an alleyway, then through a few destroyed buildings.

Confident that they were far enough away, Turner put up his slightly closed hand towards one of the carts.

And released.

Jor and the others were now walking at a regular pace back to the command post, but they turned abruptly as they heard the loud explosions behind them.

"Should we go back and check if he's alright?" Jor asked.

"He wanted us to head over to the CP, so it would be best if we did so," a soldier replied.

Jor sighed deeply, and then drew his great sword. "I'll go check on him, then meet you back at the CP."

"Be careful then," another soldier told him.

Turner shook out his hand painfully after the attack. He knew that there would be no fire nearby to use for the attack, so he had to manifest it himself.

And he knew well he would burn himself, just not as bad as he thought.

"Turner!" Jor said as he went through the smoke that now shrouded the area.

"Damn it Jor, you shouldn't frighten a soldier like that!" Turner replied, his chest heaving.

"So you blew up the exposives?" Jor asked.

"Explosives Jor, ex-plo-sives."

"Whatever, so no more of them?"

"Shouldn't be any left."

"We got attackers men!" shouted the sergeant through the smoke. Find em' now!"

"Let's go!" Jor said as he headed for where the alley should be. After going for a few meters, he crashed into something big and furry. He looked up to see a Raider with the same surprised reaction.

His eyes soon rolled back and he fell. Turner reloaded his wrist bow and helped Jor up.

"Pro tip, don't die Jor," Turner said jokingly.

"Pfft, I learnt that at age five," he replied.

Out of the smoke came several more Raiders and they wasted no time in unsheathing their swords and axes.

Jor took a heavy swing, moving forward as he did. His blade smashed into the raider's large round shield, smashing it in half, along with the man's bones.

He seemed to ignore the pain, and he launched a full on flurry with his good arm with his long sword.

Jor held his blade near his body, blocking most of the attacks. He managed to get close enough to bash the man, then whipped out his belt dagger quickly.

The raider charged forward quickly, beginning his same pattern of attacks, with Jor repeating his same patterns of blocking and deflecting.

Turner noticed the other two men were watching patiently, and he wasted no time on planting a bolt into his neck.

The other was startled and whipped out a large battle-ax, then charged for Turner. He swung high, and Turner ducked. He slammed it down overhand next, but Turner simply moved to the side.

He attempted to reload his wrist bow, but a slash from behind told him this was not the time.

Another was behind him, a bloody short sword in his hands.

Now is not the time to panic Turner, worry about bleeding out later.

"This hardly seems fair," he said. "I thought you people were stronger than that."

He saw a flair of anger in both of their eyes, then raised his hand as they did.

"Pertusus!"

A thin beam tore through the Raider's chest and he fell, the other tried another overhand slash with his battle-ax, but Turner held his sword up, but tilted it slightly. The battle-ax slid off the side of it, and Turner closed the gap between them, ending the man with a stab of his belt dagger.

The Raider Jor was fighting now swung again with the same pattern, exhausting his own strength while Jor blocked and deflected with his great sword.

"I can do this all day; the question is, can you?" Jor asked.

He saw through the man's helm that his eyes were turning red, just like Alda's when she went berserk.

"Crap, Turner I need back up!" he shouted.

The man soon took heavier, faster swings, and Jor in turn took up the idea of making as much space between them as possible.

The raider wouldn't let up, and easily matched Jor's speed.

Turner could hear more Raiders coming, but couldn't see through the smoke. He soon made his way to assist Jor either way.

Out of the smoke, Turner attacked from behind with an overhand swing.

The Raider now twisted his arm so the sword could be horizontal, and took a full spin.

Crimson blood took to the sky as both Turner and Jor fell onto the street.

As Jor tried to stand, the Raider lunged down for a finishing blow. Jor managed to roll to the side and scrambled to his feet. He quickly realized that his great sword was not in hand. He unconsciously pulled out his long dagger and met the Raider's next attack.

The sound of clashing steel echoed out through the streets.

The raider swung lightly at Jor, but he barely deflected it with his dagger. As he tried to jump back, he felt that his chainmail had been cut again. Another step back told him that he wouldn't have a chest if this man kept hacking away at him.

"Ekriksi!" he commanded quickly. The white mass of pure energy slammed into the Raider's helmet, sending his head back.

Jor heard a snap, and thought he had won at that moment, but the Raider pulled his head back up in place.

"NO!" Jor shouted as he began his own attack. He swung low with his dagger, but the raider hopped back. He stepped forward and swung high, but the raider deflected it and slammed his fist into Jor's face.

He seemed unmoved from the Raider's blow, and grabbed his outstretched arm. "We'll see how you like this!" His long dagger tore through the Raider's arm until the other end was visible, then as quick as it went in, Jor pulled it out and spun it so that it faced the Raider's body. He attempted the stab him, but it instead tore slightly through the chainmail on the Raider's arm.

The Raider now lifted his arm and drove his sword down.

And Jor caught it.

The Raider's eyes turned back to normal as he saw Jor's were now turning red. He felt the blade being torn from his own grip, and Jor hopped back to make space between them again. He soon closed the gap again, and lunged at the Raider, slightly lifting him in the air, then dropping him, the sword still in his chest.

"Turner, let's go!" he said, panting.

No reply.

He walked a few steps, then watched in horror as his friend sat in a small pool of blood.

"Turner, no!" he shouted as he ran to him.

Raiders soon barred his way again, and he picked up the battle-ax left by the Raider Turner was fighting. His eyes went blood red, and he blacked out, returning to consciousness as he stood over Turner, leaving mutilated bodies and severed body parts in his wake.

"You're not dying on me today Turner! No one will!" He lifted him up and ran for a destroyed building.

He ran over piles of rubble and low walls, through alleyways and over small craters.

"Jor...leave me....get to the CP," Turner managed to say through the blood that kept welling up in his mouth.

"No, I need you, the troops need you, and Jane needs you!"

Turner now seemed to gain a new sense of energy, then reloaded his wrist bow.

"What are you doing back there?" Jor asked.

"We got raiders behind us!" he said as he fired.

One went down, but not without sending an arrow flying. It slammed into Jor's back, and they both fell, sliding in the dust.

Turner was already halfway up, firing after the attackers. He got off two shots before an arrow slammed into the arm he used to reload.

The Raiders now drew back their bows before the two, and Turner closed his eyes and awaited his fate.

"Turner!" Jor shouted. "Behind them!"

Turner opened his eyes to see several knives come from behind the Raiders and slit their throats.

An elven man and his troops walked toward to the two.

"Wounded men of Deneaux. Help them." Gailo ordered his men.

Turner watched hazily as they helped him up, and he soon passed out.

"Get them somewhere where they can be treated!" commanded Gailo to his men.

"Yes sir!" they replied.

"You did what!?" Lyra screamed at the soldiers who had come back from their patrol.

"We didn't want to have to sacrifice anymore men in the worst case scenario," the soldier replied.

"You should have told them both to stay with you!"

"And let them blow up the city?" said another soldier.

Lyra looked up at the smoke that was filling up the sky. "Do you think they're okay?"

"They should have been back by now, unless they ran into trouble."

"We have men approaching, five elves, two of our own!" said a sentry.

Noch, who was still recovering, took over as the sentry commander. "Let them in!"

They entered and Lyra quickly ran over to the stretcher that Jor was on.

"Jor, are you alright?" She realized how badly he was torn up by the battle, as he had large red gash across his chest, among other injuries.

"Don't worry, I'll be fine, Turner is the one we should be worried about.

She turned to see how cut up he was, and that his blood was covering his stretcher.

"Where are the medics here?" Gailo asked.

"Just put them in the upper rooms, I'll get some of the others to help them out," Lyra replied.

CHAPTER 30

Den Hall

The wagon had at least given them some comfort when traveling as they went down the dirt roads that led to Den.

Will and Mark sat up front while the rest of them sat inside.

Zen looked side-long at Alda while she wasn't paying attention for probably the fifteenth or sixteenth time today.

Definitely the twentieth time, thought Illeth.

"If you're going to watch her all day, at least explain what you want," she finally said to him.

Alda turned to Zen as soon as he turned away from her.

"What now?" Alda asked.

"Oh, I was just talking to Zen Zeran here," she replied, her gaze unmoving.

Zen blushed and sunk into his seat.

"What a strange boy," Kullskash said to herself.

Zen managed an inward smile as he looked down at the small charm in his hands.

They had set up camp on the roadside, and they each took turns keeping watch. Zen waited until it was Alda's watch.

Alda leaned on the side of a tree, looked out into the darkness uncaringly.

"Hey Alda," Zen whispered.

"Aren't you supposed to be sleeping?" she replied.

"Well yes but…" he couldn't find the right words.

"Let me guess, you want to spend the night watch with me?"

"I-I wouldn't mind," he managed to choke up.

He leaned on the same tree Alda was on. He noticed how she stood calmly and almost uncaringly and copied the stance.

"What are you doing Zen," Alda chuckled as she saw him.

"The Alda stance," he replied with a sly smile.

"Stop, you're gonna mess up the watch."

"As if you were watching anything."

"Hey, I like being in my own world."

"So that's what she calls it."

"You're such a fool Zen."

"I prefer the term minstrel," he said, bowing as he said minstrel. He now realized he had Alda giggling, not something someone of her nature would normally do.

"What on Edafos possessed you to miss sleep to joke with me?"

Zen held out the necklace for Alda that had her clan emblem on it.

"What is that?"

"It's something a friend made for me to give to you," Zen replied. "Does it even somewhat look like your clan emblem?"

Alda held it in her hands and watched it closely. "I-I've never told anyone this, but I never knew my family, I was just told I was a Breach-Breaker and that was it. I never knew my mark, or my calling."

"Do you like it?" Zen asked.

The emblem showed and axe between the two towers of a shattered castle, and was brown from the varnish applied to it.

"Zen, I-I don't know what to say."

"You did say I was a fool a little while ago," he said, pretending to talk to himself.

Alda embraced him tightly, her armor making it even harder to breathe.

"I love it Zen!"

"Well, you may want to let go while you're at it, I'm slowly running out of air," he managed to say.

"Sorry," she said as she let him go. "But why did you get this for me, I mean there a lot more prettier girls here and in Deneaux."

"Well, you see, the reason is, well, because, you know...."

"It doesn't matter, I still love it. I'm going to wear it everywhere I go from now on."

"Well I'm going to get some rest; we have a long day ahead of us tomorrow."

"Goodnight,"

"Night to you too."

"Damn it Akina, why must you be such a fool?" said Dasimay as she stood on an overlooking hill. "I'll get you eventually. Then that wench Eros."

They were now back on track and making way to the capital of Den Hall, the true capital of Den.

Illeth now pondered what was going between Alda and Zen, as she noticed one would look at the other while the next wasn't paying attention. She gave up on guessing.

Akina opened the small door at the front of the wagon that allowed the driver and passengers to speak easily.

"Can you see the capital yet?"

"Keep your head in Akina," said Mark. "You see Will trying to show himself?"

Akina looked back inside the wagon and remember why it was so cramped. She turned back to Mark. "I'll still need to show myself to the leaders of Den you know."

"That's what I'm scared of," he replied.

"Pfft, who was it that got captured the first time?"

"Who was it that didn't lift a finger to fight?"

Akina tapped him on the head and ducked back into the wagon before he could act.

"Very mature Akina, very mature."

"Just steer," she replied.

The gates to Den were now visible after a few more hours of riding. The walls had a stone base but were more or less wooded with several watch towers. The city itself couldn't be seen over the large walls.

"Be ready for a fight everyone, or be able to create a mass of constructive lies to get in," Mark said.

"A big, strong Fen like you shouldn't need to resort to lying," said Will from inside.

"I can tell you're mocking me," Mark replied.

"Heh, you're smart too."

"Quiet, we're here!"

"Who are you?" asked a Fen sentry.

"I am....I am Yellow-Mark Blunt-Claw," he proclaimed proudly.

"Then state your purpose here."

"A peace mission," he said.

"How you plan to make peace then?" the sentry asked in a mocking tone.

"I have officials from the other Kingdoms that will negotiate peace."

"And how do we know you are not trying to trick us?"

"Why would I trick a Kinsman?"

"You are not a Kinsman!" the sentry snapped.

"Alright, I'm not, but will you let us in?"

"Show us the officials."

"How can I trust you?" Mark said, and the sentry raised an eyebrow.

"If you don't show us the officials, we shoot."

Mark saw a combination of spears, javelins and crossbows go up around them.

"Mark, you are a horrible liar!" Kullskash whispered from inside.

"Just get out," he replied equally.

The sentry's jaw dropped as he saw Akina and her sisters.

"Men of Kinigos wish to enter! Open gates!"

"What the hell?" Alda said to herself, loosening her grip on her axe.

"That was a lot easier than I thought it would have been," Illeth added.

Once inside the city, they were escorted to the Main Hall. The door was opened and inside was an on-going feast. It stopped as they spotted the members of enemy Kingdoms.

"Why is this little Fel child standing in my hall?" asked the big Fen at the head of the table. He was dressed simply in a red kilt bordered with many different colours, and a brown bear skin cloak—the head still attached.

"I-I-I-I," Akina couldn't manage to say anything.

"Pro tip, use your words to talk," Will whispered to her humorously.

She felt Mark's large hand on her shoulder. "Don't be scared, you're a chief too, and you have two Divines on your side. You shouldn't be scared of anything now."

Akina took a deep breath and exhaled. "I am Akina, Chief of Fel Hall, son of Akin, servant of Eros and Kinigos."

"And I am Rirjiken, Chief of Den Hall and leader of the Den council," he replied, not showing how stunned he was at Akina's introduction. "What brings you here in our times of war?"

"I am here to bring peace between our nations, then with the Fox."

"So you are to bring peace to us?" said Rirjiken as he stood up, still in awe.

"You look as if you have witnessed the impossible."

"I have, let us discuss this now! Bloodshed shall not mark what will be the new United Halls of Den! Tradition can be set in stone, but stone can always be broken."

C H A P T E R 3 1

Dodecagon vs. Se'dah

"It's the child, he is very close to Eros," Meso said to himself. He waved his hand over the orb on a table and it displayed Eros weeping madly before a small grave.

"Idle wishes are no good Meso, the real thing on the other hand..." Kinsei let it trail off.

Dianne watched and turned away, determined not to protest.

"We would need someone very capable and powerful to pull off such a skilled murder," said Keelia.

"Why not have Dianne do it?" Se'dah asked.

"No, hell no," she replied.

"Why don't you do it Se'dah, you're capable," said Delta.

"I was waiting for that," said Gregory. "I'm not the one for murdering the kids."

"Alright then, I'll be back with an obituary, and maybe we'll get front row seats at seeing a Divine crazed with grief."

Meso laughed. "Yes, yes, do it quickly, I cannot wait!"

Eros now held the excited child's hand as he bounced about.

"Toys, toys!" he shouted.

"And to think you were a dragon about a week ago," Eros said.

"This place is too small for me to be a dragon."

"I know," Eros lifted him into her arms and kissed him on the cheek. "If kids were like you I would have told Kini to give me one."

"Is that your son, miss?" asked a woman.

It wasn't too odd to see people eager to start conversations or make friends on the streets of Deneaux.

"Not quite, he is somewhat adopted," Eros replied.

"He's so cute I just want to eat him up," said another woman.

"No, I don't want to be eated!" he exclaimed. Eros and the other women laughed.

"Having fun Eros, Divine of Love and Marriage?" asked a voice.

"Who said that?" Eros asked, looking around.

"Pertusus!"

"Apsis!"

The thin beam went from the roof of a house to Dodecagon. But he put up a soul shield before harm could come to him.

Se'dah stood up in the street before them and smiled.

"Eros, it's the bad man that took the scythe!" Dodecagon shouted.

Eros put him down and faced Se'dah.

"Another agent of Meso eh? What the hell do you want?"

"Just a trial at arms with your little dragon."

"No, he is not part of my war," she said.

The black scythe he had stolen now animated in Se'dah's hand to Eros' horror.

His gaze then shifted to Dodecagon. "I'm sorry to say, but that boy is going to die, no matter what you do or say."

"Get out of here!" Eros shouted to the gathering crowd.

"I could cut them down as quick as you would have given the command, but my power over darkness is limited to the strength of my own soul. My energy is to be used on one person and one person alone."

Eros could see the dark energy flowing around him, and the same for Dodecagon.

Before she could even comprehend it, she was jabbed out of the way by the end of the scythe.

The crowd gasped as they saw that Dodecagon now held the scythe by the blade.

"We haven't had our fair fight yet, and now you've given me more reasons to crack your skull open!" Dodecagon growled, baring fangs and his skin turning scaly.

"Big talk for a six-year-old."

"Dynami Fos Ekriksi!" Dodecagon commanded.

The blast came from his mouth and Se'dah barely dodged the unexpected attack.

"Dynami Aduro Pertusus Barrage!" Dodecagon commanded again.

Se'dah expected the attack to come from his mouth, but they came his fingers this time as a barrage of shining beams.

"Tachista!" he quickly commanded. He moved quickly about to dodge that attacks, but Dodecagon wouldn't have that.

"Hermes!" he commanded.

Dust kicked up around the square, and the small groups of people peaked from behind their hiding spots.

"Don't move, they're still at it!" Eros shouted as she got up and ran for cover.

Several explosions lit up around the area, taking out buildings and houses.

Se'dah soon shot down from the sky and slammed into the cobblestone road, leaving a crater. He quickly rolled out of it as Dodecagon slammed his fist down.

He quickly got to his feet, and blocked several blows from the claws of his fast adversary.

"Boreas!" Se'dah commanded, sending a burst of compressed air in every direction.

Dodecagon went flying, and he now saw it fit to push his advantage. A rain of blows fell unto Dodecagon as he went, and in a matter of seconds, he felt himself smashing through bricks and stone.

The scene fell quiet again.

"We need someone to help the poor child!" shouted one townsman.

"Don't worry, my disciples will be here eventually," Eros replied.

"Are they Soul Knights?" another asked.

"People of far better quality."

Se'dah sat patiently atop the half crushed building waiting for Dodecagon to show himself.

"Are you done already? I was going to play with you some more before I killed ya."

A flash of light went into the sky, and out of the rubble were two shining eyes locked on Se'dah.

"No one....defeats....Dodecagon, the Dragon of Deneaux!"

Out of the rubble he came, and Se'dah could only watch horrified as he felt a rain of blows connect to him.

"Tachista!" he commanded.

"Hermes!" Dodecagon commanded in reply.

Se'dah only got a few seconds break from the blows, and they quickly began again.

"I can't be getting beat by a glorified lizard child!" he said to himself. He crashed into the cobblestone road, leaving a small carter around him. "Damn it, time to enter Hell's gate: One."

Dodecagon's eyes widened as he saw a black circle below Se'dah, and he realized half of his face went black as shadow.

"Aduro Barrage!" he commanded quickly.

The ground lit up brightly as the light energy crashed down. The dust kicked up by it disappeared.

But Se'dah was nowhere to be seen.

"Aero Barrage!" he commanded from above Dodecagon.

"Pyras Barrage!" Dodecagon commanded in reply.

And inferno lit up before both of them, but Se'dah flew through it and using his entire hand, grabbed Dodecagon's head and slammed it into the cobblestone.

"Psyche Katastrofi!" Dodecagon managed to choke up as Se'dah held him firmly down.

"Damn you!" Se'dah exclaimed with two different voices at once.

Dodecagon began to glow white, then detonated. As the explosion occurred, he was loosened from Se'dah's grip, and he ran across the street.

Out of the smoke came Se'dah again with a clenched fist. Dodecagon grabbed him by the arm and spun him, then threw him.

He slid for a few meters, but hopped back to his feet.

"Pyras Katastrofi Barrage!" Se'dah commanded.

"Aqua Hoplon!" Dodecagon commanded in reply. A water shield appeared before him to answer the challenge to the coming fireballs. The first few fireballs burnt out as they hit the shield, but the others began to evaporate it until a well-placed fireball hit its mark.

Dodecagon went sliding down the street, his clothes slightly on fire. He got up and glared at Se'dah. The fire went out instantly.

"Dynami Khthon Katastrofi!" Se'dah commanded.

Sharp stones began to rip out of the ground towards Dodecagon.

"Gaia!" Dodecagon commanded in reply. He slammed his fist into the ground as he said it, and the stones began to shift in direction towards Se'dah. He dodged, but stumbled as he touched the ground.

"Khthon barrage!" Dodecagon commanded, sending more stones shredding out of the ground in multiple directions.

Se'dah touched the top of one, and vaulted himself in the air with a flip. He landed and side-stepped another set of stones, but as he did, a second line came up to him, and one flat-topped stone shot up and crashed into his chin. He fell back into the dust.

"Come on Se'dah, I thought that little transformation of yours would give you the upper hand, but now I see your already low on soul energy," Dodecagon said.

"Don't count me out kid, Hell's Gate: Two," Se'dah replied. The other half of his face was shrouded in darkness again, except for one beady red eye that appeared on the left side of his face.

He charged forward with another punch, but Dodecagon grabbed his arm again and tried to toss him. Se'dah found good footing and reversed the move. He began to spin Dodecagon, but he managed to escape and slid back in the dust. Se'dah kicked at him, but Dodecagon crossed his arms and blocked. Se'dah began to rain blows now, but Dodecagon's arms began to glow white.

"Smart kid, use off your energy on blocking," Se'dah said sarcastically.

"It's a phase daimon, I thought you knew of it," Dodecagon replied. "Lux Lucis Psyche Katastrofi!"

The entire area lit up in a blinding light, levelling the nearby buildings.

There was now a clear crater where the two adversaries stood. Dark energy was leaking from Se'dah's body, and he knew he would soon be in deep water. He looked up at Dodecagon now. An attack that powerful after a fight that used up so much energy should have either killed him or incapacitated him.

"Lies!" Se'dah screamed.

Dodecagon stood, a bright golden circle of energy at his feet. His hair was pure white and went down to the ground. His scales became more defined. This was Half-Soul form, a transformation that could only be attained by using up vast amounts of Soul energy. While being in the form, you gained even more than you started with. It was also on the path of showing your true self, as many would act differently after reaching this form.

"This is not a lie Daimon, this is power," he replied.

"But how could you attain such a form?!"

Dodecagon ignored his question. "So Daimon, may I ask of your name?"

Se'dah spat at the ground before him. Dodecagon raised an eyebrow. "It's Se'dah, and never forget it, for it will be the last name you'll here of."

"No, now let's play this game according to my rules. Dynami Aduro Katastrofi."

A circle began to glow around Se'dah but as he tried to move, Dodecagon stopped him.

"If you really want to get out of there, you'll tell me everything. Why you wanted the scythe, why you're a daimon, and where your fellows are."

"I'm not telling you anything, H-Hell's Gate: Two and a half."

The circle around him turned dark and faded, and an eerie laugh came from him. "Now it is time we play according to my rules."

"Then let us go to battle, good luck daimon!" Dodecagon shouted to him.

"Hermes!" the two commanded. They faded, then reappeared before each other, their fists together.

Eros was standing atop a building not too far off watching the battle.

Alice, Jane, Kilan, Efiia and Adele appeared near her now.

"What's going on?" Jane asked as she looked at the large crater.

"My Dodecagon is getting naughty," Eros replied with a smile.

"I can hardly sense him," Adele said.

"He may be moving faster than you thought possible," Efiia replied.

"Kid has skills then," said Alice.

"Can't be better than the Dark Champion," said Kilan.

"I'm still pretty banged up," Adele said. "And even if I wasn't, he would still own me."

Dodecagon slammed into the ground, but hopped back to his feet and gripped Se'dah by his shirt and slammed him face first into the ground. He faded as he hit, and Dodecagon did the same. They reappeared in the air, and a swift kick by Dodecagon sent Se'dah flying. He kicked up stones on both side of him as he slid, but got up as if unharmed and raised both hands.

"Dynami Hades Aegis Ekriksi!" he commanded. A towering shield began to form up from dark energy before Dodecagon, casting a shadow over the area. "Let me see you dodge this!"

"Yperano Kapnizo," Dodecagon commanded. A thick black smoke began to pour out from Dodecagon's mouth, covering the crater quickly.

"Crap! It's coming our way!" Eros shouted.

"Aduro Ekriksi!" Alice commanded. The ball of light flew into the wall of energy and simply faded.

"Aduro Katastrofi!" Jane commanded. The bigger ball of light hit the shield, and seemed to stop it for about a second, but it kept coming.

"That thing will wreck the city if it keeps coming!" Eros shouted.

"No it won't," said Adele. He twisted his arm around awkwardly, as if trying to get it in the right spot.

"What on Edafos are you doing Adele?" Kilan asked.

"A move I worked on, but I can't remember it accurately; it's been about three hundred years since I used it." His fingers now curled over slightly as if he was holding something, and a small, dark mass of energy glowed within it. "Anti-light Absorb!" he commanded.

A stream of energy passed over into Adele's palm, and the shield began to shrink dramatically.

"Good going young one, that shield may be down before we know it," said Efiia.

Adele's veins began to show on his face and hands, and his pupil grew smaller. "Damn it, Anti-light Burst. Move everyone, now!"

"What's going on Adele?" Kilan asked, concern in here voice.

"Move it!"

The group began to move over to the other rooftops, but as they did they were sent flying by a burst of dark energy.

Kilan was the first to get up after the blast. "Adele!" she screamed.

He came limping out of the smoke. "That shield is still coming again; don't worry about me though, I just lost a bit of energy, and maybe twisted my ankle."

Efiia helped Eros up and turned to look at the shield. "A simple problem with a simple answer." He faded and appeared atop another house. "Exochos Lux Lucis Hoplite!"

A giant spear made entirely out of light appeared above him, then it flew towards the shield.

"Eros, this old man may require assistance," he said.

Eros got up and raised both of her hands. The spear was now jabbing at the shield, sparks of light and dark energy flying with their collision.

Dodecagon appeared before Se'dah and swung with his fist. The blow contacted his face and he flipped. He got up and sent a kick. It slammed into Dodecagon's stomach, but he held onto his foot.

"Aduro Keravnos!" he commanded. An electric looking surge of energy went about Se'dah, and he cried in agony.

"Anti-dark burst!" commanded Se'dah commanded quickly. The energy now flowed back out of him, and shocked Dodecagon. He cringed, but didn't let go.

He faded again and appeared above Se'dah.

"Boreas Ekriksi!" he commanded.

"Boreas Ekriksi!" Dodecagon commanded in reply. Both blasts of compressed air slammed into each other, and Dodecagon was propelled higher into the sky.

"I have you now!" shouted Se'dah. He pointed both his palms to the ground. "Boreas!"

He was propelled into the air by a sudden burst of air, and as he appeared above Dodecagon, a horrible smile crept apart his dark face, bearing crooked fangs from the abyss.

"Hades Kopis!" he commanded. A sword made of dark energy animated in his hands, and he made an overhand swing.

Dust and debris flew high into the air as Dodecagon crashed into the crater once again. He tried to get up, but stumbled and fell. He looked back and found a red gash on his back.

"No, not now!" he snarled as he began to crawl.

At that instant, Se'dah came out of the sky and slammed both his feet down on Dodecagon's back, right where the gash was. He let out a pained cry of agony.

"Who's the one losing now?" asked Se'dah in a set of crazed voices.

"You're losing it, I can sense and hear it," Dodecagon replied.

"I'll return to normal once I grind you into the cobblestone!"

Dodecagon realized his energy was slowly running out of his body in the form of blood, and Se'dah wouldn't let him move as easily.

"I hate daimons," he choked out.

He felt a sharp pain in his leg, and he realized Se'dah was stabbing into it. "I'm going to make this as painful as possible for you though, the only thing that would make this better is if Eros was watching you—no, if all your friends were watching you."

Dodecagon's eyes widened at the mention of his friends, but he closed them, realizing his mistake.

"They are here, aren't they," Se'dah said, his crooked grin growing. "Yes' they're stopping my shield! I had forgotten all about that!"

"No!" Dodecagon protested.

"Hermes," Se'dah commanded. He faded.

"We're almost through it!" said Eros.

"Well of course, did you doubt your teacher?" Efiia asked.

"I always doubt you, but that's what makes you succeed."

"Hello all," said Se'dah as he appeared behind Eros and Efiia.

"Hello to you too daimon," Efiia replied equally.

The scythe has reanimated in Se'dah's hand.

"Efiia, he has obsidian!" Eros shouted.

"Scary isn't it!" he said happily. He felt a sharp pain in his cheek as he said it.

Kilan stood atop the roof, her dagger in hand. "To get to Lady Eros, you must get through me!"

"I would gladly do so," said Se'dah.

"To get to Kilan you must go through me," said Adele as he appeared before her, his staff in hand.

"And to get to Adele, you must go through me!" said Jane.

Alice now appeared. "I suppose that gives you a choice, run or be banished to hell fire."

"I'm the strongest one here, why on Edafos would I have to choose."

"What happened to Dodo?!" Eros asked now, almost hysterically.

"Just about dead, I just wanted you to be there when I delivered the final blow."

"Eros, the shield is regaining strength!" said Efiia.

"Oh yes, and it will be very strong," said Se'dah. He faded, and Eros felt a blunt force hit her stomach. Another she felt on her face and she went flying.

"Eros!" screamed Kilan. "You're going to pay! Aduro Ekriksi!"

Se'dah tossed aside the attack, but Jane had a planned follow up.

"Pagos Hoplite!"

It was a fatal mistake. The ice spear was closing in on him, and he was definitely going to lose a lot of blood once it connected.

"Hell's gate: 3."

Eros crashed into the crater. She knew she hurt her back worse than it seemed, but she managed to get up. She turned to see a crumpled form on the ground. She crawled over to it now.

Dodecagon was silent, unmoving.

And cold.

"Dodo, Dodo speak to me," she said, holding his hand. "Dodecagon, say something!" she cried.

"Look at her, look at her at the verge of tears!" Meso laughed.

"You have a different sense of humour Meso," Gregory said, unamused.

"You wouldn't find it funny because you aren't a full daimon like us," said Kinsei.

Dianne covered her ears as she heard Eros begging for the lifeless body to do the impossible and get back up.

"Where's the fun Dianne, or are you just anti-joy?" asked Delta.

"If this is the stuff you like, I'll be anti-joy any day," she replied as she stormed out.

The moment of silence from Dianne's outburst was quickly ended.

"Meso, try zooming in with that orb, I want to see if her nose is running as fast as her eyes!" Keelia laughed.

Jane coughed up blood as she was choke-slammed into the stone wall for the tenth time.

Alice managed to get up, but his expert speed slammed her face back into the dust in seconds.

"You damned daimons!" Adele screamed as he got up and charged.

"No Adele, you're too injured as it is," said Kilan and she tried to limp over by him.

Se'dah dodged the staff as Adele swung, then grabbed him by his neck.

"Which one here was your girlfriend again? Was it the midget Fel with the dagger?"

"You bastard, leave her alone!" Adele shouted. He was slammed into the same wall as Jane, then tossed to the side.

Se'dah raised his scythe above Adele now. "Goodnight!"

"Anti-light burst!" Adele shouted.

"Wait, what?!" Se'dah shouted as the energy began to pulsate around them.

"Adele, no," said Jane as she faded between consciousness.

"Dodecagon, I can't be losing you too! Please!"

He just lay there, unmoving in a growing pool of blood.

"Dodecagon!" she cried now, her tears clearly visible.

The area lit up in a violent dark explosion. Adele and Se'dah were nowhere to be seen, but as the smoke began to clear a bit, you could see two figures fighting.

Adele lunged with his staff, but Se'dah pushed it to the side with his scythe. Adele now swung low for his feet, but Se'dah jumped and brought his scythe down on Adele. He jumped back, then quickly charged forward, closing the gap between them.

"Damn!" Se'dah managed to choke out as Adele lunged for him. The attack surprised him, and he realized his confidence was taking over him.

Or something else.

He remembered what Dodecagon had said earlier.

"You're losing it."

He felt the staff shred through his chest, and it began to drain his energy.

"No, NO! Anti-Angel Burst!" he commanded.

Adele was puzzled by the attack, but after seeing the sharp teeth on Se'dah growing, he realized what it was.

The area was soon shredded apart at the seams by the energy of Lunar Soul, the most lethal branch of Soul.

"Hell Gate: Full Release!" Se'dah laughed hysterically. His entire body turned to dark energy, and large jagged horns grew out of his head. One big red eye was in the middle of his face, and his grin showed bloody, spiked teeth that had razors along their sides. His arms had grown long like that of Meso, but his had sharp claw of steel.

Se'dah now stood atop the roof of a higher building, and held out his hands. "Hephaestus Barrage!"

Fireballs soon began to annihilate the city of Deneaux as he fired them in every direction, laughing all the while.

Efiia was now forced to abandon the spear he had sent, and the shield continued on its path of destruction. He managed to get over to Eros, who was crying over Dodecagon.

"We must leave now Lady Eros, we shall live to fight another day!" he pleaded.

"They killed my baby!" she cried, ignoring his plea.

He grabbed her hand, but she pulled away. "I'm not leaving him here!"

"But he's dead!"

The words stung her, but she already knew they were true. She held the body tightly in her arms, his blood getting all over her.

"I'll never let you out of my arms again, never, ever again!"

"Eros, he shall surely kill us!" Efiia shouted. He realized he was now completely tuned out, and to Eros, she and Dodecagon were the only two people in the world.

Dianne held her hands over her ears tightly, but failed horribly to drown out the wails.

"I'm sick of it too," said Gregory as he took a seat next to her.

"Is it worth it? I mean, what are we even doing all this for?" she asked.

"We're doing it for our Lord Mes..."

"Why are we doing this for him? All this murder and evil! I don't want to hear any crap about doing this for 'our Lord Meso!'"

"Don't let them hear you!" Gregory said.

"Or what, they'll kill me? I've been the most useless one here for years now, they would all be happy if they were rid of me!"

"Don't say that! You're the smartest one here, who says that you are useless?"

"Tell me, when would you all need my intelligence?"

"For missions in unknown territory of course, you know the history of every square inch of Cardia!"

"Why would you need Intel if you could just annihilate everything in your path until you find what you're looking for?"

Gregory couldn't answer.

"See, I'm useless and weak, now even Eros has me crying!"

She felt a hand wipe away her tears, then raise her head up.

"How many battles have you seen me in?"

"I-I don't think I've ever seen you fight before..."

"Exactly, and I'm not too good on the brains part either, and quite frankly," he looked about to make sure no one was listening, then whispered in Dianne's ear. "If it were within my power, I would have beaten the living crap out of Se'dah before he killed that kid, and I damn well mean that."

"Gregory, I-I never knew..."

"I didn't either..."

Se'dah now walked through the streets, or at least what was left of him. He was a walking murder machine, killing or destroying anything in sight. Something seemed to dawn in him as he saw the crater, and he faded and repapered there.

"Eros, it's Se'dah!" Efiia said fearfully.

"Leave me with my Dodecagon, I'll die in peace if he I die with him in my arms."

"And what of all the people you'll leave back here? What will they do?"

"Just leave me be with Dodecagon!"

"He's getting closer!"

"I don't freaking care!"

"We won't have any help!"

"Go to hell!"

"Miss Eros!"

Se'dah was now before them, and Efiia saw that he might be too quick for even him. It was then that he noticed it.

Dodecagon's hair was still white.

"If I could only hear your cute little laugh one more time, I was going to buy you toys today, remember, and you were so excited! Why can't we go back to that?!"

"We shall."

A white, glowing fist slammed into Se'dah, and sent him rolling.

Eros realized that her hands were now empty.

Efiia fell back in the dust as he watched Dodecagon in awe.

He had reached Pure-Soul mode, a transformation that let the soul out of the body and made it as a spiritual coating over the mortal body. It also revealed one's true self, and acted according. One had to be careful while it was active, as it would burn away at your mortal skin and drain your energy.

Dodecagon was only a white glow, like a ghost.

But with the pain he was about to bring to Se'dah, he would prove he was no kind of ghost.

"Hermes. Dynami Exochos Lux Lucis Katastrofi," he said simply.

As Se'dah tried to get up, his face was firmly planted back into the dirt.

"Today Daimon, I drag you and all your petty transformations to hell!"

"Never!" he replied.

"Then step into the light!"

The circle appeared around them and the light went up into the sky. Se'dah and all the demons that inhabited his body seemed to send a chorus of cries that echoed throughout the city.

"Music to my ears," Dodecagon said.

The darkness around Se'dah began to disappear until all that was left was his regular body.

"Lux Lucis Makhaira," Dodecagon said as he levitated, making sure he held Se'dah so they could see eye to eye. A short sword made entirely of light animated into his hand.

"This is called retribution."

Se'dah let out one long note of agony as the blade pierced his heart, then fell quiet as his lifeless corpse it the ground in a pool of blood.

Dodecagon returned to human form now, and struggled to stand up straight.

"Eros, I won, we won." He passed out, but fell into Eros' loving arms.

"Yes we did," she replied simply. As far as things went, that's all she could say.

They had now gone back to the sanctuary, which was now a lot emptier, tired and bruised.

"Finally, we're here," Adele said as he slumped gratefully unto the ground.

Kilan grabbed him by the arm. "You know you have a lot to answer to, we patched you up once and now we have to do it again. I'm starting to wonder if you like being injured."

"Ok, I'll stay out of the battles until I heal. You won't have anything to worry about," Adele replied.

Kilan sat down too and embraced him tightly. "Are you going to make me into one of those girls that only worry?"

"Not in the foreseeable future I hope."

"We're going to need help if Deneaux is to survive," said Eros to Efiia in a secluded corner.

"Do you think Alcino would be of some help?" Efiia asked.

"He may not want to help us."

"Then I shall try to convince him!"

Eros raised an eyebrow at him.

"Ok then, we'll get someone else's help."

"Don't worry, I'll help you," said a deep, confident voice.

"I can't believe they let you in," said Eros.

"They probably know I'm a friend."

"You are not my friend, you are my ally."

"Oh come on Eros, why can't you forgive and forget?"

Alcino now heard the tiger like growl that came from Eros, and now turned to Efiia.

"So where is my little dragon?"

"Resting from a battle," Efiia replied.

"Resting from a battle? What did he fight, a mouse?"

"A daimon at Hell's Gate: Full Release," Eros replied forcibly.

Alcino was breathless now. "Impossible!"

"Did you not notice the vast amounts of Lunar energy around the Deneaux, or even the craters left back from the battle?" said Efiia.

"Yes but..."

"You should have given Dodecagon more credit, the kid's a mortal Divine!" Eros snapped at him.

"Hi Alcino," said Dodecagon as he leaned on the doorway that led to some beds.

"You should be in bed Dodecagon," Eros said.

"It's fine Eros, I just wanted to see Alcino," he replied weakly.

"Dodecagon, I...."

"Don't worry, I'm fine."

Eros noticed he was falling and caught him before he did. "Come on little one, let's get you back to bed."

"So what do you want me to do?" Alcino asked Efiia in a meeker tone.

"We need you to help us search for Meso, and since he isn't expecting you to be here, he won't be looking out for you."

"Well of course he won't be looking for me!"

"And that will be your greatest power."

"So where do I begin my search? I mean, if you and Eros together couldn't find them, what chance do I have?"

Efiia chuckled. "You look like a street thug as it is, all you have to do is go into shady corners of the city and figure out where you can join up with the men of Meso."

"And why can't any of your mortal servants do this?"

"Alignment shows easy to people, they would be sniffed out just as quickly as they got in."

"Alright, I'll try my best, but don't look for any breakthroughs."

Battle for Keels Part 3

Jor winced for the fifth time today as Lyra poured many strange liquids on his wounds.

"You can cry if you want to," she teased.

"You know, are you sure you're healing me? Getting slashed across my chest seemed a lot less painful," Jor replied.

Lyra placed a generous amount of liquid on his chest unexpectedly, and guess who couldn't help nearly screaming the building down.

"How was that?" she asked with mock concern.

"Painful as hell," Jor replied weakly.

"You don't see Turner making that much noise."

"That's probably because he is out cold."

Lyra held up a clenched fist. "Would you like to be out cold too?"

"Very funny," Jor said as he turned to look out the window.

"Enjoying the scenery?" Lyra asked.

"It's just strange how it could take years to build something up, but only seconds to destroy it."

"Don't worry, the capital can be rebuilt. My parents said yesterday that it took less than a year to rebuild the whole of Keels after the Three Hundred Year War."

"That's probably because there were fewer Elves back then than there are now," Jor turned back to Lyra. "Your parents here?"

"Yep, they say another patrol Noch sent out found a few civilians hiding out. My parents were with them."

"Good, keep them close, never know when they might leave you."

Lyra noticed the hint of sadness in his voice. "Jor, you okay?"

"Yeah, just...It's nothing important."

Lyra held his hand. "You can tell me."

"Just my mother was killed right in front of me not too long ago and I always wondered what she would say if she saw me now." Jor laughed sadly. "I mean, I escape execution, killed a Divine, met new friends along the way; and now I'm in the army fighting a war against what could be considered my own people. Not a life I thought I would have had."

"I thought adventurers were used to that kind of stuff," Lyra said with some concern.

"I'm no adventurer, I'm just a kid that was always fighting family, and now look where that got me. Betrayed by my brothers, hated by my father, forced out of my home." He stopped himself. "But you and the others in Deneaux are my family now."

"So what, you gonna stop telling me about your life story? It sounds really interesting to me," she said.

"My life story? I never thought of myself having much of a life story."

"You've done a lot of things Jor, a lot more important and heroic deeds than 'Lyra the wild girl that no one liked'."

"Well I like you, or am I not that important?"

Lyra sighed and looked around. "Jor, you are one of the most important people to me. I can say that I li..."

"That you what Lyra?" asked Turner.

"What the hell, you're supposed to be asleep!" Lyra snapped at him in hush tone.

"And miss this epic drama? Not a chance," he replied.

"Well you know how to wreck a scene," said Jor as he folded his arms.

"If you two like each other so much, why not just say so straight out and go out with each other."

"Pfft, me like Jor of all people? Not I, no," Lyra replied.

"So mean," Jor commented.

"What did you just say?!" she snapped.

"Nothing, nothing." Jor heard Lyra snarl at him, and he decided it would be best for his health if he stopped now.

"You know, you two could make a cute couple," Turner said.

"Yep, a midget wild girl and a tall Walrus," Ifadeel commented.

"Ifadeel, if I said what I was about to say to you, you would have had to kill me," Lyra replied.

"Yeah, and you're lucky I'm in bed right now, or I would have tarnished you!" shouted Jor as he reached weakly out after him. He winced and held his chest and realized now would not be the time for shouting.

"Just watch what you say or do around the Elves, many of them have war fever, and a trigger finger for Raiders," said Ifadeel.

"Pfft."

"Alright, just keep your wits about you—if you even have any." Ifadeel went of laughing back down the stairs to the rest of the base.

"Keep laughing Elf, see if I don't drop a tree on your head," Jor said to himself.

"Wow, he has more insults than me," said Turner.

"Shut up Turner," Jor replied. "You know what, I'm going to sleep."

Ifadeel was now walking to the Elven quarters when Noch stopped him.

"Yo Elf," he called.

"Hm?"

"I hear you're troubling one of my men," Noch said, his voice turning serious.

"Actually, he has been troubling me," said Ifadeel.

"How so?" Noch asked in mock surprise.

"He's taken to my sister and..."

"You sister was Lyra correct?"

"Yes."

"Well, were you there to protect her when she was captured and forced to play dolly to a bunch of grown men?"

"No but..."

"Were you there when she was almost killed by a shot from an obsidian bolt?"

"I was defending Keels!"

"And not your sister!"

Noch's last words echoed and many turned to see what the commotion was about.

"Now, were you there by her bedside while she healed from the loss of energy from the shot?" Noch asked in a lower tone.

"So I was supposed to abandon my post?"

"No, but my point is, who are you in debt to for protecting your sister?"

Ifadeel looked around and saw that all eyes were on him.

Noch voice got a bit calmer. "Jor would give his life any day to protect her, or any of his friends for that matter, no matter what they said or did to him."

"I don't trust him..." he said quietly.

Noch grabbed his shoulder and realized that Ifadeel was taller than him, despite the fact he was an Elf. He shook the thought aside. "Then learn to trust him, he'd take a shot from an obsidian bolt through the heart for you, and if anything, you should be able to do the same for him."

"Just wait, he's still a Raider, he'll betray you all!" shouted Ifadeel as he stormed off.

"Damn," said Noch to himself. "I hate idiots."

"Well Jor, you seem like a proud warrior," said a voice to Jor.

Jor looked about the room to find it completely empty. "Where did everyone go?"

Two black axes appeared on the bed on either side of him.

"The Raiders took them; they stormed the base while you were sleeping! You must go down and stop them!"

"But my wounds...."

"They are healed child, now go before it is too late!"

Jor grabbed both axes and hoped out his bed. He stormed down the stairs to find the building infested by dozens of Raiders—some of which were his brothers. He looked down to see the crumpled forms of Noch, Lyra, Ifadeel, Turner and many others on the ground.

"No you bastards! NO!"

His eyes turned crimson as he jumped down into the crowd and swung both axes savagely. He hacked and slashed his way through the army until he reached Lok, his sworn enemy.

"Today is the day you pay for your sins Lok!" he screamed in a grizzled voice thick with hatred.

"Lok? Jor, you're supposed to be resting! What's going on?!" he replied.

"Don't play stupid, I've seen what you've did to my mother, and now my friends! I promised myself I would come back to kill you! Even if I died in the process!"

He began to charge now, but axes ready and screaming a bloodcurdling war cry that seemed like it echoed for miles around.

"That's it my son, show them that you are a true Raider!"

"Yes master Fenalph, I'll show them all who is the mightiest of the Nords! The world will be filed with blood at my dawning!"

"Yes, finish them all now!"

As Jor was about to strike Lok, a force seemed to hold him back. "W-What's going on, what am I saying?"

He now stood before Noch, obsidian axes in both his hands. They dispersed into energy as he seemed to get a greater sense of his surroundings.

"Where did the Raiders go? And how did you get up so quickly, I thought you were dead," Jor said through heavy panting.

"Raiders?! You nearly killed twelve men!"

Jor turned to see many of the Deneaux soldiers on the ground, wounded by his attacks.

"T-That can't be right, I was fighting Raiders..."

"In a dream maybe?" Noch asked.

"But what about the axes?"

"I don't know Jor, but you spouted something about Fenalph."

"Who's that?"

"Lord of the Raiders," Noch replied sadly.

"Ifadeel was right! He would betray us!" shouted one Elf.

"Damn right, and I thought he was a good kid!" said Deneauxman.

"I didn't mean..." they cut Jor off.

"How about we cut him down before he pulls another slaughter off!"

There were roars of agreement as many of them drew swords or picked up halberds.

"Noch, tell them to stop!" Jor pleaded.

"I don't know if I would be right to stop them; even I wouldn't have been able to beat you in that state," Noch replied.

"You can't have them attacking a wounded boy!"

"Your wounds are healed Jor," Noch said.

The men were now getting closer. Jor looked up to see Lyra horrified, tears running down her face.

"I'll prove I'm innocent! I'll bring back the heads of all the Raider leaders, and I'll find a way to stop this strange dream fighting!" he shouted before leaping out of a window. He managed to evade the shots fired after him and ducked in between some ruined buildings.

Lyra ran downstairs to Noch, who was still staring out of the window.

"This can't be happening," she said, breathing heavily.

"I told you he was a traitor!" shouted Ifadeel. Several others spoke up in agreement.

A stinging slap went across Ifadeel's face. "I don't care what you say about him damn it! He will be back, and I hope he kills you first!" Lyra screamed at him. She slumped down to the ground and cried loudly.

"What happened to you Jor," Noch asked himself. "I know you couldn't have summoned obsidian yourself..."

"What the hell is going on," said Jor. "That really couldn't have happened!" He remembered what he had said before leaving, and Lyra's face.

He looked at his chest to find that his wounds were in fact healed.

And that meant he could fight again.

"I'm not going to let this beat me, I'm getting at those raiders, and the same way I stormed through them in my dream, I'll do the same now. And I will succeed."

He realized he left back his crossbow and great sword.

"Even if it costs me my life," he said with a sigh.

"Roseanne, see any Raiders?" asked the King.

She had been using soul sight for the last few minutes now and had come up with nothing.

"There!" she said.

"This must a road block," said the King.

"Are we going by a plan?" asked Roseanne.

"Nope, just charge through, blowing up anything in your way!" the King shouted. His horse reared up on its hind legs and began to gallop.

Roseanne sighed and followed along.

"Gaia Katastrofi!" the King commanded. The raiders stood puzzled at why the ground below them rumbled.

Roseanne heard several screams as large stone spikes shot out of the ground.

"You're letting them know we're here!" she shouted.

"That's the idea Mystic!" he called in reply.

They came upon another road block as they got farther into Keels, and they dispatched it as quickly as they did the first.

They had slowed their horses' paces and returned to a normal march until they appeared on a hill overlooking Keels.

"This is it then," the King said to himself grimly. "I can now see the Three Hundred Year War with my own eyes..."

"This is madness, how on Edafos could they have sacked the capital?" exclaimed a soul knight.

"I don't know, our Lord Efiia said that a Divine even more powerful than him has laid siege to here, but if we have faith in our abilities, we shall overcome, and prevent a second war from plaguing our lands." He raised his sword high and it gleamed in the sun. "Today, we charge into battle the men of Deneaux, mighty warriors of the North!"

There was a rallied cry from behind him, and they began their charge into Keels.

Jor picked up an axe left back by one of the raiders that were killed in his ambush on a small patrol. He never realized he could do so much damage by not being seen.

He now listened closely. He could have sworn he heard hooves thundering, but dismissed the thought. No one should have escaped Keels.

The sound came louder and he climbed up over some rubble. He looked up to see men charging down the hill.

"Men from Deneaux!" he said happily.

A wall of fire burned across the bottom of the hill to Jor's horror.

"Who dares to lay siege to my new fief?" thundered a voice.

"The Men of Deneaux dare do so!" the King shouted in reply. He lowered his blade to the fire, and it was dispelled.

"What?! Men cannot do such things!" the voice said.

"Well you have just met one that can!"

Raiders soon began to pour out from the buildings and several alleyways, and more began coming from the camps that had been set up.

"You may have dispelled the fire, but can you dispel my mighty army?"

"Only a fool stands against the might of Deneaux, have them charge!" the King challenged.

"They will do so!"

The hundreds of Raiders began to charge, and the men of Deneaux did the same.

"Good, go fight; that gives me plenty of time to get your leaders," Jor said to himself.

The priest from the attack on Fort Letry and the Sergeant from the attack of the wagons now stood atop a tower and watched the battle.

"I wish we could make bets and such things like these, but then we would all bet on the Raiders and get no money," said the priest.

"True, I'm just glad I don't have to go down there to get slaughtered," the sergeant replied with hearty laughter.

"You'll get slaughtered up here too," Jor said suddenly.

They both turned to see a shirtless boy holding two axes in his hands. They assumed he was another raider since he wasn't wearing any of his armor.

"Who will be able to slaughter us up here? I don't see any Deneauxman storming the tower," said the sergeant.

"Pray to Fenalph, for this will be your last hour!" Jor shouted as he attacked.

The sergeant was slow to draw his sword and fell as the axe hacked away at his chest. The priest had an iron staff and blocked Jor's second attack. Jor swung again and he parried with the staff.

"You're determined aren't you," Jor said.

"I don't have to be determined, as a priest of Fenalph, I am invincible!" he replied.

"Let's see you live through this then!" his eyes flashed red and he swung with both axes at the center of the staff, shattering it to pieces instantly.

The priest stepped back in horror, and stopped as he realized he was at the edge of the tower.

"Where are the rest of the leaders?" Jor asked, his voice showing no sign of humanity.

"Why should I tell you?"

"Well, how about we test your immortality? Your face versus the ground below."

"P-Please, they are waiting at Bearded Run!"

"I think you're lying."

The priest's eyes showed nothing but true terror now. "I'm telling you the truth!"

"Tell it to the dust."

Jor grabbed the man by his robes and tossed him off the tower. As he turned, he realized that there was a blade aimed at his heart.

"I have you now!" said the Sergeant.

"Khthon Katastrofi!" commanded Roseanne. Sharp shards of stone broke away from the ground and punctured anyone nearby. Others behind her were giving the same commanded, killing five or six raiders at a time.

"My King," Roseanne called.

"Don't interrupt me when I'm using soul my dear, you forget who I am and what I could do," he replied. "Exochos Psyche Gaia Katastrofi!"

The roots from many destroyed trees shot of the ground, ripping through many of the raiders, then detonating, causing many casualties among the raiders.

"That's our King!" shouted a soul knight. Many of the other Knights shouted in agreement.

Roseanne now noticed that the Raiders were now routing a bit at a time.

"My King, the Raiders are retreating!"

"Then let them go, it is Fenalph I want," he replied.

"So boy, you must feel grown after scaring that priest half to death, but now I want to see you scream and beg for mercy," said the sergeant.

"I'm not dying here," Jor replied.

"Oh yes you are, unless you beg."

Jor held up a black, round object up to the torch. "So would you risk exploding just to hear me cry?"

"You're mad boy! Do you even know what you have in your hands?!" shouted the sergeant.

"I have your life in my hands, and I choose to toss it away." Jor punched the man dead center in his face, then hauled him over the side of the tower with the grenade.

He heard a scream cut off by an explosion and walked off.

"Fenalph, prove to me that you are not a coward and fight me!" the King commanded as he got off his horse.

No one dared question his challenge.

Before them appeared Fenalph, Lord of the Raiders. He had a beard that seemed to go to the ground, and long hair that stopped a little below his shoulders. Both seemed to be golden.

He wore no shirt but wore a fur kilt. In his hands were two obsidian axes.

"Finally, I get to lay eyes on the being greater than Efiia," the King mocked

"So mortal, if your Lord Efiia is lesser in power to me, why do you wish to face me yourself?" Fenalph asked in a voice thick with the Nordic accent.

A blue and white aura floated about the King, and strange runes began to glow in a circle around him.

"You may not know this, but I am far more powerful than Efiia. The power of the Kings before me flows through my veins. That should be enough to dispatch you."

"Then come at me old man, give Efiia my regards when you meet him."

The two charged toward each other, both giving a mighty war cry.

"Impossible!" shouted Noch. The two sentries beside him were startled by his sudden shout.

"What's going on sir?" one asked.

"The King is here—and he's facing off with a power far more magnificent than that of any enemy we will ever face!"

"You know if Jor is nearby?" Lyra asked.

"I don't know," Noch replied. "This energy is fogging up my senses."

Jor turned to see the two adversaries charging after each other and frowned. "You better not blow up Cardia."

Their weapons clashed now, sending a blast of air that knocked down several nearby Raiders. The King's men however were not moved.

"So we plan to play swords or what?" asked the King.

"I planned to leave only your ashes to be honest," Fenalph replied. "Hephaestus Katastrofi!"

"Reflect!" commanded the King in reply. A mirror shield appeared before the large fireball and sent it back.

Fenalph was caught by surprise and was caught up in the blast. He managed his way out of his own fireball and fell into the dust.

"So you haven't heard of King Carel before have you?" he asked.

"Why should I care," Fenalph said as he got up. "You're about to become history." His black aura began to show now, and it was one Carel had never seen before. It wasn't an elemental or a magic aura.

"Selene Barrage!" he commanded.

Carel raised his hands. "Lux Lucis Barrage!"

The masses of lunar energy sent by Fenalph passed straight through the attacks sent by Carel.

"Oh, and Reflect," said Fenalph. The shield appeared and the light energy came toward him.

"Selene Aegis!" Carel commanded. The dark blue shield made of Lunar energy formed up before him, and was hardly able to beat back the attacks from Fenalph.

"Selene Pertusus!" Fenalph commanded again.

Carel hopped to the side as the piercing beam shattered his shield.

"Selene Gaia Katastrofi Barrage!" Fenalph commanded.

"King Carel!" Roseanne screamed.

The ground began to rip, and veins filled with lunar energy began to show. Stone after stone shot up around Carel.

"Selene Hermes!" he managed to command. He dodged the stones as they came and detonated. "Pertusus!" he commanded as he neared Fenalph.

He stood still and the beam tore through his heart.

But he remained unmoved.

"Impossible!" shouted Carel.

"I'm a god, mortal. I will survive through anything you throw at me!"

Carel faded again and appeared right before Fenalph, as blade raised and ready to strike.

"Hermes."

Carel slammed down with an overhead slash, and kicked up stones as it smashed into the ground. "I missed?"

"You missed," said Fenalph. He grabbed Carel by his head and slammed him into the ground. "Not so powerful now?"

Carel got up as quickly as he went down. "My dear boy, the fight begins now. Selene Barrage!"

Fenalph saw that nothing came from the man's hands and was puzzled. Right then, a blast of lunar energy slammed into his back followed by twenty more.

Carel faded and reappeared a few feet away from the blast zone. "Lux Lucis Katastrofi Barrage!"

"Reflect!" he heard Fenalph choke out as the attacks continued to hit him.

"No you don't Anti-mind Burst!" Carel seemed tired as he gave the command, but he returned back to his ready state. "Hades Barrage!"

Light, Lunar and Dark Soul now slammed down from the sky into Fenalph, and Carel seemed to show no sign of stopping.

"Ready to surrender yet?" he asked.

"Never!" Fenalph replied through the smoke.

"Ok then, Ishis Exochos Hephaestus Katastrofi Barrage Ekriksi!" Carel commanded.

The sky had become shrouded with dark clouds, and through the clouds now came a fireball as big as a castle.

"I gave you a chance Fenalph, and you gave it up!" said Carel.

"What do you mean; you're the one about to lose your head!" Fenalph replied.

Carel faded and reappeared behind his new enemy. It was an Orc, he could tell, but this one was different. They faded also.

Carel blocked swings that seemed to come from every angle at him.

Jor was a good ways away from the battlefield, and even he could feel the bursts of air as their steel clashed. "Nice, level the city why... don't...you...." He looked up now the see the fireball coming down. "We're screwed."

Titus had let up on his attack for a moment to get his bearings, but as he did, Carel was already lunging at him. He parried the first two slashes, but the third went across his knee. He went down and watched as Carel swung for his neck.

Several buildings went down after the sonic blast of air swept through.

Fenalph now stood by Titus. Having blocked Carel's attack completely, he helped Titus up.

Carel jumped back after Fenalph had stopped him. "So you both wish to take me on?"

"We do, and we will kill you," said Titus.

"Then come at me and spare me your idle words."

"Hephaestus Ekriksi!" Titus commanded.

Carel swung his sword and dispersed the flames. "You must do better than that!"

"I have," said Fenalph as he appeared behind Carel. The two faded, but you could still hear the sounds of their clashing blades.

Noch stared intently at the fireball in the sky. It was just like the one that had destroyed the forest around Fort Letry, but it was clearly different in a way.

"Who's winning?" Ifadeel asked.

"Well, I think another person entered the fray," he replied.

"You still can't tell?" asked Gailo.

"Nope, but I feel like I may have faced off with the one that just entered.....The Orc! That's who has entered!"

"So it's Fenalph and the Orc versus your King?" Ifadeel asked.

"Probably, I just hope the King can handle it," said Noch.

Carel slid across the ground as he disengaged Fenalph. He was panting terribly now.

"It seems your body cannot keep up with you energy, or are both of them wearing out on you?" Fenalph said.

"I'm...Fine!" he managed to say.

"How about we just both attack him?" asked Titus. "All we need to do is scrape him with the obsidian and we win!"

"Eh, alright Titus, we'll kill him now," Fenalph replied with a shrug.

"The King can't keep taking this," said Roseanne. "We need to help him!"

A Paladin stopped her. "The King is fighting a duel and it would be wrong to interrupt."

"It would be wrong to let him die too!"

"We'll get cut down in seconds if we went out there!"

"Then what do we do?"

The paladin made sure his voice was as loud as possible. "We cheer our King on to victory!"

About a hundred voices roared behind them, and then they began to chant the King's name.

Jor now found himself nearing the battlefield again. "Hmm, he has a loyal army."

Noch and the others could hear the echoing shouts and they began to look to each other for the reason why.

Two axes and two battle picks came from every possible and impossible angle at the same time, and Carel was doing everything in his power to block and parry them. As soon as he parried the attack aimed for his neck, he had to block the other three aimed for his heart and the other ten aimed for ten other places.

"He's low on energy," said Roseanne.

"Then cheer him on even greater, our King shall not be defeated!"

The blasts of air began to get greater each time, and now the men of Deneaux found themselves being pushed back by it.

"Watch out!" shouted Roseanne as she realized the fireball was going to touch down.

"Everyone get down! This is gonna rock the whole of Keels!" shouted Noch as he put his hands over his head.

"Crap," Jor said as he braced himself.

The fireball now slammed into the ground, right unto Titus, Fenalph and the King.

"How does it feel to be bested by a mortal?" asked the Carel.

"Bested? I am not yet defeated," Fenalph replied.

The three of them stood inside of the fireball, but now Carel watched in horror as the two Divines stood up and approached him through the inferno. Carel now charged for them, and the last moments of the fated duel began.

"Noch, did it hit?" asked Lyra who was hiding under a table.

"It hasn't exactly made it down, so stay..." Noch was cut off as the area began to shake violently.

"Now's my chance!" said Jor. "I'm heading down to the shores while all this has everyone's attention."

Carel was forced back with every strike made by the two Divines. Stopping four weapons with one was hell enough, but now he was fighting in a fireball that was sucking up his energy.

"Pity that you two must both fight to defeat me," he taunted.

"You foolish mortals still don't get it do you? There is no such thing as a fair fight or fair duel! One man will always be stronger than the next, and only the strong deserve to survive," said Fenalph darkly.

"Deneaux is an ancient Kingdom, it's about time it fell," Titus added.

"Never!" Carel shouted. "Hephaestus Ekriksi!"

Fenalph and Titus were both caught off guard by the attack and were sent back by the fireball within the fireball. Carel kept sending them, one by one at the two Divines.

"We need to fall back, soon enough we're going to get burnt to a crisp!" shouted Roseanne.

Many of the others didn't want to leave the King's side, but they saw it necessary to fall back.

Jor stood atop the hill at Bearded Run and looked down at the beach to see the Raider's ships. He slid down and ran for the beach, then ducked between the longboats that were pulled up on the shore. He could see light coming from a ship not too far out from the beach. He located a small rowboat and made his way to it.

"Was that Fenalph I heard there?" asked Gulnar with mock surprise.

"Must have been, who else would cause that much racket," said Faen.

"Are you insulting our Lord Fenalph?" asked Gulnar.

"No my Jarl, just saying that he is a true Nord!" said Faen. He had known of Gulnar's bad temper, so he became good at making up quick explanations to things he said or did that would please his Jarl. "I mean, we make people know we're here whenever we are."

"Good," Gulnar said. "Now, back to the subject of where I will build my glorious hall."

"You won't build it anywhere; get off my land before I haul you off myself!" Jor shouted.

The two turned to see the berserker boy standing before them with two bloody axes.

"Who are you and how did you get past my guards?" asked Gulnar.

"I simply cut them down. I would have thought you would have defended your ship with good men," Jor replied.

"I assume your identity isn't important?" said Faen.

"I am Jorigsveer of the mighty clan Great-Blade."

"I've never heard of you," said Gulnar as he got up and drew his shining steel long sword. "Where are you from?"

"I'm from Denhoec and I am the last true son of my clan," Jor replied.

"Oh, the Great-Blades! Your brother must be the one in charge of the advance from Denhoec into Deneaux."

"Wait, what?!"

"It was meant to be a little surprise see, Fenalph has all the details on one of the greatest coupes that will ever sweep this land. Deneaux is crumbling from the inside out, and once we take that, no one nation will be able to stop us!"

"Well I will stop you, right here and now," said Jor.

"And how do you expect to do this? You're just a clanless boy with no friends or family willing to back you up!" laughed Gulnar.

"And your just a fat walrus who's about to be headless, with no neck to hold it up. Get ready Gulnar!" Jor shouted. His eyes flashed red and he charged after him.

He spun circles around Gulnar, swinging both axes viciously. Gulnar blocked each strike in reply with his sword. Jor put a bit of space between them, then made a heavy overhand strike.

The room was small and Gulnar was a big man. Faen had already run out the door. Jor had all the advantages here, so the battlefield would have to change, and quick.

Gulnar moved to the side, but hit the wall. Jor's strike was off, and the axe cut across Gulnar's arm. Jor swung the other axe overhand, and at that moment, Gulnar grabbed his arm and tossed him through the door.

The two were now on the deck of the ship and glared at each other.

"I like a spacious environment, don't you?" said Gulnar. Jor growled in reply and swung for Gulnar.

Carel sunk to his knees now and dropped his blade.

"You're done already?" asked Fenalph.

"You were really boring," Titus added.

"No, I'm not done yet," Carel choked out.

"Yes you are mortal." Fenalph now stood before Carel and smirked. "Not everyone can win can they?" He kicked Carel in his neck with his large, muscular feet.

And the mighty King Carel the Joyful of Deneaux fell onto the muddy ground of Keels.

"No, it can't be happening!" shouted Noch. He got up and tried to open the door, but the other units stopped him.

"We can't let you out, not now at least," said one Halberdier.

"But the King, I can no longer sense him!" Something dawned in his eyes. "I'm sensing Jor though, but in two different places."

"But how?" asked Lyra.

"Now one Jor has two different energies, while the other has just one powerful mass of it..." Noch stopped again.

Lyra could see his mind was racing, but over what?

"Is it possible for a Divine to take over one of their subjects?" he asked finally.

"I believe so, why?" said Ifadeel.

"When Jor was attacking us, I sensed a second energy, and now I can see that that energy is the same that is in Fenalph."

"And how do you know it's not the Orc you're sensing?" asked Ifadeel.

"He has a different energy than Fenalph."

"Do you know where Jor is?" asked Lyra.

"He's fighting—at Bearded Run?" Noch said.

"What? We must get him back here before he hurts himself!" said Gailo.

"That is why I am going," said Noch.

"It's too dangerous!" warned the halberdier.

"And that is why I'm going myself. Let me through, and that's an order!"

Steel clashed with steel as Gulnar and Jor kept up a steady stream of blows on each other. Anyone on shore could see sparks fly now and again, and the sound of the two war cries.

"You have a lot of energy boy, who trained you to fight?" asked Gulnar, who was now panting.

"Life in Denhoec will teach anyone how to fight," Jor replied. "I bet you went to a hundred different mentors just to lift a sword."

"I had the best mentors in the country, and there were many people I had to kill to take the throne. Fighting came natural to both of us then."

"Maybe so, but this is something I'm sure you're not used to. Ekriksi!" Jor commanded.

Gulnar hardly dodged the mass of soul energy as it smashed through the cabin they were just in.

"Ekriksi!" Jor commanded again. It slammed into Gulnar's chest this time, and sent him into the side rail of the ship. Jor stood above him now and raised his axe.

"Don't think you'll win this one, Jorigsveer," Gulnar spat to him. "Turn around why don't you."

Jor turned around to feel sharp steal on his neck. Faen held a steel Great-Blade to his neck.

"Something told me to kill you first. Not the first time I let this happen."

"How does it feel Jorigsveer? How does it feel to stare death in the face?" asked Gulnar.

"Death looks pretty wimpy to me, besides, my reinforcements are arriving," Jor replied.

"Ekriksi!" Noch commanded. The mass of white energy sent Faen flying back into the cabin.

Noch was using soul energy to skate with the water, and now he vaulted himself onto the ship.

"So you forgive me?" Jor asked.

"We forgive you," Noch replied. "So what are you doing here anyways?"

"I was killing the Raider leaders, and this guy here seemed to be one.... Where did he go?"

They both turned to see him on the rowboat, half way to shore. "I hope you two like explosions, because you're going to be part of one!"

The now looked below them into the ship's hold to find it was filled with the same explosives used while Turner and Jor were on patrol.

Jor picked up Faen and turned to Noch. "We have to get out of here, now!"

"Right, Hydro!" Noch commanded. He hopped off the side of the ship and landed on top of the water.

"How the hell do you expect me to do that?" Jor asked fearfully.

"Just do the same thing I did," Noch said.

"Rest in peace Jorigsveer Great-Blade," he said to himself. He jumped over the side. "Hydro!"

Gulnar fell out of the rowboat and unto the sand, then put his hands over his head as the ship behind him exploded.

"Yes you bastards! Burn in hell!" he shouted. He now turned his attention to the approaching beings in the water. "Impossible! Those two are supposed to be dead!"

Noch now appeared right before him. "Pretty nice coward move, might have to remember it."

"Fenalph, come to my aid!" he said. Noch grabbed him by his shirt as he did, but then Gulnar disappeared in a white mist.

"What the..."

Jor now skated ashore and walked to Noch's side. "Where's Gulnar?" he asked.

"Not here, now let's get back to the King's men before the Raiders block our path again."

The King's army was camped in the forests a mile or two from Keels. In the main tent, the mystics were using their best knowledge of soul healing they had to help the King.

Many eyes opened as they saw Noch walk into the camp with a raider boy and another small Raider man over his shoulder.

Roseanne came out of the tent and embraced Noch.

"Whoa, easy Roseanne, you forget I have a girlfriend already," he joked.

"The King is dying," she replied. He noticed now that there were tears coming down her face.

Noch now looked up at the main tent and raced towards it.

"Wait Noch; what do you want me to do?" Jor asked.

"Bring the others here!" Noch told him.

"Walk two miles in the dark carrying a raider who almost killed me a few hours ago?"

"I'll go with you," said Roseanne. "It's the least I could do in Deneaux's aid."

The two were now headed down the forest path. Roseanne held a small fireball in her hands which lit the way for them.

"You know anything about that girl that's with Noch?" she finally asked.

"You mean Alice? Why do you need to know anything about her?" Jor replied.

"Was just curious, that's all."

"Well, she's the girl that trained me to use soul, plus she's a love oracle."

"What?! She must be using some special technique to make him love her!" she shouted.

"No, she's just, well, Alice," Jor replied, blushing.

"No tell me, what makes Noch want to choose her over me?"

"Well, she's just....well...she's just naturally infatuating."

"And I'm not?!"

"She's a very likable person then..."

"And I'm not very likable?!" The fireball in here hands grew in size very quickly.

"Well, once she caused a huge brawl in Deneaux. Almost twenty men were fighting over her."

"Ah, so she's a wench...."

"No no no, she just talks with you in a way that will make you like her."

"Is that not a wench? Or should I use a more specific term."

"Look, I'm not the person to handle these love issues. Go to Eros if you need help in it."

"You talk like I could meet her directly."

"She's been hanging around with us in Deneaux for a while now."

"Oh really?" Roseanne said sarcastically.

"Haven't you seen all the Divines coming down? It shouldn't surprise you if Eros did too."

"I guess I'll take your word for it."

"Look, we can see Keels again," said Jor. "Let's head for the big building over there, that's where we've been hiding out."

CHAPTER 33

Alcino and Meso

Alcino ducked into an alley when no one on the street was looking. He kept going down the twisting and turning alleyways until he stood before a boarded up door. Two armoured men stood before the door, one got up as he spotted Alcino.

"What are you here for then?" they asked.

"I'm here to talk to Meso," he replied sternly.

"And what makes you think he's here?"

"Let me through or I kill you both."

Both men drew their blades, but Alcino stood strong.

"You're a brave man, I'll give you that," said one of the men.

"Metallos," Alcino commanded.

The swords in the men's arms were pulled away from them, and flew into Alcino's hands.

"You two are very brave fighting a Divine. Now let me in before I give these back to you."

"Give them...back to us?" asked the other man. The blade flew from Alcino's hand and into the man's leg.

"Do you want yours back too?" he asked to the second guard.

He shook his head quickly and stepped out of Alcino's way.

"Good." The bars were only an illusion, and Alcino could easily see through the trick. He walked through the doorway and went down some steps. At the bottom he opened a door and found himself in Meso's sanctuary.

"I better now blow this, a lot of bribes and assaults were needed to get me here."

He could here crying coming from another part of Meso's sanctuary and headed towards the sound.

Se'dah was lying in an open coffin, and Delta was crying over him.

"Excuse me, but do you know where Meso is?"

She turned and pointed to her left. "D-Down the hall, it's the big room, you won't miss it." She turned back to Se'dah. "Like how I miss Se'dah!" she continued crying, and Alcino left her too it.

As soon as he was down the hall, he heard his voice.

"Ah, Alcino, what brings you down here?" Meso asked.

Alcino turned to see the large room Delta had told him about. Meso was sitting on his throne and smiled at him.

"I'm here to join you Meso, I know I was supposed to own Deneaux, but Efiia cheated it out of my hands, all I want now is to get back at him!"

"Oh yes, I remember that game of dice you two played, you used cheat dice and still lost!" laughed Meso.

"I'm telling you that Efiia cheated me!"

"Efiia actually didn't cheat you, the cheat dice cheated you."

"Wait, what?" Alcino knew he would have to play along with certain things Meso would say or do, but now he was speaking on his own, free of trickery.

"So you really thought that the old fool cheated you all this time? Efiia may be wise but he is not smart." Meso looked into an orb he held in his hands. "Now let's get down to business. I need that obsidian crossbow at the Pantheon castle; don't worry about too much resistance, as all the soul users have left for Keels. Do you think you can do this?"

"Why not; I mean I have nothing else better to do," Alcino replied.

Jane and Eros were now waiting inside of the Pantheon castle. The plan was that Meso would bring all of his followers there, and they would memorise the power of each, then leave undetected. But they realized now that they had expected too much.

"Why on Edafos did they choose you to come with me?" asked Alcino.

"Because Meso knows he can't exactly trust you," Dianne replied.

"Could he not send someone like the guy from Changquan? I mean, I need someone cool at my side, not a whining cry...."

"Alcino, may I remind you that I can manifest the obsidian scythe at any given moment," Dianne said, her face showing no sign that she was making idle threats.

"Whatever, just keep walking."

"Hear that Eros, she can manifest the scythe!" whispered Jane.

"I heard her," Eros replied. "So change of plans, we get her to manifest the scythe, and then take it from her. That will weaken Meso's force greatly."

"Ok, just that girl's voice sounds so familiar..."

"Which way now?" asked Alcino.

"Around this corner and through the door if this floor plan is correct," Dianne said, her face buried in some papers.

"Aqua Ekriksi!" commanded Jane and she swung around the corner. A medium sized water ball shot out from her hand and struck Dianne. She slid back down the hall, but got up, taking no damage.

As she got up, she raised up her hand, as did Jane, and they both commanded.

"Pagos Ekriksi!"

The water that was on the floor in the hall froze up in both directions until both streams of ice collided and formed a small tower of icicles in the middle. The two girls looked up at each other now.

"Jane?!"

"Dianne?!"

"What are you doing here?" asked Jane.

"I would have asked the same thing of you, what are you doing in the pantheon castle of all places?" Dianne replied.

"You know, I met some people and things happened, then I end up here at the Panther Castle or whatever you call it. So where's Delta?"

"Mourning the loss of someone, and I really don't care that she is."

"Who died?"

"The guy the kid Dragon fought against, his name is Se'dah, strongest daimon under Meso's command."

"So you're helping Meso?"

"She is helping Meso; I'm going along because I'm not strong enough to make my own decisions."

"You have plenty of strong people here in Deneaux to help you now though."

"Not when Meso has the scythe."

"What if the scythe was taken from you in battle?"

Dianne smiled fiendishly at her. "To think of it, my combat was getting a little rusty." As she finished the sentence, the scythe animated in her hand.

"Tahitita!" Jane commanded. Almost like a flash of lightning, Jane took the scythe straight from Dianne's hand.

"Seems like you have beaten me Jane Pagos," she replied with a smirk.

"I have, but won't Meso say anything about losing the scythe?" asked Jane.

"Well, Eros and her powerful follower showed up and ambushed us, what were we going to do?"

"You're a smart girl Dianne."

"Pfft, I'm just the average book worm," she replied.

"Yes, yes, things seem all good now, don't they? Eros gets the scythe; Dianne doesn't get in too much trouble; but what about me? What excuse do I have?" asked Alcino.

"Well, can you Divines transform?" asked Jane.

"Of course we can, why?" said Eros, who had now come from the corner.

"Well, what if we had Alcino transform into a pile of obsidian bones, and wait here for the others to show up?" Jane proposed.

The four of them looked at each other, then at Jane.

"They got Alcino and the scythe!" shouted Dianne as she shambled into the sanctuary.

"What?! Why did you let them get it?!" shouted Kinsei.

"And how did they beat Alcino?" asked Keelia.

"Eros was there, along with her followers. They had an obsidian staff and dagger with them, and they had obsidian swords and axes!"

"You're alright though, right Dianne?" asked Gregory.

"I ran while they were fighting Alcino since I knew I wouldn't be of any help," Dianne replied. "Thanks for asking though."

"Lane, where are you?" called Meso. The daimon girl animated before him at his calling.

"What do you want now Meso?" she asked.

"Accompany Keelia, Dianne and Delta to the Pantheon Castle, you protect them and don't get in their way, simple enough?"

"Yeah, sure," she replied, somewhat bored.

"Well let's go," said Keelia as she picked up Kinsei's scimitar. "Mind if I use this?"

"You can use anything of mines," Kinsei replied.

Keelia smiled at him. "Such a sweetheart."

"So if we play our cards right, we should be able to take out the daimons and absorb their energy?" asked Eros.

"Adele was able to return to life by absorbing the energy of Mortha using his staff, so a daimon or two should be able to supply you with the energy you need," Jane replied.

"Want to set up the stage?" asked Eros.

Jane smiled. "Of course I do."

"It was down this way that it happened," Dianne pointed.

"That looks like it may lead to a throne room," said Gregory.

"Exactly, and that is where the obsidian crossbow is," said Dianne.

With one mighty flap of her wings, Keelia blew the door opened. She looked up now to see Eros sitting on the throne with Jane on the ground beside her.

"Hello men of Meso, how goes your day?" she asked.

Gregory felt a firm thug on his hand and turned to see Dianne. "What?"

"Nothing, just nervous as all," she replied.

Eros noted the movement and saw that her only targets now were Keelia and Lane.

"This room is pretty cold," said Keelia. "Lane will heat it up though."

Lane was examining a suit of armor for signs of life, and Keelia sighed at the sight.

"Damned fool. Lane, heat up the room!"

"Do it yourself, I'm supposed to protect you, not be your living torch," she replied.

"Jane, will you catch that bird for me? This cat feels a bit lazy today," Eros said.

Jane got up and spun the staff experimentally. "So Andras, what are you after?"

"I want those obsidian weapons back Perialite," Keelia replied.

"You'll have to take it from me."

"I'll gladly do so."

"I'll let you have the first move then."

"I'll have the second."

Jane tightened her grip. "Okay then, here I come!" She ran forward and swung the staff left and right.

Keelia had drawn the large scimitar already and parried the simple attacks easily. "You must have more than that."

"Aqua Ekriksi!" Jane commanded.

Keelia took the air and the water ball completely missed.

Even though the ceiling was not too high up, Jane was out of attacking range of Keelia.

"Hydro Barrage!" Jane commanded again. She fired many small water balls at Keelia, but she danced on the winds, escaping all the attacks.

"Dianne, you stay here, I'll help Keelia," said Gregory.

"I thought you wanted to be free from Meso's control," she replied.

"What are you saying?" Gregory asked.

"Pretend to attack Jane, but only use water and ice soul, we have a plan going."

"Whatever you say. Aqua Ekriksi!" The water ball crashed into Jane and she fell back.

Keelia now swooped down to Jane, her scimitar ready to plunge deep into her chest.

Jane rolled to the side and got up, and as she did, Keelia pulled up and continued flying.

"Aqua barrage!" Dianne commanded. She fired water ball after water ball after Jane now, until she was up against the wall. "Now end it Gregory!"

"Pagos Ekriksi!" he commanded. The water that had hit Jane now froze over, encasing her in ice.

"Oh dear Jane, seems you weren't as powerful as I thought you to be," said Eros. "Might as well take my leave."

Keelia landed right before Eros and put the blade to her neck. "You're not going anywhere."

"Dynami Pagos Ekriksi!" commanded a voice.

A large shard of ice rocketed towards Keelia, but her quick reflexes saved her again.

But not her left wing. It was coated in ice.

Keelia turned to see Jane with the staff held back in her left hand and her right hand extended. The room was now getting chilly too.

"No problem, I can fight without my wings," she said.

"To be honest I really would have wanted to fight Lane instead, but she doesn't seem to be up to it right now, so you'll make a decent replacement," Jane replied.

"Anemos Ekriksi!" Keelia commanded. She sent a burst of air towards Jane, but it seemed that it missed its target. "Anemos Barrage!" she commanded again.

"Aqua Barrage!" Jane commanded in reply right then. The balls of water seemed to burst mid-air as they hit Keelia's nearly invisible bursts of air. "Soul Technique: Ice Prison!"

Shards of ice began to form around Keelia, but what seemed to be a tornado swept up around her.

"Soul Technique: Wings of the Eagle!" she commanded in reply. Her wings both beat back powerfully, shattering the ice on them. She shot back up into the air, and Jane stopped the ice prison.

"I was sure I just had you," she said.

"You...You'll never be able to stop me," Keelia said through panting.

"I can see your tired, might have to trap you quickly."

"You'll never catch me. Aerio Ekriksi!" She fired a blast of wind from her hand, but Jane waved it aside.

"For shame daimon, for shame."

"Shut up! Aerio Ekriksi!"

Jane waved the attack aside again. "Do you want me to make this easier for you and take you down right now?"

Keelia spun the scimitar in her hand and flew down towards Jane. She lunged for her chest tiredly, and Jane knocked the attack aside with the obsidian staff. She tried overhead, but Jane stepped aside and punched her. She fell, but as she tried to get up, a cage of ice formed around her.

"You'll never beat Meso!" she shouted.

Jane pointed to the pile of obsidian bones right next to Keelia. "He's my second Divine slain so far, Meso will probably be the third."

"Lane, help me you oaf!" she shouted angrily.

"Alright, I'm coming," she said, a flaming aura lighting up around her. It was instantly dismissed as two large arms wrapped around her.

"Alcino?!" she and Keelia exclaimed.

"I'm not the fool Meso thinks I am, and I'll prove it today," he said.

"Lane, take him down!" Keelia commanded.

"Sorry, I don't do suicide missions. Two Divines and a tower associate would be too much for even me to handle," Lane replied.

"Gregory, Dianne!" Keelia called again.

"Meso has no place in my heart Keelia," Gregory replied.

"I never asked to join Meso and really disliked everything he did, also I'm actually smarter than him meaning he's a Divine not worth following," said Dianne.

Eros now held the staff in her hands and stood above Keelia. "Are you sure you don't want to switch sides? I would hate to kill such a lovely girl."

"Kill me? You forget I am just like Se'dah. Hell's Gate: One!" A dark aura began to flow around her, and she broke free of the ice prison.

"I forgot all about that," said Eros. "Now I see why Kini said it was a bad idea that I left the thinking to him."

"Aqua Pagos Ekriksi!" Jane commanded.

"Pyras Ekriksi!" Keelia commanded in reply. The ice and fire attacks collided, and steam began to fill the room.

"Fantastic, now I'll have to be careful," said Jane sarcastically. "Everyone may need to find cover, because what I'm about to do is going to shake this place."

"Oh no you don't!" Keelia exclaimed in multiple voices. She flew down and swung repeatedly at Jane with her scimitar. Jane managed to duck out of the way of the first attacks, but got cut across her arm. Eros soon came in the way and blocked what might have been a death blow.

"Bad things happen when you mess with my followers!" she hissed, taking up the obsidian staff.

"How ironic, the Divine of Love, fighting of all things!" Keelia laughed.

"You forget that I'm a Divine and you are a mortal."

"Mortal? I am a Daimon!"

"Then come and show me what a daimon is made of!"

Keelia began a barrage of blows on Eros, but she blocked, and soon after began her own string of attacks with the staff.

"I have a question about you daimons," said Eros. "Can all of you enter Hell's Gate?"

"We all can, we just can't be like that fool Se'dah and go to the verge of losing our souls to Hell's Gate," Keelia replied, parrying an attack.

Eros deflected an overhead slash. "So Se'dah is the only one that can reach Gate three?"

"Maybe, Maybe not."

"So are you Daimons really resistant to damage?"

Keelia side-stepped a lunge by Eros. "We're on the verge of immortality."

"Then this shouldn't hurt at all!" Jane shouted. "Dynami Pagos Hoplite!"

Eros leaped out of the way and a large spear made entirely out of ice shot through Keelia, who was still surprised about the sudden development.

She hit the wall and as she did, she placed both her hands around the ice spear. "Pyras!" she commanded. The ice quickly began to melt as she applied to heat, but now she realized that she would quickly bleed out from the wound. Her only hope would be to try and regenerate, and that meant her only hope would be...

"Hell's Gate: Two...." Before she could finish, the ice shard was melted, but a staff took its place in the hole in her side.

Eros stood above her now.

"No! This can't be happening!" she shouted in multiple voices. Half of her face fell to shadow, and the skin around the wound began to close itself.

Right on the staff.

Black lightning began to shoot around her body and then around Eros. They both began to scream loudly in agony until it was finally over. Keelia's body lay slumped by the wall.

Eros pulled the staff from her body. "A daimon is a daimon I suppose; I just didn't think they were this young at times."

"It's over then," said Gregory as he looked at Keelia.

"I guess so," Dianne agreed.

"So you're a daimon too huh?" Alcino asked Lane.

"Yes, and the shadow cast by that suit of armor is right on my toe, meaning..."

"Alcino she's going to fade into the shadow and escape!" Jane exclaimed.

"Too late to stop me," Lane replied and she sunk into the shadow and disappeared from the room.

"How you feeling Eros?" Jane asked.

"Strong enough to beat the living daylights out of Meso, and if I can get his energy too, I'll be able to beat Toxotes and Dasimay and get back my Kini."

"Great, so what will we do about these two?"

"We take them to the sanctuary, if they are willing to come."

"I wouldn't mind I guess, it would mean a place to hide out from Meso," said Gregory.

"And it's a good place for us to catch up, right Jane?" said Dianne.

"Yep, now let's go."

"Damn it!" Meso shrieked as he slammed his fist down on the arm of his throne. "Keelia is dead!"

"What?!" Kinsei exclaimed. "She can't be!"

"How could I have fallen for this?! And when did Alcino become smart?!" Meso shouted. "I let him in here because I assumed he was still an easily manipulated fool! And now look at me!"

"I'm going to the Pantheon castle," said Kinsei. He stopped by the doorway. "What about the two kids?"

"Their energies have just disappeared, so they were probably killed along with her," Meso replied.

"Why is Eros doing this? I never knew her for such things!" Kinsei said before leaving.

Kinsei ran through the halls at full speed, ignoring the pains in his side. At last, he turned the corner and threw open the throne room doors. He looked around to see the room was covered with shards of ice. There were signs of fighting with soul energy here, even the untrained would know that that was not normal ice.

He turned to see Keelia's body leaning on the wall. He ran over and fell by her side. "Keelia, this cannot be."

There was no reply.

"Why must this happen to my beautiful angel Keelia? Why?!" A black aura began to spark around his body. His kissed her on the cheeks and stood up. His face was now becoming covered by a white mask animated from soul energy.

Thousands of voices spoke at one at that moment, all of them speaking only of rage and intense hatred.

"Hell's Gate: Hell's Great Oni!"

Through the halls echoed the laughter of thousands at once, crazed sinister, forever hating.

CHAPTER 34

Fox Hall

The group led by Akina now had a day camp set up nearby Fox hall. It would be about a day's journey to it.

Everyone had stayed in camp except for Zen and Will, who were having a ride around the area.

"So that horse of yours, does it have a name?" Will asked.

"His name is Kenta. He's been with me for a good while to be honest," Zen replied. "Stuck with me all through the war."

"The war? Which war?"

"You never heard of the wars being fought in the west between the Zeran and Ayan Saudi?"

"Well yes, but I always assumed they were small time battles and skirmishes."

Zen chuckled sadly. "The battles we fought in turned the sand red for sometimes miles around, but I got used to it after a while. I don't wish to be thought of as an emotionless killer, but it seemed natural to pass by thousands of dead bodies nearly every day." He paused, uncertain whether to continue, but did. "I lost many friends in the last battle. Now I may never return to my home."

"And why is that?" asked Will.

"Sahra'a, the Divine of the Deserts, banished me from it. I-I don't know what I would have done if I hadn't met up with Alda and the others."

"Why would the Divine of the Deserts banish you? You seem like a nice enough kid."

"It was him and his servants that killed my warband, and when I questioned him on this, he banished me."

Will looked up at the sky and rubbed his stomach. "You think its lunchtime yet?"

"Why don't you catch something and eat it?" asked Zen.

"Do I look like an animal to you?"

Zen looked at the Fox male, and upon examining him, he replied. "You should know my answer."

"Tch, let's just go," said Will as he rode off.

Zen wheeled Kenta around and rode for the camp.

Several hours had passed now and it was getting late. The group had chosen to sit around the campfire and hold conversations to pass the time. They were usually for fun, but tonight was about planning.

"So what do I do when I go to Fox Hall, are there any special laws or rules I have to go by? Am I dressed correctly? Should I carry my weapons? Should I...."

Will cut off Akina mid-question. "Do the same thing you did at Fen Hall for starters. Everything is about the same throughout this country, so no special rules. No, you're not dressed correctly, you look sorta like a savage, but since you're a Fel, they'll ignore that fact. You might want to carry your weapons if things turn for the worst, but they shouldn't. Finally, you need to stop panicking," Will finished.

"I really don't see what you have to worry about," said Mark. "You're the Chief of Fel Hall."

"I'm the chief of a broken Kingdom."

"That's still something," said Illeth.

"I'm a child."

"Did the Chief of Fen Hall think so?" asked Mark.

"No, but...."

"You need to stop doubting yourself Akina, it's not healthy for a ruler."

"I'm not my father."

"I can clearly see that."

"This is not a laughing matter Mark!"

"I'm trying to lighten things up to help you relax."

"I shouldn't be relaxing at a time like this!"

"Then stress out and lose sleep. Then when we reach to Fox Hall, pass out right in front of their chief."

Akina frowned thoughtfully and sighed, unsure what to say next.

"I sense that there will be a romantic situation soon, I recommend it be taken further away," said Will.

"Shut up Will!" Mark shouted as the others laughed.

Akina blushed vividly and Illeth pinched her cheek. "I knew something was up with you two."

"Nothing is up! We are just good friends, that is all!" Akina protested.

"Friends she says," said Kullskash. "Is that what you young kids code it as nowadays?"

"Apparently so," Illeth agreed. "Right Zen and Alda?"

"Pfft, me going out with that...guy?" Alda couldn't find a good enough name to call him by. "Don't make me laugh."

"Then why are you wearing that necklace he had a few days ago?"

Alda looked down at the necklace and looked away. "I just didn't want to turn the kid down, so I said I would where it, and that was all!" Alda snapped back.

"Why I love you too Alda," Zen said sarcastically. "I hope you know you're a terrible actor."

"I am not!"

"So you agree that you were acting?" asked Akina.

Alda looked up angrily and saw that she was genuinely inquiring. "No, just..."

"Come on, just say you like Zen, no one would penalize you," said Will.

"It is funny that no one is commenting on Illeth, Will or Kullskash," Akina pointed out. Mark couldn't help bursting out into laughter.

"I'm over with the Guardsman Akina, and you know it!" Illeth exclaimed.

"What about you two then, Will and Kullskash?" Zen asked.

"I'm married to the battlefield," Kullskash replied.

"And I have no need for a wife right now," added Will.

"So sister, what happens when the battles are over?" asked Akina.

Kullskash's eyes widened. She never thought of life after the wars were finished. "I actually don't have an answer to that."

"When all this is over I'll be starting another caravan. I could hire you as a guard," said Will.

"Hire her as a guard," Mark repeated to himself. "He has a true motive behind that offer."

"Real mature Mark," Will replied.

"Just saying."

"Am I interrupting?" asked a voice.

Akina turned to see Dasimay coming out from the darkness of the night.

"Dasimay?! W-W-What are you doing here?!" she asked, inching away on her seat.

"So I can't hang out with my own sister? What has the world come to?"

"Akina, this is your sister?!" Mark exclaimed.

"Don't you see the family resemblance??" Dasimay asked.

"Well yeah but you're so...shapely and Akina is so....."

"Men are normally attracted to me, but I've never found one that truly loves me..." she said, licking her lips at him.

"Shut up Dasimay, there was a reason you didn't become chief," snapped Kullskash.

"You and Illeth are bastards, you could have never taken to the throne," Dasimay replied.

"So, you were legitimate, but you gave it all up," said Illeth.

"I wanted to have a little fun, and I got it. Does that really make me any different from our dear father?"

"Dasimay, you don't have the right to speak about that man," said Akina firmly.

She continued on, ignoring Akina completely. "I mean really, he had the choice between three women, he brought them to bed, made himself comfortable and chose the best one as his wife, and I'm pretty sure there a lot more kids like you running about. King's Kin they call them," she said with a laugh.

"Dasimay!" Akina cried.

"Alright, that's enough!" growled Mark.

"Good grief, I mean, I only did it with one man, but he did it with three different girls! I mean, I followed his legacy a lot better. Shouldn't I be chief?"

"Dasimay, this is going too far, you're making Akina cry," warned Illeth.

"I'm a grown woman for crying out loud, now that I'm back, I should be chief! Oh wait, my lover is now since he took it from Kinigos. He's a real leader, the people have to do whatever he says, or boom! They go up in flames!" she laughed again. "And what would you do when they disobey you? Cry to daddy? He's dead. Cry to Kinigos? He just about doesn't exist anymore. Your situation is priceless sis!"

Akina's eyes went blank at that moment, but it was different in Kullskash's eyes. The pupil had turned thin as she drew a dagger.

"How about we settle this?" she challenged.

"Kullskash, the little warrior. I remember how you would beat up all the boys in training! I remember when that one said you would probably never get a husband and you clocked him with a wooden great sword. Then you went home and cried the whole night! If I remembered correctly you had a crush on him. I think he was killed though when I attacked the town."

"Ren'Kai, no..." said Kullskash as she lowered the dagger. She gripped it tightly once again. "You'll pay Dasimay!"

She began to charge, but Dasimay held up her hand. "Ekriksi."

The attack hit and Kullskash slid through the dust and remained still.

Will and Mark soon got up, but Dasimay stopped them. "If you two even try to lift a finger to harm me, I'll blow you all up, or maybe I'll just blow Akina up." She looked at Mark and smiled seductively at him. "I was listening in on your little conversation. I'll make sure Toxotes learns of this, then I'll make your trip a living nightmare. Bye, bye." She faded back into the darkness.

The camp was now silent.

"At least it's not raining," said Will. A loud thunderclap sounded, and a torrent of rain came down on them.

"Get to the tents!" said Illeth. "And get Kullskash!"

The night seemed to drag on forever as the rain came down relentlessly.

"You know, I always wonder how I got myself into this situation in the first place. I should be home with my niece and nephew, reading them a bedtime story," Will said.

"My situation doesn't change much," said Zen. "If I weren't here, I would be lopping of heads in the deserts."

Mark's ears twitched, and Will's did the same.

"You two hear something?" asked Zen.

Mark got up in the small tent and went for the door. "I'll be back."

"Better not come back smelling like wet dog," Will remarked.

"Very funny Will."

Outside the rain was still coming down hard, with the occasional lightning and thunderclap.

Will looked around until he found the source of the noise.

It was Akina. She sat crying on a tree stump.

"Akina, you should be in a tent!" he said.

"I should be dead Mark, I should be dead!" she cried.

"Don't say that before it happens! Remember the rain?!"

"I couldn't lead Fel Hall by myself!"

"When we unite the country, you won't be by yourself."

"How will we unite the country if I don't even have my own? I've just been going around pretending to be chief! I can't get my Kingdom back! And even if I did, who would listen to a little girl?"

"Did the people not listen to you before?"

"That's because I had Illeth and Kullskash with me, they have a real influence over people, not me."

"I don't have time for this, let's go Akina!" growled Mark as he grabbed her hand.

"I'm not going back!" she shouted as she yanked it away.

"Then what do you plan on doing huh? Will you just stay here the whole night?"

"That's exactly what I'll do, and no weak, lost puppy is going to change that! I mean, you've been driving me on all these weeks, but yet you can hardly even defend yourself!"

Mark was ready to protest, but knew it was futile and hung his head in resignation. "So this is how it's going to be then? Good night Akina." He said as he left.

She watched him walk off and even more tears streamed down uncontrollably as she realised she just drove away one of her first friends. She lowered her face into her hands and sat there in tears.

Then she felt that the rain had stopped. She looked up to see that Mark was putting up a tarp over them by tying it to the smaller nearby trees. He wrapped a blanket around Akina and sat silently on a nearby log. She sat silently for a few seconds, unable to say anything.

"I dislike you even more now Mark," she said softly. "I reject and belittle you, but you still come back and help me. You're just making me feel even guiltier."

"I'm doing this out of love Akina, I don't need love back in return," he replied.

Mark couldn't figure out when she moved, or how fast it happened, but Akina embraced him.

"I'm sorry Mark," she cried. "I'm really, really sorry." She partly took off the blanket and wrapped it around Mark.

"If you realize the size of your own body, you'll know you'll need to keep all of it to stay warm," Mark said.

Akina looked up at him and smiled. "I'm doing this out of love Mark; I don't need love in return."

Mark held her close. "I'll give you love back, always."

Will awoke the next morning to see that the rain had stopped, but Zen and Mark were nowhere to be seen. He exited the tent and went outside to find Zen sitting atop the wagon.

"What are you doing up there Zen?" he asked.

"Akina and Mark are missing," he replied. "Illeth and Alda said they couldn't find them anywhere around the camp."

"Found em'!" shouted Alda from away.

"Seems so," Zen said to Will.

Alda, Zen, Will, Kullskash and Illeth now stood before a sight.

Mark and Akina were sitting upright on a log wrapped in a blanket, sleeping.

"Should we wake them up?" asked Illeth.

"I would've given them a few more minutes," said Will.

Alda frowned as she put down the sword and shield she were about to bash together.

"You're a very mischievous girl Alda," Zen said with hushed laughter.

The two seemed to awaken at the same time and upon seeing their friends standing around and realizing they were still wrapped together, they pulled apart from each other.

"This is not what it looks like!" Mark exclaimed.

"Oh really," said Illeth.

The two of them got up and looked at each other, then at the group.

"So let's get to Fox Hall, we have a good amount of hours and the sky is clear," said Akina.

"Yeah, we should get going," Mark agreed.

"Once we step into the wagon, you'll never hear the end of it," said Will.

"Real mature Will, real mature."

Fox Hall now came into view, and Will couldn't help grinning. "I'm happy to be home," he said.

Zen was riding to the front of the wagon to help him steer. "So this is Fox Hall?"

"Yep, my niece and nephew will be thrilled to see me like they always are."

As they neared the city though, all was quiet. You couldn't hear the familiar sounds of blacksmiths pounding out tools, or the loud talking and bartering from the market places. Sentries weren't even guarding the front gate.

"What on Edafos...?" said Will as he looked around. "Where is everybody?"

"Maybe sleeping or something?" Zen replied. "We'll probably see people when we reach the main hall."

They left the wagon and their horses at the stables and hurried to the Hall, but then they saw her at the square.

"Nice day for peace talks isn't it?" she asked. She was sitting on the steps to the palace with her obsidian longbow at her side.

"Dasimay, what the hell do you want?" Akina asked through a growl.

"Oh, little sister grew a spine," she said.

"I'm not even going to bother with you," said Akina as she went up the stairs past her.

"Who do you think you are?"

"Akina Akin, chief of Fel Hall, and more importantly, chief of you."

"She has a spine and spice, I like that, too bad I have to kill you."

"I'd love to see you try," challenged Akina.

"Katastrofi!" Dasimay commanded.

Akina grabbed the invisible blast and it turned white in her hand. "I learned a few things while I was in the North Country, like how to redirect soul attacks, and soon, I was able to catch and keep them."

"So you think these kinds of battles are about pitching and catching? For shame little sister."

Before Akina could even comprehend it, an obsidian arrow was coming straight for her. "Tahitita!" she commanded hastily. She was able to dodge the arrow, but as it hit the stairs behind her, it exploded violently.

Mark nocked and arrow and fired after Dasimay.

"You're going to have to do better than that Mark!" Dasimay caught and snapped it, then sent an entire volley after Mark in a few short seconds.

The group managed to move out of the way, but the ground lit up in violent explosions.

Akina drew two sharp daggers made of bone. "Alright Dasimay, that's enough. I'm the one you want, not them."

"Akina, you're asking for a death wish!" warned Will.

"Listen to the Fox Akina, fighting me on your own is impossible," Dasimay said as she turned to her.

"So what, is that supposed to frighten me? I'm the mighty daughter of the great warrior Akin! Nothing strikes fear into my heart!"

"Now she's losing it, might as well kill you now." Dasimay sent a volley of fire arrows straight for Akina.

She stepped forward and slashed away two, she ducked out of the way of the third. The other two missed and exploded nearby.

Dasimay looked up at her now, and for a second, Akina saw a quick look of fear in her eyes.

"You could never be father," she said.

"Of course I couldn't, that's why I'm going to be Akina," she replied simply.

"You and him both are fools, and just how Toxotes put an arrow in him, I'm gonna put an arrow in you!"

"It was Toxotes that killed Father?" Akina asked, her features softening.

"Yes, shot him in the middle of battle and disappeared. It actually was quite funny watching you cry, no, wail over his death for days and days on end."

Akina chuckled.

"What the battle turning you mad? That's just what I expected from you."

"I'm laughing because all this time, I thought he was killed in camp, but if the battle had already started there, he died doing what he loved." Akina held the daggers up again. "Eros has wanted a rematch with you and that coward Toxotes, but now I really don't want her to.

"Then again, I don't think Toxotes is worth fighting, I mean, why is it that he leaves the dirty work to his little wench Dasimay? Can't he do it himself like a man? My father always charged into battle first and always chose hitting you in the face instead of stabbing you in the back."

"You don't know what you're talking about Akina! I'll make sure Toxotes gets your head!"

Akina now saw the rage was taking Dasimay over, and she knew that was one of her weaknesses. "Then bring him here and tell him to take it off himself."

"He doesn't hit little girls," Dasimay said, trying to take control of the situation. She felt something cut across her face and saw that Akina was now behind her.

"Neither do I," she said.

Dasimay put her hand on her cheek and realized she was bleeding.

"I'm going to murder you Akina, there will be nothing left to bury!" she roared.

Dasimay swung her bow at her and their weapons locked.

"You're really, really mad Dasimay," said Akina. "If you keep this up, you'll let me win."

They both hopped back.

"You won't, Toxotes Barrage!" Dasimay commanded as a wall of arrows appeared before her. "I told you I would have your head, and I always get what I want."

"Is that what Toxotes tells you? For shame sister," Akina replied.

Dasimay waved her hand and the arrows went flying.

Akina spun with the daggers, snapping arrows in two as she went. The volley had seemed to disappear, but something felt wrong.

Very wrong.

"Akina!" Mark screamed.

"What Mark?" she asked. She looked down at her chest to see that an obsidian arrow had gone all the way through.

Eros fell down screaming in agony, black lightning shooting around her body.

"Eros, are you alright?!" said Alice as she got near.

"Obsidian...." She managed to reply. "Akina has to have been hit."

"Akina? Who would want to hurt Akina?" asked Kilan.

The lightening intensified.

"Dasimay!" she coughed. "And Toxotes!"

"You see how it felt Akina?!" laughed Dasimay. "Dying abroad, never getting to see his daughters grow up!"

"Akina!" Mark shouted again as he ran to her side. She had fallen quickly as the black lightning shot around her body.

"Seems I let one slip past me," she managed to say.

"We have to get that arrow out of you!" he said.

"It's hooked and barbed Mark, the only way to get that out would be the take out a few organs with it."

"Watch helplessly Mark, watch your lover bleed out before you!" Dasimay said. "I'll give her props though, she's living quite long."

"Akina, I can't lose you!" Mark said.

Akina looked up at the sky, and then to Dasimay. "I don't think I may survive this one."

Mark noticed that she was smiling. "What's so funny?"

"Nothing, it's just that I get to die by your side."

"I don't want you to die Akina," Mark said as tears began to stream down his face.

He felt Akina's hand touch his face. "It seems silly that I'm only telling you this now, but I love you Mark."

"You're just saying that to make me feel better," Mark replied.

She kissed him on the lips and seemed to lose an immense amount of strength. "I meant that will all my heart, or at least most of it."

"What about the rest of it?"

"Dasimay's arrow took some of it away," She looked up at the sky again. "I'm losing my connection to this world."

"I'll never give up on you Akina, never!" Mark said. He kissed her, and felt that she went cold.

Eros struggled to her feat, the lightning still shooting around her. "Good thing they remembered love gives me strength as a Divine."

"What's going on Eros?" asked Adele.

The lighting broke away from Eros' body as she got back to her feet. She dusted herself off.

"Dasimay, when we meet again, I'm erasing you from Edafos," she said to herself.

The amulet Akina now glowed, and the gem at the center shattered. Light returned to her eyes and she got up.

Dasimay almost dropped her bow in horror.

"What's wrong, you look like you've seen a ghost," she said.

"But the arrow, it's in your heart!" she exclaimed.

Akina let the tip of her dagger touch the arrow, and it seemed to absorb it. The wound instantly healed itself.

"You're not a Fel, you can't be!" Dasimay shrieked.

"I am," said Akina. "You scared Dasimay?"

"Tachista!" she commanded. She moved quickly, dashing over rooftops and over the city wall, disappearing into the wilds.

"Is she gone?" asked someone from the hall.

"Dasimay is gone," Akina said as she sheathed the daggers.

A Fox man came out from the Hall. He was wearing a chainmail shirt and plate legs made of steel. On his head was a crown made of silver.

"Who might you be?" asked Akina.

"That's the Chief of Fox Hall Akina!" Will replied quickly.

"What?! But my hair is in a horrible state, and my clothes are cut up and blood soaked and....."

"Calm the hell down Akina," Mark said putting his hand over his face.

"Yes, right," said Akina as she took a deep breath. She turned to face the man before her. "I'm Akina Akin, daughter of Akin, follower of Eros and Kinigos, chief of Fen Hall and the bringer of peace to this land."

"So what, you want us to just remake the council and reunite Den? Do you think I would agree to that so quickly?" he said.

"Yes," Akina said simply as if he was to see her point.

He quickly ran down the stairs and fell by her feet. "You have done the people of Fox Hall a great thing! We have been hiding out form that horrible woman all morning until you came!" He motioned to the Hall and Akina could see several heads peeking from the side. "We must have a feast in your honor!"

"Will my friends be able to come too?" she asked.

"Of course my dear! They are all welcome."

Once the feast started, Akina could see why the Fox could afford such good equipment for war. Their hall was twice the size of hers, and the entire city's population seemed to fit inside it. They had given her a simple dress with a patterned border to wear instead of the blood-soaked clothes she previously wore.

"Hey Akina, meet my niece and nephew," said Will as he brought them forward.

"Hello young ones," she said as she snapped out of her gawking.

"Is it true that you made the bad lady run away by yourself?" asked the young boy. He looked like Will but was still small, about five or six years old. He was dressed in a blue simple cotton shirt and trouser.

"Not exactly, I had help from everyone," Akina replied. She felt the other child tug and her foot. She was dressed in a tiny pink dress and Akina could see that she was about four.

"You're a nice lady," she said.

Akina patted her head. "I am it seems, though I wasn't always like this."

"Seems all it took was a little hope to get us to this point," said Will.

"I know, it's a bit surprising to see that we made it this far." Akina looked around and turned to Will. "Where is Mark?"

"Must be outside," he replied.

Mark was out on a balcony, looking up at the night sky. He found it hard to resist the temptation to howl for some reason as he looked at the moon.

"Mark, there you are," said Akina.

"Here I am," he said softly.

"What's wrong Mark, why aren't you inside enjoying yourself?"

"I'm just a little worried as all, I mean, Dasimay may come back at us at any moment and I know all of us combined couldn't..."

Akina kissed him on the lips and held his hand. "Weren't you the one that told me not to stress?"

"I suppose so," Mark replied with a sad smile. "I just don't like the idea of being at death's door."

"I had my first kiss, I can die in peace any day," she laughed. "Now come on, they'll be calling us up to make a toast and I want you holding my hand as we go out."

"I think I'm a bit too shy for that."

"No you're not, now come on," Akina said as she pulled him away.

C H A P T E R 3 5

The Fall of Deneaux

"Hey, are you guys there?" asked someone from outside."

They awoke Kilan, who was sleeping when she was to guard the door. "Who's there?" she asked.

"You should know my voice by now Kilan."

"Name. Now," she replied sternly.

"Noch from Sepal, Jorigsveer Great-Blade, Lyradel from Keels...Must I continue?"

"Well come on in," said Kilan with a smile.

"Noch, you're back!" Alice said happily as she embraced him.

He picked her up and spun her. "I'm glad to be back alive and well!"

"Hey Pagos, you miss me or what?" asked Turner.

Jane held his face. "Turner, you're cut up," she said.

"Jor and I got in a bit of a bad situation when the Raiders were going to bomb the place," Turner replied.

"You're too brave Turner," she said as she kissed him on the cheek.

Jor turned to Lyra. "Why don't I get hugs or kisses?"

"My dagger would gladly hug and kiss you. I've been with you the whole time in Keels, I don't need to act like you've been gone for years."

"I'm glad to be back home," said Jor. He now called Eros over. "So what's happened since I was gone?"

"We had some brutal battles here in Deneaux," she said sadly. "Just the other day we were forced to kill a girl around your age."

"Why?" asked Lyra.

"She was a Daimon, one of Meso's warriors."

"Anything new with Meso?" Turner asked.

"He's on his last legs, one more hit and him and all his followers will be gone," Eros replied.

Jor glanced up at a perialite girl and a boy that stood away from the commotion. "Who's the pretty one with the books?" Jor asked as he winked at her. He saw her blush.

"That's Dianne," Eros said. "They used to work for Meso but switched sides."

"She looks like a geek," Lyra said with folded arms.

"She's pretty," said Jor in reply.

"You have no taste Jor."

"Is that jealousy I hear?"

Lyra's eyes widened and she grabbed Jor by his collar. "I am not, and will not ever be jealous for you."

"Just wait until I find your diary," Jor said.

"I have none."

"Then your journal..."

"You'll never find it....if it existed," she added hastily.

"Jor, Turner and Lyra, we're heading out again," said Noch.

"Where are we going again?" Jor asked.

"The King, he has a proclamation to make..." Noch said sadly.

The four of them now stood outside of the Pantheon castle. It was quite a large castle, but there was a balcony lower down that allowed officials to speak to the people.

"We're going up since down here will be filled to the brim with people," said Noch.

"So wait, what is this proclamation about?" Turner asked.

Jor noticed that there was serious concern on his face, and Noch looked reluctant—nearly unable to answer.

"We'll see once it starts..." Noch replied.

The four of them were acting as guards where the King would be speaking.

He now came in, being helped by two other Paladins, and behind him came a boy with short, blonde hair and burgundy clothes.

"Who's that?" whispered Lyra.

"That's the Prince, Albain," Noch replied.

The crowd outside went silent as the King went outside. All eyes were on him now, and he looked down sadly.

"As it seems, my years are catching up to me, and my body is quickly weakening," he said. He coughed horribly. "That is why on this day of the year one thousand thirty five, on the third day of the seven day week on the eight month, I declare Albain to be the new King." He took off his crown and placed it on his surprised son's head.

"Father, what does this mean?" he asked.

"My son, I am dying soon, and you are my only heir, you must take the crown," he replied.

"I shall wear it proudly Father, you will not be disappointed."

A white aura began to glow around the King and his son.

"The only thing that has been keeping me alive these few days was my own energy, my body had died at Keels and my soul was still trudging along the mortal plane."

"Father, you can't leave me!" Albain cried.

"Forgive me son, what is being passed is the power of the King's, and mines will be passed along as well...Goodbye son, and goodbye Deneaux, the good Empire of the North...."

The area was engulfed in a large flash, and the king was gone.

"Albain, will you be okay?" Noch asked.

"Yes, I just need to go to my room to rest, all this is coming too fast."

Noch escorted him there and patted him on the back. "You'll be a good King, Albain," he said.

"Thank you," he replied.

He quickly entered the room and locked the door behind him. There in the room was his sister Caroline.

"Are you King yet, brother?" she asked. She wore a burgundy dress and had small tiara. Her hair was blonde and was tied into a ponytail that fell to her back.

"Carel no longer walks with the living, and now Cardia is mine," Albain replied.

"So when do we get to move into the other lands?" Caroline asked.

"We must wait sister, once the Raiders reach here from Denhoec, I'll have them invited in, and from there we'll conquer Cardia and divide the land between us."

"So we get to keep Deneaux?"

"We keep Northern Cardia and they take the south," Albain said with a nod.

"Aren't you worried about them betraying you?"

"They could never, because we have the strongest walls, the strongest military and the bigger armoury of obsidian weapons."

"Are you talking about us betraying Meso?"

"We will, and then we'll kill Eros and her followers, or better yet, we could force both sides to do our bidding."

"And how do you plan on doing that?"

"We'll use Fenalph and Titus to our advantage, and we could just simply storm both their sanctuaries."

"You're so smart brother."

"Would you expect anything less from the Emperor of Cardia?"

"So what happened out there?" asked Kilan.

"The King's dead," Noch replied, still unable to believe it.

"So what now?" Alice asked.

"I suppose they'll have us called back out again," said Noch, soldiers like Turner and Jor will get leave, but I'm too valuable a commander."

"You may not get that chance," Eros said. "Raiders are coming...."

"From Denhoec," Jor added with dark realization.

"Good, we know which wall to defend," Noch said quickly.

Eros stopped him. "You're not going to stop them," she said. "The whole force is arriving."

"Well they can't get through to our walls, it's impossible!"

"Then go, my foresight can't go any further."

Noch quickly left the room, and all eyes turned to Eros.

"What's going on?" asked Jane.

"Something, though I'm unsure what. It will change this country and this continent forever though...."

"I need crossbowmen along here! Hurry up, it's not as if I'm getting any older!" Noch shouted.

"Yes sir!" several men chorused as they went up against the battlements.

Noch grabbed the arm of a sergeant that was passing nearby.

"Are my pikemen set up by the gates?"

"Yes sir, they are all waiting and ready for battle."

"Well let's keep it that way. I see men on the horizon!"

"Ready, aim....."

"Hold fire," said Albain.

"My King, where did you come from?" Noch asked, surprised to see the boy on the walls.

"I was here to foresee the Raiders' safe arrival to Deneaux," he replied.

"Safe...arrival?" Noch repeated in disbelief.

"Everyone, as your King I demand that you lower your weapons!"

The units did what he said slowly, unsure on his meaning, and watched painfully as their enemy marched before their gates.

"Welcome friends, to the Grand Empire of Deneaux!" he called to them. He turned to men at the gatehouse. "Open the gates!"

They did as he said, and the Raider army marched into Deneaux.

"King Albain, what is this?" Noch asked. "Why are you letting these animals into our home?"

"I don't recall you ever being a man of Deneaux Noch, weren't you from some country far way? Either way, you are relieved of duty."

"What?"

"I can't command you to do my bidding like the other soldiers, and you just questioned my decisions," Albain said.

"Why would you want the men to do your bidding? Don't they already do it?"

"As a King of Deneaux, I have the almost godly ability to take over the minds of my men, you are not of Deneaux blood, so I cannot command you, and I know I could never get you to take over the lands of others."

"Take over...land?"

"Are you simple? I'm taking over Cardia! I'm using Deneaux's and the Raider's strength to take over. With both of those powers, I'll be unstoppable! Now out of my sight before I have you executed!"

Noch trotted into the sanctuary and fell to his knees.

"Noch, are you okay?" Alice asked as she ran over to him.

"I've been relieved of duty," he managed to say. "I've been refused the right to defend my country because of my nationality."

"Come on Noch, you can't let this stop you," Alice said, trying to comfort him.

"What else will I do then? All I've known how to do is defend people, what else will I turn to?"

"You could hang out with me in the mean time until you find something to do," Alice said with a reassuring smile.

Noch looked up at her. "Yes, Yes I would like that."

"But what about the Raiders moving into Deneaux?" Jor asked Eros.

"We're not in any imminent danger, so we might as well continue fighting Meso," she replied. "Though it would be reasonable for you all to leave Deneaux and walk other paths."

"I've come to grow on a lot of you guys, so I'm not leaving any time soon," said Jane.

"Well, I might try going over to the tower again, I just hope they'll reaccept me," said Dianne.

There was a sharp banging on the stone wall door of the sanctuary.

"Seems that the Chief is back from her mission," said Eros.

"It's actually Melvin," Kilan replied.

"Melvin?" Jor asked.

"One of my priests, he knows where the sanctuary is located," Eros replied. "Let him in."

The man dressed in brown monk's robes rushed in and fell on his hands and knees before Eros. He had papers almost falling out of his already packed satchel.

"The King! He is launching investigations into the fighting between you and Meso, and he says he will execute anyone involved.

He is also banning the worship of every deity except for Titus and Fenalph!"

Eros seemed to be taken aback by the news.

"What's wrong Eros, you seem to be in pain," Jane said.

She turned to her. "Did it ever occur to you that I am a Divine and am able to speak with my people unlike many others?" she asked.

"Well no, but can't Divines do anything?"

"Not exactly, under normal circumstances, it would take up energy to stay in this world, but once I have people worshiping me, it takes up less energy to stay. As you can see, I'm praised by thousands of people in Deneaux and other places in Cardia, but now that my worship is being banned..."

"You won't be able to stay in our world," Kilan said sadly.

"Same with Efiia too."

"Then why don't we stop the King?" Gregory asked.

"Good idea," Turner said. "We'll all go up against the kid with the power to stomp on a Continent and two super powerful Divines!" he finished sarcastically.

"Didn't take that into account," Gregory replied, embarrassed.

"So does this mean, that this is it?" Lyra asked.

"I suppose so," Eros said sadly.

Jor noticed that something sparkling came from Eros' eye.

"So then where do I go?" Jor asked. "Unlike the rest of you I have no life to go back to."

"A life to go back to Jor? You've seen what Albain is doing. Anyone from Deneaux doesn't have an old life to go back to," Turner said. "I'm leaving the army and the guard if it means helping to conquer the lands I don't own."

"Then I guess I may have to go back to that damned tower!" Jane said, her voice quivering.

"And what's so bad about this 'tower' you and Dianne keep speaking of?" asked Eros.

"I have no problem with going back there, it's just that Jane has a few parental and social issues there," Dianne replied.

"What if I come with you?" Turner asked Jane.

"You would make things go from disastrous to Catastrophic," Jane replied.

"What's that supposed to mean?"

"My parents are..." Jane couldn't find the right word that would describe them and left the sentence off there.

"So Jor, you plan to go along?" Lyra asked.

Jor's face went dark. "I was planning on going over to Denhoec, had some things to do back there again..."

"Like what Jor?" asked Lyra.

"My brothers and I have a thing to settle."

"And you plan and beating them all yourself?"

"I could easily handle them all, except for Lok, he is the one I want the most."

"So you don't know if you can beat Lok?" asked Turner.

"I would be wrong for me as a human being to let him win."

"Well try fighting him later when you're sure you can beat him, no point in losing your head too early," said Efiia, who had just come in.

"Then what do I do in the meanwhile?"

"Come with us to the tower," said Turner. "The trip might make you stronger."

"You. Are. Not. Coming. With. Me." Jane said.

"Who said we're going with you?" Lyra replied. "We're going along for the ride."

"Don't you belong back in Keels?"

"That pile of ash and rubble? I can't go back there."

"Alright, you all can come..." Jane said defeated. "I'm going to regret this though."

CHAPTER 36

Ichor

Ema watched as she let the gold coins fall through her fingers. As the last of it fell into the pile on the ground, she scooped up more.

"You seem bored," said Haima, who was lying on a hammock between two palm trees.

"I am, I mean, how do you enjoy hanging out in the sanctuary all day?" Ema asked.

"I like gold and seeing a lot of it is entertainment enough for me," she replied.

"I want to fight again."

"Then go to one of those little desert towns. Fenalph said he would be coming down here to take it over in due time, so the least you could do is make it easier for him."

Ema's face lit up quickly as she got up. "So I really get to destroy another village?!"

"Yes Ema, go break a leg, or break their legs."

"You see any of the Zerani?" asked one Ayan Saudi soldiers on a camel.

Another looked through a seeing glass, looking into the empty desert. "Nothing, they aren't making any moves."

"Smart idea to give us a twenty man troop just to scout around," a third soldier said sarcastically. "Let's move."

"Zeranian! Or at least I think they are Zeranian!" cried the soldier with the seeing glass.

The other men began to pick up their lances and sabres, but the on soldier stopped them.

"It's a girl it seems."

"We'll let her come to us then."

"Hello!" she said as she waved.

"Good day my lady, what makes a pretty girl like you want to cross the deserts?"

Ema had changed form from a small child to young woman around eighteen. She was dressed in clothes that seem more exposing than normal, and it marked her as either an enchantress or belly dancer.

"Well, I've been taking up jobs around Zeran and the smaller little hamlets in the middle of the desert, but when I saw that there were soldiers, I realized I could use my greatest talent to earn money..." she said with a wink.

"How good are you?"

"Good enough for you I'm sure."

"Care to give us a demonstration?" another soldier asked.

"Patience, tonight."

The twelfth soldier had left the tent that night grinning brightly, and the next entered soon after.

Ema lay in a bed and looked to the soldier who had just "finished".

"So it's only twenty of you out here?" she asked.

"Yes my dear, getting tired?"

"I could go for a while more, but I think now is the time for carnage."

"Excuse me?"

Blood began to gather below Ema's feet as she got up, and she smiled maniacally at the soldier. "Ema Ekriksi!"

The body of the soldier tore out the side of the tent, and the rest watched in horror as Ema approached them.

"Ema Barrage!"

Sharp projectiles made of blood shredded through the unarmed men. One managed to get away and grab his lance, but Ema stopped him.

"Metallos Ema," she commanded. An iron spike ripped through the chest of the soldier, and he fell promptly into the sand.

Ema looked at the small camp and smiled. "Pyras Katastrofi Barrage!"

The camp lit up brightly in flames, so much so that it could be seen for miles around. With it was the sound of sharp agony that rang out even further.

The man dressed in desert robes and wielding a scimmitar at his side slammed his fist down on the wooden table inside his office in the town of Kurd.

"What do you mean the scounting party hasn't made it back yet?!" he exclaimed.

"I don't know Captain, all that I do know is that our sentries have reported seeing bright lights far out in the desert," replied a man in a type of armor made of robes and chainmail. He was a Mamluk, one of the most elite of the Ayan Saudi army. He was dark-skinned and bald, but still had a look of youth to him.

"Well why didn't you go out and check?!" the captain shouted.

The Mamluk replied meekly, "I didn't want to risk any men, and I just assumed that they would be alright...."

"You assumed? You assumed!? I ask for a field commander and they give me a—a—an assumer!"

"I doubt that is a word sir...."

"Get out their and check on that unit! I don't care what it costs, I just need those men!"

"Y-Yes sir!"

He quickly exited the room and a young boy sitting on a brightly colored cushion on the ground ran to him.

"Daddy, was the mean man mad?" he asked.

The soldier patted the boy's head. "Is he ever not?"

"You going to stay home now?"

"Not yet it seems, I have to go ride into the deserts to check on the other warriors."

"Will it take long?"

"I should be back before nightfall young one, we shall eat dinner together at least."

"Okay," he replied, a hint of sadness in his voice.

"Amec, you really can't have us going out there, bright lights in a shrubless desert do not bode well," said a soldier.

"It probably just had a few shrubs that got struck by lightning, or maybe some person out there was lighting a fire and it got a little out of hand," the Mamluk from earlier replied.

He was with a unit comprised of five riders from the town garrison that were dressed and armed lightly in robes over chainmail with bows and sabres. They could handle small ambushes and quick skirmishes but not long drawn out battles.

"But still, are you not a little fearful? The desert is a dangerous and mysterious place, and the legends of the monsters that inhabit the deeper parts of it are still spoken of and shouldn't be ignored," another soldier warned.

"We will be fine, all we do is ride out, see the scouting unit and come back," Amec replied.

The riders left town quickly and made their way in the directions of the lights. It was mid-day, so the sun was at its peak, beating down on the riders. They would have left at another time when the sun wasn't so merciless, but the Captain was an impatient man, and keeping him waiting wasn't a feasible option.

They eventually met up with a large sand dune after hours of riding, and as they slowly made it over, they dismounted their camels and stood at the top.

"Impossible..." a soldier said slowly in awe.

The camp was completely destroyed, the charred remains scattered about.

"Come on, there must be someone left alive," Amec said as he ran down the dune towards the camp.

"Wait sir, it's getting dark!" one soldier shouted.

"I know, so the quicker we search, the quicker we get to go back."

As they slowly walked through the remains of the camp, one of the men vomitted at a gorey sight.

A body was on the ground, his chest shredded apart by a shard of iron. Not to far from him was a man riddled with small holes.

"How is this possible!?" the soldier shrieked.

"Must have been the vultures, nothing more..."

"But what about the one with the object in his chest?!" the soldier interrupted Amec.

"Maybe the Zeran have some kind of new iron shooting ballista," Amec said, trying to remain calm.

Another man was torn clean in two across his waist, and another straight down into two parts. After them was one unit burned to nearly a crisp, his charred, black skeleton blowing away into tiny particles by the wind. Nearby him were small collections of metal on the burnt ground that could hardly be identified as soldiers.

"What could have done this?" a soldier asked.

"Maybe...maybe it was an attack by the Zeran, it had to be!" Amec exclaimed.

"But do the Zeran burn men to nothing and chop them up into pieces?"

"They are our enemies soldeir! They will do anything to kill us and will do so in the most brutal ways! We are at war soldier! Atrocities like this are common, and if you head out to the real battlefield, this will be all too common!"

There was a soft giggling noise that blew through the camp.

"What was that?"

"Probably nothing."

The sound came through again, a little louder this time.

"Someone here is alive! Get to looking!" Amec commanded them.

The units were about to go off and search when they saw the tent up ahead. They drew their sabers and walked ahead slowly, Amec being the one taking point. They entered the tent and saw a small bed, and someone was under the sheets.

"Who's under there?" Amec called.

Ema slowly rose up and smiled at them. "Good evening soldiers, have you come to this little girl's rescue?"

The soldiers sheathed their sabers and relaxed a little.

"Are you okay miss?" Amec asked.

"Yes, why are you asking?"

"Well, it's just that this whole camp has been destroyed and everyone is dead except...you."

"I'm fine, but feeling...a bit lonely," she said as she looked longingly at each soldier.

"How can you be thinking of that at a time like this?" Amec asked, somewhat in awe.

"Well, I've finally gotten some freedom, and I want to spend every moment of it by enjoying the greatest of the mortal pleasures," she replied.

"Do you know what happened here?" a soldier asked.

"Oh, I was giving the gentlemen here some enjoyement after such boring duties in the deserts, I was on the eleventh man I think when I got a little bored with them, so I decided to play a new game."

"Excuse me?" Amec said.

"I killed them! Making art with their bodies, imbuing them with my soul and creating all manners of monstrous beings!" she shrieked joyusly. "Do you know how wonderous blood is?! How it is the essence of life, but yet is shown as a symbol of death! The sight of blood makes me get happy and excited, I can hardly stand due to the pleasure it brings, but you mortals hold it so greedily, and panic when it is spilled, but I want more. Ema Ekriksi!"

One of the soldiers' chest exploded with a bright crimson colour, and one could see that all traces of humanity in Ema's eyes had vanished.

The other soldiers looked down at their fallen comrade and saw that his blood was also splattered on them, they quickly began to panic and rushed out of the tent. Amec followed.

"To the camels!" he shouted.

Several mounds of sand began to rise up, and they gave a whistle-like screech that threw horror into the men that heard it.

Out of the mounds came skeletal hands, dried to the point that there skin was stretched with every movement. Out of one came the black, dusty skull of some atrocious humanoid, and it began to shriek loudly again.

Amec ran towards it with his sabre drawn, screaming a mighty war cry as he did.

"Geo Ekriksi!" the being commanded.

A sharp shard of compressed sand shot out of the ground at Amec, who managed to dodge it. It struck a man behind, but the cry was short, and Amec knew looking back would only show another atrocity.

"Geo Barrage!" another commanded. The shards of sand began to come out of the ground rapidly at Amec and his men.

They managed to get past the flying shards and bolted up the dunes. Another man went down and rolled down the hill.

Amec and his men made it to the camels and mounted, then charged off in the direction of Kurd.

Ema stood atop the hill and gently extended her hand in their direction and smirked. "Exochos Haima Katastrofi," she commanded, her voice echoing softly across the far sands.

Out of the sands came sharp spikes made of a black liquid that stood like a solid. Amec knew he could smell blood, and that was no doubt the blood of men who died from thousands of years ago shooting out at them. He could now see streaks of it ripping its way through the sand, and in front of him he could see that they would form some kind of barrier. He urged his camel on.

"Amec, what is happening?" a soldier asked, the terror in his voice replaced by complete confusion of whether this was reality or a dream.

"I do not know, now hurry!" he shouted in reply.

Amec quickly rode past the black lines being made in the sand, but the men behind him weren't as lucky. The black sand rose up to form a wall, and all that could be heard were brief shrieks of an agony far beyond comprehensible, and then the complete and utter silence of the dark desert.

Amec turned to see only pieces of clothes left. The camels had disappeared completely, but he knew this wouldn't be the time for wondering. He wheeled his camel back around and headed for Kurd.

It was late at night and he could see over the horizon that there were lights. He could easily tell they were from Kurd though, so he urged his camel on to reach his destination faster. He was hungry, tired and exhausted, and he sighed as he got over a dune nearby.

That is when he saw it.

Kurd was burning, and you could hear the men fighting for their lives inside. He dismounted his tired camel and drew his sabre and charged down towards the town. As he entered, he saw the same sand men as before cutting down men with stones. He hacked down several of them that weren't paying attention and made way for the square.

At the square, he could see a makeshift barricade set up, and he ran towards it. Someone was already reaching over to help him up, and he took the hand easily.

"Amec, you're alive!" a villager said. He had the scimitar of a soldier that had already died and looked over every once in a while. "I don't know what the hell has been going on, but it makes no sense at all!"

"I encountered these beings in the desert. Where is the commander for that matter?" Amec asked.

"Blown to dust in the wind, a great ball of fire just crashed down on him directly and the town went to chaos from then." Another fireball crashed down and a house disappeared in a matter of seconds."

"Where is my son?!" Amec cried, realizing that he had been so distracted by current events.

A side of the barricade lit up, and at the villager's call, several soldiers began pouring down from a building and waited behind the barricade.

"I don't know, most everyone is dead or hiding, so I cannot say."

Amec hauled himself to the top of the barricade. "I'm going to look for him!"

"Do not go Amec, that will only mean certain death for you!"

"And what about my son?"

"He is probably already dead.

"I refuse to believe this!"

"Then let the Divines be with you Mamluk."

Amec vaulted over the barricades and ran through the on-going battle. He was forced to avoid the fireballs that came crashing down from the sky and sharp rocks sent by the sandmen. He had to avoid tripping over the mangled, burnt bodies of the dead and the undead. All the while he was shouting the name of his son.

"Father!" a voice called.

"Aman?" he called again in reply.

"Father!" the voice shouted almost hysterically.

He ran through some burning rubble until he made it to an area that was surrounded by burning houses but was relatively clear of debris. There the boy sat, cowering.

"Aman!" his father said happily as he ran over to him. He picked up his son and embraced him tightly, but Aman pushed himself clear.

"You must get away father! Or else..." the sentence was cut off and the boy went silent.

Amec looked at the body to see that a dark spear went through both of them. It faded quickly as it was made of energy, and Ema came walking towards them.

Amec and Aman fell to the ground and struggled to get back up, but she was already upon them.

"Ah, so this is the father of such a cute child," she said with an extremely convincing warm smile.

"Please, leave us alone, we did nothing to you and wish to be left alone," Amec managed to say, holding his wound.

"If I were to leave you all alone, my life would be so boring, so I kill you all for some entertainment, among other things..."

"What do you want?" Amec asked again.

"Just what every girl wants, some fun," Ema replied. She grabbed Aman by his leg and tossed him aside. "I think I have plans for this one."

Amec could see the blood pooling beneath him, and the world was becoming darker and darker.

Ema placed her hand on Aman and began whispering softly to herself. As she seemed to finish, darkness began to envelop the boy. It faded and he stood up. His back turned to Amec.

"Aman, please be okay," Amec said through his dazed state.

Shards of darkness seemed to rip out from the boy's body, and darkness enveloped him again. Now he stood up tall, an entirely different being.

His body was a full shadow, like that of Meso, but he was an even more nightmarish form, as his limbs seemed more like the branches of a tree. They were also freakishly long. His eyes were two white circles that broke out from the darkness, and what could have been his mouth looked like a white zigzag line drawn across his face.

"So this is how it must be like to have a child of my own!" Ema said as she put her hands together and smiled.

"Aman," Amec called. "Do not leave me Amec," he said, his voice fading.

"He's already dead, so that means that now means he's mine! All mine!" Ema replied. "I think I'll name you Ichor."

Amec now found himself trudging though the endless sands of the desert, as if he had awoke from a bad dream.

He looked up blankly and directly at the sun and frowned, then kept walking, his understanding dimmed.

"I will find Aman," he whispered. "Must find Aman."

CHAPTER 37

Freelancers

One would have seen the group of people that walked down the road and thought them to be a small army, all armed and ready. And it truly was an odd mix up of people, but adventurers were always odd. The previous day, they had escaped Deneaux by sneaking out under the walls and through secret entrances, then met up at one point and walked down.

They all walked in groups, rather than all together. Jane, Turner, Dianne and Gregory made one group, then it was Adele and Kilan, and finally Jor and Lyra in the back. Noch and Alice said they would be leaving for somewhere nice, or would stay in Deneaux. Dodecagon said he would go back to his cave to rest and regain his strength.

Jor bumped Lyra on her arm, and she staggered a bit to the side.

"What the hell was that about," she asked as she rubbed her arm.

"Didn't mean to tap you so hard," Jor said. He was wearing casual clothes instead of the Deneauxic armour, which comprised of a brown long shirt with a belt and brown pants with a cloak. Lyra was dressed similarly.

"We're two completely different sizes Jor, I'm a speck and you're a freakin' giant. Your tap is like being smacked by a damned bull," she replied.

"I'll take note of it," Jor said. "It's just that you're always lost in thought."

Lyra exhaled calmly. "Just being in the forests is relaxing by itself, the falling leaves and the sound of the shaking trees."

"You should see how it is in Denhoec, nothing but snow and ice unless you're on the tundra lands, and that place is grey."

"Can't imagine a forest like that," Lyra said. "I've never been away from the greenery of the forests."

"And just when I thought that you were just a box of nails, you're a pillow Lyra," Jor said with bellowing laughter.

"Do you want this pillow to cut you?!" Lyra shouted.

"Pfft, cut me. I know you like me too much."

"I do not!"

"Come on Lyra, I know you really and truly like me, you just don't want to say it nearby any of these guys."

"No, I don't."

"Well does it make it easier that I like you?" Jor asked.

Lyra stopped and saw that the group ahead of them were staring to set up a camp.

"Well, I suppose we could, I mean I could do with a walk, j-just so I wouldn't have to help pitch the tents. Want to come Jor?" she asked.

"Why not, it's not like I've been walking all day already," Jor said as he put his hands behind his head.

Jane looked around as she took up a wooden peg.

"Where's Jor and Lyra?" she asked.

"Probably on some wild adventure in an attempt to ditch work," Adele said.

"Wild adventure is right," Kilan giggled. She was dressed in a short black robe with a cloak.

Adele elbowed her side. "You have a dirty mind for a servant of Eros."

"What do you mean? Two lovers go off alone in the forests..."

"I still think they are ditching work."

"Well they better get back from whatever they are doing before they miss lunch," said Gregory. "Right Dianne?"

Dianne's mind seemed to be far away and she turned to Gregory as she snapped out her trance.

"Sorry, something's just a little odd."

"What do you mean?" Turner asked. He was wearing a black surcoat over his chainmail from his regular armour, and carried a simple round shield.

"It's just that something seems off, like something is unbalancing the soul energy of the area," Dianne said.

"We may need to have up more lookouts tonight," Turner said. "That means less sleep. Kilan, go get those two."

"Why do I have to go get them?" she asked.

"You're the smallest in the camp, so we may not particularly need you right now," he replied.

Kilan folded her arms and went off.

Lyra and Jor walked through the evening forests together. Jor once or twice had hit his head on a branch or tripped on a log while Lyra seemed to glide about easily and happily. Jor had never seen her smile like how she was now.

"So you really like the forests here?" Jor asked finally.

"Yeah, they always help me relax," she replied in a calm voice. "Don't the trees just fascinate you?"

"Trees? Fascinate me?" he said, trying to understand.

"Well, don't you ever wonder why nature is so wonderful?"

"I've actually never tried really..."

"Shhh, listen," she told him. A breeze blew through and shook the trees gently.

"I suppose this is why I was called a wild girl. Good thing I'm not with my parents in Deneaux, because if I was, I would be in some tight long dress sitting at feasts for hours on end."

"You'll visit them at least?" Jor asked.

"Why should I?"

"Well—you never know when you might lose them, like how I lost my mother."

"Oh..." Lyra replied. There was a silence between them, but another gentle breeze set the trees to motion, lessening the tension.

Jor realized that Lyra took his hand. He looked down at her and she smiled softly at him.

"How do you go on with such a terrible loss?" she asked.

"I can go on because I know she would want me to, and I have too much already to give up," he replied. "You and the others are what help keeps me going."

"Well, it's good to see that I'm needed for once."

They stood in silence for a little longer, but no wind seemed to come.

"You know, this may be the closest I've gotten to a girl ever," Jor said.

"And this is the closest I've gotten to a boy who likes me," she replied.

"Well I don't know what to say," Jor said, blushing

"Well I know what to do," Lyra replied. Her lips came closer to his as she spoke, and at that instant there was a short gasp.

The two stepped back and Jor began to animate an orb of soul energy in his hand. Lyra had pulled out two belt daggers she kept.

"Who's there?" Jor called.

"It's Kilan!" she said as she walked forward with both her hands up.

"Oh, you had me thinking that there were bandits," said Jor.

"Did you see anything?!" Lyra asked.

"See what? I'm pretty sure there's nothing to look at in the middle of a forest," she said with a wink.

"Tell anyone and I swear I'll..."

Kilan cut her off. "Or you'll what? Everybody knows you like each other, no need to hide it."

Lyra put her hand over her forehead and let out a deep sigh. She then shook her head and glared angrily at her. "I was just examining a bee sting on his face! You know, wasps everywhere? It's a forest."

"Yeah...bee sting?" Jor said weakly.

"Come on sealskin, we have to get back to camp."

"Wait," Kilan said, and they stopped.

"What?" Jor asked.

"I'm sensing some energy around here, and it's not normal energy."

"So what could it be then?" Lyra asked.

"If it's the worst case scenario, it may be a monster of some kind, but I believe it's just a pile of latent energy in the environment."

"It's energy," Jor said reassuringly. "Now let's go."

The three of them walked into the camp to see that there was a simple soup being cooked in a pot over the fire.

"There you are Jor, you'll be the first guard tonight," Turner said. "Along with Lyra."

"What?" Jor asked. "I thought you only needed one lookout.

"Not when there might be strange things on the loose. Besides, you two skipped setting up camp so you have to have some kind of retribution."

"Alright," Lyra said with a sigh.

"Come, get a bowl and sit," Dianne said. "Gregory cooked up this mystery soup himself."

"I'm not sure whether it's a curse or a blessing to not know what I'm about to eat," Jor said as he sat down on the ground and took up a bowl.

That night, everyone went to sleep except for Jor and Lyra. They would stay up for a few hours until it was time for a switch.

The moon shone brightly that night, and that made things a bit easier.

"I guess there won't be much to talk about tonight," Lyra said.

"True, unless you want to talk about...you know," Jor replied.

"I want to sleep tonight Jor," Lyra replied simply.

An hour passed and there was no sign of intruders, so naturally they both began to relax.

Until they heard the growling.

It was somewhat lion-like, but it seemed to echo out in every direction.

"Lyra, hand me my short sword," Jor told her, his eyes still darting through the trees.

She quickly gave it to him and he held it tightly.

"Swords won't save you mortal," a ghostly voice echoed.

Lyra drew one of her long daggers and got near Jor.

"Neither will staying together," the voice added.

"Who's there?!" Jor called. "Show yourself coward!"

"Are you sure mortal? I have been known to instil great horror in men's heart, and on more occasions men have died at the mere sight of me."

"Better hope I don't take your head off with all those threats your making," Jor shouted.

Out of the dark came a ghastly being. It had the body of a lion, the tail of a scorpion and the head of a man. The face was so atrocious and monstrous that Jor fell back upon seeing it. It was twisted and thorn, broken and put back together again by other patches of skin. He smiled and showed many sharp teeth.

"Get away!" Lyra screamed.

The beast stepped forward. "Or what? You'll attack me?"

Jor got up and energy began to form up in his hand. "Ekriksi!" he commanded.

The ball flew towards the creature, but it simply moved its head to the side to dodge. It moved closer.

"Everyone, wake up!" Lyra shrieked.

The beast soon faded into the shadows as the others could be seen leaving their tents.

Lyra rocked herself slowly as she refused to release her grip on the dagger.

Jor sat with his head down on one of the logs setup around the fireplace.

"So what did you guys see that was so terrifying?" Gregory asked.

"A monster, a horrible monster," Jor could only manage to reply.

"I-It had the body of a lion, and the tail of a scorpion, and the head of a..." Lyra burst into tears at that moment. Jane put her hand around her shoulder.

"Don't worry, you can rest now," she said.

Jor stood up angrily. "How the hell do you expect us to sleep while that thing is around? I can't rest till that thing is dead!"

"Well we can't go for it at night, we'll look around in the morning," said Turner.

"And what if it tries killing us during the night?!"

"We'll have people on watch."

"That...thing...said it could kill men if they looked upon him, and the amount of things he had on him that could kill us..."

"I think that may have been a Manticore," Dianne said, cutting Jor off. "They aren't the most pleasant kind of beast."

"So how do you kill them?" Jor asked as he turned to her.

"It's not that hard really, just kill it like you would any other monster."

Jor picked up his great sword and slung it over his shoulder and looked into the forest. "I'm going."

"You're sure as hell not," Turner replied equally.

As Jor began walking, he felt a firm hand on his shoulder.

"We'll go after it in the morning," Turner said, trying to sound as calm as he could. "You and I know better than anyone that we make the best team, and no Manticore could beat us together."

Jor let a small smile go across his face. "You're trying to make me sound strong. That's just how I got my brothers to do what I wanted. I'll stay, but first thing tomorrow is when we're leaving."

"Anybody else plan on coming?" Turner asked.

"No telling how strong that thing will be," Gregory said. "I'll keep watch in case anything weaker comes to the camp."

"So everyone else will watch the camp?" Jor asked.

"We won't interrupt on your boy's day out," Kilan said. "Besides, better to keep Jor and Lyra away from each other."

"Shut up you stupid cat!" she snapped at her.

"That's enough for the night, Gregory and Adele will take next watch," Turner said, and the two sighed.

CHAPTER 38

The Battle for Fel Hall

Several Fox in chainmail wielding halberds, swords and crossbows ran silently through the light brush near the tree line. They could clearly see the wooden walls of Fel Hall through the dim light of dawn.

"We need someone to scout the inside of the city," Zen whispered. "Any volunteers?"

"I wanna go," Alda whispered in reply.

"No, you'll make too much noise, these men are light on their feet, even with armor on."

"I can be light on my feet if I wanted!"

"No, I will walk in, with Mark and my sisters of course, but you all stay in quick reach of the city," Akina said.

"Do you know how dangerous that will be for you?" Will said. "They'll try and tear you apart, even worse if Toxotes and Dasimay are in there."

"Even better if Toxotes and Dasimay are in there."

"This recklessness will be the death of you," Zen said. "I have seen many men die that way."

"A Chief must be willing to die for her people, just as my father had."

"Then may the good Divines be with you," Zen said.

The Main Hall was abuzz with activity, as an on-going feast was made to the current chief, a fat Fel merchant ready to give out gold to all that would aid in his rise to power.

The door flew open, and the hall instantly fell quiet.

"Who is the nice, giving fellow that has been keeping my throne?" Akina asked suddenly with a loaded crossbow in hand

The merchant, upon seeing who was at the door, shouted for the guards, but as he did, a Fen and another Fel dropped the unconscious bodies of the makeshift militia.

"Please don't hurt me," the merchant cried as she approached. She continued until she stood before him, and he dropped to his knees and kissed her feet.

"Filthy rat, you dare take the throne without even having the ability to fight for yourself. My Father would have killed you," Akina snarled.

She kicked him away and stood before everyone.

"I am Akina Akin, daughter of the Great Chief Akin, and proud Chief of Fel Hall!" she exclaimed.

The nobles and other high officials were caught off guard by the powerful entrance of the once weak ruler, and were only able to bow down in awe.

"So we've retaken Fel Hall," Mark said as he bowed his head. "Now all that's left is to fend off Dasimay and Toxotes if they come."

"When they come," Akina corrected him.

"That's not a good line of thinking," Illeth said.

"What do you mean, I want to face them now, and maybe we'll be able to find Kinigos."

"Seems we may get that chance," Kullskash said. "We have visitors."

Will and several other Fox soldiers rushed into the Halls, panting hard.

"What is it?" Akina asked.

"The two Divines are coming," Will managed to get out.

"We'll fight them in the fields to the West of the city; I do not want a massacre here again."

Toxotes sat on a throne of vines atop a small hill, Dasimay at his side.

"Look at the city, my city," he said. "Taken over by that wretched spawn of Akin."

"Do we get to sack it again?" Dasimay asked. Toxotes put up a hand.

"We won't, yet. Look," he pointed to the bottom of the Hill to see Akina, Mark and Will.

"Well, if it isn't my lovely sister, you have grown, haven't you?" Dasimay said.

"I'm not here for you Dasimay, I'm here for him," she said, pointing her dagger at Toxotes.

"Oh no, I'm so terrified I might cry like a little girl," Toxotes mocked. "I should probably kill you where you stand for even looking upon me."

"I should have you write me a formal apology for looking at my city, but we don't get everything that we want," Akina replied equally

"Your city?" Toxotes asked, somewhat confused. "This is my land, and that is therefore my city, whether you claim it or not."

"Then show me your proof of ownership," Akina challenged.

Dasimay pulled Toxotes over and whispered in his ear, "Why are you playing along with her, just kill her and wreck her precious city."

"I have a better idea. I'll destroy the city and all her friends before her, then maybe torture her a bit and kill her, slowly and painfully."

Over by Akina, the same whispering was going on.

"Akina, I really don't think you should be making threats like this," Mark warned.

"I agree with Mark," Will said. "He could destroy us with the snap of his finger if he wanted."

"And he won't, now get back to the city, quick," Akina said.

"And leave you out here?!" Will exclaimed.

"Toxotes hates me, not the city. If we can defend the city, he'll get tired and go after me."

"And what if you get killed then, huh?" Will asked.

"At least I'll die protecting my Hall."

"Well Akina," Toxotes said, turning to her. "Seems we're going to your Hall after all."

Will and Mark were already far off, riding towards the city.

"I would rather you not," Akina said.

"Too bad little sis," Dasimay said as she stood next to her. "But we're going."

A black circle with different markings glowed under them. Black energy began to surge up around them and they appeared on top of the main Hall.

"Do you see all this Akina?" Toxotes asked.

"Clearly I can," Akina said in a stating-the-obvious tone.

"Ishis Pyro Ekriksi!" Toxotes commanded, sending a large fireball crashing into a building.

"Why'd you do that for?!" Akina shouted.

"Because I own it, and because I own it, I will destroy it!"

"Over my dead body!"

"Soon Akina, soon there will be a dead body," Dasimay said. She picked her up and tossed her over the roof of the hall. She created a whirlwind below to cushion the fall.

Fireballs soon begin dropping out of the sky, and a burning arrow slammed into the wooden gates of the city's walls. It erupted in a heavy explosion, tearing a large hole within it. Ants began surging out from it, sending the nearby civilians into a panic.

A hand was extended to Akina, and as she looked up, she saw it was Mark's.

"Come on Akina, you can't fight a battle from there," he said.

She got up and surveyed the scene. It was surely morning, but the sky was dark from the black clouds overhead.

"We're going to need to take care of those ants," she said. "Those imps are said to be more dangerous than they look."

"Well I can't find Will, and I'm not going to look for him myself."

"Get more men at that intersection! Don't let the ants get through! More crossbow ammo over here!" Will shouted at men in different directions. They were trapped in the pottery district of the city, and they were forced to set up barricades in the street and post crossbowmen in the houses.

"Sir, the North-Western barricade is down!" a Fox soldier shouted. "The next barricade doesn't have enough men to withstand another attack!"

"Then get more men posted there!" Will shouted back. He turned to several men hauling a cart full of crates. "Take it to the eastern building, the men there are low on ammunition!"

"Ants!" a soldier screamed before being slashed across the neck by one.

Will drew his rapier and raised it in the air. "They've broken through, everyone, on me!"

Several Fox soldiers jabbed at the first line of ants with their pikes and halberds, but their numbers increased and they began to overwhelm them. At that moment, Will and his men charged in, hacking at the horde of ants with all they had.

"Crossbowmen, volley!" he shouted at the top of his lungs.

A heavy stream of bolts could be seen flying overhead and they crashed into the ants, killing many of them. Before they could reload though, another horde was rushing towards Will's men on the ground.

"Force them back to the barricades, then close them!" Will commanded.

"Won't work, my scouts say that have flooded the streets and alleys near the two destroyed barricades," the field commander said to him.

"Can we flank them?" Will asked.

"Only if the Eastern and Northern streets are clear, which I seriously doubt."

"Commander Will, the North-Eastern barricades are under attack by a large horde, we're holding on but barely," a soldier said as he approached, blood covering his arm.

"You're wounded, you need to get to the medic," Will told him.

"I can't sir, my unit is already three men short," he said before running off.

Will hacked down an ant that approached him and turned back to the commander. "Go follow him, I need someone watching that barricade."

He turned back to the battle at hand and charged in, rapier still drawn.

"I can't see a way through this," Kullskash said, watching the ants intently from the balcony of the inn.

"We'll have to, Will and his men will surely die if they stay bottled up in there," Illeth replied.

"And then what happens when we get trapped in there?" Zen asked.

"We hack our way through!" Alda exclaimed. "My bloodlust is already kicking in!"

"We will break through that," Mark said, determination set heavily in his voice.

"And break through it we shall," Akina said. "Where are your soldiers Kullskash?"

"They're about, I'll have to find a way to rally them," she replied.

"Why now cry out for them to rally to you?" Zen asked. "Worked pretty well in the deserts for me."

"I doubt they'll all hear me, this is a big city you know."

"WARRIORS OF FEL HALL, UNITE UNDER YOUR LEADER KULLSKASH!" Alda shouted at the top of her lungs.

The other held their ears in discomfort.

"That set my ears to ringing," Illeth said.

"Yeah, thanks Alda," Kullskash said sarcastically.

"Warriors of Fel Hall, unite!" one voice shouted.

"To arms, to arms!" another exclaimed.

"Rally at the square, our leader will surely be there!"

"That was totally worth losing my voice over," Alda said hoarsely.

Kullskash stood on the side of a fountain at the square, looking at her troops intently.

"This looks like the full army. Now we'll have some fun," she said, and they shouted in reply.

"Today our proud chief has retaken the throne, but now our city is once again under attack by the evil Divine Toxotes. We shall fight harder than we have ever fought, and we shall do it the name of our chief, our country, and for Kinigos!"

"For Chief, Country and Divine!" the soldiers replied proudly.

"Now, we charge for the pottery district in a flanking sneak attack. Our new allies from Fox Hall need us," she pointed her spear in the direction of their intended targets. "And help them we shall!"

Will hacked endlessly at the horde of ants, men on either side of him being cut down by the ants' dark blades.

"What the hell are those?!" a soldier shouted.

Will kicked away and ant and saw at the edge of the barricades that a new enemy were approaching.

The shadows of the soldiers that died during the wars in Den.

They were a mixed group of Fel, Fox and Fen, and were staring intently on their living counterparts.

"Everyone, they're stepping it up!" Will shouted. "Form up!"

The men formed several rows, the first with halberdiers and swordsmen, the second with pikemen and more halberdiers and the third with reserve troops that would take the place of their fallen comrades.

The undead warriors surged forward, lunging and killing several of the men in the front row. The pikemen lunged back, but their attacks were deflected easily.

Will jabbed at one of the undead warriors, and they deflected easily like that of the pikes. They swung in reply but Will blocked and lunged again. It pierced the shadowy exterior of the being and it disappeared in a black mist.

"Fall back to the buildings!" he commanded.

The troops did so, charging into any of the nearby potteries and sheds.

Will shut the door behind him and pushed several heavy crates in front of them.

"We need help, and fast," he said.

"Where is the Fel army?" a soldier asked.

"I don't know, but what I do know is that they're probably getting ready to push their way through those hordes," Will replied.

"CHARGE!" Kullskash commanded, pointing her spear to the ant horde.

Warriors flooded the area, from houses and alleys they came, then in one great push, they collided with the horde. It was flanking at its best as even more warriors came through other smaller alleys to the ant hordes. Longbow men began to position themselves in the houses and porches directly above their enemy, raining on them arrow after arrow.

"Alda, are you ready for battle?" Kullskash asked.

Her eyes had already turned red, and she was losing herself more than she usually did. "I'm always ready for battle."

The two charged into the horde, Kullskash swinging her spear and Alda making wide arcs with her battle-ax.

Dasimay and Toxotes stood atop the Hall, watching the battle unfold before them as if it were a play.

"Look at them Dasimay, they're trying to fight back," Toxotes said, humoured.

"It almost looks like they might win," Dasimay commented. "But we have thousands of those ants; no way they'll survive a ten year siege."

"You're sickening," someone said from behind them.

They both turned to see Mark and Akina standing before them.

"What makes us sickening?" Dasimay asked. "The fact that we cannot be defeated?"

"That fact that you find war and destruction enjoyable," Mark replied.

"What? That's the most enjoyable part of life! Don't you mortals love taking each other apart?"

"I would love to live in a world where I don't have to worry about it, but frankly I don't. But if we were to get rid of you two, that would make the world an even better place."

Dasimay's bow animated in her hands and at the same time Akina drew her two daggers. Mark and Toxotes already had their longbows ready.

"This is not the kind of fight someone as frail and limp as you would survive," Dasimay said to Akina.

"And this is not the battle where you stream endless threats from your mouth," Akina replied equally.

Toxotes and Dasimay fired several rapid shots, but Akina was able to glide away from them. Mark raised his bow and fired, but missed.

"Pyras Ekriksi!" Toxotes commanded. The medium sized fireball rocketed towards Mark, but he managed to roll out of the way. It crashed onto the roof of the Hall, leaving a hole.

"Katastrofi Toxon!" Dasimay commanded. Several white arrows began to float above her, and then flew towards Mark and Akina.

"Down!" Mark shouted as he grabbed Akina and went through the hole in the roof. They both landed inside the attic of the Hall. It was filled with old war relics, and unneeded items.

"We need a plan of action Akina," Mark said. "We can't fight a Divine on brute force alone."

"Then let's set up and ambush," she replied. "It worked for me when I captured you."

"Very funny."

Dasimay and Toxotes came through the roof and looked about the dark attic.

"Still as dusty as I remembered it to be," Dasimay commented.

"Don't start getting sentimental on me," Toxotes said.

"Pyras Ekriksi!" she commanded. Several nearby crates and display cases went up in flames. "Don't worry, I hated this place."

Akina sat quietly, her normal short bow ready with an arrow. She turned to her side to be paralyzed.

There it was, the arrow that killed her father.

She froze up, unable to stop the flow of memories, the sense of inadequacy.

And fear.

"Ready Akina, Dasimay and Toxotes are coming," Mark whispered. He noticed that she was still, and called to her again.

"Akina!"

"I can't do this Mark," she said without looking at him. "The same arrow that pierced the heart of my father will pierce mines, and black blood will again flow on the floors of the Hall."

"Akina..." Mark noticed now that they were getting closer. "Get to your senses, quick!"

"Father, why couldn't you be here to fight this battle while I stayed in my room like I always did? Why did you leave me alone with an entire country to rule?"

"Damn it all," Mark said to himself as he shot out from behind some piled crates. He fired but the arrow was simply caught be Toxotes and burnt away in his hands.

"You're horrible at this game," Toxotes said as he turned to him.

Mark turned to see Akina still in her frozen state, then as he was about to turn back to Toxotes, a firm hand went around his throat.

"Now where is that little girl you're always with?" Toxotes asked.

"As if I would tell you..." Before he could fully finish, the grip got tighter.

"Why wouldn't I kill you? Answer me this."

"You wouldn't kill him," Dasimay said. "Because I'm sure Akina is watching, and if we beat the spirit out of him before we kill him, it'll break the poor girl's heart."

"Okay then Dasimay, we shall torment him," Toxotes said. He tossed Mark to the side, knocking down several heavy crates that fell on him.

Dasimay walked up to him and kicked him in the face. "Where's Kinigos to save you now?" She kicked him again. "Where's your precious Eros to revive you?" She kicked him even harder. "Where's your precious friends?" She slammed her foot into his snout, and it began to bleed. "Where's your Chief to save you?!"

Mark grabbed her leg before she could go again and sent her crashing into a display case. He pulled himself up and turned to her, but he felt a searing pain in his back and lurched forward. He turned to see Toxotes tossing a fireball between his two hands.

"It takes a lot of courage to hit a man's spouse in front of him, just be ready to take punishment afterwards," he said. "Pyras Ekriksi!"

Mark side stepped the attack and slammed his fist into Toxotes' face, though to little effect.

"Don't think this is over yet," he said.

"This is over," Toxotes replied. He grabbed his throat and picked him, then tossed him again across the room.

Before Mark could even get his bearings of where he was, he felt Toxotes' rock solid fists slowly crushing him with each strike.

"You should be thankful that you get to die by the hands of the Great Toxotes," he said.

Mark grabbed one of his fists and punched back in reply, but Toxotes merely ignored it and hit him even harder.

Dasimay got up from where she had hit the glass display case and saw that she was cut up. She frowned at the idea that she was actually bleeding.

She realized now that she could feel Akina's presence, and began moving to where she could be.

She turned a corner to see here there, grief stricken and frozen by the sight of the arrow.

"Lovely, isn't it? The arrow shot by the greatest archer in the land is what killed our father. I'm proud to be honest, aren't you?"

"Why do you enjoy his death?" Akina asked, confused.

"Because when he died I knew you would be in line, and such a pathetic being isn't even fit to be ruler of her own sad life, that is why you must die too."

"I don't want to die like father."

Dasimay opened the case and held the arrow between them as if it were a rose.

"This black stone is said to be the weapon capable of killing a Divine in a single hit. Our father was no Divine, so this arrow was supposed to instantly destroy him, but somehow he kept on going."

"He did, and he died right in front of me."

"I'd like to say he held on just to see his daughter one last time, but he probably just wanted to see if he could get his last moment of pleasure with the tavern girls or servants."

"Why Dasimay, why do you torment us, what is your goal?"

"To see you suffer."

"But why me..."

"Because you were father's favourite after he kicked me out of the family! I was supposed to be chief, me! But you just had to be the child of his second wife, and therefore next in line, not me! I mean, you hardly even knew how to read much less rule a kingdom, but yet you went on, and no matter how much dumb crap we put in your way, your 'friends' would always come to the rescue, encouraging and loving you like no one else but father could!"

"And your jealous of me, the same one you call pathetic and useless," Akina said, her voice rising.

"I could never be jealous because you never deserved the things you got!"

"Don't tell me a damn thing about what I deserve!" Akina shouted back. Dasimay took a step back as she did. "I deserved to be loved by father, because I loved him back, and my friends are always there for me because they know I will extend that same love when possible. And one thing I do know is that if I'm ever staring death in the face, Mark would shield me from it, staring back at the void with equal conviction, unlike that dog Toxotes that will hide behind you while you wreak havoc on my people, MY PEOPLE! You're jealous because I have and deserve everything, and you have and deserve nothing."

Tears began to roll down Dasimay's cheeks, and she balled her hand into a fist. "You don't know anything Akina! And soon all that you deserved will lie in ashes!" She swung at Akina, but she grabbed her hand.

"Just go Dasimay, and we won't have to fight like this, and then maybe, just maybe you might have something," Akina said.

"Never!" Dasimay shouted as her other hand went to get her dagger. Akina grabbed her head and slammed it into the display case, then threw her back and kicked her into a pile of crates. Dasimay tried to get up, but saw a spear and picked it up. Akina came up to her, and she lunged, but the attack was deflected easily.

Dasimay rolled to the side and got up, letting both her palms face Akina, "Pyras Ekriksil"

Akina side-stepped the fireball and grabbed her by the arm. She tossed her on the ground and walked towards her.

Mark, now bloody could see Dasimay on the ground. He and Toxotes' hands were locked, and neither seemed exactly able to overcome the next quickly.

He noticed that Dasimay was holding up her hand as Akina approached, but couldn't figure out why.

"You can't win, you cannot survive, I can't let you!" Dasimay said.

"I must survive, for the sake of my people," Akina replied.

Dasimay's hand began to glow with a nearly black aura. "The obsidian arrow doesn't think so," she said with a smile.

Mark twisted Toxotes' arm with new strength and slammed his fist into his face. He stepped to the side from the unexpected blow.

Mark charged forward and pushed Akina out of the way, and as he did, the obsidian arrow flew past, driven by Dasimay's energy.

"Let's move Mark," Akina said. They both ran to the ladder that led to the Main Hall, but as they neared it, Mark fired several shots off.

Three arrows landed in Toxotes' back, and he shouted in pain.

Dasimay got up and picked up the obsidian arrow. "Toxotes, we're killing her, now!"

"What happened my dear?" he asked her, seeing her bloody face.

"Akina thinks she's better than me, she says I have nothing," she couldn't stop the tears from flowing as she said it.

Toxotes moved to embrace her, but she pushed him away.

"I want her dead, now!"

"Then we'll kill her."

Mark and Akina ran through the hall when Akina stopped him.

"Mark," she said.

"What?" he asked.

"You—you promise to love me and support me no matter what, right?"

"This may not be the time..."

"Answer me!"

"We all love and support you Akina," Mark said hastily.

"And do you love me?"

He stopped and answered. "You know I love you Akina, and nothing, even death, will stop me from doing so."

"Good, because we may be facing death," Akina said as she turned to face Toxotes and Dasimay.

"Well if I'm going to die, at least it's with you."

All four of them held and arrow ready on their bow strings, staring at one another with a steady glare.

Will jumped as he heard heavy banging on the door. He grabbed his rapier and stood on its side, ready to stab at anyone who came through.

"Any Fox men in here?" a voice called from outside.

"Who's there?" Will asked.

"Zen Zeran," he replied.

"Open the door up," Will commanded his men.

Outside the battle was raging, but Will, Zen and the other soldiers were able to be clear of it.

"So I suppose we have flanked them?" Will asked.

"We have, and Kullskash and Alda are going wild out there," Zen said with a smile.

"Now I'm sure we're winning. What happened to Akina and Mark though?"

Zen's face darkened. "They're taking on Dasimay and Toxotes."

"B-But they're Divines!"

"Still, I don't think they'll be taken down like that."

"So they plan for us to fight a battle while I'm worried sick about them?"

"Don't worry about them, their fight is their fight. Just clear the district and we'll think about taking the Hall."

A new horde of ghostly warriors and ants came in, walking slowly and menacingly for their enemies.

"Let's win this war," Zen said as he drew both sabres.

Will, Zen and the Fox troops charged in, ready to continue battle.

Three arrows slammed into the wall next to Akina in a rapid succession, and she swung around and fired.

Dasimay managed to tilt her head out of the way and fired.

Akina rolled behind a chair, and as she did, the nearby wall lit up in a heavy blast.

Mark raised his bow while Dasimay was distracted, but an arrow flew past him and he ducked back behind the chair.

Dasimay looked about searching for Akina, but couldn't find her. An arrow soon flew past her, grazing her skin. She heard Toxotes let out a shout of pain, and she turned and saw an arrow in his leg. The second he reached for it though, another slammed into his arm, and he cried out in pain again.

"How dare you harm my poor Toxotes!" Dasimay shouted as she looked about. No one else was in the room but them now. "Damned cowards, always running."

"I haven't felt this much pain in years," Toxotes moaned.

"Hurry up, before they get away!" Dasimay said.

"Do you not see the arrows in my body?"

"Pull them out and let's go!"

"But it'll hurt!"

"And I don't give a damn whether it hurts or not! You'll feel better once Akina is dead!"

Mark and Akina ran down the stairs in front of the hall.

"How long can we keep up this game?" Mark asked, panting.

"As long as it's needed. I know we can't fight them with brute strength, so we'll use as much tricks as we can," Akina replied.

The black circle from earlier appeared over the ground of the square in front of the hall, and Dasimay and Toxotes appeared in it.

Dasimay had the obsidian arrow drawn on her bow string, and she smiled manically. "Looks like I win Akina."

"No, you haven't won yet," she replied.

"What makes you say that?"

"Because I'm better, haven't I already told you that?"

"You won't be better when this rips through your heart."

"Tch, even in death I'm still better, I mean, I'll be remembered as a legend for years to come, and you'll just be another speck in history."

"Keep talking and you'll be history!"

"I already am history," Akina said with a bow.

"Dasimay, don't let her get to you," Toxotes warned.

"She'll miss either way," Mark said.

"You, shut up before I have to rain another set of beatings on you!" Toxotes shouted at him.

"You're really stepping it up Toxotes, now you're actually fighting for yourself instead of sending your servant girl."

"Shut up! Both of you just shut up!"

Akina spread her hands and stood straight. "Or what, you'll shoot me? I'm right here."

Will and Zen hacked through the lines of spiritual warriors and ants, aided by the troops from Fox Hall.

"How much of these things are there?" Zen asked.

"Hundreds," Will replied briefly before ducking to avoid an attack by an ant.

Zen hacked through several more ants until he saw an axe swing towards him. He bent back, the blade only grazing his nose.

He got back on his feet to see Alda in front of him.

"Alda, it's good to see you," he said.

"Nice to see you too Zen," she said, the aggressiveness of berserker mode still in her voice.

"Where's Kullskash?" he asked.

"Over there, taking part in the gaining of glory!"

Kullskash seemed to be in a berserker mode of her own, stabbing and beating back at any opponent with her spear. Many of the Fel warriors could be seen at her side, fighting just as fiercely.

"Are you ready to make the push for the Hall," Alda asked Will and Zen.

"My men need to get the hell out of here. Let's go!" Will said.

"Kullskash, we need to get the wounded out of here!" Alda shouted to her.

"Okay then, warriors of Fel Hall, charge!"

There was an echoing cry from the warriors as they turned and charged wildly into the enemy.

"Well, what are you waiting for, you scared?" Akina asked.

"Dasimay, relax, do not fire a hasty un-aimed shot," Toxotes warned again.

"Never! Akina Akin dies today!" she shouted as she released.

Akina watched as the arrow came towards her. Time seemed to slow as she watched the sharp obsidian projectile fly towards her.

"Tahitita!" she commanded as she turned to the side and grabbed the arrow by the feather on the end of its shaft.

"You messed up again, Dasimay," Akina said. She quickly fired the arrow, and it slammed heavily into its target.

Dasimay closed her eyes, as if awaiting the horrible pain that seemed to take Divines when they are struck by obsidian.

But there was no pain.

"GAH, NO!" Toxotes shrieked in pain. The arrow was firmly planted in his chest, right in his heart.

"Oh no, Toxotes," Dasimay managed to say as she dropped to her knees beside him.

"Help...me," he said, reaching out with his hand.

"No Toxotes, you can't be dying!"

"I am damn it! Can't you...see...I'm losing energy...help me you fool!"

"What do I do," Dasimay asked frantically.

"Give me your energy, and I may be revived."

"B-But, I'll die if I do that."

"I don't care about you, I never cared! You were just a tool for me to use, now as you're told and help me!"

Dasimay got up and dropped her bow, her hands over her mouth and tears streaming down her face.

"All those years we spent together, all the nice things you told me, everything you did was just to keep me beside as a tool?!"

"Are you stupider than you sound? Help me!"

"But, why?"

"Because I don't want to have to go out and fight on my own...Ow... Pain is too much for me!"

"No, this can't be happening," she said to herself over and over.

"It is," Akina said as she dropped her bow and drew her daggers.

"You, you did this!" Dasimay shouted as she turned to her.

"I think that's pretty obvious."

Akina charged forwarded and lunged with both her dagger at Dasimay. She blocked with her obsidian bow. Akina swung again, and the blade slashed across her cheek. She slashed again, cutting and Dasimay's body repeatedly.

Dasimay was able to block with her bow again, but Akina kicked at her knee. She stumbled a bit, then was sent sliding by Akina's fist.

"Dasimay, this all ends here," Akina said as she walked slowly up to her.

"Sorry, but Meso disagrees," a voice said.

Lane fell from the sky and landed next to Dasimay. She picked her up and held her over her shoulder.

"Who are you?" Akina asked, puzzled.

"I'm just a friend of Meso, and you are...?"

"Akina, now give me back my sister."

"No can do, Meso needs her to be able to take control of Cardia since Toxotes is about to die, bye bye."

A black circle came around Lane, and she disappeared with Dasimay.

"All this, and I still don't have my sister back," Akina said, a hint of sadness in her voice.

Toxotes reached for his bow with the last reserves of his strength, but Akina stepped on his hand. With the last of his strength gone, he turned into a pile of obsidian bones.

"Akina, look!" Mark called as he ran to her. "Thus sun is beginning to shine again!"

She looked up to see the black clouds overhead diminishing.

"I suppose it is."

Zen, Alda, Will and Kullskash were near the final line of ants and spiritual warriors when they began to burn out in the sunlight.

"That makes our job easier," Will said as the last of the ants burnt up. "I need my wounded to be cared for, hurry!"

"Seems we achieved glory again," Zen said to Alda.

Her eyes returned to normal colour and she smiled brightly at Zen. "We did, didn't we. I think it's your little charm that made me fight so fiercely."

"Come on, it's just a clan emblem made out of some kind of stone," Zen replied.

"I'm a Breach-Breaker Zen, meaning I can break through any Fort, Castle or even enemy lines, and showing a symbol of your clan in battle is considered good luck."

"I'm glad you feel that way about it. But what now?"

"I don't know, but now that the battle is over, I'm looking to hang out with my best friend."

It was now late afternoon, and many of the warriors had flocked to the square to celebrate the victory. There was great happiness as men, women and children danced around a large bonfire. Minstrels played music and sang, and the cooks had prepared a large feast.

Akina sat on top of the stairs of the Hall, watching what was happening.

"Akina, shouldn't you be down there?" Mark asked as he approached her. He had just come from checking up on below.

"I should be, I just wanted to talk to you," she said.

Mark noticed she was averting her eyes and blushing. "What you wanted to talk about?"

"Well, you see, it's about my father and the stuff he did, and..."

"Are you talking in code?"

"No, I'm just trying to say, well ask, well..."

"For the love of the Divines, what is it?! You're killing me with anticipation!" he said, not able to stop himself from smiling afterwards.

"It is obvious that she won't get it out in this life time," a voice said from behind them.

"Kinigos!" Mark and Akina exclaimed in awe.

"In the flesh and speaking. You act like you've seen..."

"Yes a ghost, we know," Mark said.

Kinigos got up and he embraced to two of them, causing Akina to suffocate a bit.

"Don't forget about me," Eros said as she approached.

Akina ran up to her and embraced her warmly.

"I see my little warrior is in shape still. I'm still a little weakened from when I had to revive you."

"Sorry, I wasn't so careful," she replied a bit meekly.

"No problem, though we may have to make this quick. My energy is slowly running out, since I can't stay too long in this world."

"Why?" Akina asked, sounding a bit hurt.

"The new King of Deneaux, King Albain, has outlawed my worship, and most Divines can only stick to this world when they are worshiped."

"Oh...But what if you were to be worshiped here?"

"Well that was actually why we're here. Since Toxotes was defeated, all I had to do was travel to his realm and rescue my dear Kinigos."

"Yes, that's all good, but what were you trying to say to me Akina?" Mark asked.

"Too much people around now, maybe I'll ask you later."

"No such thing as later," Eros said sternly to her.

"Don't worry, Akin can say it himself," Kinigos said.

A ghostly being appeared before them, and as he turned, he smiled at Akina.

"There's my favourite girl," he said.

Tears streamed down Akina's face. "Father!"

"I wish I could have been at your side through all this, but if I was alive, you would have never had needed to go on this journey."

"That's true. I'm just glad to be able to see you again."

He turned to Mark now. "I know my time here is short, so I'll go straight to my purpose. Yellow-Mark Blunt-Claw, mighty archer of the low Fen a fellow saviour of Fel Hall, would you be interested in marring my daughter?"

"What?!" Illeth and Kullskash exclaimed as they walked in.

"This is grand, now I get to speak with all my beautiful daughters," Akin laughed.

"Remember, I can't keep you up for too long," Kinigos said.

"Yes, yes. Now what do you say Mark?"

"I-I don't think I'm ready for all that!" he said, still getting his head together from the sudden question.

"Well, you can't blame a guy for trying, but you're the only one I trust."

"Then maybe one day, Chief Akin," Mark said meekly, rubbing his head.

"Alright Kinigos, let me return," Akin said. He slowly faded, a warm smile on his face as he watched his young daughter, or now, proud chief.

"That's so sweet of him," Eros said.

"I know," Akina said. "But why not Mark? We're a happy couple already?"

"I don't know, I just feel that we may be facing something bigger in the near future, and I don't want to die knowing I left you alone in the world."

"Well maybe you'll change our mind eventually. Let's go to the party and have fun while we're still around. And I just remembered we have to meet at Den Hall later to remake the council, and repair the city, and..."

"You know, let's just go to the party," Kullskash said. "Illeth will handle those things."

"I'll do what? I'm just her advisor!"

"Well I'm the head of her army, therefore I'm not smart enough for those things."

"Okay," she replied in defeat.

"See you Kinigos and Eros..." Akina didn't get to finish as she realized both of them had disappeared in the commotion.

"I guess they had to leave for their reunion," Mark said.

"I guess so. Now let's go to that party, it won't get good unless the chief is in it!"

CHAPTER 39

Turner and Jor vs. The Manticore

Turner had a crossbow slung across his back and a sword at his side. He wore a shield on his right hand, fearing that they could be attacked at any time and he'd need to defend quickly.

Jor was dressed in the same clothes as before, as he didn't feel the need to be armoured. He had his longbow and great sword slung across his back.

"You sure you're going to be alright?" Jane asked them both.

"We'll be fine," Jor said. "We faced down a squad of Raiders together, nothing else should be a problem for us."

"You were half dead when you came back from fighting the Raiders," Lyra said.

"Pfft, we're stronger now, and no four legged weirdo is gonna beat us today," Turner replied.

"Alright..." Jane said uncertainly. "Just be back by nightfall."

"We may be still searching for that monster by nightfall," Jor said.

Jane kissed Turner and Jor on the cheek. "Just please be careful, Dianne says manticore are far stronger than they look."

Lyra punched Jor on the arm in turn. "Just make sure you don't hurt yourself too bad again. I'm not too good a healer."

"I'll be fine," he said, rubbing his shoulder. "Now let's stop with all the farewells as if we're going to die. You're all scaring me."

Jane glanced sidelong at Lyra as they walked off, and Turner the same to Jor.

"This doesn't seem well," Adele said. "I can sense amenity returning to them again."

"They had troubles with each other from before?" Dianne asked.

"You should have seen them in Deneaux. They were a drama off stage," Kilan said.

It was now mid-day and Jor and Turner were still walking through the forests.

"Why doesn't it show itself," Jor said, clearly frustrated.

"Maybe it only comes out at night," Turner said.

"I feel insulted that you call me an 'it'," a voice echoed throughout the forest.

"Damn it," Jor said as he drew his great sword.

"Show yourself," Turner called. "I have ways to locate my enemies and they usually don't like it"

"Soul tracking with an attack? Shameful, utterly shameful."

"Alrighty then, Fos Ekriksi!"

A spark of light energy went flying into the forests, then disappeared.

"It's that way?" Jor asked.

"Yep," Turner replied. "Let's move."

As they moved slowly in the direction of the soul attack, they heard echoing laughter.

"That thing is getting annoying," Turner said.

"Pyras Ekriksi!" a voice commanded.

A large fireball flew towards Turner and Jor, but they were able to avoid it, but just barely.

"What the hell?" Jor said to himself.

"Pyro Barrage!" the voice went again.

"Move Jor, this attack isn't a joke!" Turner shouted.

Many fireballs began slamming into the ground and nearby trees, catching easily on them.

"Ekriksi!" Jor commanded in reply. The white sphere of energy animated into his hand, and he fired it in the direction of the incoming attacks.

"Apo Pano Ekriksi Barrage!"

Blasts of soul energy came flying through the forests, tearing down any trees in their path.

"How strong is this guy?" Jor said as he ducked behind a rock.

"I don't know, but he isn't a regular monster, that's for sure," Turner replied.

After several minutes, that attacks ceased.

"Have you had enough?" the voice asked.

"I could take a few more rounds if you want," Jor called. Turner elbowed him in his side and he decided not to continue his taunting.

"Perhaps I can give you several more rounds. Pyras Ekriksi!"

"Good job big mouth! Now we're pinned again!" Turner shouted.

"Sorry, okay!" Jor replied as he turned and watched the fly fireballs. They were going somewhat downhill, but were all scattered and never hit the same points.

"That's it!" Jor exclaimed.

"What's it?"

"Those attacks aren't aimed, meaning it's just trying to scare us!"

"That bastard is doing what?!" Turner exclaimed as he got up and charged up hill. Jor followed.

Turner dodged and blocked the incoming attacks with his shield, while Jor ran directly behind him.

"What are you doing?" the voice said, somewhat confused.

"Coming to finish you!" Jor shouted back.

The two of them ran until they broke through the heavy brush at the edge of the forest.

They now saw that they stood in a clearing before a cave. At the center of the clearing was the Manticore.

"I see you've come to my humble abode. Please make yourself at home," he said, his face stretching out awkwardly into a dark grin.

"Watch yourself, we're in the position of power this time," Turner said as he pointed his sword at him.

"Position of power? I'm the Manticore, one of the half-blood of Edafos."

"Half-blood?" Jor asked.

"Half mortal—half Divine," the Manticore replied, the grin growing unnaturally wide.

Jor stepped back, his face showing a flash of fear. He realised it at that instant and pulled his cloak halfway over his eyes. He unslung his bow from his shoulder and reached for an arrow, but not before the Manticore could get to him first.

"Pagos Ekriksi," he commanded. A large shard of ice flew towards Jor, and his eyes widened as it neared.

Turner came in at the last second and the ice shattered on his shield. Jor, seeing his chance, readied his arrow and fired.

The Manticore jumped out of the way, and was about to open his mouth to give a command when Turner charged up to him. The Manticore was only able to dodge his swing, but he looked up to see another arrow come his way.

He leapt back again, and commanded while in mid-air. "Pagos Wall!"

A wall of ice grew up towering high above them.

"What, too scared?" Jor asked. Turner elbowed him.

"Keep your guard up, never know when he might..."

"Pagos Barrage!" the Manticore commanded angrily.

"What was that everyone used to say? Hoplon!" Jor commanded.

A white wall appeared before them this time, the hundreds of shards of ice slamming into it and shattering.

The wall of ice dropped as their shield fell.

"Damn," Jor said as he lurched forward.

"You okay Jor?" Turner asked.

"Used up more energy than I should have...but at least we're alive."

"Not anymore!" the Manticore exclaimed, his face showing only pure madness. "Pyras Barrage!"

Jor dropped his bow and drew his great sword at that instant, and as the fireballs flew in, he swung at them, making them dissipate into invisible energy.

Turner did the same, blocking and slashing away every and any attack.

"Pagos Rain!" the Manticore shouted.

Ice shards began falling out of the sky, falling point first onto the ground.

"Pagos Barrage!" the Manticore shouted again. More shards of ice appeared around him, and they flew towards Jor and Turner.

Turner hopped to his left to avoid a falling shard, and then to his right to avoid a flying shard. He put up his shield as he saw another shard coming from above. It hit his shield hard and twisted his arm back.

He dropped backwards to the ground and cried out in pain, but he was soon cut off as he saw a large shard coming his way.

"Turner!" Jor cried as he ran towards him. His eyes began to glow, the right was red and the left was blue.

He swung his great sword in a mighty arc, slicing the shard of ice in two.

"Come on then Manticore, I'm waiting for your next move!" he exclaimed in a rough, grizzled voice. He picked up Turner's blade.

"Holding a great sword in one hand and a sword in the other? You must be incredibly strong," the Manticore joked.

Jor took a simple step forward and broke into an instant charge at that second.

The Manticore, caught completely off guard, leapt back, only to barely avoid the one-handed overhand slash made by Jor. The ground shattered when it hit.

The Manticore gasped, and opened his mouth for another command when a blade ran down the center of his face.

He cried out as he felt his tongue split at the front. Blood also began to run down his face.

Black blood.

"Don't cry yet, I'm not done!" Jor shouted. Turner's sword was covered slightly with blood.

"You can't be normal!" the Manticore shouted.

"I'm not," he said as she charged forward again.

The Manticore watched as the steel cascaded and glistened before him, then felt surprisingly light.

The ground was covered with black blood, and Jor sat down in it next to the Manticore.

"It's done," he said.

"Yes, you have bested me, now if only I could congratulate you on your victory…"

"You're sucking up way too much, now I know you're still plotting," Jor said. He looked up and saw several large shards of ice surrounding him.

"Pagos Ek…"

Before he could finish the command, Jor put his hand on his face. "Pagos."

The ice energy flowed down from Jor's arm and froze the Manticore's body. The ice extended all the way up to the floating ice shards, creating what looked like pillars.

Jor got up and turned to the cave. Something seemed important about it but he had completely ignored it during the fight.

Turner had gotten up and approached Jor, but was taken aback by his discoloured eyes.

"You look like the Manticore just returned to life," Jor said jokingly.

"Hm, those bad jokes mean you're still somewhat normal," Turner replied.

They both entered the cave, and were both appalled at the volume of items they found. There were many bags of gold, and a horde of weapons and armor. There was also a chest, but something looked different about it. It was covered over by a red fabric, but between the torn patches and holes, you could see it was black.

"Well I'll be damned. It looks like a chest made of obsidian," Jor said to himself.

"Might as well look inside," Turner said. "You go on ahead and open it. I think my arm's broken."

"And the money?"

"Considering we're traveling with teenage girls, we may need more than that," Turner replied jokingly.

"I'll get it then," Jor said as he lifted the chest up and put it over his shoulder with nearly no effort.

Turners' eyes widened at what Jor did, but Jor only raised an eyebrow in reply. "It's light, that's all."

Jane poked at the fire they had set up with a stick, waiting patiently for Jor and Turner to arrive.

Lyra was sitting across from the fire, holding her legs close to her chest.

"They plan to stay like this?" Gregory asked.

"Seems so," Adele replied.

"We got three entities inbound," Kilan called.

"Three?" Lyra and Jane asked at the same time.

Out from the dark of the forests came two glowing eyes, one blue and one red. It seemed to be on the body of something as tall as a man.

"Ready yourselves!" Adele shouted as he picked up his staff from a nearby tree.

Jane and Lyra both stood up. Gregory drew his sword and Dianne stood beside him, her hands emanating an icy mist.

"That's no way to greet your wounded warriors!" Jor boomed mightily.

"Raiders!" Adele shouted as he stepped back.

Turner and Jor now became visible to them, and the group relaxed.

"Jor, you're back!" Lyra exclaimed as she ran to him. She stopped in front of him as she saw his discoloured eyes.

"Don't worry, I'm fine," he said.

Before he could finish, she had already embraced him.

Jane moved to embrace Turner, but he put up his hand.

"Watch it there, my arm is a little broken," he said, but soon regretted.

"It's broken? We should get it checked out and treated, we should probably get to a nearby town..."

"Jane, we're in the wilderness, meaning no villages or towns nearby. I'm going to have to work out some field first aid," Lyra said as she took up a flat piece of wood and some bandages from one of the bags they carried.

Dianne came up to Jor while everyone else was either resting or getting things ready.

"So what's with your eyes?" she asked.

"My what?" Jor replied, absentmindedly.

"I'm asking why your eyes are different colours, and why are they glowing a little."

"Oh I don't know, they just got like this and have been stuck like this for a while now. Only thing I'm feeling is a bit of regret for killing that Manticore so quickly."

"Why is that?"

"I just wished I got a longer battle...like on that would last for hours, or days, or years..."

"Are you okay Jorigsveer?" Dianne asked.

He grabbed his head and lurched forward, grunting through grit teeth.

"Jor?" Adele asked as he ran over to him.

He soon recovered from his state and looked at him, both his pupils red. The glow had also disappeared.

"My name is Jorigsveer, boy, do not discredit me with this 'Jor' pet name," he said sternly.

"Excuse me?" Adele said as he raised his eyebrow.

"A...Deneauxman...a man of harmony..." Jor said to himself.

"Are you okay Jor," Adele asked again.

Both his eyes turned blue and began glowing slightly.

"I don't think so, something feels wrong," he said. "I feel like when my mind was taken over by that Nordic Divine in Keels."

"Seems your ethnicity is clashing," Turner said from where he sat. Lyra was still wrapping the bandage around the splint and his arm.

"What do you mean by that," Jor asked.

"Well, those glowing blue eyes of yours are only used by Deneauxmen. It's an ability called 'Noble heart'."

"It grants you the ability to deflect many physical attacks at once, though it takes up a good deal of energy," Adele added.

"And I guess the red is that berserker mode Alda had whenever we got into a battle," Jor said.

Dianne nodded. "So it seems you have two enemy races inside of you fighting for control and you're stuck in the middle of it."

"Well that's fantastic..." Jor said sarcastically to himself.

CHAPTER 40

The Tower

Before Kinsei was a barren field of small craters and bumps. It was void of any kind of grass or vegetation, as well as fauna. It was also chilly here, as this was the site of a major battle in the 300 Year War.

"So Wintella, you've fought so viciously with ice soul that you're icy touch is still here. I would kill for that kind of power, and it seems that that is what I'll get," he said to himself.

A hard wind blew on his face, and he noticed that frost had gathered around him.

Don't underestimate you're opponents, the wind seemed to say.

"You sense them too?" one robed figure asked the next.

"Yes, and it seems we may have to put a good bit of effort in eradicating them."

Jor and the others watched appalled at the empty field before them.

"Seems this is the beginning of the end," Jane said.

"Come on Jane, I'm sure you'll find something you like to do in the tower again," Dianne said.

"Only in my dreams. Let's just hurry up and get there."

A Perialite man stood before a crowd of robed people. He seemed to be in his late forties, and there was a symbol of ice on the back of his robe, a snowflake.

"It seems we may have another fight on our hands today," he said. "And this time, it's with a Daimon."

There was fearful muttering throughout the crowd, but they became silenced when the man spoke.

"I'm not forcing anyone to risk their lives today, I just wish to have some assistance if we cannot negotiate with the beast."

"I'll go," said one young man with a fire symbol on his robe, a twisting flame.

"Then I'll go too," said a girl with a symbol of a white flame, the symbol for neutral soul.

Several others spoke up after them, and the man made a determined smile.

"You all are serious about this tower, and I will make sure that we get rid of this threat, whether it be by peaceful means...or the means in which only daimons may understand..."

The small group of adventurers walked across the cold, empty plain. After all these years, the craters almost seemed natural.

"An odd place isn't it?" Jor said.

"I know right. Looks like a whole nice place that got wiped out," Gregory replied.

"And that's the problem with ice, it's cold and unforgiving, and the land is always devoid of life when it comes. And worst of all, people hardly survive the winter," Jane said sadly, almost to herself.

"Sounds like you've had some bad experiences with the cold," Turner said.

"Well, more of dreams than experiences."

"But dreams are as important as experiences," Lyra said wisely. "Why not tell us about it?"

"Well," Jane said, taking in a deep breath. "When I was eight, I started getting strange dreams and visions, but I could at first only see light blue and white, and then being taken over by a powerful chill. Soon, I began to hear the shouts of men and the clattering of armor and weapons, and after that I could hear rowing and the sounds of the sea."

"I see where this is going," Adele said.

"And not too long after, while I was training at the Tower, I passed out. I awoke before an army of thousands of warriors, beside me was a woman in the same colours I described before, and as she put up her hands, an even greater chill overtook me, and all the men before us were frozen solid. The blocks of ice shattered with the men, and frost took me over.

"When I awoke the room was covered over by frost, and I was pale and almost frozen. I was sick for the next few weeks, but the chills stopped... until I fought against Meso in Deneaux. I felt I was at the end when a cold hand reached out to me, and I felt as if nothing happened to me previously."

"Sounds tiring," Kilan said. "I'm glad I don't have to deal with all that cold."

A chilly wind blew hard against them, setting Kilan shivering.

"How on Edafos could you be shivering? You have fur!" Adele said.

The rest of the group laughed.

"Hey, Fel Hall is regular temperature, nice and mild, but here is as cold as hell...cold as whatever I can compare it too," she said, trying to amend her last statement.

"Hell can be a cold and unforgiving place also," said a voice.

Everyone looked up, and it was Dianne to give the first cry of surprise. "Kinsei!"

He smiled evilly at them from the small hill he sat on.

"How long has it been, Dianne and Gregory? Your absence had made the sanctuary such a boring place. Delta is still shaken up over our valiant leader's death, and I have also been mourning recently..."

"We have to get out of here," Dianne said to everyone with growing urgency. "We have to get out of here now!"

"No little one, you must face punishment for killing my poor Keelia, my corrupted Angel!"

Jane, Adele and Kilan stepped forward.

"You all want a fight? Then you all will die! Pyras Barrage!" Kinsei commanded as many fireballs lit up the sky.

"Teresa Barrage!" Adele commanded in reply, filling the sky with dark sphere of energy.

"Pagos Ekriksi!" Jane commanded, forming a large shard of ice before her.

"Erebus Pertusus!" Gregory commanded as he fired a thin black beam from her hand.

"Anemos Makhaira Barrage!" Kilan commanded as many clear coloured daggers animated around her.

"This is gonna light the place up," Turner said. "Best we get behind some cover."

The three of them ran and slid in the dust until they made it behind a small bump in the landscape. They could hear the sounds of heavy blasts that shook the area.

"Pagos Ekriksi!" Jane commanded again as she tossed an ice shard after Kinsei. He shattered it with the back of his hand, and charged towards her.

"No you don't, Erebus Ekriksi!" Adele commanded, sending a mass of dark energy slamming into Kinsei's side.

"Don't let him near you," Adele warned. "He is almost unbeatable in close combat!"

Just as Adele said it, he saw a kick coming his way, and was only able to duck at the last minute.

As Kinsei realised he missed the kick, he saw a quick follow up kick come from Kilan.

It sent him sliding a bit on the ground, but he instantly hopped back up.

He turned to see Gregory approaching with a soul sword and shield.

Kinsei kicked high for his neck, but he ducked and lunged. Kinsei was ready and already had his other foot in the air, and in one movement he slammed his leg into Gregory's shield.

He spun out of the position and landed on his feet. He knew now that he couldn't fight them unless he knew where each one of them would come from.

"Anemos Barrage!" Kinsei commanded, sending a heavy gust across the field.

The others were knocked back by the sudden attack, but Kinsei chose it as the perfect opportunity for attack. He drew his sword and commanded. "Tahitita."

Kilan looked up to see Kinsei had appeared over her in a matter of seconds, and rolled to avoid is downward lunge. She got up quickly, but she saw the gleam of the blade across her face. She leapt back, but felt blood running down her face, her forehead cut.

Behind her was Kinsei, and she leapt again in another direction.

Kinsei was fast, she thought, almost too fast for her to catch herself...

She blocked the incoming strike with her dagger, the blade only inches from her hand.

Adele looked up and saw that she was in danger, but he was already feeling that he was weakening.

"The things I do for love...Tachista!" he commanded.

Kinsei felt a burst of energy crash into him, and went sliding across the hard ground, but even before he finished, he felt an iron fist slam into the centre of his chest, stopping him.

He rolled to the side as he felt the obsidian staff near him, barely avoiding it as it broke through the hard stone ground.

Gregory and the others got up and watched as the two of them fought. It was hard to pick up their movements at such speed.

But they knew, Kinsei had the energy to keep going, but Adele was running out.

Kinsei swung his large scimitar, but its arc stopped halfway as Adele unexpectedly blocked it. He leapt back, but felt a firm fist in his chest.

He spun mid-air and landed on his feet.

"Give it up," he said simply.

"No," Adele said as he limped forward, his great speed lost.

"Then I will have to end you," Kinsei replied as he charged after him.

"This is my last chance," Adele said. "Noble Heart!"

His eyes both began to glow blue, and he blocked Kinsei's heavy scimitar strike.

"Seems you're pulling all kinds of cards today," Kinsei said.

"I'll gladly use my whole deck if it means beating you. I've died once and I'm not too scared to do it again," Adele replied darkly.

Kinsei struck at every angle at Adele, but he blocked every attack easily. Every overhand, every lunge, every slash seemed to be deflected by Adele.

"Isn't anyone going to help him?" Gregory asked.

"Well, I'm trying to but I'm accumulating the right amount of ice soul from the environment," Jane replied. Frost was beginning to grow at her feet, and the area was getting chillier.

Dianne ducked behind the same bump Turner Jor and Lyra were behind and startled them.

"You don't do those things Dianne!" Jor exclaimed.

"Sorry, I just don't want to be stuck in the middle of all that!" she replied.

"Then I guess we'll all stick around here for a while," Turner said.

Adele weakly blocked each strike. Kinsei on the other hand, seemed to be enjoying himself.

"Are you feeling tired now?" he asked.

Adele didn't reply, but continued to block the blows with his staff.

"Come on Adele, just hold him for a little bit longer..." Jane said.

Adele's eyes returned to normal and he fell to the ground. As Kinsei raised is sword for a final killing blow, Kilan charged out from nowhere and slashed at him with her obsidian dagger.

Kinsei dodged it and tossed her aside, but she got up and out spread her hands, then closed her fists.

He turned to see many soul daggers fly towards him. He dodged the first two, but the next three dug themselves into his upper arm and thigh. He turned at that instant to see Kilan lunging from behind.

Though it pained him to do it, he side-stepped the attack, receiving a graze, but a graze from obsidian was usually deadly.

Black sparks and streaks of black lightning surged around the wound, and he fell to one knee. He quickly pulled himself up, only to find he was staring straight at Kilan.

"Aduro...Ekriksi!" she commanded tiredly.

Kinsei's eyes widened as he felt the heavy light burn into him. It sent him flying into the dust again, but this time he seemed to stay down.

Kilan wiped the blood from her face. "That's it? After all that brandishing and taunting of yours you're finished?"

Kinsei appeared over her, half his face covered by a mask. "I'm not done yet!" he shrieked in an otherworldly voice.

Kilan felt a heavy blow on her head, then darkness.

Gregory was about to charge up an attack when he saw a flash of darkness before him. As soon as he did though, blood flew from his chest, and he fell to the ground.

"Gregory!" Dianne shouted as she ran forward.

"No Dianne!" Jor shouted as he ran after her.

Turner looked at his injured arm and back at his friends, and then made his decision.

"Fos Ekriksi..." before she could even finish the command, Kinsei was upon her with his large scimitar. Dianne watched as she stared death in the face.

This can't be how it ends, she thought.

There was a heavy clanging of steal, and Dianne opened her eyes to see that Jor had stopped the attack with his great sword.

His eyes began to glow with separate colours again, one red and one blue.

"Dianne, get away from here before you get hurt. I'm about to go on a rampage," he warned in a grizzly voice.

Kinsei seemed to disappear and reappear before Jor, but he easily blocked the attacks. He spun mid-air and lunged down, but Jor stopped it with the broad side of his sword and leapt back. But in two simple motion, he felt like he had blocked a thousand strikes.

He landed, a bit unbalanced by the unexpected strikes, but swung in defence to the coming blow.

He saw blood fly and Kinsei leapt back, but not before charging forward again, issuing terrifying slashes complimented by his famous martial arts moves.

Jor made his way back and tripped in a crater.

It was a fatal mistake.

Kinsei lunged down at him while he wasn't prepared, but he put up his sword and blocked it. He fell to the ground and rolled, then quickly got back up, but as he did, he felt a heavy force under his chin.

Kinsei had given him a powerful kick, and Jor noted that a modest amount of blood began to pour from the sides of his mouth.

"You're good at this," he said.

"I'm perfect at it," Kinsei replied.

Jor shook his head. "No one, especially you, is perfect."

"We'll see about that," Kinsei said as he ran forward with blinding speed. Jor put up his great sword to block again, but Kinsei slammed his knee into it and sent it spinning away.

"Not so powerful without your sword," he taunted.

"I'm just as powerful."

Jor grabbed Kinsei's leg and slammed him into the ground, but Kinsei used his other the leg to kick Jor away. He got up and swung over hand for Jor, but he clasped his hands on the blade before it had a chance to slice him down the middle.

"You can't hold my blade forever," he said.

"I don't have to," Jor replied evenly.

A ball of light came flying out of nowhere and slammed into Kinsei's side. He moved over, letting go of the blade, but Jor was right there to catch it. "Thanks Turner!" he called without looking around.

Kinsei regained control over himself, but it was too late as he saw Jor coming towards him.

"Teresa katas…" he didn't finish the command before Jor came down upon him with an overhead slash, cutting his tongue.

"That look fits for you," Jor said. "You make me think of a snake more than anything else."

"Y-You'll pay!" Kinsei exclaimed with three high-pitched voices. The mask had fully covered his face now, and one large red eye was at the center of it.

Jor felt his hand twisted and realized that Kinsei had flipped him in a matter of seconds.

"Now you die…"

"Now you die!" Jane shouted in reply. "Dynami Yperano Pagos Hoplite!"

A giant spear made entirely out of ice formed above them, then in that instant it came upon Kinsei.

He tried to move away, but felt Jor's firm grip.

He pulled himself to the side in one last ditch effort, but the blade shredded apart his left arm completely. The ice crashed into the ground and broke into many individual pieces.

"Damn it…" Jane said as she collapsed.

Kinsei surveyed the scene. Everyone was down, but now he remembered that there were more people that were supposed to be present.

Lyra ran to where Turner and Dianne lay hiding.

"What happened?" she asked.

"Everyone is down, even Jane and Adele," Dianne replied.

"And we're next if we don't be quiet," Turner warned.

"Too late," Kinsei said as he stood before them. "Erebus Barrage."

Several dark spheres of energy flew towards them, but in an instant, Turner drew his blade with his good hand and hacked them away.

"You two need to get out of here!" Turner shouted.

"But what about you?" Lyra asked.

"I've been dead weight since my arm broke, you don't need me. Now go!"

Dianne and Lyra got up and ran but Kinsei was faster and appeared before them.

"Not so fast," he said, dark energy beginning to animate in his hand.

Turner seemed to surge forward with almost unnatural speed and slashed Kinsei down the center of his face.

The mask split, and a heavy knockback of dark energy sent he and Lyra flying. Dianne was unaffected since she was a daimon.

"Damn it," Kinsei said to himself as he stepped back.

"Kinsei…" Dianne said as she tried to reach out to him.

He fell to one knee and coughed up blood, then looked at her with eyes that showed only a deranged rage.

"Get away from me! Hephaestus Ekriksi!"

A large fireball lit up the sky above them.

"Please Kinsei, don't do this," Dianne said.

The mask returned, as well as the red eye in the center of it.

"Ah, much better," he said in relief. "Pain is something I need not feel or fear."

The fireball came down upon her, and she closed her eyes and awaited her fate.

Strangely though, she could only feel the heat, and not the burning of her flesh and following coldness.

Two robed warriors stood before her, holding up the fireball.

"What?" Kinsei began in awe. "Where did you come from?"

"None of your business daimon!" one of them shouted.

"May I at least know your names?"

"Our names are not important here, but if you must know, we are the students of the Tower."

"We?" Dianne said to herself. Kinsei thought the same thing.

He was only able to dodge to large shards of ice before a stone shot out the ground and slammed into his jaw.

He stepped back, but only met two literal iron fists on the hands of more robed figures.

He mask was cracked again, and he panicked for a second too long.

A shard of stone shot through the ground through his side, and he watched in horror as his blood began to flood beneath him.

He shattered the stone quickly and tried to get a grasp of the situation, but a powerful gust of wind hacked at his skin and sent him sliding a few meters.

"That's it, I can't fight like this," he said to himself. "I'll get my revenge when I'm farther from death."

He got up and began to run, and as he made his first step, he moved so fast that he almost seemed invisible to them.

The robed people cheered as they watched him retreat, but a few of them had ran off to tend to the wounded.

Jor awoke to find himself in a small room. It contained four bunk beds, and a small chest next to each of them. There was a window at the back of the room with a flower pot on the window sill.

He got up and opened the door, then looked out to see if anyone was there.

No one.

He began to move around the lobby area quietly until he met up with another door. He opened it and began to hear voices. He snuck out and moved down the hall until he found the source of the voices.

He opened the door slightly and saw several robed figures standing around a bed.

"You may come in," the tallest one said.

He exhaled and opened the door, and the man smiled at him. He was the same one who was talking to the others and organized the attack.

"Who are you and what's going on?" Jor asked.

"Don't you young ones believe in good manners nowadays?" the man replied.

"I'll have good manners when you tell me what the hell I'm doing here and where the hell my friends are."

"They are resting and are safe, I assure you."

"Where's Lyra then, I mean the elf girl," he said making it easier for the man to know of who he was speaking of.

"She's been at the main Hall of the tower for hours now," he said.

"Where's the Hall?" Jor asked instantly after the man finished.

"Just go down the staircase at the end of the hall until you reach the ground floor, go any lower and you may regret seeing what's down there."

"Alright, thanks old man," Jor said as he turned for the door.

"Jor...is that you?" Jane said groggily.

Many of the robed figures moved from by the bed as Jane got up.

"Finally my daughter, you are awake!" the man exclaimed as he embraced her.

"Jane, that's your father?" Jor said in surprise.

"Apparently so," she said wistfully.

Lyra frowned thoughtfully as she sat near a table on the ground floor. She couldn't tell how long she had been waiting for.

"Lyra," someone called from away.

She turned to see that Turner was approaching, looking a bit confused.

"Thank goodness someone is here," Lyra said as she got up. "Where's Jor?"

"I was gonna ask you the same thing and where Jane was."

"So you don't know where anyone is then?"

"Nope," he said as he sat down. Lyra sat back down next to him. They sat in silence for a few minutes.

"That was some pretty cool swordplay you had out there," Lyra said with a small smile.

"You really think so? Turner replied. "I was just trying to save you and Dianne's lives."

"Well yeah, you don't see much people able to do that with a broken arm. I mean that was just amazing."

Turner laughed a bit weakly. "I wouldn't call it amazing, I would call it desperate."

Lyra put her hand on his arm. "Come on, modesty doesn't get you anywhere with me mister, be proud that you could tell your kids and grandkids that you fought off a daimon with a broken arm!"

"They'll think I'm stupid then, is that what you want?" Turner replied jokingly.

Lyra winked and poked out her tongue at him. "I always figured you were a hard warrior, but you seem just as light-hearted as Jor."

Turner couldn't help blushing a bit. "Well, to tell you the truth, all the joking I do used to get to Jor and we used to fight a lot, but after fighting in Keels, we kind got used to each other."

"Well...I hope I can get used to you too..." Lyra said to him.

Turner raised an eyebrow to her, but she turned away briskly, realizing what she said could be interpreted wrong.

"Okay, what I meant was different from what I said," she quickly amended.

"Don't worry, I know what you mean," Turner said, trying to calm her. He himself was unsure what she meant.

Chapter 41

The King and the Chief

The sounds of heavy pounding could be heard from miles around. Trees could also be seen falling in the forests around Fel Hall.

Fel Hall was currently under repair after the large scale battle that occurred there not too long ago. Much of the walls and houses had been damaged or destroyed during the battle, and the bodies of those who had died were still being buried.

Akina watched from the top of the stairs of Fel Hall at the rapid repair done by the workers.

"This better be the last battle we have for a while," she said to herself.

"Should be," Kullskash said as she came from inside the Hall. "It's not like we have any more enemies."

"Yes but...what about those Raiders who attacked Keels?"

"The Deneaux military probably took them out by now, no way they'll let some foreign enemy destroy their 'sacred honour'."

"But still, they're not invincible Kullskash, anyone can be defeated."

"Don't talk that way Akina, the Men of Deneaux are our allies now."

"I know...but still..."

A bell was set to ringing at the front gate. That was the city alarm, and that meant some unknown or unexpected force was coming.

"Want me to ready the militia?" Kullskash asked.

"No, I can't risk more fighting, just get a few guards and meet me at the gates."

In a large horse drawn carriage, the King and several of his advisors were speaking. They had several large units of Deneaux pikemen and swordsmen, and a small unit of highly trained crossbowmen.

"That is why we brought this much men, in the case they fight," Albain said.

"They won't fight my lord, all these men are just a waste of our resources. You're already the most powerful mortal, why bring soldiers?" his advisor replied.

"To assert my authority over these...beast-men. After all, the only thing animals understand is fear."

"I thought you said we were going to assert our authority and keep our diplomatic status friendly?" his diplomat asked.

"I lied. I knew you would never agree to anything like conquering a nation, so I had to sugar it up, but it seems it got turned into a lie at the end." He opened up the side door and looked out to see Fel Hall come into view. "Oh, it seems these animals are smart enough to build walls."

Akina folded her arms as she watched soldiers come into view. She had Toxotes' obsidian long bow slung over her shoulder. She knew it would never make her look threatening considering it was bigger than her, but it served its purpose in combat.

The large carriage soon came into view, and when it finally came before her, Albain exited. He and two soldiers approached.

"Move girl, I wish to enter this encampment," he said without looking at her.

"You first disrespect me by not making eye contact, then you insult my city. Who are you to say such things?"

"He is the King of Deneaux!" his diplomat snapped as he approached her. "Who are you supposed to be?"

"The Chief of Fel Hall, and keep your distance, we have some of the best archers in this city." She nodded in the direction of two of the guard towers and two readied bows reached out from them.

"Impressive, they may not be as skilled as my crossbowmen, but still, impressive for a tribe of beats," Albain said.

Kullskash, Mark and Illeth came to the gate now with several militiamen behind them.

"Who's this?" Kullskash asked.

"King of Deneaux apparently," Akina replied.

Mark looked puzzled. "What's he doing here? Shouldn't he be heading to the capital for political business?"

"He should," Akina said, loud enough for the King to hear.

"Look here beast," Albain started angrily.

Akina nodded up to the bowmen, who were still ready.

"Listen, Chief of Fel Hall," he spat the title indignantly. "I've come here because the people of Den Hall seem to look up to you, despite the fact that you are not head of the council. That being said, you're basically in charge of the country."

"Well I'm not in control, you want to go on a diplomatic mission, then get your facts straight."

"Damn it! I'm not some kind of fool to look down on, I'm the King of Deneaux..."

"This isn't Deneaux," Akina said flatly, interrupting him.

That was the final straw for Albain. His face turned red and he shot off a fireball at one of the guard towers. The archer inside was able to escape the blast, but just barely.

"I am the King of Deneaux, the harsh equivalent being the King of both Northern and Southern Cardia! I have the military strength to own the world just about, and I won't have some little girl telling me what's what!"

Akina looked up at the burning tower, then at the archer. Several villagers carrying buckets were putting out the flames, while the others helped the archer up. She decided she would not continue insulting him.

"What is it that you want then, King of Deneaux," she said, looking away from him.

"That's much better," Albain said. "Now, on the terms of giving up Den Hall to the Empire of Deneaux..."

"What?! What is this that you speak about?!" Akina exclaimed.

Albain smiled sinisterly and chuckled to himself. "Don't you understand? I want you to give up the country and give it to me."

"And if she doesn't?" Mark asked now.

"I take it all by force."

"You really plan to risk the lives of thousands of your own soldiers to conquering other people's lands?" Kullskash asked in utter amazement.

"Once I get a hang of my powers, I would do it myself, but as of now, I'm still learning."

"But she doesn't have the authority to give up tor annex the country," Illeth said.

"Then give me Fel Hall, I'm not leaving empty handing."

"Go to the council," Akina said quickly. "Only they have the authority to give up Fel..."

"No! I know and you know that you have the power to sign it off!"

"But I can't give it up, I can't!"

"Aero," the King commanded, and behind her, Akina could her Illeth gasping for air.

"I believe that is your advisor, and sister?" Albain asked.

Akina turned to see Illeth struggling for air desperately.

"What are you doing?" Akina asked.

"Simply sucking the air from her lungs, now give up the Hall or she dies."

"No King, please don't do this!" Akina begged.

"Give up Fel hall."

"I can't!" Akina cried, tears beginning to well.

Illeth began to choke as she clawed at her own neck. "Don't give up... the Hall..." she managed to say.

"Yes you will, do it now, or she, and the rest of your friends and family here meet an untimely end."

"I'll give it up!" Akina said, but quickly felt numb after hearing what she had just said.

Illeth fell to her knees and gasped in as much air as she could.

Albain chuckled to himself again. "What kind of chief are you anyways? I risk the life of one of your followers and you give up the whole city. The people here are supposed to look up to you, but, that's what is to be expected from a mere child. You are a terrible chief, and will be remembered as the last one. The one that lost her country."

As Mark ran to her side, she wept loudly, unable to mask her sadness. He embraced her tightly, but it hardly helped.

Albain walked into the Hall and swept his hand across the view of the city.

"Now, diplomat, this is how you be a real King, you rightfully take advantage of your power and use it because you have it!"

Now, on to the capital, so I make annex this grand building area to myself!"

"Building area!" the diplomat exclaimed. "You can't just build over these people's lands. They aren't our enemies, as far as history goes, they are some of our greatest friends!"

"Are you telling me what to do?" Albain asked without turning to face him.

"I-I'm just advising you. The other leaders of Cardia won't like your actions."

"I don't care for the other leaders. I'll kill or capture them if they don't annex their lands. Didn't you know I'm taking over Cardia?"

The diplomat froze.

"Now, let's move out, and let's take our little princess chief with us."

A soldier slammed the back end of his halberd into Mark's head, and two other soldiers hauled Akina up.

"Mark! She cried. "Don't let them take me!"

Several halberds went up around Mark before he could act, and a ring of fire went up around Kullskash, Illeth and the militia.

"Oh, and I want her sisters to come with us, the rest stay here," Albain said.

"You can't do this damn it!" Mark shouted. "This is wrong!"

"I have the power. Everything I do is right," Albain said.

"Y-You can't take Akina from me!"

"I will my friend, because she is now my Akina."

Zen and Alda watched this exchange from afar in the attic of the Main Hall.

"We're going to need to stop him," Alda said. "I may not be as good a diplomat at most, but I know this kind of stuff can't go unchecked.

"I know, that's why we're going to meet up with Jor, Turner and the others. If they did all the things they said they did, then together we may have a chance." Zen replied.

"So what, we're going to Deneaux again?"

"Yeah, but we'll ride there on Kenta."

"They won't be there," a voice said from behind.

They both turned fearfully and saw it was Eros.

"How did you get here?" Alda asked, still surprised.

"That's not important, what's important is that Jor and his friends are North of Crill in a tower. Go there and meet them." Just as she finished speaking, she faded away.

"Seems we have a job to do. Let's get going," Zen said.

Akina looked sadly out of the side of the carriage they were in. The land was bright green and beautiful, just as it had always been.

"Don't worry my dear, soon we'll be out of this miserable jungle and in the lap of luxury at the pantheon castle," Albain said.

"I don't want to be in a castle," Akina replied. "And I'm not your 'dear'."

Albain held her chin and turned her head to face him. "As of now you are, and soon, you'll be my servant at the castle, doing my bidding."

"I don't want that," she said weakly, looking down.

"It's for the best you know, you get to have the honour of living in the Castle of the most powerful man in the world, and you may even get to be the first to have my child..."

"No!" she cried as she knocked his hand away. "I'm not doing in any of those things!"

"But you will, or your precious Hall, and your precious friend Mark goes to the sword."

Akina wept silently for the rest of the trip, curling into her own corner of the carriage.

Chapter 42

Life

The whole group of friends sat in the auditorium of the Tower. The chairs went back for many rows, showing that the Tower had many students, but it seemed that only a few teachers were there, along with Jane's father at the podium.

"Welcome, my fellow instructors. I feel this is a very momentous occasion, due to the safe return of my daughter," he said happily.

Many of them clapped, and a few cheered.

"And as a reward to the brave warriors who brought her here, I give them the privilege to join us as students, free of charge."

Jor and Turner looked at each other.

"I've never been to a school," Jor said, almost nervously. "What do they expect us to do?"

"Probably attend boring classes maybe," Turner replied.

"This is a lot more fun than normal schools, I'll tell you that," Dianne said to them.

"Yeah, I guess..." Jane said weakly.

"I know give you your soul robes, to signify your class, please come to the stage."

The group came up, and as they did, Turner and Jor approached Mr Pagos.

"Um, excuse me sir, but we may have a problem," Turner said.

"What is it, friend?"

"We don't particularly use soul, we're more warriors of the sword, soldiers," Jor said.

"So you have a commander to report to later then?" Mr Pagos asked.

"Well, a corrupt King has taken over in Deneaux, so we've been out of the job and adventuring around," Jor said.

"So you plan to leave us already?"

"No, no, we're just saying we may not be able to fully attend in the future," Turner said.

"No problem, many of our students come over for a few months and leave, so we have no problem with you leaving us every once in a while."

"Oh, well—I wouldn't mind getting that neutral Soul cloak over there..." Jor said as he went over by the rest of his friends.

"So...does Jane take the ice classes?" Turner asked.

"Why yes she does," Mr Pagos said, looking at him oddly.

"Oh good, then I'll take the ice classes..."

"Why not take light? I sense you are an avid user of it."

"That's more of a reason to leave my comfort zone."

Mr Pagos' eyebrows furrowed as he barred Turner's path. "What are you getting at, because I feel my daughter seems to have taken a liking to you."

"Oh, you've noticed," Turner laughed weakly.

"I have, and I may have to ask you to not play around her too much. She must attend to her studies and doesn't need some boy meddling with her."

"I can assure you, I've never meddled with your daughter, and I've been a good friend to her. Ask her yourself."

"I can't take her word for it, now, get a class or get out and leave for Crill. I heard there is some kind of fighting going on down in Crill, and you mercenary types seem to like that kind of activity."

Turner looked at him angrily.

"What are you going to do? Swords won't hurt me."

"I don't need my swords, neither do I need to start a fight," Turner said as he turned and grabbed the light class cloak.

Two days had passed since then, and everyone was starting to adjust to their new life at the Tower. Many of the Soul users, like Adele and Jane, had an easy time with classes, and sometimes worked as assistants to the teachers.

Jor walked tiredly into the lobby on his floor and sunk gratefully into one the soft chairs nearby.

"Looks like you had a hard time today," Jane said.

Jor was surprised to see Jane sitting across from him. "Looks like you had a rough time too."

"Every day is a rough day here," Jane said sadly. "It's even worse that Turner seems to be ignoring me."

Jor's eyebrows shot up. "Why, you two have hardly ever been apart since we came back from Keels, why would he suddenly start ignoring you?"

"I don't know, that's the problem."

"Well, I did see that Turner hasn't been all too happy since we got the cloaks, and he and your father seemed to be angrily discussing something at the time."

"Discussing what?" Jane asked quickly.

"I don't know, I wasn't paying attention."

"Do you ever?"

Jor opened his mouth to protest, but decided not to say anything.

"Sorry," Jane said after a short pause. "I just feel stressed."

Jor sat next to her and put his arm around her. The both of them knew each other for over a couple months now, and they were very close when Jor lived in Denhoec. He felt a need to at least try to lighten up the situation.

"You know if Turner sees you, you're dead right," she said with a small smile.

"Bah, Turner knows I would never take you from him. He wins any woman, remember?"

Jane chuckled at the memories of when they stayed in Deneaux, and the constant fights between him and Turner. Now though, they were like brothers.

"Now if he could only conquer his own problem and actually show up and talk to me."

"Well, I could talk to him..."

"You would!" Jane exclaimed, cutting him off.

"Hey, he may not tell me, so I might not get any results," Jor warned.

Jane hugged him tightly. "I'm sure you will, now hurry!"

As Jor exited the lobby, Lyra stopped him.

"Oh, hey Lyra," Jor said as he was about to go off.

"So, what were you doing in there with Jane?" Lyra asked flatly.

"Just talking to her," he answered. He was about to walk off when Lyra stopped him again.

"That hug didn't look like you were just talking."

"Wait, wait. Are you...jeal..."

"Hell no! I'm not jealous!" she exclaimed in a hush.

"You look and sound like it, and my uncle always said, 'if it quacks like a duck, and looks like a duck and moves like a duck, it's probably a duck'."

"I'm not a duck, I'm a person, and I say I'm not jealous!"

Jor laughed. "It's almost written across your face, look, J, E, A..."

"Jorigsveer Great-Blade, I am, and never will be jealous of anyone!"

"L, O, U..."

"Jor!"

"What's going on out here?" Jane said as she opened the lobby door.

Lyra glared at her and then at Jor. "Nothing," she said, and walked off.

"Don't worry, she'll get over it," Jor said, and he left for Turner's classes.

Turner and the light class teacher sat cross-legged in the center of the empty class room. Large windows were open there to let in the sunlight, and there was a view of the beaches of Crill from there.

"Now, I need you to feel the warmth of the sunlight," the teacher said, closing his eyes.

"Isn't that for fire Soul?" Turner asked.

"Well yes, but fire soul and neutral soul make light, so you must have full understanding of both. Now meditate..."

Turner closed his eyes and felt the warm of the sun on his back. He smiled a bit at how it felt.

"Now, doesn't that fill you with some kind of respect for light? It's what guides many through darkness, and without it, we could not survive."

"So I need to feel some kind of confidence to properly use light soul?" Turner asked.

"Correct! How did you come to that?"

"I had spare time, so I read up on some stuff," Turner said broadly.

"Well you keep it up, now let's get back to meditating."

After half an hour, Turner left the room, and turned to see Jor sitting on a bench outside.

"Hey Turner, can I talk to you?" Jor asked.

"What is it?" Turner asked.

"It's about Jane."

"What about her?"

"Well, she says she wishes she could see you more, and can't figure out why you refuse to talk to her."

"Don't worry why, just know I'm not allowed to," Turner said, a hint of anger in his voice.

"I need to know why, and Jane needs to too," Jor said, standing before him. "We're friends Turner, and I don't leave my friends behind."

"I'm not going to hurt Jane and tell her what's what."

"But not telling her is hurting her right now, and I don't want to see that happening.

"It's better she doesn't know, I'm telling you."

"So you're not gonna tell me then," Jor said.

"No, I can't, I'm sorry."

Jor exhaled. "Jane won't be too happy about that."

"I know, but I wouldn't want to hurt her feelings. It seems like no matter what I do, I'm still screwed."

Jor put his hand on Turner's shoulder and went on his way. Turner watched him go down the hall, then turned to go his own way.

"So he won't say," Jane said sadly to herself.

"No, he said he can't say!" Jor said quickly.

"Same thing, he probably doesn't like me anymore, or maybe he found a more interesting girl..."

"Not true, Turner would never do something like that, especially with you..."

"But you talk like you've known him from birth. How do you know he's not just off with someone else?"

"Because Turner would never give up an amazing girl like you, I know I wouldn't," Jor exclaimed.

Jane turned to him in utter surprise. "Amazing?"

"That's the first thing that struck me when I met you in Denhoec. Amazing, and as I got to know you, even that word couldn't describe you."

Jane chuckled softly to herself. "Is that really what you think of me Jory?"

Jor couldn't help blushing, realizing what he had just said.

"You sound like you want to go out with me," she continued.

"No, I'm just trying to say..."

"I've never heard anyone call me amazing, I always thought I was even more boring than average, but you think...that I'm amazing..." she said to herself.

"Lyra's gonna kill me if she hears any of this," Jor said. "I can already feel the cold steel of a knife in my throat."

"Let's not worry about her right now," Jane said as she sat down next to Jor. "I just want to hang out with my good friend Jor."

"Good, now Turner and Lyra will want to kill me," he said. "I really don't think we should be sitting so close."

"Don't worry about all that, we have enough to worry about."

"Worry?"

"I ran from this tower to escape from all the worry and stress of the classes. I hardly had any freedom at the time, but then I was free to do what I want and go where I wanted. Yes I may have had a few bad run ins and had to work hard for small amounts of food, but getting to see the world seemed to make up for that fact."

She ran her hand across Jor's cheek. "And it was during one of those run-ins that I met with someone special..."

"So you thought I was special..." Jor said flatly.

"Well, I just felt...safe around you for some reason. You just had that... well, Nordic confidence I guess. You just kept going no matter what happened, and if you felt like you had no purpose, you made one for yourself."

"I-I don't know what to say..." Jor said, inching away at the same time.

"Jor...I think I might..." she stopped herself from continuing.

"You think you what? Say what you're saying," Jor said.

"I think I've been in love with you, okay."

Jor looked at her with wide eyes, but she looked down.

"It's unfair you know, I like two guys. Seems kind of nasty, don't you think..."

"I'd be lying if I said that was a yes or no question. I can't answer it."

"Oh..."

"But you should like Turner, he's an honourable guy, even more so considering he's a Deneauxman. I'm half Raider, so I doubt I'm all that."

"You are all that, and more—I just can't decide."

"You'll have to go for Turner—"

Jane kissed him before he could finish, and Lyra happened to open the door slightly to check on them. She hastily closed it at what she saw, and was hardly able to believe it herself.

The next day, Lyra walked past one of the training rooms sadly. She heard the sound of tired grunts and it sounded familiar.

She opened to see Turner attacking a training dummy with his sword. His shield arm was still in the cast, but he hardly needed it to fight.

"Don't you think you should be resting with that arm of yours?"

Turner turned to her and smiled. "I couldn't go another day without practicing. I don't want to get rusty."

He returned to hacking and slashing at the dummy. Lyra noticed, despite having a broken arm, Turner still had some finesse when attacking.

"You're more skilled than you look," Lyra commented.

"Nah, I'm just always practicing," he replied. "You know, have you seen Jor lately?"

He heard muffled sniffling come from Lyra, and noticed that she looked down trodden.

"What's wrong?"

"Nothing," she said.

"Come on, you can tell me."

"No."

Turner put his sword back in its scabbard. "So have you seen Jor then? I wanted to know about him and Jane..."

"To hell with both of em'..." Lyra said to herself.

"Whoa, whoa, whoa, what was that?" Turner asked her. "And I swear, if you say 'nothing'..."

"Jane and Jor," she spat the last name. "Aren't on my good side."

"What did they do?"

"Jane used to be your girlfriend, ask her."

"Used to be? She still is."

Tears welled in Lyra's eyes, but she wiped them away quickly and only showed reticence.

"What happened damn it," Turner said. "No use in keeping it bottled up."

She took a deep breath and closed her eyes.

"Good grief, where's Adele when you need him. He's good with this kind of stuff..."

"I saw him with Jane. They were kissing..."

"They what?!" Turner said in complete awe. "Jane, and Jor for that matter, would never do anything like that, I know them!"

"I don't want to believe it either," Lyra said, trying to force back more tears. "But it's what I saw."

Turner frowned in thought. "I'll go have a talk with them then."

"Just don't fight," Lyra said. "I can't deal with the thought of anyone getting hurt over this."

"Don't worry."

Lyra passed sadly through the halls until she passed by a balcony and decided to get some fresh air. It had been a while since she's been outside she thought.

"Morning Lyra," Jane said as she and Kilan approached.

"Hello Kilan," she replied.

"I'm here too you know," Jane said.

Lyra ignored her. "So Kilan, what class have you taken up?"

"Neutral Soul, same as Jor," she replied.

"Oh," Lyra said as she bowed her head sadly.

"You okay Lyra?" Jane asked, the concern clear in her voice.

"I'm fine, now stop talking to me Pagos," Lyra snapped at her.

"Hey, what did I do?" Jane asked.

"You know what you did."

Jane's breathing got a bit faster. "What did I do?"

"You kissed Jor, that's what you did," she said in a low growl.

Kilan's eyes widened and her eyebrows went up. "Okay, normally I like to hear about this kind of stuff, but this is a little too much," she said as she ran off.

"I never kissed Jor!" Jane quickly defended herself.

"Once in the forests, and once here, and you look like you really relished that last one!"

"Okay, I admit to that first one, but not the second!"

"Don't act innocent! You're just a little harlot too scared to say you are."

"I am not Lyra, I don't know what you're talking about."

"I saw you Jane, I saw you at the door. You can't hide it."

Jane stepped back at this. "I-I."

Lyra punched her, but as Jane fell to the ground, she looked at her clenched fist.

"Jane, I'm sorry, I didn't mean to..."

"You didn't mean to? That punch seemed very deliberate!" Jane exclaimed, holding her cheek, though hardly fazed by it.

Lyra fell to her knees and embraced Jane.

"Why Jane, why?"

"I just couldn't decide, I know it was foolish, I just...couldn't decide..."

"Do you forgive me?"

"Of course I do Lyra, I know I somewhat deserved it," Jane said. "It's just both he and Turner seem special to me."

"And that is worth breaking my heart over? I know we aren't that good friends but..."

"No, I shouldn't have done the things I did, I'm sorry Lyra."

Lyra gave her a weak smile. "I'm sorry too."

Jor was walking towards a staircase on the ground floor when he heard Turner call him from behind.

"Hey Jor, I hear you've done something Lyra doesn't like," Turner said.

"Is that so..." Jor said nervously.

"Okay, I'm not going to play around with you, Lyra said she saw you and Jane kissing, did you or did you not do it?"

Jor saw that Turner wasn't in the mood for anything other than a truthful or straightforward answer.

"In the event that I did what you think I did, what would you do?" Jor asked nervously.

"Answer my question and you'll see what I'll do. Don't answer and I'll make you look like me." He saw Jor's eyes dart between his cast and his own arm.

Jor's nervousness went away and stood to face Turner. If anything ever happened, he knew Turner would have to tell him, so he felt a heavy conviction to do the same.

"Yes, I did what Lyra said. I tried to tell her, but we both failed at keeping away from each other," Jor outstretched his arm. "If you plan to break it, make it quick."

Turner chuckled to himself. "We won't be seeing neither Jane or Lyra for a while."

"Why is that?" Jor asked.

"I can't see them talking to us for a while, especially with Lyra and you."

"Oh yeah," Jor said, a bit sadly. "I doubt she'll forgive me after this."

Turner put his hand on Jor's shoulder. "Eh, we could do without them for a while, considering we'll be heading out to Crill soon."

"Crill? Why?"

"I just wanted to visit it, you know, see the great Crillic beaches everyone seems to talk about."

"Good, who are we taking along?"

"I was planning on bring Adele with us, maybe even Gregory. Once we're gone for long enough, the girls will miss us and maybe feel more accepting."

"Not Lyra," Jor remarked.

"Well, it's better than doing nothing."

C H A P T E R 43

Raid on Deneaux

It was a rainy day at the Pantheon Castle, and the Fel sisters and Albain were sitting at a table in his private quarters.

"So Akina, tell me, did you live in such a magnificent building in Fel hall?" Albain asked.

"Well, this Castle is quite big but...Fel Hall has its memories..." she replied sadly.

Albain reached his hand around her shoulder.

"Well now you get to make memories with me..."

"We don't want memories from you, we want it from our home," Kullskash said. Illeth had a fearfully look on her face from her sudden outburst.

"Well aren't you spicy," Caroline said as she entered. She sat next to Akina.

"So how is my favourite little Fel doing today?" she asked, playing with her cheeks.

"Depressed, and the rain isn't helping," Akina replied blankly.

"Then what do you want to do for fun?" Caroline asked brightly.

"Going back home would be nice..." Illeth said weakly.

"This is home now," Albain said.

"Ah ha, I know what we can do for fun!" Caroline said. "Akina can get us our drinks!"

"Drinks?" Kullskash asked.

"Wines and spirits of that kind, you know."

"But I don't drink," Akina said.

"Well today you start, and maybe that will get you in a more... agreeable mood," Albain said with a sly smile. He saw a flash of fear in Akina's eyes.

She quickly got up and went for the cellar.

She entered the dark, musty room filled with cobwebs and moss growing around the some of the leaked liquids. She was far past her fear of the dark and quickly grabbed a keg. It was heavy, but that hardly seemed to make a difference to her. Life was done for her as far as she knew. Neither pain nor embarrassment seemed to bother her.

"Hey, Chief," a voice called.

She turned to see a dark figure leaning on a wall.

"Who are you?" she asked.

"I'm Alcino, a friend of Eros and Kinigos."

Hope seemed to glow inside of Akina. "What are you here for?" she asked quickly but quietly.

"To get you out of here first, then settle a debt," he said.

"But how will you get us out?" Akina asked.

"I'll bust up the place, simple as that," he said.

"But aren't you scared of the King?"

"That brat can hardly even handle himself, much less his own powers. There are only two I'm close to fearing here, but they're too intoxicated by the things of this country."

"So what do you want us to do?"

"Well, Mark and Will are on their way here with a small raiding party. They've successfully snuck in, and I'm guessing they'll have some way to break out."

"Then let's go," Akina said.

Akina brought in the heavy Keg and smiled at Albain.

"Hmm, have you been drinking Akina?" he asked before breaking into laughter.

"No, I'm just glad I'm in a room with you," she replied.

"Oooh, Albain, what have you been doing with this one?" Caroline asked.

"Nothing yet, maybe tonight is the night…"

"Hey, Albain! Get out here and face me you blue-blooded bastard!" a voice shouted from outside.

Albain looked outside to see Alcino standing in the castle court yard.

"Don't worry, the guards will take care of him," Albain said as he turned away. He soon heard the sounds of many men having screams cut short, and as he looked out the window, he saw twenty of his best guards lying unconscious.

"Now get down here!" Alcino shouted.

"No, I'll simply let Meso have his way with you, but maybe I could humour you a bit," Albain said as he leapt out the window. The rain gathered on the ground and made a water cushion for him.

"Neat trick, hope you can do more," Alcino taunted.

"I can do far more. Aqua Pagos Barrage!" he exclaimed. The rain gathered into spike-like shapes, then froze over into razor sharp shards of ice.

"Using the rain to your advantage eh? I'll still win."

The ice shards flew towards him, but he shattered them with his bare hands as they approached.

"Geo!" Alcino shouted.

Albain hardly dodged the stone spike that shot up at him, and lost his balance as he stepped back. Alcino took that opportunity to send a rock hard fist flying his way, making his tumble down and slide off the wet cobblestone.

Albain looked up and saw Alcino coming down with another punch and rolled out the way. The ground shattered.

"Ekriksi!" Albain hastily commanded. Alcino knocked aside the ball of soul energy and grabbed Albain by his collar.

"Now Meso, I've defeated your ally and I expect you to appear post-haste," he said aloud. "Come now or I will kill him, and you lose the piece of grand bounty he said he would offer you…"

Before he could finish the sentence, a dark hand came before him, and he briskly dodged it.

Meso and Delta now suddenly stood before him.

"Fantastic," Alcino said with an evil grin. "I've got both of you here, now that evens the odds a bit."

"Alcino, I don't know what you're playing at because I certainly know you cannot defeat all three of us," Meso said.

There was a roar from above, and out of the sky fell Dodecagon in child form. He slammed his fist in the ground as he landed, and Albain knew he felt a heavy vibration.

"Delta, I believe you know Dodecagon," Alcino said. "He's the one that killed Se'dah."

He saw a flash of rage in Delta's eyes, and an aura of darkness and fire seemed to float about her.

"You and Eros have killed enough of my followers, it's time you lose someone," Meso said.

"Wait!" Dodecagon shouted. His body glowed white, and he changed into an older form of himself. As he did, the obsidian scythe formed in his hands.

"That's better, now I'm as big as Jor!" he said, pretending to pump up his arms to show his muscles. He was in fact now the same age as Jor in body, not so much in mind though.

"No matter how old you get, I will still kill you, just like how you killed my precious Se'dah!" Delta cried. "Black-Fire Burst!"

A ball of darkness and fire flew towards Dodecagon, but he leaned back to dodge it.

Meso frowned as he realized that Alcino had gotten behind of him in the heat of the moment.

"Seems I win this fight," Alcino said.

"Not until I go back to hell," Meso replied. A ring of dark energy rose around him, and Alcino only barely dodged it.

Albain scrambled to his feet, but quickly fell to the ground as two stone shards broke through the wall behind him.

"By the Divines, Albain!" Caroline cried as she ran for the window.

"'By the Divines' this!" Akina shouted as he grabbed her by her ponytail and tossed her across the room.

She scrambled to her feet and pulled out a dagger, but Illeth had grabbed her hand and sent three blows to her face.

Caroline fell to the ground, crying and holding her nose.

"Whoa hell Illeth, since when could you fight?" Kullskash asked, her eyes sparkling with admiration.

"I always could, I just never did," she replied.

Will and Mark sat patiently in the tavern near the castle. Several Fel warriors were around the area and had their weapons stashed away.

"What's taking that Alcino guy so long?" Will asked.

"I don't know, I just hope he gives the signal soon enough," Mark replied.

"The Pantheon Castle is under attack!" a man shouted as he burst through the tavern door.

There was a bit of confused muttering going on between the people in the tavern now.

"Well, here we go," Will said.

Mark got up and howled loudly. Several of the Fel inside the tavern got up from their seats and screamed mighty war cries. The others outside did the same, and soon they charged for the Pantheon Castle.

Mark shot at a crossbowman at the top of the road, killing him on the spot. Another popped out from an alley, but a javelin struck him in the chest and he fell, leaning against the wall.

Some other guards up the road were forming up, but before they finished the Fel warriors were upon them, making quick work of the unorganized band.

The road ahead was blocked by more guards, but these were ready.

"Don't stop!" Mark shouted. "Storm the Castle!"

Three fireballs flew Dodecagon's way, but he avoided them all, and raised his palm to Delta. "Aduro Ekriksi!"

The ball of light burned at her side as it grazed her, and struck Albain dead center in his chest. He screamed in agony and put his hand over the charred area.

"Almost had you Theta," Dodecagon said.

"It's Delta!" she exclaimed.

"Where?" he asked.

She screamed out in anger. "Hephaestus Barrage!"

"No Delta, that will take too much energy!" Meso shouted.

"Pay attention!" Alcino shouted.

Meso flipped backwards at the impact of the punch, and before he could act again, and shard of stone ripped through his body.

"That hurts, doesn't it?" Alcino said.

"Shut up you fool," Meso coughed as he tore it out of his body.

"Khthon Barrage," Alcino commanded calmly, and three more shards of stone shot into his body.

The large fireballs that hovered above Delta now crashed into the ground around Dodecagon, but caught and dismissed each attack.

"This is how you make fire," he said as he inhaled deeply. He breathed out and blew and inferno at Delta.

She screamed in agony as the fire burned away at her. It died away, and she lay there, unable to move.

"Meso, I can't move," she said weakly.

"Well that's you own damned fault!" he said, ripping the last stone shard out his body.

"Dodecagon, finish her!" Alcino shouted.

"She can't fight, so I can't hurt her," he replied.

"Dear Lord," Alcino said, shaking his head. "Fos Ekriksi!"

Meso caught the attack in the palm of his hand, but it caused him considerable pain.

"So you do have a heart," Alcino joked.

"Shut up Alcino, before I take out yours, Teresa Ekriksi!"

Alcino was stuck at close range by the ball of dark energy, and slid back a few meters before letting it fly into the air.

"Now you're dead for sure," Alcino said as he ran forward.

"Yperano Teresa Katastrofi Barrage!" Meso commanded.

"Whoops, better move!" Dodecagon said as he ran for cover.

Alcino ran through the shower of exploding dark energy, and slammed his fist into Meso's face. A hail of blows soon followed.

Albain frowned as he watched what was happening. "Where is Fenalph and Titus when you need them?!"

Kaisan and the others snuck across the outside wall of the Pantheon Castle. They heard a voice shout out to them, and their hearts sank as they taught it was a guard.

"Chief Akina!" A Fel warrior called to them.

"Good, let's move," Akina said, and the others followed.

Mark smiled as he saw Akina. He handed her her obsidian bow. She kissed him on the lips.

"Couldn't wait for me to escape on my own eh?" she said.

"Of course not, now let's get out of here."

"What about Alcino?"

"He'll live, but we won't if we don't move!"

A warrior handed a spear to Kullskash. Illeth frowned at this.

"Where's my weapon?" she asked.

I see a halberd by that dead guard," Kullskash pointed.

Illeth went over by the body and picked up the halberd and a sword he carried.

"These are a bit heavy but they'll work."

They rushed the streets and any of the guards that got in their way. Before they made it past the arch way to another district, a rain of bolts landed before them.

"Get into the alleys for cover, go!" Mark commanded. The Fel warriors did so, ducking into alleys while Mark stood, firing straight for the crossbowmen.

Before he could release the next shot though, a halberd went through the side of one.

Illeth charged forward, slammed the back end of the halberd into the crossbowman's toe. He shouted out, but his head was soon lopped off by the axe end of the halberd.

She avoided a shot and leapt into the air and landed on a crossbowman's neck. She twisted her feet and snapped it, then lodged the axe end into another soldiers' kettle helm. She swung under him and got between two of them.

She drew her sword and lunged it through the back of one. The other tried to attack, but she used the first as a meat shield. She pulled the blade out and the two locked swords.

He flicked his blade to the left, and she lost balance. She rolled before he could do anything and grabbed a crossbow. His eyes showed a quick fear, then were glazed as the bolt landed deep in his neck.

"Catch me!" she called.

Kullskash caught her as she jumped from the high arch.

"Move, all we have now is the gate!" Mark shouted.

Meso slowly stepped back. He felt the strength of Alcino's powerful punches, and knew this could end badly for him soon.

"This is it Meso," Alcino called. "Lux Lucis Katastrofi!"

A beam of light began to charge up in Alcino's palm.

"Damn you!" Meso shouted as the beam hit.

Albain covered his eyes as the bright light filled the courtyard, and as it slowly died away, he felt as if things were surely over.

Meso had used Delta as a living shield from attack. She was burned horribly all over.

"Why Meso?" she asked weakly.

"You've served your purpose," he replied.

She coughed up a bail of blood, and it seemed to run from her mouth, eyes and nose.

"Damn you Meso, damn you to hell...I'll be sure to meet you there..." She finished her last sentence and her head hung low.

Meso tossed her limp body aside as if it were nothing and turned to face Alcino.

"That attack looked like it took a lot of out of you," Meso said with an evil smile.

"Damn you Meso!" Alcino said as he stepped back. He realized now that he was in fact getting low on energy.

"Alcino! Watch out!" Dodecagon shouted as he ran forward. "Aduro Ekriksi!"

Two masses of light went flying. The first flew past Alcino and struck Albain, right when he was about to sneak attack him.

The second tore through Meso, creating a large hole in his torso.

"Now I've got you for sure!" Alcino roared as he charged forward. He put his hand in the hole, and Meso's skin regenerated around it.

"Lux Lucis Katastrofi!"

A circle made of light and covered in strange runes and light formed around Meso.

"No, no, no! This can't be happening!" Meso cried, clawing at his face.

"It just did," Alcino said in a grizzly voice. "Best regards to all your allies in hell!"

Meso cried out in great agony as the shining light shot up from the circle. The blood chilling cries could be heard from all over the city, but as quickly as it came, it faded.

Meso's destroyed body stood there facing Alcino. It slowly broke apart, the dark matter touching the ground and dissipating until the wind blew the rest of his body away.

The ashes floated in the wind, and faded.

Alcino fell to one knee, and Dodecagon hurriedly caught him before he fell.

"Alcino, please be okay," he said.

"I'll be fine once you get me out of here you damned fool!" he coughed.

Dodecagon hefted him onto his back, and ran as fast as his feet could take him for the gate.

The Fel warriors had now escaped the city with no casualties. They were already back on the road to Fel Hall.

"So you actually led that whole battle?" Akina asked Mark as they walked together.

"Yep, Will thought up of the plan, but I executed it," he replied.

"You were brave out there you know," Akina said softly.

"Yet my name is Yellow-Mark."

"You're certainly not yellow, that's for sure," Akina said as she turned and gave him one long kiss on the lips.

Akina felt a firm hand grab the back of her kilt and drag her away.

"Come on, save that for when we're at the halls," Illeth said as she let go.

"I don't think she can wait that long," Kullskash said, and the two of them laughed.

"We're now officially at war with Deneaux now you know," Akina said to Mark.

"Then that means they'll have to take on the armies of Fel, Fen and Fox Hall. Let them come," Mark said.

CHAPTER 44

Crill

Turner, Adele and Jor walked into the city country of Crill. It was very sunny and green here, despite it being several miles from the Tower. The city had no walls, but guards seemed to stand at every corner. The docks seemed vibrant and alive with activity as people moved goods and fished.

Up and down the coats, beautiful beaches seemed to go for miles with shimmering water.

"So this is Crill eh?" Adele said, looking about. "I always heard of it, but I never actually got the chance to come here."

"Well I'm glad we did," Jor said. "It's a welcome change from the chilling winds outside the Tower."

"Just be careful okay, Jane's father said there was some kind of rebellion going on down here," Turner said.

"A rebellion? In such a beautiful city?" Jor asked as he spread his hands.

Just as he did, several cloaked figures pulled crossbows from behind crates and from slung positions on their backs.

The guards, caught by surprise, picked up their crossbows in return. Three of them went down in the attackers' first volley. They fired back and one of the attackers was hit in the leg. Another came to his aid, but was shot in chest.

And guard rushed up to the wounded man and raised his sword.

Jor and the others cringed and looked away as they heard a short scream of agony.

The attackers ran into the alley ways and disappeared.

Five men lay dead nearby, but everyone hardly seemed troubled by it. They went about their daily business again, walking around the bodies as they went.

"You know what, let's head to a tavern..." Jor said as he led the way, steering clear of the bodies.

The tavern was full of many dirty and criminal-looking types, drinking and dancing to the bright shanties played by the bards there.

Jor and the others got a seat.

"See what I told you," Turner said.

"I wish I hadn't, what's going on here?" Jor asked.

"Maybe gang warfare or something?" Adele suggested.

"Or a rebellion," Jor said.

"Both of those are likely, but let's keep our noses out of whatever is happening here, agreed?" Turner asked.

"Agreed," Adele and Jor replied.

"So, what's it today...Oh, foreigners..." the tavern girl said. She had tan skin and black hair that fell to her shoulders. She was dressed in a bright red vest and wore a skirt that seemed to end far above her knees.

The sight of her knocked the air out of Jor. Adele found himself in the same situation.

"So, did you need anything?" she asked with a bit of an accent.

"Um...we could do with some ale...non-alcoholic you know," Turner choked out.

"I like your accent," Adele said, but soon regretted saying it. He got the thought of Kilan slitting his throat.

"I get that a lot from foreigners," she said, winking at him. "Bernie, los extranjeros obtener sus bebidas!"

"Alright girl, I'm getting it!" the tavern keeper shouted back.

"I'll be right back," she said as she elegantly turned and went to the some of the other customers.

"Holy crap she's hot," Jor said in a hush.

"And what if Lyra heard you say that?" Turner asked.

"He'd get beat up," Adele said.

"You shouldn't even be talking! 'Oh, I like your accent'," Jor mimicked.

"Hey, I'm just admiring her accent, that's all!"

"That's what they all say," Turner replied.

"And you Turner, your mouth was dryer than the Ayan Saudi deserts!" Jor joked.

"Jor, don't make me tell on you…"

The girl had arrived at their table and dropped the ale in front of them.

"Anything else?" she asked.

"Your name would be good…" Jor said, but was quickly cut off.

"I'm Arielle, nice to meet you, you know you're some of the first foreigners I actually got to speak to, where are you from anyways?" she said rapidly.

"Well, I'm from up Deneaux, that guy there is from Denhoec and this kid is from Harmony," Turner said.

"A Deneauxman with a Raider? He's your prisoner?"

"Oh no, he's only half Raider, the other half is Deneauxman. He's cool…every once in a while," Turner joked.

"Very funny," Jor said as he folded his arm and sunk in his seat.

"So you're from Denhoec? How is life there? Did you ever go on a raiding trip? Did you ever have a beard? Where's your giant battle-ax…"

"Slow down, please," Jor said. "Now, yes I'm from Denhoec, my life there was crap so I moved away. No I've never had a beard and it doesn't seem like it wants to come, I've never been on a raiding trip and I can't lift a battle-ax for more than ten seconds. Anything else?" he answered with the same speed she did when she came by their table.

"Cool," she said, pulling a chair and sitting next to him. "You ever had been in battle at least?"

"I fought with my friend Turner here in the Battle of Keels. We were driven out by the Raiders, and left when Albain took over. We've been traveling around ever since."

"So you're sell-swords?" she asked.

"Nope, we've never fought for money since we left the army," Turner replied.

"Oh...Well maybe you could come by after dark? I want to ask you something in private..."

"What could you want to ask us in private?" Adele asked suspiciously.

"Sssh, there are eyes and ears all around. Nowhere is safe nowadays."

"Arielle, we need more ale over here!" someone shouted from across the inn.

"Coming!" she called as she got up. "I'll see you all later..."

"Well?" Adele asked as he turned to Turner.

"I say we not go, who knows what she wants. I mean, with a dress so short, she could be in the business of..."

"I say we at least see what she has to say," Jor said, cutting Turner off.

"Oh, so you plan to cheat on Lyra again?" Turner asked angrily.

"No damn it, I just feel like she needs some kind of help, and we could give it to her...and I wasn't cheating!"

"Okay Jor, but I anything happens, you're on your own."

That night, Jor and the others headed to the tavern. The door was locked, but as they reached to knock, they heard movement.

"Put your hands where I can see them!" a cloaked man said.

"I don't think that'll work for me, I don't need my hands to fight," Adele warned.

"Hook, are these the three you wanted?" the man said to the shadows.

"Bring em' here," a woman's voice said as she walked them into an alley. They were shoved through a side door and entered the tavern.

"So, you've decided to come after all," Arielle said as she pulled back the hood of the cloak.

"What's this all about?" Turner asked.

"Hook, why did you bring one with a broken arm? What could he possibly do for us?" the tavern keeper, Bernie, asked. He was older than them, but not by a wide margin. He was Arielle's skin tone and had sideburns and short black hair.

"Depends, first though, we have to tell them what's going on," Arielle replied. She turned to the others. "This is the headquarters of the Crill Rebellion."

"And why are we here?" Adele asked.

"Well, you see we need help, and the people here are too scared of our corrupt leaders to do anything. Foreigners are usually the ones that join our ranks, and you three seem very skilled."

"That may be true, but why would we want to be part of your rebellion?" Turner asked.

"We're desperate for freedom," Bernie said. "We'll ask anyone for help, as long as we can win our freedom."

"But do you know what happens after a rebellion?" Adele asked. "You have to re-establish some form of leadership for the country, then you have to clean up the mess you caused while fighting...I've read about this kind of stuff, and seen the results."

"We already have a few ideas floating around on how to rule the country of Crill correctly," Bernie said. "But right now we can only focus on winning the war."

"By murdering guards in public? That doesn't seem like the actions of freedom fighters. That seems like the actions of criminals." Jor said.

"Then what do you expect us to do?" Bernie asked.

"Get to the hearts of the people. No more guards will be recruited for the country once the people decide to come to you," Adele said. "That's how I was able to help defend my country many years back when their spirits was weakened."

"Then you have to win key battles," Turner said. "No point in losing men unless you have something to seriously gain from it, like when we tried to hold the capitol in Keels instead of attacking the Raider's landing."

"Brilliant!" Bernie said. "You do this stuff on a regular basis?"

Turner smiled weakly. "I actually only know the outlines to winning a war, I've actually never planned a battle, only fought in them."

"Well, I doubt we can do those things ourselves, would you mind joining up?" Arielle asked.

Jor frowned at this now. "Well, we have no right to join in your war, and we really don't know what kind of stuff the leaders here are doing."

"Then go out and see, and maybe you'll have a change of heart," Arielle said. "But I'm telling you, what you see tomorrow will scar you..."

"Well, see you around," Adele said as he turned for the door.

The next day, the three of them were walking down the streets as they saw a large crowd assembled at the square.

"What's going on down there?" Adele asked.

"I don't know, let's go," Turner said.

As they neared the crowd, they heard any people weeping and crying. They then saw a raised platform, a block put up and a man standing with a large axe.

"Looks like an execution," Jor said.

Just as he said it, a group of guards came up on the platform.

With them was a girl, only a bit younger than them.

"What the hell...?" Jor muttered to himself.

"Something's wrong here," Adele said.

One of the guards now spoke.

"On a count of treason to the King, this young woman is to be executed at the block on the count of treason!" he proclaimed.

"She's just a girl!" a woman cried.

"Silence wench!" the guard shouted. "Let the execution commence..." He stood there on the platform, completely frozen, then fell back silently.

A bit of dark energy glowed around Adele's finger after the sneak attack.

"Move!" Jor shouted as he drew his great sword. The crowd parted at its sight. He ran forward and leapt to the platform.

The two guards let go of the girl, but as they did, Jor swung mightily for them, cutting them down. The executioner hefted up the heavy axe and slammed it down before Jor. He easily stepped back and evaded it, then made another mighty swing, taking the executioner's head right off.

"Get the hell out of there!" Turner shouted.

Jor grabbed the girl and jumped off the platform. He, Turner and Adele ran up the street, the crowd cheering all the while.

The tavern door swung open and the four of them walked in. The place went silent at the sight of Jor's bloody sword.

"Arielle!" he called.

"Yes Jorigsveer?" she said, quickly coming from the back room. She watched in surprise at the girl that was supposed to be executed today.

"We're in," Jor said.

Chapter 45

Inbound

It had been a few days since Jor, Adele and Turner had left, and Jane was getting worried. They said they would only be there for a short time, but what was a short time?

She walked across the crater filled fields that were before the Tower. She felt the cold wind hit her, but she ignored it

"Just hurry up and come home..." she said softly.

She heard hoofbeats and looked up. The fog that surrounded the area obscured her sight, but they sounded oddly familiar.

Out of the fog came Zen and Alda riding Kenta. When they got close enough, she could see that they were exhausted.

"Jane Pagos, it is good to see you," Zen said tiredly.

"Zen? What are you doing here?" she asked.

"Albain has attacked Fel hall. We've ridden and walked here non-stop to tell you, he has taken Akina and her sisters hostage."

"What? Why?"

"Because the bastard's strong enough to take what he wants. We've come to you hoping that you and the others could help us," Alda said.

"We can try, just come to the Tower and rest up, then we can start something," Jane said to them.

"So what is the current objective?" Turner asked the crowd of rebels. They were all gathered in a small cave outside the city.

"To kill government officials," one rebel said.

"Now, that's where you're going wrong. We should start by speaking to the people."

"With all those damn guards around?" Bernie asked.

"That's why we're raiding the armoury too," Jor said.

"The armoury?" several people said, muttering excitedly.

"Yes, I'm leading the attacking group while Turner and the others head for the town square."

"So what will I do?" Adele asked.

"You're with me Adele, your problem solving skills have saved us enough times," Turner said. "Now arm yourselves, we're moving out."

Jor and his group of fifteen rebels sneaked towards the armoury building. It was a pretty normal looking stone structure, but inside would be the Crill military's arsenal for this part of the city.

"We're going to need to make this as loud as possible. I don't care if we can get in, all we have to do is catch their attention," Jor said. He unslung his bow from over his shoulder and took an arrow.

One of the patrolling guards walked about the building, as he neared the front, an arrow landed before him. He was about to draw his sword when another struck him in the chest.

The guard nearby ran to the other side of the building and began blowing a bugle.

"Good, now, attack!" Jor shouted as the rebels swarmed past him.

The guards at the square and around the city heard the alarm, and ran for the armoury.

Turner, Adele, Bernie and three other rebels waited in the alley until they were all gone.

They then ran out and ran up on the raised platform from a few days ago.

"People of Crill, we beg that you hear us!" Bernie exclaimed in his language.

Many of them turned to see what they had to say, and others watched from their windows.

"Do they speak Deneauxic?" Turner asked.

"Not all of them, I'll translate for you as you go, now speak," Bernie said.

"Alright, people of Crill, we hear your country is under the grip of cruel leaders, and we have come to aid in its liberation."

Bernie translated it, but many of them gave Turner odd stares.

"Yes, I may be a foreigner, but I'm not here for control. I'm only here to help you, then I will leave. The other rebels are your fellow countrymen, and are hoping that others may join their ranks for a better future."

A townsman asked a question in Crillic, and Bernie translated.

"He asked what we will do to save them," Bernie said to Turner.

"Well, our friend there," he said, raising his hand in the direction of smoke. "Are fighting to keep the guards distracted while we speak, soon enough they will have to leave and we'll be forced back to our base."

He saw the looks of fear in the people's eyes after Bernie translated.

"What we will do is fight for key points, and make sure we keep you clear of the fighting. No more will you see random acts of violence, but organized charges. We will defend you as long as we breathe, and your interests will come first."

As Bernie translated, people began to mutter, almost excitedly.

"This conflict will end quickly, and we will make sure that the corruption is ended."

There was the sound of bugling off in the distance, and Turner knew that the attack was repelled.

"Well, seems our time is up, let's move!" Turner said, and the rebels followed.

Everyone was stuck waiting at the base for half an hour when Jor and his group returned. They were all blood-stained and tired looking, carrying pikes, swords, halberds and many other weapons with them.

Turner smiled as he saw them approach. "You couldn't help plundering the place, could you?"

"Come on, I got everyone out in one piece," Jor said.

"They look a little bloody to be in one piece," Adele said.

"That's just the blood from the guards. There were a lot, but they weren't very strong," Jor said. "Hasty training I'd say."

"Either way, get those weapons in the back. We could use them for the new recruits," Arielle said.

"Great, see how good my Raider instincts are?" Jor said to Turner.

Arielle patted him on the head. "Just don't go in over your head, even Raiders can die too."

"Great-Blade!" a voice shouted from away.

Jor turned to see Zen and Alda approaching on horseback.

"Zen, what are you doing here? Weren't you in Fel Hall?" Jor asked.

"I was until Albain came. He's annexed Fel Hall, we've ridden here for days to get to you," he answered.

"Albain is the big King and I'm the little soldier. What do you want me to do, raise an army and lay siege?"

"That's not a bad idea..." Alda said slowly.

"I can't do that, I'm just Jorigsveer. I'm helping out here and I believe that I'm going to be here for a while."

"And that's why I came," Alda said as she dismounted. "I wasn't going to let a fellow Raider steal the glory of war, so I'm here to help you in battle."

"Do you even know what we're fighting for?" Turner asked.

"No, just point me in the direction of the enemy, and I'll cut him up. That's the basis of fighting and what I'm best at."

Jor and the others looked at each other, then back at Alda.

"Okay, just try not to wreck the place. We're going by stealth, not brute strength," he said finally.

"No problem," Alda said.

"That means no heavy steel plated armor or your huge battle-ax," Arielle said.

"Well..." Alda said. "That's a different story then..."

"So you joining or not, we're wasting valuable time out here as it is," Turner said.

"I'll join, I'll join," she said. "Just gimme some 'lighter' equipment and I'll fall in."

CHAPTER 46

Skippers

Ferdinand frowned to himself as he sat on his throne. He was beginning to notice that the rebel activity had suddenly increased, and instead of being small skirmishes to kill his guards and soldiers, they were attacking key-points in the country.

He also realized that the one girl he was executing was able to escape by being rescued by foreigners, and that was when the rebel activity...

"That's who it is!" he shouted. The servants who were cleaning the red velvet rug in the large hall were startled by the sudden outburst.

"Servants, send for my generals!" he said.

As quickly as he said it, several men dressed in steel plate armor rushed in. They knew that keeping him waiting was the quickest way to be executed, and wasted no time in literally sprinting across the castle.

"Yes my king?" one asked.

"Rico, I need you to find out information about several foreigners that entered the country. Seth, I need you to be on call for any attacks. Make sure you keep the most guards posted at the square, I don't want another speech. Carlos, I want you to get on those smiths, that raid on the armoury was a little too damaging and I need more weapons."

"Anything else sire?" Seth asked.

"Yes, kill any and every rebel you see, and anyone who sides with them too."

"Alright then sire, we shall make our leave," Rico said before the three of them saluted and left.

"So what's another point for us to take?" Turner asked the group of rebels.

"There's the barracks," one suggested.

"No, too heavily guarded. That's for when we want to start striking decisive blows, and we don't have that kind of momentum yet."

"We could start getting momentum if we attacked the barracks," Jor said.

"No, I've seen the barracks, the worst of the worst in the countries army could be garrisoned there and defend it. You need explosives to get past it," Bernie said.

"Exposives?" Jor asked. "Like those things we saw used in Keels?"

"Explosives Jor," Turner corrected. "And you really have those here?" he asked, turning to Arielle and Bernie.

"Well, I think they are being imported from the west. They say the dwarves over there have all kinds of dangerous items," Arielle said. "I also believe the ones in southern Cardia also sell those kinds of stuff."

"So why not take it from them and use it for ourselves?" Alda asked. She had now changed into the same cloak and regular clothes as the others. She wore shorts since she said she would not accept the same short skirt Arielle wore.

"That would be stealing Alda," Zen said. He wore his old Zerani clothes from before. "I don't think these people are interested in that."

"Well, aren't those explosives headed for Deneaux?" Jor asked. "If the Raiders were using them in Keels, I'm guessing it was Albain who ordered and sold them."

"That's actually true..." Turner said, a smile forming on his face. "Seems we have some ships to raid."

Several of the rebels nearby shifted away from Alda nervously as they saw her eyes flash bright red.

Jor smiled at her and did the same.

"The old Raider Berserker mode, I'm actually beginning to like it," Adele said.

"But where are *we* going to get ships from?" A rebel asked now.

"We have some fishermen friends who are willing to borrow us their boats. If anyone asks, say we stole them," Arielle said. "We'll use the smaller boats to take a bigger one, and hopefully use that one to go on more raids in the future."

They moved later that night, sneaking across the docks. They noticed that more guards were posted than usual, but they forced their way instead between crates and boxes out of sight. They finally made it to the smaller boats and shoved off in five groups, five men each.

Jor noticed that Alda had her teeth gritted together and her fists clenched tightly. She had a wolfish grin on her face.

"You look funny you know, almost cute..." Jor said.

"Hey, Alda Breach-Breaker is not cute, I'm just excited, that's all," she replied.

"Oh good, because I am too," he said, both his eyes turning red once they neared the first boat.

They snuck aboard the first. They crept across the crates, ducking away at the sight of any deck hands. They were all drunk or tired, Jor noticed. They wouldn't put up much of a fight.

They made their way to the cabins, then kicked the door in, pointing crossbows at everyone inside.

"So, what's your problem?" The captain asked. He was a muscular man, and had a scimitar at his side. He had a beard growing down to his chest.

"I want you hand over the ship. The two other ships are already under our control, so all that's left is you," Jor said.

"You do realize I was ready for you? I mean, I'm always expecting trouble, and even worse for you is that this ship could easily blow up sky high with one cannon shot."

"Cannon? What's that?" Alda asked.

"Turn around and you'll see..."

As they all turned around, they saw that the big, black tube shaped weapon was pointed at them.

"You're not getting away with this on my watch, Ekriksi!" Jor commanded.

The shot of soul white soul energy went into the cannon, forcing it upward. It fired, tearing a hole through the top of the cabin.

Two crossbow bolts slammed into the torso of the two men that were operating the cannon.

The captain drew his sword and charged for them.

"Ekriksi!" Jor commanded again. The attack struck the captain in his chest, and as he recoiled, Alda's sword went straight through his thigh.

He shouted in pain, but Alda pulled the blade out and cut across his throat in the same motion, killing him.

Jor and the others ran outside to see that two more ships were coming their way.

"Those must be the escorts," Jor said. "We're going to need to find a way out of here."

"Looks like we'll have to fight," a rebel said.

Several of the sailors were coming at them now, armed with swords, spears and halberds. About three of them had crossbows.

"Fun," Jor said sarcastically. "Now, Ekriksi Barrage!"

The white spheres appeared overhead and crashed down on the deck. The sailors, frightened, scattered across the deck for cover.

The rebels fired at the enemy crossbowmen as they ran. Two of them dropped but the other got behind a crate.

"Charge!" Alda shouted as she picked up a fallen sword and ran. Several others followed.

Alda hacked down two men with a spin with both swords. Another approached and struck at her, but she parried it and sent his sword sliding across the deck. The frightened sailor ran, only to have a crossbow bolt hit him from behind.

Two men with halberds stood before her now. One lunged at her. She side-stepped it, but soon realized she was in the path of the next. She crossed both swords in front of her and blocked the attack, but just barely.

She took a step back and smiled wolfishly at the two sailors. They took a step back themselves, intimidated by the girl before them.

Alda surged forward, swinging both blades. The first man leapt back, but the second instead tried to raise the long weapon. Alda was already too close and easily cut him down. The first now lunged at her, but she side-stepped it and broke the halberd as well as cracking her own sword.

The sailor only had a brief glance at her blood red pupils before a sword went through his chest.

She smiled to herself and charged to engage more targets in the fighting.

Jor had stayed back, firing soul attacks at anyone he could reach. Out of the corner of his eye, he saw a crossbow come up and followed its path to see it was aimed at Alda. He swung his hand around and let his palm face the enemy.

"Pertusus!" he commanded, sending a piercing beam across deck, the through the crossbowman's head. The hit jostled his body, and he pulled the trigger on the crossbow, sending a bolt flying across the deck.

Jor watched in horror as the hood of Alda's cloak tore at the area by the neck. She fell to one knee and stayed that way for a few seconds.

"Alda!" Jor cried.

She stood up, and laughed heartily.

"Good show sailors! Now bring me more enemies!" she yelled, running into battle again.

"My condolences to Zen," Jor said sarcastically to himself before drawing his great sword and charging into battle.

Hook's group had been successful in taking one of the ships. They surged forward, attempting to outrun the other battleships that approached.

"Bernie, do you think we can make this?" she called.

He glanced back at the approaching ship to the left.

"Not likely, we may have to fight," he replied.

"What? But how do you suppose we do that? We can't use those weird smoke makers!"

"Cannons," Bernie corrected.

"I don't care what the hell they are! Just sail!"

Jor and his crew were now doing the exact same thing.

"Okay, so how do we do this?" Alda asked.

"I'll figure something out," Jor said quickly. He looked around the cannon for a trigger or lever of some kind. He found nothing except a string...

"That's it!" he exclaimed. "Point it at the battleship!"

The rebels pushed it over to face the ship, and Jor placed his hand around the string.

"Pyro," he commanded. The string lit up, and burned slowly away. Jor stepped away, and it fired off a cannon ball into the battleship's hull.

"Aim the rest of them!" Jor shouted. The rebels did so and pushed them towards the ship. Jor ran down the line of six broadsides, setting them all off.

The first two tore the masts off, and three of them crashed into the hull right above the water. The last fell short and fell into the water.

The smaller battleship slowly fell back behind them, then slowly began to sink.

"Bring this thing around so I can get over to Hook's ship! I'm not leaving anyone behind tonight!"

The ship increased its pace and went ahead of the other two merchant ships. Jor realized now that it would take too long to maneuver.

"Watch out guys, don't go for me if anything happens, just get to Hook's ship," Jor said as he went to the side.

"What are you talking about Jor?" Alda asked.

"Aqua!" he commanded, then jumped over the side of the ship. He began to skate over the water, to Alda and the other rebels' surprise. Alda shook herself out of it fastest.

"Well what are you looking at? Get to sailing!" she shouted, and they quickly went to work.

Jor skated over the water. He was quickly making way to Arielle's ship, though at the cost of some of his own energy.

"Get down!" he heard someone shout.

As they did, Jor forced himself to the side, moving out of the way of a cannon ball. Water splashed up on him, but he shook it off and kept going.

Several more fell around him, but he expertly dodged them. The last one broke off the rail of Arielle's ship and fell before him. He was knocked back and fell in.

"The commander!" a rebel shouted.

"Keep going!" Alda replied.

Jor resurfaced to see Arielle's ship still under attack. He coughed up a bit of water.

"Better make my last bits of energy worth it! Aqua!"

He rose out from the water and began skating again until he made it to the ship. The water pushed him up until he made it on deck. He fell to his knees and panted tiredly.

"Jor, how did you get here?" Arielle asked.

"I soul-skated here on the water, took up a lot of energy," he replied.

"But why come over here? Don't you need to watch your ship?"

"I do, but I'm here to tell you how to fire the cannon things."

"You know how? Tell us!" Bernie said, ducking as a cannon ball flew overhead.

"Point it at the battleship, then set the string on fire."

"You heard him, light up those cannons!" Arielle shouted.

The rebels did so, using one of the torches that was mounted on the masts.

The seven broadsides went off, all of them hitting their mark.

"That didn't look like it did much," a rebel said, looking at the still approaching battleship.

As he finished the sentence, the ship erupted in a large explosion. It soon began to sink, a large, burning mass.

"Yes!" Arielle shouted as the rebels erupted into cheers. She embraced Jor.

"Hey, be careful how you go about me, I have a girlfriend already," Jor warned.

"Relax, it's not that kind of hug, I'm just happy we're alive!"

"I'm surprised *I'm* still alive," Jor said as he fell back on a crate. "That water skating was a little too much for me after this battle."

CHAPTER 47

Red Raiders

"What happened to my bombs?!" Albain shouted in disbelief.

"The ships were taken by the Crillic rebels. All the explosives are in their hands now," the messenger said.

"Then go tell the King over there to bring those damned rebels. I want their heads on a silver platter!"

"Okay sir, they said that they are already seizing foreigners."

"Why?" Albain asked, puzzled.

"They said that the rebel activity came alive after three foreigners entered the town and attacked the guards there during an execution. One was a Raider with a two-hander, the other is a countryman with a broken arm and the last was a boy who could apparently manipulate soul."

"Hmm, they sound oddly familiar. I'll take a look into these foreigners in the meanwhile, you need to get to Crill, now go!"

The messenger saluted and went out the door.

"So you all claim to just be adventurers?" King Ferdinand said to the assembled foreigners.

"Yes sire, we just came here for the beaches," one woman in armor said.

"Yeah, and the women," another large, bearded Raider added.

"I was just passing through," a tall man said.

"And I came from visiting family in Deneaux," a Zerani man said.

"So how do I know you're telling the truth?" Ferdinand asked.

"Well...how do you know if we're lying?" the tall man asked.

The King noted that he wasn't mocking him, and continued.

"You've made your point," he said. "Now send them to the dungeons."

"What?!" the large Raider bellowed.

Several guards grabbed them and hauled them off to the dungeons.

"Now, all we do is put this grey powder into a case and set it on fire," Jor said to the assembled rebels.

"So all we do is light and throw?" Turner asked.

"Yep," Jor answered. "It's a lot simpler than you think."

"So do we get to attack the barracks now?" a rebel asked.

"Well...we have the explosives, so..." Arielle let it trail off.

"We go tonight," Jor said. "We'll give the people of Crill a show they'll never forget."

Several fishermen were walking down the street, taking about the current events.

"I'm telling you people, if we join the rebels, we could get added benefits from winning the war!" one said.

"Not so loudly," another one whispered. "And joining would mean certain death. There are way more guards than there are rebels."

"So what, they could still win," the next said.

"Not until they start gaining an advantage..."

Before he finished the sentence, the barracks building down the street exploded.

"What the hell?!" one shouted before running off. The rest followed.

"Keep throwing the explosives until I give the word!" Jor shouted.

"Alright commander!" several rebels said.

"When did they start calling me commander?" Jor asked, turning to Arielle.

"I don't know, they just give people nicknames according to what they do," she replied.

"Then why do they call you Hook?"

"Because I used to fight with two hook swords. They're broken now, but the name sticks." She said. "They probably call you commander because you scream the most commands in every battle."

"Oh," Jor said. He chuckled to himself. "And to think I was only a foot soldier in Keels."

"Don't let it go to your head, we still have a battle to win," Arielle said, hitting him on the arm.

Several guards could be seen charging from the flames, swords high in the air.

"Looks like our cue, let's go!" Jor shouted, charging forward with the rebel force.

He swung mightily with is great sword, hacking down the guards. Alda was at his side, doing the exact same thing with her battle-ax.

"You gotta teach me that," Jor said to her.

"When the battle's over," she said as her eyes turned red. Jor's did the same.

"Let's go!" he roared as they threw themselves at the enemy.

"Erebus Astrape Pertusus!" Adele commanded. A bean of black lighting struck several guards, and they all fell. He turned to see Arielle surging through many guards with two daggers. She flipped, slid and spun gracefully past them, then as she made it to the last one, she vaulted over them, flipping in the air and landing on her feet before tossing a knife in his back.

All the guards quickly fell, blood already pouring from them.

Bernie tossed a bomb at a large group of approaching guards, and they were torn apart by the blast.

"Watch it Crillic!" Zen shouted as he shielded himself from the nearby explosion.

"Sorry," he called.

The fighting ended as quickly as it started. Jor slowly walked through the burning rubble of the barracks. He placed one foot on a raised bit of stone and looked around.

"We're going to need to be careful next time," he said to himself.

"Hey Jor, nice work!" Arielle said as she and the others approached.

"Yeah, I suppose it was good, but we need a few more good pushes before we achieve victory," he replied with little joy.

"So does that mean we have a good chance?" Adele asked.

"I doubt this Revolution will last any longer now that the barracks are gone. Turner probably knows what should happen next."

"A Raider?!" Ferdinand shouted. "How the hell could a Raider be in charge of the Revolution?!"

"Well sir..." the fisherman said weakly. "I also saw a girl from here, and a Zerani and a Deneauxman..."

"What, so which one is the leader?"

"Maybe it's the girl. The Raider was the one that looked like he was leading the battle though..."

"Guards, free the prisoners, and peasant, tell me how he looked or I'll cut out your tongue!"

"Okay, okay," the fisherman said fearfully, then began describing each.

Jor, Turner, Adele and the others sat in the tavern, happily recounting the current events.

"So you really skated on the water?" Turner asked, completely surprised.

"Yep, it was a trick I learned from Noch."

"You two looked like you learned a lot from Keels," Adele commented.

"We learned many things in that hell hole. I just hope they can get it rebuilt," Jor said.

"Then Lyra will go live with her parents and you may not get to see her for a while," Turner said.

"I doubt she wants to see me now," Jor said weakly.

"They all must be missing us," Zen said.

"Aw crap, that realization hit me like a war hammer," Turner said, putting his hand on his forehead. "Jane's gonna kill me, and if she doesn't, her father will..."

"Her father? What does he have against you?" Adele asked.

"Oh damn...I gotta learn to watch what I say..."

"Is this what you wanted to hide from Jane?" Jor asked, his mood turning serious.

"Don't worry about it..."

"And that's your problem, you don't want help. At some point you'll have to talk, why not do it now?"

"Can't, I think I forgot something all the way at base, I'll go get it..."

"Nope, you say it now, or we could spend the next few days waiting in the tavern until you talk," Jor said.

"Okay damn it! I'll talk!" he exclaimed, taking a seat.

"You want to be alone?" Arielle asked.

"Nah, you can stay," Jor said.

"Okay," Turner now said. "What happened to me was that Mr. Pagos says that I'm no good for Jane."

"Well he's full of crap," Jor said bluntly. "You're like Jane's other half."

"I tried to tell him, but he said all I'm good for is fighting and killing, and as you can see..." he let it trail off, lifting up his broken arm in a sling.

"Hmm, once this is over, we're going to the tower to see Mr. Pagos about this. I'm not leaving you hanging as I said before."

"You won't change his mind."

"Then I'll change it for him."

"He's the school's headmaster, he must be full of all kind of powerful soul energy!"

"Turner, I've killed a Divine, staring down a powerful Perialite won't be that hard."

"You've killed a Divine?" Arielle and Bernie said in surprise.

"Well, Adele killed her, and it was only lesser one," Jor said.

"Her name was Mortha, a necromancer," Adele said.

"Like from the stories eh? Then how'd you beat her?" Bernie asked skeptically.

"Well what we did was..."

"Good day citizens and foreigners," a guard said, walking up to their table.

"Hello," Arielle said, turning to him.

The guard tried not to look at her and her short dress. "We need you to write your names for the local census. We also need the names of the foreigners, for records you know."

Jor and Turner whispered to each other now, then turned back to the guard.

"We'll sign it," Turner said distrustfully.

Each of them signed it and the guard went on his way.

"This better not backfire on us later," Zen said.

"I hope it doesn't," Jor said.

Chapter 48

Jane vs. Lane

Jane and Dianne were walking together around the empty fields. It had become a practice for Jane to go walking every day, hoping that Turner would come from Crill.

"You need to stop worrying and relax, I'm sure he's fine," Dianne said to her.

"I don't know, I mean, what if he broke his other arm? What if he..."

"Don't start with the 'what ifs', they'll only cause you to worry more. Both Jor and Adele are with him so I'm sure he's fine."

"Yeah, I guess...I just wish I knew why he didn't tell me what was bothering him..."

Dianne froze up where she stood.

"What's up Dianne?" Jane asked.

"Lane..." she was about to say. An arrow flew and slammed into her chest. She silently fell to the ground.

"Dianne!" Jane screamed as she ran over to her.

"Don't even try," someone said.

Jane angrily turned to see Lane standing before her.

"What the hell did you to that for?" Jane cried.

"I'm helping her to go back to her sister," Lane said. "Reuniting the living with the dead is something I've been very good at lately."

"Delta...dead?" Dianne said slowly.

"Yep, Alcino burnt her up along with poor Master Meso. It hurts to say," she said, pretending to be sad.

"So you're here for revenge?" Jane asked.

"Nope, I'm just bored and thought killing you would be fun. And now that Dianne is here it makes double the fun." A flame went up around her now. "Three, two, one go!"

Jane hardly dodged the flaming punch that came her way. She turned and raised her palm. "Pagos Ekriksi!

"Pyro Ekriksi!" Lane commanded in reply.

The shard of ice and the fireball collided, making a bit of steam.

Jane ran from the area, and Lane followed.

"Pagos Barrage!" she commanded, sending many shards of ice Lane's way.

Lane knocked them away. "Apo pano Pyras Pertusus!" she commanded.

A straight line of fire flew Jane's way, but she flipped over it. "Pagos Ekriksi!" she commanded again.

Lane caught the ice shard and laughed. "Don't you have any new tricks?"

"Yeah, this!" Jane shouted. "Pagos Prism!"

The ice began to go up Lane's arm, freezing over her.

"Well that's crappy," she said, shattering the ice as her arm ignited.

"Don't you know you're elements? Fire always beats ice!"

"Shut up!" Jane shouted. "Hydro Pagos Ekriksi!" A large water ball manifested before Jane, then it froze over into a large ice shard. She let it fly towards Lane, but it was cut into two by a fire blade on the side of Lane's forearm.

Lane laughed again. "I'm having so much fun!"

"You know you're demented!" Jane said angrily.

"You know you're not as hot as me?" Lane replied.

Jane watched Lane carefully. Her only chance right now would be to either wear Lane out or get in a decisive blow.

Neither seemed possible.

"Don't you have someone else to kill today?" Jane asked.

"Nope, just you."

"But I'm sure there's someone else out there with a lot more power."

"Yeah, but I want to fight you."

"But..."

"Three, two, one go! Pyras Barrage!"

Jane was hardly ready as the fireballs crashed down around her. She ran a few feet, then rolled on her side and put up her hand. "Pagos Hoplon!"

A shield made of ice formed up around her, stopping the fireballs as they came.

Lane happily tossed fireball after fireball at the shield of ice. "Come on little turtle, get out of your shell!"

"Come on Jane, think of something," she said to herself. She thought about using a speed command, but Lane would just copy the command and get to her speed. Making a weapon would work, but she was never good at hand-to-hand.

The shield shattered to pieces, and she got up and ran as it did.

"Ready to die yet?" Lane called as she tossed another fireball.

It crashed into Jane's back and she fell. Her cloaked had a hole burnt into the back, but she felt she hadn't been seriously injured.

"Pagos Barrage!" she got up and commanded.

They both fired their elemental projectiles at each other, filling the area with steam.

"Pagos Kopis," Jane commanded quietly. Two swords made of ice formed in her hands.

She quickly put up the swords, all most by instinct, as a flaming sword came from the fog.

She spun, feeling like she was deflecting a hundred weapons from every corner.

"Enough!" Jane shouted. "Kapnizo Katastrofi!"

Dianne watched from away as the mist erupted in a large explosion.

"I'm seriously not sitting this one out," Dianne said as she forced herself up. She held the arrow in her chest and realized it was made of energy. It faded as she pulled it out.

Jane fell to the ground and rolled several meters until she lay flat. Her clothes were torn up pretty bad, she realized, and she was bleeding from her lip, nose and head.

"Stupid daimon girl," she said to herself.

"That wasn't nice," Lane said as she approached. Her injuries were similar to Jane's.

"But it was true," Jane said as the ice blades returned in her hands.

"You're a fighter Jane, I can respect that," Lane said, the fire swords already in her hands.

They both ran to each other and swung. Each attack burnt away at Jane's swords, but she kept going anyways, despite the growing steam.

"You can't keep this up," Lane taunted, swinging to her left.

Jane parried it and lunged, but Lane blocked it. "I can so!"

As Jane struck at her, the ice blades shattered. She quickly leapt back.

"Dynami Yperano Kapnizo Katastrofi!" Dianne commanded.

Lane leapt through the mist to attack Jane, but it erupted into an even larger explosion.

"Here's your chance!" Dianne shouted to Jane.

"Pagos Spatha!" Jane commanded. A large, flat bladed sword animated in Jane's hand, made completely of ice. "Pagos Tachista!"

A trail of ice animated as Jane surged forward at a blinding speed. Lane now got up and saw Jane quickly approaching.

She anticipated the next attack and put up her swords, blocking Jane's overhead slice.

As she stopped it though, Jane heard a heavy crack, and Lane's arms trembled.

"Still having fun?" Jane asked.

For the first time now, Jane saw something in Lane's eyes she never thought she would see.

Fear.

Jane wasted no time in bringing the heavy cleaver up and slamming the blunt end into Lane's side. She flew several feet and slid on the hard ground.

She screamed out in complete agony as she hit the ground. Her fire swords dissipated instantly.

Jane approached her, hearing her sobbing in pain.

"Damned hypocrite, you like killing but never knew how it felt to be cold. I know what cold is, and soon you will too," Jane said darkly.

Lane opened her mouth to speak, but as she uttered a sound, she felt her lungs collapse on her and a sharp pain go through her ribs. She only sobbed quietly as Jane stepped on her chest.

"You aren't really going to kill her?" Dianne said as she limped over.

"I'm considering it," Jane said. She looked at her ice sword and saw her reflection, then back at Lane. "She looks just like me."

"She's your split, of course she's going to look like you," Dianne said.

"And then there's the problem, she's almost like my sister."

"I guess you could say that..."

"Damn you Pagos," Lane said weakly. "Let's see how merciful you are when I kill you..."

A black circle went up around her, and she disappeared, reappearing behind Dianne with a flame sword.

"Dianne!" Jane cried.

Dianne spun around and held the sword. Lane teleported again, only to have Dianne go with her.

There were blurs of movement around Jane as the two disappeared and reappeared.

Finally, Dianne slammed Lane down to the ground, both their fists covered in flames.

More blood came from Lane's mouth as she hit the ground. She tried to scream, but she only choked on the blood that was coming up right after.

"So you must be that last piece of Meso," Dianne said. "The only true surviving member of his little syndicate, not counting Kinsei..."

"Please, I don't want to die," Lane begged weakly.

"Shut the hell up! I don't want to hear you say that!" Dianne shouted. "You've killed enough people already I'm sure, and all of them probably begged for mercy the way you did!"

Lane was shaking her head before she finished.

"But...but..."

"But what daimon? But what?!"

"I can't go yet, I just can't!" Lane managed to say. She soon regretted it and blood came pouring out again.

"Dianne, the sun's gone down," Jane said.

"So what?" she asked, the realization hit her.

Lane slowly slipped away in the darkness, and Jane noticed that she went south.

"Crill, she's heading for Crill!" Jane shouted. "We have to get there now!"

"You go then, because you aren't apparently wounded!" Dianne shouted. "Use your sense before you use your fists!"

"Okay then," Jane said sadly. "But I'm going to Crill, no matter what anyone says."

CHAPTER 49

The Siege of Castle Steel-Hold

Jor and the others were at the old underground rebel hideout in the woods behind Crill when Alda rushed in, panting heavily.

"What's wrong Alda?" Jor asked.

"We're up on the wanted lists, it seems people are beginning to notice that the rebellion quickly became effective."

"The guard's note," Zen said. "That was probably a ploy to get us."

"Well, how do they know we just weren't passing through like many of the other people?" Adele asked.

"Well, we did stop a public execution, while in public," Turner said. "It wouldn't be hard to find twenty-odd people as witnesses."

Jor took the wanted poster from Alda and burnt it in his hands.

"Well, we've been at this rebellion for a while, and at the rate we're going at, it hardly matters if we're wanted."

"And why is that?" Adele asked.

"Because, we're about to win."

"And how do you suppose we do that?" Turner asked, a grin coming across his face.

"We storm Castle Steel-Hold," he said. "And we take the King out of power."

"But Jor, how do you expect us to do that?" Bernie asked now.

"Yeah, how do you expect us to take a fully garrisoned castle?" Arielle asked.

"We have explosives, don't we?" Jor asked.

"Yes," Bernie agreed.

"And we have many skilled crossbowmen and archers in our ranks?"

"True," Arielle agreed.

"And we have the spirit to match our blades?"

"Hell yes we do!" Alda exclaimed.

"Then what in Edafos is stopping us from attacking? I mean, with all we have done we should be allowed to walk in there and take the King!"

"And because of our recent activity, we've probably lowered the moral of the enemy," Turner said.

"So then what are we waiting for, let's get the King!" Adele said.

The crossbowmen on the walls went about on their daily patrols of the castle on the foggy and overcast day.

"What's the point?" one asked another.

"We have to make sure the rebels don't make it here."

"The rebels? What the hell do they have with this castle?"

"They might attack."

"Yeah, they'll attack when an arrow fired from the forest line over there hits me," the guard joked as he pointed at the tree line, nearly a mile away.

"Don't joke like that, you never know..."

An arrow slammed into the head of the guard, dropping him to the ground.

"Attack, we're under attack!" the other guard shouted, running to warn the others.

Jor slowly lowered his bow.

"You shouldn't waste ammunition with crazy shots like that," Turner said.

"You never know, it could have hit..." Jor said with a small grin.

"Yeah, when pigs fly."

"Careful what you wish for."

The castle garrison began to form up where the shot had been fired, their crossbows loaded and ready.

Little did they now, the rebels were coming from the back with ladders and ropes.

"Is everything going as planned?" Turner asked.

"Umm, I think I can see the garrison up and ready, but I don't see our...there!"

The garrison was now flanked, and standing on the narrow walkway by the battlements, Alda surged forward, hacking them down with her battle-ax.

The men turned to run in the confusion, only to be met on the next side by the other half of the rebel force.

"Okay, ladders!" Jor shouted, and out from the forest line came many rebels, some holding ladders and the others wielding bows to help cover their allies.

From high above the battlements on another tower were more crossbowmen. They fired a volley, wounded and killing several rebels. Soon after, the rebels fired a fast return, and kept firing.

"The towers held, the initial battlements are captured and all that is left to get into the keep, which is probably loaded with warriors," Turner said.

"Good, I'm going to deal with the garrison inside, stay safe," Jor said as he waved to Turner and left.

Alda pounded angrily at the door to the Keep with her fists. She still had berserker mode active and attacked relentlessly.

She felt an arm on her shoulder and instantly calmed down.

"I have this," Jor said to her.

"Okay, help get this door down," Alda said.

Jor frowned at the large wooden double door. It was probably made of reinforced oak and barred on the other side while the garrison inside kept it forced shut.

"Everyone may need to move, and I'll need to get some explosives," he said.

Ferdinand sat quietly inside. He knew the rebels were outside, and he pondered what they would do to him if they caught him.

"Sire, it seems like the rebels are unable to get past the door," one guard said.

"Good, let's keep it that..."

The door exploded violently, killing the men nearby. Out from the smoke and debris, Ferdinand could see two eyes.

One blue, and one red.

He watched in horror as his men fell silently to the ground before him, and a great, arcing sword being swung around his hall.

"A boy!" he shouted as he saw Jor charging in.

A guard swung for Jor's neck, but he easily ducked under it and drove the blade through the guard. He tore it out and cut down two more with one swing.

One guard picked up a crossbow and desperately fired.

Jor caught the bolt.

"What?!" Ferdinand cried.

"We must make our leave sire!" a guard shouted, grabbing the King.

"No, I will use my gifts from the West!" Ferdinand replied.

Alda and the others rushed in, cutting down any of the other left back guards.

"Good show rebels," the King said, clapping.

"Why thank you," Hook said, putting down swords taken from some dead guards.

"Too bad your rebellion ends here."

"And how do you plan to stop it?" Jor asked.

Two figures appeared suddenly in the hall, covered in rags. Their bodies were not visible.

"Meet the Metallos Anthropos!" the King exclaimed.

"Metal men?" Adele asked, throwing back his hood.

"Correct."

"But what do I have to fear of metal men?" Jor asked.

"This."

The men in rags surged forward, and ten rebels were cut to pieces behind Jor.

He turned, only to have a vice grip go around his throat, slamming him to the ground.

"You guys, go! Adele and I will take these guys down!" he shouted in between gagging.

The rebels did so, running out the keep as fast as they could.

"Erebus Ekriksi!" Adele shouted.

The metal man holing Jor looked up and was blasted by the dark energy.

Jor leapt to his feet and raised his hand to it. "Ekriksi!"

The metal man dodged it, and Jor moved easily in turn, dodging the attack made by the second metal man.

"These guys have some speed," Adele said.

"They still can't hit me," Jor said as he ran forward.

He swung for the metal man, but it jumped and stood on his blade. He pulled it from under its feet, but it only back flipped and landed on its feet.

"Attack," it said in a mechanical voice. "Metallos!"

"Many iron limbs shot out from the rags, almost hitting Jor. He dodged most of them, and leapt back.

"Duck!" Adele shouted.

They both did so, and a metallic arm came flying above them from the other metal man.

"Game plan?" Jor asked.

"Don't die," Adele replied.

"Good, just how I like it. Ekriksi Barrage!"

"Erebus Barrage!"

White and Black spheres of energy floated around the room above them.

"Sel Barrage!" the metal men commanded, and strange spheres of dark purple floated above them.

"Damn," Jor said as he leapt out of the way.

The shots began falling around them like rain, destroying anything nearby.

They were all forced to dance around the raining projectiles.

"Teresa Ekriksi!" Adele shouted, firing a shot of dark energy. The metal man dodged it, but went into the path of another attack. It was hit in the back, but it recovered and sent its hand towards Adele.

Jor forced his way through the rain of energy and grabbed the metal arm. He pulled the metal man towards him as energy began to charge up in his hand.

"Apo Pano Ekriksi!" he shouted. A large ball of white energy struck the metal man, sending him flying across the room.

"Metallos Barrage," the other metal man said, and almost twenty arms shot of from between the rags.

Adele used his staff and hacked an approaching arm down the middle. He grabbed both parts of it.

"Teresa Astrape Katastrofi!" Adele commanded. Black lightning went up the metals hand, and he shook as it hit him. He exploded in a blast of dark energy.

Adele was only able to see as the arms of the other metal man hit him. One stabbed him in his arm, and the other cut across his cheek.

"Adele!" Jor shouted as he cut off the two arms.

The metal man charged forward, but Adele hastily put up his staff at the last second. The metal man hit it, and more black lightning surged around him as his energy was drained by the obsidian staff.

He fell to the ground, and as he did, the rain of energy subsided.

"Where is Ferdinand?!" Jor shouted as he looked around the room.

"Down that way!" Adele exclaimed as he pointed down the way of the dungeons.

"Don't worry, he won't get far," Bernie chuckled.

"And why is that?" Jor asked.

"Because, we had a group leave from here and go to the dungeon exit at the opposite forest line."

Jor's eyes returned to normal and he panted heavily.

"Hell, you've made a mess of this place," Hook said.

"We've just won the most important battle of our lives and you're worried about the condition of the floor?!" Jor exclaimed.

Arielle pushed back her hood and kissed Jor on the cheek.

"Loosen up, I'm still trying to believe it's over," she said.

"Jor, what did I tell you?" Turner asked as he folded his arms.

"Hey, she kissed me, not the other way around..."

Turner burst into laughter and embraced Jor. Jor did the same.

"So, when do we get to put up our banner?" Zen asked as he now walked in.

Alda frowned. "I thought we were going to put it up now."

Everyone looked at each other, then smiled.

Celebration and cheers could be heard from the rebels as they raised their own banner of Crill high on the main tower.

People began proclaiming their freedom in the streets, and large festivals seemed to break out from nowhere.

"Crill is free!" someone shouted from atop their house, waving the new country's banner.

Jor and the others now sat in the tavern, reviewing the events that had happened, now three days ago.

"So, what do you plan to do?" Jor asked Arielle.

"Well, I think we should have a fairer monarchy with some kind of assembly of people."

"Like the council of Den Hall?" Adele asked.

"Yes! That's it, we'll form a government just like that!"

"Well, you still need someone at the head," Turner said.

"So what? You expect me to be the Queen of Crill?"

"Well, you could be the High Counselor or something," Adele said.

"Not a bad idea Adele," Arielle said, considering it. "I'll go over it with Bernie and the others. In the meanwhile, where do you all plan to go?"

"Well, we might be heading back up north to the Tower. I'm sure Jane is in a wreck," Turner said.

Adele looked up quickly.

"What's wrong?" Jor asked.

Jane and Dianne forced open the tavern door, both of them tired and panting.

"Jane!" Turner said as he got up and approached her.

"Turner, I can't believe it's you!" Jane said as she ran to his warm embrace.

"What are you doing here?" Turner asked.

"Lane, she came this way after I fought her a few days back. I thought she might have come looking for you!"

"Is Lyra with you?" Jor asked now, getting up.

"Everyone came," Dianne said. "We thought we might run into trouble and brought back up."

Lyra came through the door and her face remained reticent as she saw Jor.

They slowly approached, and as Jor spread his hands apart, he received a stinging slammed across his face.

"I told you she was still mad," Jor said to Turner as he rubbed his cheek.

"How could you do things like that to me Jor? Am I that kind of girl to you, the one that you can just throw away?" she snapped at him.

"Lyra, I've been through hell and worse with you, how do you expect me to toss you away?" Jor replied equally.

"You're lying."

Jor seemed hurt by the words and shook a bit.

"H-How could you expect me to be lying Lyra, I wouldn't do that to you..."

"You already did."

"But I won't again, and I swear and my mother's grave..."

"And how do I know you wouldn't lie to her to?"

She felt Jor's tight grip around her shoulders.

"If I lie to my mother, I would be just as bad as that wretched bastard Lok, and I'll never become that person. If I do, I want you to slit my throat, and if you can't kill me, make sure you get someone who can."

"Oh Jory," Lyra said a she embraced him, tears coming from her eyes.

"I'm sorry Lyra, I didn't mean to do anything to hurt you. It's just that some things...happen."

"All this drama," Kilan said as she walked in.

"Oh damn," Adele said as he remembered the scar on his cheek.

"What's wrong?" Arielle asked.

"Kilan is gonna kill me when she sees the scars," he replied.

"Oh, so she's your girl, this gets interesting by the second."

"Adele, it's been so long," she said, taking his hand.

"Yeah, it has," he said, not taking his other hand off his face.

"What, something on your face?"

"No, just..."

"You're not a good liar you know," Kilan said as she pulled off his other hand.

She gasped. "What happened to you?"

"I was just fighting some metal men, that's all," Adele said.

"I don't care, it's just that you got hurt!"

"He also got stabbed in his left arm," Arielle said idly.

"Damn it," Adele said to her softly. She blew a kiss and winked at him.

Kilan rolled up his sleeve and saw that the area was bandaged up.

"That's it, I'm not letting you out of my sight again, not my Adele," she said, kissing him on the forehead as if he were a young child.

"I'm fine Kilan," he protested.

"That's what the dead people say before they get infections!"

"Oh Eros, save me today if you could!"

CHAPTER 50

The War Begins

Albain frowned on his throne. It had been several days since his messenger left, and he was sure that the trip shouldn't have taken that long. He knew his bombs were already stolen from him, but after that, the current events were unknown to him.

"Good Morning," someone said as they entered the throne room.

"And who is this coming to me unannounced?" Albain replied.

It was Joralkar, one of Jor's older brothers. He was dressed in a chainmail shirt and plain brown pants of linen. He had on a simple Raider's skullcap.

"My name is Joralkar sire, I'm the one of the heads of the military in Denhoec," he said.

"So why are you here then?"

"Because I have come from Crill," he said. "And I have seen that the King has been defeated, his army broken up and his castles under new management."

Albain turned red in that instant. "Under new management?! By who?!"

Joralkar took a scroll from the satchel he wore on his side and opened it up.

"Jorigsveer Great-Blade is one of the foreigners who aided in the Crillic Rebellion," he said angrily. "He is my brother."

"Oh, interesting," Caroline said as she strolled in. "This is a family conflict gone too far."

"Yes it is," Joralkar said. "He left us in Denhoec and just disappeared after the undead army slew our Jarl and we were forced to fight in the city. We thought he had died, but a castle guard went missing and it was found that they headed down through the secret exit of Palace Shatter and left."

"Ah, so a lonely Raider and a castle guard running off," Albain said, following the story carefully.

"And they had a witch with them; a Perialite."

"I believe that was a soul user," Albain corrected him.

"Whatever she was she killed two of our warriors with the help of Jor, and we had them sentenced, and as you know the skeletons attacked and they escaped."

"Well, now I know the name of one of the leaders, now I have a favor to ask of you," Albain said, putting his hands together maniacally.

"What is it you ask King? You give the word and it is done."

"I want you to take some soldiers and head down there. I'll try and give you some Soul Knights and Paladins, but if not, you can take your best men down there."

"So what will I do once I reach?"

"Tell them that the King of Deneaux requests that you send them the heads of the rebel leaders."

"And what if they refuse?"

"Destroy the city, or force them to annex to us."

"Then I shall go and do as you say. Good day King Albain..."

About two weeks had passed since the end of the Revolution and the meeting between Albain and Joralkar, and things were moving smoothly in Crill.

The docks were busy with fishermen and the streets filled with busy shoppers and merchants.

Arielle stood outside on the balcony of the Centro Ciudad Villa, a castle located in the middle of the town. It was much friendlier and open than Castle Steel-Hold, and it allowed an easy view of the ocean.

Arielle was now dressed in the clothes of a noble, with a red dress that stopped at her ankles.

"I never expected any of this," she said.

Bernie, who she had noticed just came in, frowned at what she said. "You didn't expect us to win?"

"No, I didn't expect for us to free Crill without destroying half the city."

"Oh yes, that was something that surprised me very much," Bernie replied, nodding.

Arielle looked at the clear, blue water that bordered the Crillic shores. It sparkled like a sapphire in the sun, and one could see the many ships that were out in the harbor.

"Jor was out there, right Bernie?" she asked wistfully.

"Yep, he's out helping the fishermen," Bernie replied.

"Funny, he went from random foreigner to war hero to fisherman. He doesn't even seem to brag about the battles he fought in."

"Well, he said he was here to help, and that's what he's doing," Bernie replied. "He's one of those kind of men that only show up every couple hundred years."

Arielle chuckled to herself. "By the Divines I wish he was single!"

"I thought you said you were just friends?"

"Well, if I was given the opportunity, I would have gone deeper into the relationship. But he has that elf girl so I'm in no place to take him."

Bernie also chuckled. "Don't worry Arielle, one day you'll find that special person."

Jor struggled as he and the other fishermen pulled in a big haul. As they finally got the net on deck, hundreds of silver-tails, the fish found most abundantly in Crill, poured out on deck.

"I don't think we'll be able to sail back to port," Jor said jokingly. "We might just tip over before we make it."

The other fisherman laughed heartily. "You know, if it weren't for you and the rebels, we would only be able to have a few of these and some bread. Ferdinand would always sell them off for profit," one said.

"Well, now you have an all you can eat buffet for three hundred years!"

They were about to start laughing when they turned to the horizon.

"Now what in blue blazes is that?" one asked.

Jor put his hands over his eyes to shield them from the sun.

"Looks like a longboat," he said. "What could one of those be doing down here?"

"I don't know. Should we warn the city?"

Jor flagged over a smaller boat. "Go to General Gales! Raider ship!" he bellowed from away.

He saw one of the boaters nod and they rowed back to port.

Dianne and Lyra both had a greenish aura about their hands as they hovered them over Turner's arm. They had both worked on their healing skills at the Tower, and now was the perfect time to use them.

The door to his office was thrown open.

"General Gales, a Raider ship has been seen on the horizon!" the one boy said tiredly.

"What?! Who told you this?" Turner asked, completely surprised.

"General Jorigsveer told my grandfather and brother, and when they got to the dock, they told me to get to you as fast as I could."

"I'll go get the boats out then," Turner said. He turned to the two girls. "If Jane asks, I've gone out to the harbor to check on something."

Jor and the other fishermen had already returned to port, and soon after, Jor left with Turner to intercept the boat.

"Looks like we have company," Joralkar said, looking through his small looking glass.

"We attacking them?" the first mate asked.

"No, let them come. I have an idea of who will be there."

The ships soon reached each other, and Jor stood at the bow.

"Who goes there!" he bellowed.

"A friend of yours," a voice replied confidently.

Jor's heart fell as he saw Joralkar at the bow staring at him with an evil grin.

"What's wrong Jor?" Turner asked.

He stepped back slowly. "It's one of my damned brothers, those damned monsters..." he managed to say.

"What's your business?" Turner asked.

"We are here to annex this country in the name of the Great King Albain of Deneaux! We will be forced to attack violently if you do not agree to our terms!"

Turner looked to Jor now. "What now?"

Jor regained himself. "We burn them...destroy the ships..."

"You sure about that? I mean Albain is not someone to be messed with."

"Well we either sink them or all the lives we've lost in the revolution mean nothing."

"Then when Albain sends the rest of the fleet to raze the city? Think Jor!"

Jor stopped and rubbed his chin thoughtfully. They fight and lose, or don't fight and lose. That meant that they had only one other option.

"Turner, tell the sailors to go aboard the other ships and tell them that I've gone away."

"What are you talking about Jor?"

"I'm going to sail this ship down the coast in a diversion."

"But it' Crill they want, not you."

"I'm the one that Joralkar wants, and I doubt Albain will be happy if he doesn't see my head on that platter."

"So you plan to sail this ship by yourself?"

"I'm a Raider Turner, I've helped sail ships since I was seven," he said with a smile. His mood quickly darkened. "Tell Lyra I love her, and my regards to the people of Crill. I'll be off."

"Are you done talking yet?" Joralkar bellowed.

"Just a few more moments," Jor shouted back.

After nearly ten minutes of waiting, Joralkar had enough.

"Alright, give me an answer!" he shouted.

"You're a big loser just like Lok, Horrin and Skall! Catch me if you can!" Jor replied as his boat began to move.

Joralkar, caught by surprise, turned to his crewmen. "Well what are you waiting for? After him!"

The Raider ships started off slow, but they soon turned to go after Jor's ship.

"Damned fool," Turner said angrily to himself as they sailed away on smaller rowboats. "You better not die and leave all of us behind."

Jor was thinking something similar as he dealt with the rigging and rushed to the wheel, then back to the rigging.

"Don't worry guys, I'll be back."

"He did what?!" Lyra and Arielle both shouted. They were all now in the private meeting chambers of the villa.

"He's gone off to stop his brother, just as I said," Turner said.

"Where's he going?" Arielle asked.

"South."

"To the deserts?"

"Wait, deserts?" Lyra asked.

"To the South of us is the country of Zeran, then after that is the nation of the Ayan Saudi," Bernie said.

"Does Jor know this?" Zen asked.

"Nope, he just said he'd go until he finds a port, then he'd stop there and get a plan going," Turner replied.

Lyra fell back into a chair and sighed. "Jorigsveer, always running off! When will I ever stop worrying about him?"

"Don't worry Lyra, I'm sure Jor will think of something," Arielle said, putting her hand on her shoulder. "I mean, the guy has helped us win the Revolution. I'm sure he could handle a few Raiders."

"Oh yeah? Jor had an army when he won those battles! Does he have an army now?"

"You ever saw Jor with his shirt off? With the muscles he has there he is an army," Arielle said.

"True that," Jane agreed. She backed away shyly as she got an odd look from Turner.

"And what happens if he gets another girl down in the desert?" Lyra asked now, almost looking panicked.

"He won't Lyra, I'm telling you," Turner said. "Knowing Jor, he'll be back here before you know it."

"Funny, because I was planning to go back to the deserts myself," Zen said.

"Why on Edafos would you do that?" Alda asked.

"I live there..." Zen replied, questioning himself on why Alda would ask such an ill thought out question.

"But what about me—that's fine," she said, quickly amending her statement.

"You all could come along if you want. I have a fight to win, and Jor inspired me to continue it."

"You can't seriously go back to fighting that silly war with the Ayan Saudi," Dianne said.

"I'm not going to fight them, I'm going to unite them with me against Sahra'a and his Pantheon of Divines!"

"Whoa, whoa, whoa, how on Edafos do you think you'll bring the Zeran and the Ayan Saudi together?"

"Didn't you know I'm an heir to the throne? I have the right to rule, but before I do all that, I have to settle my score with Sahra'a and Ema."

"Now who is this Ema you speak of?" Alda asked quickly.

"A Divine who murdered everyone dear to me," Zen said bitterly.

"And you plan to fight them?" Dianne asked.

"Well...that's why I was hoping you all would come along. I mean, you killed a Divine already, right?"

"Because she was weak and cocky," Adele said.

"So is Ema, well, the cocky part at least."

"Well, wherever you go, I'll go," Alda said.

"I'll go to rescue Jor if anything," Adele said.

"And I'm not leaving Adele alone in the deserts," Kilan said.

"I might as well go too, though I'm not going to fight some super powerful Divine. I just hope Lane is down there," Jane said.

"And I'm finding Jor so I can give him a piece of my mind," Lyra said as she got up, a determined look on her face.

"You people are really serious about this," Turner said.

"Well yeah, I mean it's Jor we're talking about here," Adele said. "He's like the one who started this all off."

"That's kind of true," Jane said. "If it wasn't for Jor, I wouldn't have met you."

"And I wouldn't be alive," Adele said.

"And I would still be a castle guard," Alda said.

"I don't even want to think what those soldiers would have done to me if Jor hadn't fought for me at the border post," Lyra added.

Turner chuckled to himself. "Then count me in. I'll never give up on my brother."

"So it's to the steppes of Zeran?" Arielle asked.

"Well, do you have a problem with us going?" Turner asked.

"We're good on our own for now, you guys on the other hand need to start finding your friends," she said.

"Let's gather our things then, I plan to leave tomorrow," Zen said.

The Den-Deneaux War

From away, many of the people of Den Hall could hear the shouting and debating from the Den Council. For hours already they were debating a course of action to take against the Kingdom of Deneaux over their attempted annexation of Fel Hall.

"We should not rush to war!" one of the elders from Fox Hall shouted. "A war with Deneaux almost certainly means defeat!"

"Then let us go for peace!" a Fen said.

"We cannot go for peace," Akina said. "We already attacked the city and raided their Capitol Castle. No way in hell they'll let us off with a warning."

"But we cannot fight them!" another Fel diplomat said.

"But we can defend against them," Mark said.

The Hall went silent.

"And how do you plan to do this?" the Fen Chief asked skeptically.

"Well, when the Fel Chief raided my caravan," he said indicating Akina. "They were able to take everyone down in a matter of seconds. We had armed cavalry and guards with us in full armor, but yet we were quickly defeated. If we can manage that many times during a single day or week or month, then what's stopping us from being able to stop a Deneauxic advance?"

"Well, we must consider those Soul Knights and Paladins that they have," Illeth said. "We cannot have much camouflage in the bush if they burn it down with their powers."

"Well, you must remember that they are mortals. One shot and they'll die like the rest of us," Will said.

"But it's a problem to get in that one shot when they start putting up their shields," Illeth replied.

"So why not get these soul warriors ourselves?" a Fox elder asked as the debating began again.

"Do we look like we have those kinds of men at our disposal?" a Fen warrior shouted.

"Then I'll find us one!" Akina said, and the Hall went quiet again.

"And where do you plan to find one?" Mark asked, looking towards her, surprised.

"Many of the soldiers from Albain's army have been deserting him. It wouldn't be unlikely that one of them left with the rest of the deserters."

"And you think you'll find some in the near future."

"I know I will," she replied confidently.

Roseanne forced her way through the thick vines that covered wherever she was. It was not too long ago that she was enjoying the luxury of civilization, but now it was only the hard outdoors and her.

"So Soul Knight, what makes you think that you can quit the job?" Albain asked her.

They were both seated in one of the large offices of the Pantheon Castle.

"Well sir..." she stammered out. "I was hoping you would let me off after the war in Keels you know...I just thought that after all that..."

Albain laughed. "You have many more battles ahead of you Soul Knight, now get back to your quarters."

Roseanne left quietly, formulating her escape plan in her head.

Now she was out again running for her life in unknown territory on her own at night. Knowing her own strength she believed that there was nothing out there she couldn't handle, but it was still scary.

After bounding over a stone, she landed heavily on the ground, feeling a pain in her ankle. She nearly fell but kept going. A vine was in her path, but she forced through it, but a spikier and tougher vine awaited and cut her leg. She fell from the sudden sharp pain and went down what could have been a hill or cliff.

Then darkness.

The next morning, the Fel diplomat's caravan was going down the country dirt road.

"These are tough times," Mark said, staring out the window.

"Yeah, and I have to find that Soul Knight," Akina said as she sighed.

Mark turned to her. "You actually want to find one?"

"Is that not what I said?"

"Well yes, but I just thought..."

"That finding one would be impossible?"

"Yes."

Akina put her hands on Mark's face. "I thought you had absolute fate in me."

"I do, it's just I didn't think you could do it."

"I will, I'm telling you, I just have a good..."

"Human!" the driver shouted as the caravan stopped.

Akina and several other Fel warriors exited the carriages and gathered around the being on the road before them.

"Is she alive?" Illeth asked fearfully.

Kullskash was on her knees and checking her pulse.

"She's just out, that's all," she replied.

The warriors put up their spears and swords as they heard her begin to cough. She opened her eyes to see many angry, furry faces.

"Oh my," she said as she began to get up.

"Stay down human," one warrior said.

"Now who are you?" Akina asked.

"Roseanne Pree," she replied from her sitting position.

"And where are you from?" Kullskash asked.

"Deneaux."

"Deneaux? What are you doing down here then?" another Fel warrior asked.

"The King is corrupt there. I've been trying to escape for a few days now," she replied.

"The King has something against you?" Illeth asked.

"I'm a Soul Knight, and considering how valuable we are to the crown, Albain won't let us leave."

Akina's face was already lit up as she helped Roseanne to her feet. "You're a Soul Knight?!"

In her right hand, a fire burned and in the other was a ball of shining light. "Yep, born and raised just to be one."

Akina turned and winked at Mark, whose jaw was dropped. He quickly shut it.

"So human, are you interested in helping in the war?" Kullskash asked.

"War? What war? I thought the Den Revolution was finished," Roseanne asked.

"This isn't a civil war we're dealing with, it's a war with Deneaux," Akina said.

"Don't reveal our plans!" Illeth exclaimed.

"Hey, it doesn't matter if they know or not. War is war."

"Okay, so if I agreed to join you in this 'war', what would you have me doing?" Roseanne asked.

"You could help us in raising Den's own Soul Knights," Illeth said. "Or, that's what I think they want."

"Well...why not? I can't get into any more trouble than I'm already in."

"Yes! I told you I would get one!" Akina said.

"I never doubted you for a second," Mark said as he turned back for the carriages, still in disbelief.

"I thought so," Akina called at him, but he kept walking.

Albain kicked over the table in one of his offices, knocking over many papers and documents. In the angry King's hand was the Den Council's Proclamation.

"This is an outrage! Who are those beast men to think they can go demanding I pay for the damages done to Fel Hall? They should be paying me for attacking my Kingdom!"

"Well sir," the diplomat nervously started. "You kidnapped one of their leaders…"

"So? I had already claimed her as my private property!"

"W-Well sir, all of this doesn't change much…I mean we still have to pay…"

"No, I refuse to yield to them. I want war and I want it now!"

"But sir, wouldn't it be easier if we just pay…"

"Go fetch my Generals! I have land to conquer!"

"I-I'll take my leave then," the diplomat said as he ran out the room.

Caroline soon entered. "Albain, you sound mad."

"I am mad!" he said. "Those beast men are declaring war on me, the most powerful man in Cardia!"

"I don't know about most powerful," she said as she took a seat on the arm of a chair. "This Jor fellow is whipping something up down west."

"He's not dead? I thought his brother had made it their already."

"He has, but they say Jor has led him away from Crill."

"To where?!"

"Zeran I guess," she said, somewhat uncaring.

"Messenger!" he called, and the man entered the room soon after.

"I need you to go down to our allies the Ayan Saudi and tell them that we want the Raider Jorigsveer Great-Blade dead or alive."

"I'll do so sir," the messenger replied and left the room.

"Now all I have to do now is plan this war," Albain said.

"Good luck then Al, you'll need it," Caroline said as she left and several highly decorated military men entered.

CHAPTER 52

Xegel

Jor panted as he tiredly pulled rigging and ran to steer the ship. He had not eaten or slept in, well, a while now. He had tried to keep track of how much time had passed, and with the way the sun was down and it was dark, it could either be evening or dawn.

Joralkar was still behind him, and that was all that mattered. That and finding a port.

"I'll be back Lyra, I'll see you again," he said for the tenth time. He had been repeating this for hours now, and that was what kept him going.

"Joralkar, I see lights on the horizon," the first-mate said as he approached him.

"I see, maybe this is where our friends will stop," he replied.

Jor felt like he was on his last legs when he happened to look up. Before him were lights, and light meant a city or town. He quickly pulled himself up and saw he was now too far off.

"No time to put this in the harbor," he said weakly. He rose to his feet and rolled the wheel, turning the ship hard left for the coast.

"Captain, they're going for the coast," the first mate said.
"What, why?" Joralkar asked.
"I'm not sure, we'll have to wait and see."

Jor felt as the ship skid across the ocean floor. He was hoping that he wouldn't hit a reef before he reached shore. The ship was now on a collision course with land, and before it hit, and strong wind blew into its sail and forced it up onto the coast.

Jor was knocked about with the sudden impact and rose weakly. He could feel the blood running down his face but paid no mind to it.

"Suck it up Jor," he said. "You've been through worse."

He leapt off the side of the ship and hurt his legs as he hit the ground. He kept going despite this. Ahead of him were the steppes of Zeran. He could see down the coast the city and limped towards it.

"Shipwrecked?!" Joralkar shouted. "How?"

"I don't know Captain," the first mate said, slightly annoyed. "Maybe they hit a reef."

Send a party down that way, I want the heads of everyone onboard!"

Jor could see now that smaller boats were approaching the ship, but they were only taking the bait he left. He could now get help at the town and later go back to Crill.

"See, nothing to worry about," he laughed.

The town was quiet, and only a few people were outside, putting out any of the lamps and torches left outside.

Several of them were startled by the appearance of the bloody boy.

"My dear child, what happened to you," and elderly woman said as she approached.

"I was saving my friends from a Raider attack and ended up wrecking my own boat and limping all the way here."

"Don't worry, come inside, we'll fix you right up."

Jor was brought inside the small hut made of a thatch roof and clay brick walls. There was an opening in the roof and a fireplace in the middle of the floor.

Several of the members of the family were startled by the appearance of this wounded stranger.

"Now who's this?" an elderly man asked as he got up from his bedroll.

"A wounded boy who needs our help. Bayara, get some bandages!"

A girl about Jor's age quickly did so, reaching into a crate of different items.

"Jagu, help your sister," the old woman ordered, and the young boy did so.

The girl was wrapping the bandages around his head while her brother wiped off the blood on his face.

The girl was covered in dust, and wore a dress made heavily from furs. Her eyes were narrow, just like Zen's. Her hair was grown down to her back.

Her brother had hair that went down to the bottom of his back, and also wore furs.

"What country am I in?" Jor asked.

"Shh, rest warrior," she said. Jor liked how soft her voice seemed.

"You're in Zeran," the boy said. "The village of Xegel."

"Good," he said simply.

Several hours had past and Jor was sleeping soundly. The villagers had known of the newcomer's arrival early in the morning and were curious about him.

"So Bayara, who is this person you have here?" one village girl asked. They were standing right outside their hut.

"He's a Raider from the West," she replied.

"Is he cute?" another girl asked.

"Why do you ask?"

"Well, I always dreamed someone from the West would take me to the big Deneaux country."

Bayara laughed. "Sorry, that is not your knight in shining armor. To tell you the truth, he looked pretty disoriented when we found him."

"Well how is he now?" the third girl asked.

"Sleeping. Want to watch him sleep?"

"Yes," the second girl agreed quickly.

"I was joking…"

"Bayara is it?" Jor asked as he now approached. He almost hit his head on the doorway, and the girls giggled as they saw him.

"Yes, that's me," she replied.

"Well, do you have anything to eat around here?"

"The mess hall is ahead if you want food," she said, pointing to it.

"Okay, and thanks for the patching up you did," he said, indicating the bandage around his head.

As he left, the second girl, Denai, sighed wistfully.

"He's tall," she said.

"Yeah," Bayara agreed.

"And handsome..."

She grunted in reply.

"And appealing..."

"I get it Denai," she said, annoyed.

As Jor entered the mess hall, he saw that several of the elders were arguing about something.

"I'm telling you, the bandits will eventually leave once they get tired of us!" said Chuli, the head huntsman.

"They won't leave, they can take as much from us as they want as long as we keep producing!" said Simsay, the old man in the house with Bayara. "We need an army."

"All our young men have gone to war Simsay, we have no one to fight with!" said Tuluy, another village elder.

"What Tuluy says is true," the village elder, Gali said.

"So we'll just give the bandits everything we have? What happens when they start to take our women and children, what then?" Simsay said.

"We may just have to let them go. That is the way it may have to be," Gali said sadly.

"Did you say you have a bandit problem?" Jor asked as he walked in.

"Yes outlander," Gali said. "They've been stealing from us for years and we have not been helped."

"How much bandits are there?" Jor asked.

"We couldn't ask you to fight for us in your current state outlander," Tuluy said.

"I heal fast," Jor replied. "And once I do, I'll help with the bandit problem."

"Where's your army then?"

"I have my sword, my bow, my hands and my soul. Those are all the soldiers I'll ever need."

"I hope you know these men are mounted, and there are many of them," Gali said.

Jor laughed. "I've been through the battle of Keels and the Crill revolution. I can handle a simple skirmish with bandits."

"So you're a soldier?" Simsay asked.

"Solider, adventurer, freelancer, student...I'm a lot of things."

"That's good then," Gali said, shaking Jor's hand. "Just know we'll be in your debt for saving us if you can do this."

"I've saved my fair share of people, I don't need anything from you in exchange for helping."

Bayara and the other girls were still talking when Jor approached, a large piece of meat in his hands and mouth.

They went quiet as he passed, and he stopped and awkwardly turned to them.

"Did I do something wrong?" he asked, food still in his mouth.

"No Raider, you can go inside," Bayara said, somewhat embarrassed.

"Hi," Denai said nervously.

"Hello..." Jor said.

"So, where are you from?"

"Denhoec. Very, very far from here."

"So how did you get here?"

Jor looked around at the expectant faces. "I have to sit down for this one, because my story is long as hell."

Many of them giggled as they followed him inside.

Several hours had passed as he told them about what was happening up North and of his adventures, and as he spoke, more and more villagers came.

"So you really fought alongside an heir to the throne?" Denai said, mystified.

"I really don't know if he is, he just claims to be," Jor replied.

"I still can't believe you fought Divines!" Jagu said.

"But what possessed you to fight in Crill?" Bayara asked now.

"I just saw a place that needed help and helped. I hardly have a real purpose nowadays, so I do what I can."

"And after all this you're still single?" Denai asked.

"Nope, and I've gotten in enough trouble with her already."

"So, how long will it be until you're up and running again?" Simsay asked.

"Maybe three days or more, I still have to catch myself, but once I do, those bandits will be on their knees."

CHAPTER 53

Steppes of Zeran

Zen frowned as he looked through his small looking glass. The steppes were flat and empty, except for a few short bushes and the low grass that sometimes grew here and there.

"We may cross to the capitol," Zen said to Turner and the other. They were all mounted, as going about the steppes on foot would mean trouble.

"What's wrong with crossing the capitol?" Turner asked.

"Well, young and powerful Zeranians such as I are prime targets of recruiters, and I don't plan on fighting my way out of the city to avoid being drafted."

"So we're just skipping it and going ahead?"

Zen pointed to the ocean, which was down a hill about half a mile away.

"We'll stay on the coasts, Jor should be in one of the seaside villages."

"Adele!" Turner called. "Where's the nearest village?"

"Xegel in the south!" he replied after carefully studying the map he held. "It's several miles off."

"There's a problem then," Zen said.

"What's the problem?" Alda asked.

"We may have bandits traveling around there, and I don't think you all are versed in steppe warfare."

"What's so hard about swinging a sword and bashing skulls?" Alda said, folding her arms, nearly sliding off the saddle.

"They ride and shoot with bows and arrows, and will make quick kills with sabers, spears and javelins. They're merciless, so killing Adele or Kilan isn't above them."

"Good thing I've had cavalry lessons in Harmony," Adele said.

"Oh, planning to use Soul while mounted?" Jane asked, her interest growing.

"I could try something if the time comes, for now though, let's go."

They began riding to the South, but for some reason, the place was quiet...far too quiet.

"Birds," Zen said finally after half an hour of riding.

"Excuse me?" Lyra asked as she stopped her horse.

"I haven't been hearing any birds."

"Well we're on a steppe with hardly any trees, why would there be birds?" Turner asked.

"You would occasionally hear them overhead every once in a while, but the place is silent," Zen replied. His eyes widened as he saw what lay down a hill in front of them.

Bird cries could now be heard from away.

"There are your birds," Kilan said. "Now can we get moving?"

"Those aren't regular birds," Zen said grimly. "Those are vultures."

"Oh," Alda said. "Let's go over there and check it out then."

Zen put his hand up.

"Are you sure you want to go check it out?"

"Yeah we're sure," Turner said.

"These aren't like bodies you would see on a normal battlefield, the Zeran and Ayan Saudi themselves disregard each other as animals for slaughter and extermination, and will savagely mutilate each other... and there are also many 'other' things in the deserts that will tear apart anything they see. One of those being Ema."

"I'll stay back," Kilan said nervously now.

"Same here," Lyra said.

"I'll stay back with the girls to, you know, protect them," Adele added nervously.

"Chicken," Jane laughed. "I'm coming."

"Let's head for it then," Turner said, and they rode off.

On the scene were the bodies of what seemed like caravan guards and merchants, but they were all cut up badly in the chest and neck, among other places. Nearby, the dead corpses of bandits lay in the dust with similar wounds.

A few horses were not too far off and were grazing. They all had equipment on them, showing they were used by either the merchants or the bandits.

"Either they fought this battle hard," Alda said. "Or there was a third, really powerful opponent here."

"All this blood makes me think of Ema, and this does not seem above her," Zen said.

"And you're right," a voice said from behind.

Zen turned to see Ema, in her older form standing atop a chest, several gold coins flickering around in her hands.

"Now who are you?" Turner asked.

"Just your average steppe cutie, and who are you? My brave and gallant knight?"

"Cut the crap Ema," Zen said, drawing his sabre.

"Zen, is that really you?" she said as she got off the chest and walked to him. "It's been about what? A year and change since you've been gone! Did you miss me?"

"Did you not hear me say cut the crap? Besides, I want Sahra'a, not you."

"So uptight and mean, but I can fix that."

"You'll be fixing your face when I'm done with you!"

"And what are you gonna do? Cut me?" she taunted as she winked at him.

"I have little reason not to," Zen replied flatly.

"Well my face is right here to draw sweet scarlet blood from. You could give me a kiss too if you wanted."

Zen swung at her angrily, but as the blade neared her face, it stopped midair.

"Who is that?" she asked, pointing at Alda.

"Someone you shouldn't be worrying about!" he replied, grunting as he tried in vain to finish the strike.

"Tell me or she blows up," she said, her mood turning dark for a second.

"Alda Breach-Breaker, my friend," he said in defeat, loosening his grip on his sabre.

Ema waved him away, and he was thrown through the air and landed hard on the ground.

"So, you're Zen's friend eh?"

"Yeah, you have a problem with that?" Alda asked, trying her best to show that she wasn't moved.

"Well, I was hoping I could have Zen, seeing he is one of my people. I mean, you're a Raider and all, and Raider girls need to be with their big huge bear-looking counterparts."

"I prefer to hang around Zen," she replied, inching away.

"I'd prefer you'd go back to the North with Fenalph where you belong."

"This is no good," Jane whispered to Turner. "We should really get out of here."

"What, you scared?"

"Hell yeah I am, she's no ordinary Divine. Even Eros would have a hard time with her."

"Well we can't just leave Zen and Alda alone with her."

"Then why not hang out with me," a familiar voice said from behind.

Jane turned fearfully and her heart dropped in that instant.

"You look like you've seen a ghost," Lane laughed.

"What are you doing here?" Jane asked angrily, an icy wind blowing about her.

"I'm hanging out with my new friend Ema! She's teaching me all kinds of fun moves, and she knows a lot of cool things."

"Fun moves?"

"I can blow up people from the insides now! Isn't that great?"

"You realize those people don't appreciate dying."

"That's why you make them feel good first..."

"Seduction," Turner said with a chuckle. "You people make me sick you know, you're just like sirens."

"Enough of this," Haima said as she approached over a small ridge. "It's getting late and I want to get back to my gold throne."

"You all go," Ema called. "I'm not done with my girl's day out."

Lane went with Haima, and disappeared in a black teleportation ring.

Ema tickled Alda's chin and laughed.

"You should just give up now, you know you couldn't get Zen."

"And what makes you say that?" Alda replied, stepping forward.

"Zerani want house maids that pop out litters of children, not warriors."

"Shut up!" Alda shouted.

"Or what?"

"I'll do worse than cut you!"

"I have the power of regeneration. I'm the ultimate Divine you know."

"Just go away then. If you're the ultimate Divine, why waste time with us mere mortals?"

"I love destroying mortals physically, but now I get to destroy one emotionally. It's a skill I've always wanted to practice."

"Just leave me alone for once."

"Go home then and forget about my Zen Zeran."

"I refuse."

"Listen Raider, I own every man in Zeran and Ayan Saudi. Are you trying to steal from my collection?"

"Your collection?! Zen is not some object to be collected!"

"Well, he looks like a fun toy to play with, maybe I could get more use out of him than most."

"He's not your toy," Alda said, the anger welling in her voice.

"Then who does he belong to?" Ema challenged.

"Zen is his own man, and he does whatever he wants whenever he wants."

"Still, I guess I'll just seduce him to my side."

"You'll fail."

"Why is that?"

"Because—Zen loves me more!"

"Loves you? A big bear of a Raider, we already went over this. Zerani want cattle, not warriors. Just look how he's knocked out over there, I could just pick him up and go home with him if I wanted," she said as she began walking over to him.

"No, don't!" Alda shouted, her hand going to her hilt.

"You're willing to fight for Zen?"

"Yes I am," she replied equally.

"I'll give you there first swing. I win, Zen is mines, you win, Zen is yours. To make it fair, I won't even use my powers."

Alda drew her sword and swung at Ema in a fraction of a second. Ema dodged it like she was a feather in the wind.

An arm hit Alda in the back, and Ema's leg went between hers and she tripped her. Alda landed face first in the dirt.

She tried to get back up, but Ema placed her foot on Alda's back, and she couldn't get up no matter how hard she tried.

"Zen is mines," Ema laughed.

"No!" Alda shouted, her eyes turning red from entering berserker mode.

"Oh please, that foolish mode hardly even helped them in the 300 Year War, how on Edafos would you expect that to harm me now?"

"Get off, I'm not done yet!"

Ema placed her finger on the back of Alda's head, and she suddenly exited Berserker mode.

"Checkmate," Ema said as she walked off to retrieve Zen.

"Don't take him," Alda cried, reaching out in vain.

"Why shouldn't I?"

"We've been through too much together for me to lose him so quickly," she said, the tears running from her eyes.

Ema pulled the necklace that Zen had given Alda from around her neck telekinetically and held it before her.

"What's this? I didn't know you Raiders were into fashion."

"It's a necklace..."

"From Zen," Ema laughed as she put it around her own neck.

"That's enough Ema," Turner said as he approached her.

"I don't think it would benefit you to get too close, you might just break another arm."

"Just calm down, we don't have to do things we'll regret here."

"I regret nothing I do!" Ema laughed.

"You'll regret this," Turner replied seriously.

"And who'll make me regret this?"

Turner wanted to answer her challenge, but he knew that could mean an instant death on his part.

Zen leapt up and put his sabre to Ema's neck in an instant.

"This is where your cockiness has gotten you!" he shouted.

A spray of blood flew through the air as his blade went through her neck.

She choked desperately for air, then fell silently into the dust.

"Now I have avenged my warband," he said sadly. "All that's left is to avenge myself."

He heard laughing, and as he looked down, he saw Ema still cracking herself up. She rose, the wound in her neck healing.

"You're the first person to actually make me bleed in so many years... could you do it again?"

The words hit Zen to the point that he staggered back and fell in fear.

"Y-You're not real! No one sheds blood so easily in Zeran!"

Ema laughed loudly, a bit of madness almost evident in it. "You people make me laugh, honestly. Don't you mortals love the sight of each other's blood, the satisfaction that you've struck the right vein and the feeling of cutting through flesh? Isn't war beautiful to you? Isn't suffering one of your fine arts? I've walked Edafos since it was just a giant stone with no living beings, and watched how you have all evolved.

"You've all evolved through the need to be better than one another, making better weapons and armor, just to hack and kill each other when neither side can seem superior, and deem it as a righteous act. I watched when they founded the Deneauxic Empire through blood, and rose it from the dirt through blood, and watched as it expanded by blood, only to see it is still bleeding!

"You're all in for a war, and a great bloodshed, and you'll see me at the forefront. First we shall take Edafos, then I'll kill Albain and any heirs. The Kingdom will fall into chaos, and I'll be free to get Fenalph and Titus, and after them, I'll get Eros and Efiia, who'll be trying to hold their dear Kingdom together. Soon enough, we'll be back to the good old days of blood and bronze, where men knew only rage, and felt no love for the Divines.

"Killing is your fine art, and I've adopted it and made it beautiful beyond imagination. I want a world were the ocean that you see to the West of here will be red. We will know of the sight of the beautiful scarlet for all eternity, and I will be praised for it! Praised for my art!

"But really, in the end, you brought it about, angry, malicious, destructive, vicious, blood stained mortals."

A black circle appeared underneath Ema, and she disappeared soon after, a broad smile on her face.

"We can't beat her," Zen said fearfully, holding his head in his hands. He looked up to see Alda, and ran to her.

"Are you okay Alda?"

Alda reached out and embraced him tightly.

"I don't want to lose you Zen, I never want to lose you!"

"You won't Alda, I'll be around for as long as you need me."

"Then do you promise to love me for who I am?"

"I always loved you for who you were. Now promise me you'll never let Ema get to you."

Alda only cried in his arms, while Turner and Jane stood afar.

"We better find Jor soon, that kid is going to get us killed," Turner said.

"Well let's ride back then. The faster we find him, the quicker we get to leave."

CHAPTER 54

Uhuran Bandits

Jor swung his great-blade mightily, cutting down three hay targets at once. He turned, lunging the sword through the head of the target. He got another down and stabbed his sword into it, leaving it there and drawing his bow.

He quickly shrugged it from over his shoulder and fired at the targets at the end of the field. Several of the shots were off, but most roughly hit their mark.

He quickly threw down the bow and drew a dagger, viciously lunging it into several nearby targets.

"Ekriksı!" he commanded, sending a shot of energy into the last standing target, tearing it apart.

"Good job Great-Blade," Jagu said, clapping.

Jor picked him up playfully and put him on his shoulder.

"It's a gift I supposed. I would much rather talk with the bandits, but it seems most bandits usually understand only violence."

Jor stopped as he saw Bayara now. She picked up a bow left behind one of the houses and took up a quiver.

She took careful aim and fired.

The shot hit the head of the target, the bucket helmet skewered on by the arrow.

She fired a quick volley, moving up and down the range, the shots hitting head and body. She took aim once again and fired the pretend sword off a target, and shot the helm off another.

"Bayara!" Simsay shouted as he approached her.

"Oh yes father," she said, quickly putting down the bow.

"Young ladies do not need to be shooting," he said sternly.

"How so?" Jor asked as he approached.

"Oh, Jorigsveer. I was just telling my daughter that combat is forbidden among young ladies."

"And that is why I asked why," he replied, putting Jagu down. Several people saw that something might be developing, and watched what would play out.

"Well, do women where you live fight in wars?"

"They do not fight in wars," Jor said. "But many that I know are well versed in combat. Some are even more powerful than I."

"Are any of them archers?" Bayara asked, but Simsay silenced her with a wave of the hand.

"That's the only reason many of them are alive. I know a girl by the name of Alda, and she was there with me in the battle for Crill, along with another named Arielle."

"Well we do not need our young people fighting."

"But it would help for them to know how. If bandits attack, you'll want people who can defend you..."

"We have no more men to spare!"

"Well women can fight just as well if needed, and to tell you the truth, I doubt there's anything harder to break than a line of angry women. One was hard enough for me to get past," he laughed. "But seriously though, Bayara has skill with the bow. Why not let her practice for the fun of it?"

Simsay looked around to see the expectant faces of the many villagers. "I'll be home if you need me, let's go Bayara," he said, defeated.

Soon enough, night was upon them, and Jor stood at the town center, a torch in his hands. He wore his cloak, as it was a bit chilly out.

"You'd think that bandits were a bit more active at night," he said to himself.

He heard hoof beats off in the dark, and soon enough, he could see the bandits riding in. They entered the center, circling him and brandishing their weapons.

They all stopped, and an older, bearded Zerani man rode up before Jor.

"Name yourself peasant, I do not recall your face."

"Jorigsveer Great-Blade of the High Clan Great-Blade," he said proudly.

"A Raider eh? What are you doing here?"

"I'm here to talk to you."

"About what?"

"Well, I've heard you've been aggressive towards this village, and I may have to ask you to stop."

"Or what?" the bandit leader asked, laughing with the rest of his men.

An arrow slammed into the head of the man next to the leader, their body sliding off the side of the saddle.

"Or that will happen," Jor said.

"Kill him!" the bandit leader shouted angrily, his horse rearing up as he gave the command.

Jor drew his great sword and swung at an approaching bandit, hitting them a glancing blow in the arm. They slid off the saddle and rolled in the dust.

Another bandit swung out at Jor, but he blocked it. They rode around for him again, and he side-stepped at the last second and swung, slicing through his furs and hitting his ribs.

The bandit that had fallen off their horse had gotten up to face Jor now. Jor looked behind him to see an approaching mounted bandit.

"Bayara!" he exclaimed.

A shot flew from seemingly nowhere and hit the bandit in the back. Jor turned in that instant and put up his hand.

"Ekriksi!"

The shot slammed into the bandit's chest and sent them flying.

The bandit leader came from behind without Jor knowing. He quickly turned and put up his sword, but the leader was able to knock it from his hand with ease.

He drew his dagger.

"Come on Jor, you must have gotten some bit of skill from Lyra," he said to himself.

A bandit was quickly approaching, and he flipped the dagger, holding it by its tip. He tossed it, and it slammed into the bandit's chest.

They fell nearby him, and he picked up his sabre.

He quickly swung, deflecting an arrow that was fired by another bandit.

"Ekriksi Barrage!" he commanded, several shots of energy floating around him.

They flew in every direction, hitting anything in their path. Three bandits went down in the barrage.

"Jorigsveer, behind you!" Bayara shouted as she ran out from the cover of the village barn.

Jor turned to see the bandit leader swing at him. He fell back, avoiding the slash, but before he could get up, the leader had leapt off his horse and approached his downed opponent.

Bayara dropped her bow and charged at him.

The leader turned, only to see a heavy boot before blacking out.

Her kick had hit his temple exactly, and he fell over soon after.

"I could have killed him right then and there you know," Jor said as he got up and dusted himself off.

"Well...I just wanted my moment of glory, you know," she replied, punching him on the arm.

Simsay gasped as he saw the village center. It was laden in the bloody bodies of the dead bandits.

"How on Edafos do you expect us to clean this up?!" Gali exclaimed.

"You clean it up? I'm the one that ended them and I should be the one who should clean them up," Jor said with a small smile.

"But you've done so much already," Tuluy said.

Jor picked up one of the bodies and held them over his shoulder.

"I'm about to do more too."

Bayara came up alongside him and picked up another dead bandit, one that was much bigger. Jor's eyes widened at her strength.

"I shot down a few of these guys, I might as well take half the load," she said.

"Well, I suppose I can't change your mind then," he said. "Hey Simsay, you have a shovel?" he called.

"I-I'll get it," he said, appalled.

CHAPTER 55

Intervention

The band of warriors rode over the steppes at a slow canter. Zen looked about, while the others quietly spoke amongst themselves.

"Crap! Stop!" Zen shouted.

Turner and the others pulled on the reins, immediately stopping the horses.

"What is it?" Alda asked.

"I see one of our ships," he replied.

"The one Jor took," Turner said darkly.

"What if he's still onboard, or hurt?" Lyra asked fearfully.

"Then he's screwed," Zen said. "It seems our Raider friend has beaten us to it."

"Joralkar is gonna pay if he puts a hand on Jor," Turner said angrily. "Allons-y!" he shouted as he got ready to charge."

"We would have seen a few bodies if Jor was there," Adele said. "That guy has far more resilience than he shows."

"So we just keep going on like nothing?" Jane asked.

"It would be best I suppose, besides, I'm sure Jor is at some town, having all the local girls at his feet," Kilan laughed.

"Allons-y!" Lyra shouted angrily as she charged down the coast.

"You're good with manipulating people, aren't you?" Adele asked, smiling at her.

"I'm one of the best," Kilan laughed.

"So that's when I decided I didn't need the shovel to scoop up the snow, but boy, was I in for a surprise," Jor said to several of the village girls that were gathered by him. "I never got buried by snow before, but it was cold."

"Oh my gosh Jor, you're so cool," Denai said.

"I was a lot more than cool that day though," he said to them, and they all giggled.

"Lame pun Jor," Bayara said as she passed.

"They don't think so," he argued.

"Well I do," she said as she winked at him and walked off.

"Excuse me for a second ladies," he said as he got up and followed her.

"So Bayara, you ever wondered about leaving the village?" he asked.

"Sometimes, why?"

"Well, I was planning on leaving soon and going back to my friends in Crill, and I didn't want to risk going out there on my own..."

"And you see how good I am with a bow and want me to be part of your little band of adventurers?"

"H-How did you know?" Jor asked, surprised.

"You're not a very complicated person," she replied.

"Are you trying to insult me Bayara? You really seem to be implying something."

"Exactly my point, besides, you think I'm hard to get."

"I'm not interested in getting you, no offense," Jor replied.

"Then why abandon your fan girls and come to me individually?"

"Because you're full of surprises, and not the kind where Denai throws hot soup on me by accident," he said, and they both laughed.

"So...when you heading back out?" she asked now.

"Maybe today, or tomorrow, I don't really know."

"Well, this is a thank you gift for helping us," she said as she embraced him.

"Hey, I don't get good results in these kinds of situations," he said quickly.

"Just enjoy it, you're girlfriend isn't around..."

"JORIGSVEER GREAT-BLADE!" someone shouted from away.

He turned fearfully to see a rider approaching quickly. Bayara let go of him and watched as the horse stopped before them, rearing into the air before coming to a full stop.

"L-L-Lyra?" Jor said weakly.

"So, you can't stop messing around for a few weeks," she said with folded arms.

"She's just a friend!" he argued.

"Oh really? Then why was she hugging you like that?"

"Because..."

"I don't want to hear it," she interrupted as she got off the horse.

"You're an elf?" Bayara said in complete surprise.

"You have a problem with elves?" she asked aggressively.

"No, but it's just hard to take you seriously now that I see you're so... short..."

"Jor, what's her name?" she asked.

"She has a mouth Lyra," Jor said, putting his hand of his face.

"I'm Bayara of Xegel, nice to meet you," she said, extending her hand.

"Well who are you to be hugging Jor?" she asked now.

"I'm simply his friend, and I was hugging him to show how happy I am for him saving our village."

"Hey Bayara, who's this?" Denai asked as she approached.

"Lyra, Jor's girlfriend apparently," Bayara replied.

"You're Lyra? I was expecting someone more...fitting to someone like Jor..."

"You think I'm not good enough for Jor—I'm not his girlfriend!"

"Oh good, I know he would need to be with someone gorgeous like me," she said, tossing her hair back.

"When I'm done with you," Lyra said. "You won't even be able to be matched with a mud brick!"

"Hold on there," Jor said as he grabbed her and held her back. "Let's just all calm down here."

"You're learning problem solving for once without a sword," Turner laughed as he approached with the rest of the group.

"It's not as easy," he replied with a weak smile.

Jor packed up his supplies in the saddle bag and began mounting the horse.

"Hey Jor," Bayara called.

"Don't get me killed Bayara," he said, quickly putting up his hands in a mock fighting stance.

"So, where you headed now?"

"Deep in the deserts," Zen said as he walked over by them.

"But the Ayan Saudi..." she said to him.

"There are things much worse than them out there, trust me," he said.

"That's not it. The Ayan Saudi has been getting the upper hand, and now they are on the first provinces. They're going to lay siege to Zeran soon."

"So it's a siege again, but this time we're defending," Alda laughed.

"You'll have a hard time defending the entire city yourselves."

"Why is that?" Jor asked.

"The Emperor is dead, and his armies scattered and in fear of the powerful force that destroyed him and his best soldiers. Something vile and dark attacked them, and I fear it has the power of a Divine."

"Ema and Sahra'a are behind this," Zen said silently to himself.

Jor mounted, and he helped up Lyra as she approached.

"We may meet again one day I suppose," Jor said to Bayara.

"Maybe we will," she replied. "See you, Jorigsveer Great-Blade."

"Bye Jory!" the crowd of girls cried nearby.

"Good bye, tell Simsay and Jagu and everybody else that we'll save Zeran!"

"Ready to go, fearless leader?" Turner asked.

"Leader? Since when did we have one of those?" Jor asked as he obliviously turned and looked behind him.

"You're the one who started this whole adventure Jor, it's only fair that you be leader," Jane said.

"But it's Zen's quest, so I'll leave him in charge for now."

Zen nodded to him and smiled. "Well as a first order, we'll go check on Zeran. I want to make sure my country is safe first, then we'll see about Ema..."

CHAPTER 56

Amec

Amec was still wandering aimlessly, unsure what was going on, and unable to get a grasp of his emotions or good sense.

Shadows seemed to appear on the horizon, but they were hard to see over the desert heat.

The whole world seemed to be enveloped in this shadow, and everything went blank from there.

"Aman?!" he shrieked as he awoke suddenly.

Kilan and Lyra fell backwards in the tent is surprise.

The man looked about nervously, trying make sense of what has been going on.

"So, you're awake," Kilan said. "I thought you were dead for sure."

"I-I, where am I?" he replied.

"A tent in the middle of the desert," Lyra added.

"How did I get here?"

"We found you passed out," Kilan said.

"Oh..." he said, looking down sadly. "That means all that happened was a reality..."

"Well lay down then, panicking won't help you at all."

"May I see that dagger you're wearing?" he asked Lyra.

"Why?" she asked.

"So I may end my life here. I've failed as an Elite Mamluk warrior, and I've failed as a protector of my village and what's left of my tiny family."

"How about we talk about it instead. Digging a grave in the sand is the least I want to do right now," Kilan said.

Zen, Jor and the others were waiting outside when Jane approached them.

"This guy has met up with Ema before, and it seems she recruited his son to her dark cause," Jane said.

"Oh really," Zen said. "Then we have something in common."

"You going to check on him?" Jor asked.

"Yep," he said as he went over to the tent.

The man's eyes widened when he saw Zen enter, but Zen only smiled in reply.

"You two girls can leave the tent now," he said to Kilan and Lyra.

"That's a nice way to say get out," Kilan said as she exited, followed by Lyra.

"Kill me if you need to," the man said.

"Nope, I've come to talk."

"About what? Zeranians don't talk, they kill."

"I was told the exact same thing about the men of the Ayan Saudi," Zen said, chuckling to himself. "But I've come to talk about your loss and my loss to that girl."

"Her," he said as he clenched his fists.

"Yes, she killed my entire squad and killed my closest friends. She also killed your son and destroyed the village you were stationed at."

"So you know what it's like then," he said sadly. "I never thought I would be actually connecting with an enemy..."

"We're all family here, my name is Zen Zeran, I was a warrior in this war, but I soon saw how futile it was, and now I want to make things right."

"And how do you plan to do that?"

"First I'm going to help defend Zeran and try to get some recognition there. Since the Emperor is dead, the people will want someone to look up to..."

"But that sounds like you're trying to seize power from possible rightful heirs…"

"I am an heir, but I want to seize power so I can finally make peace with the Ayan Saudi, and soon after we'll come together and defeat Ema and her vile League of Divines."

"Then first thing's first. How do you plan to get the people's approval at Zeran?"

"Maybe defending the city will make them join me? It's a plan in the making. Ideas will come when the time comes."

"I suppose…" the man said wistfully. "Oh, and by the way, my name is Amec."

"Well nice to meet you then," Zen said, shaking his hand. "Let this be the first of the new bonds that will be shared among the Zeran and the Ayan Saudi."

CHAPTER 57

Dasimay's Melancholy

Ema laughed uncontrollably as she sat on a stool made of solid gold, looking into a pool of water in the Sanctuary.

"Look at the Zerani, they're losing provinces like crazy. I wouldn't kill them to fight back a little, but then again, it would!" she laughed.

"Ugh, don't you ever get bored off all that fighting? That stuff is tiring," Haima said, playing with the gold coins scattered on the floor.

"You know I'll never get tired of it. Hey Lane, want to see?" she called.

Lane appeared out of nowhere and landed on her lap.

"What's all that?" she asked.

"It's the battle for one of the last provinces of Zeran. It seems now that the war will be coming to an end."

"Seems like a lot of killing for no reason," Lane said, watching as a line of infantry were cut to pieces by charging cavalry.

"Yeah...but it's fun to watch."

"So what about when all your Zerani play things are dead?" Dasimay asked, leaning on a wall in a dark corner.

"I'll probably get them to hate on the people of Crill, or better yet, maybe Sahra'a has a better idea. Big brother always finds the time to get me more entertainment."

"So be it then," Dasimay replied. "I'll be leaving soon, so don't bother looking for me."

"You'll only get killed like our friend Toxotes if you take on your sister again," Haima warned.

"Toxotes is the last thing on my mind right now. My sister is the one who needs to die. Someone from such an unworthy bloodline must be killed before they can make another heir."

"Your own goals conflict with what is right."

"So did my Father's, but no one said anything, and there he is six feet under with four daughters from four different mothers."

"He atoned for his sins before death Dasimay," she said, approaching her. She spoke quietly now. "I don't know about the rest of them, but I value some life, and you losing yours won't help the world very much."

"I won't die Haima. You're starting to sound like that wench Eros. She's going down right after Akina and her friends."

"We may need you here, we have several people moving through here that aren't push-overs...I think they may be the ones who killed Mortha."

"Well, can't you handle them?"

"The future is uncertain. These mortals are stronger than one would think, and soon it may seem, they could start hacking their way through here again, with men with the powers of us Divines."

"Well I'm only a half-blood, so I don't need to dabble in the affairs of the Divines. Good day."

"Dasimay, don't do this! We have all that you could want in here!"

"There is no revenge in here. That is all I seek."

"That only leads to death. You know that Dasimay!"

"Well, death follows death does it not? I'm just continuing the cycle."

"Come on Dasimay..."

"I already said no, now good bye Haima."

Dasimay walked out slowly, slinging her obsidian bow across her back.

CHAPTER 58

Back to Arms

Zen sat on his horse high on a dune overlooking the city of Zeran. Its walls were high and made of hardened clay and chiseled stone. The houses were also made of the same material.

He frowned as he saw that barricades were set up around the town gates, and several trebuchets and catapults, among many other siege machines were in the outlaying fields.

Amec rode up alongside him now.

"So what do you plan to do?" he asked.

"I'll take out the siege machines," Zen replied.

"Oh really now?" Amec said, a bit of humor in his voice. "And how do you plan to do it?"

"I'll burn them down."

"With what fire?"

"You'll see when I do it," Zen said as he began to ascend the dune.

"Wait, let me come with you," Amec said.

"In your condition? I don't think so. You have no armor or weapons."

"Not true, I'll be back soon enough," he said as he turned and rode away.

"So Zen, where are we going now?" Alda asked, riding clumsily up to him.

"We have siege machines on the horizon, it'd be best to get rid of them before we enter Zeran."

"Let me come, I wanna break some skulls!" Alda exclaimed.

"Not risking that Alda, you're not the world's best rider, and you certainly are not equipped with weapons to be used on horseback."

"I could watch your back."

"These Ayan Saudi are not normal opponents Alda, they have tricks you wouldn't believe. They are probably waiting for someone to attack, only element I have over them is surprise."

"How do you have the element of surprise if they know you are coming?" Alda asked, scratching her head.

"They won't be expecting a single rider to attack."

"Zen, now am I in the state to fight?" Amec laughed as he approached.

Zen's jaw dropped as he saw him.

Amec was dressed in a full chainmail body and leggings comprised of chain and plate knee pads. His face was covered over with a pointed helmet with chainmail that was draped over his face. The only part of him you could really see was his eyes.

"Where did you get all that from now?" Zen asked, still in awe.

"A fellow Ayan Saudi Mamluk was killed in battle it seems, and I looted this off his body. Of course I gave him a proper, but shallow, burial. The only thing I didn't take was his sword."

"Well, considering you're in all this, I guess you can come, just don't die."

The Ayan Saudi soldiers lazily sat under their tents and tarps, awaiting the command to prepare for the siege. They knew no Zeran defenders would come attacking, and so, they were relaxed.

"Qulyat, when's the commander going to give the order?" one Ayan asked.

"Pfft, I dunno, maybe he's just waiting so long to build up some suspense, you know this will be a defining point in history Hakim."

"Yeah, but I'm itching to kill some Zeranians, you know, in the name of Sahra'a and all."

"When the time comes Hakim, just wait a little bit and..."

"Qulyat, what's that?" Hakim asked, pointing at a cloud of dust.

"I look like I know? Probably more units arriving for the siege."

"Zerani!" Hakim shouted as he ran to get his spear.

An arrow slammed into his back, and he fell into the sand. Qulyat panicked and began to ring the signal bell.

Amec threw a javelin into his side, and he also fell into the sand.

"For Zeran!" Zen shouted.

"For Aman!" Amec shouted.

The two drew there sabers and cut down any Ayan Saudi they saw.

"Pyro Ekriksi!" Zen commanded, sending a fireball into a catapult. The other Ayan Saudi ran to put out the fire, only to be put down by Zen's arrows.

"Come on Kenta, we need some real speed," Zen said to his horse. It whinnied and picked up speed.

"Pyro barrage!" he shouted, and the fireballs slammed into the battering rams and trebuchets nearby.

"What are you boy?" Amec exclaimed as he rode up next to him.

"I'm Zen Zeran of the family of Zeran, tenth son of the Khan Temu of the Zeran bloodline," he replied proudly.

"And now we're taking back the throne you want?"

"I used to want it, but now all that matters is the peace in the sands, whether I live or die to bring it about."

"Well just don't die then. Spear wall," he said quickly.

Zen turned and took a sharp intake of breath as he saw the Ayan Saudi set up in a spear wall. He turned Kenta quickly.

"Warn me earlier, okay!" he shouted to Amec.

He only laughed in reply. "Use your eyes more often."

"Ready to go? The siege machines are more or less gone," Zen asked.

"We've had enough blood in the sands, let us go," Amec replied.

They turned back for the dunes, but a javelin struck Amec's horse in the side, and he fell with it.

A unit of Ayan Saudi rose out from under the sand, armed to the teeth.

Amec rose to his feet, holding his spear ready.

"A fellow Saudi is attacking us?" one Mamluk asked.

"He is a fellow Mamluk!" another replied.

"Amec!" Zen cried out.

"Go back, I'll be fine!" Amec replied.

Several axes flew past his face, missing by only inches. He tripped back, getting up quickly and lunging at the other Mamluk.

They dodged his strokes, but then stepped into Amec's last lunge, killing one Mamluk as his spear went through his eye slits.

He lunged at another, but they deflected the hit. Another grabbed his spear and chopped off the head with an axe.

He spun it to the blunt end and tossed it into a Mamluk's face. It simply bounced off their helmet. Before they could realize, Amec charged forward and grabbed him, then hefted him up and dropped him on his head. There was a cracking noise, and the Mamluk remained still.

He picked up his sword in time to stop a downward slash from another sword.

"Why are you betraying us Mamluk?" one asked.

"There is more to life than killing. An end to the war is what is needed," Amec replied.

"And that is what will happen, look, the capital of Zeran is right before us. We shall destroy it and end this war!"

"Forgive me brother, but it does not need to be this way..."

Amec put up his hand, and Zen caught it, helping him up on Kenta as they rode off.

"We shall bring peace to this land!" Amec shouted, holding his sword in the air.

CHAPTER 59

Ambushing General Skall

Akina and the other Fel warriors waited, hidden in the forests of Den Hall.

On the road was a large force of Deneaux soldiers, armed and ready for a siege.

"Hold, we shall take them soon, I just want to see their general. Illeth, warn Will and the others that we shall move soon," Akina said.

"Yes Chief," she said as she ran off.

In the center of this force was Skall, Jor's brother. He rode triumphantly on his horse, dressed in full chainmail with a shining steel sword decorated with gems at the center of the hilt.

"He doesn't look like he's ever used that," a Fel warrior said, and the other snickered.

"Shh, attention!" Akina said.

"Akina, the Fox and Fen are ready," Illeth said as she shrugged her bow off her shoulder and stooped down next to her.

"A Raider, and he looks...familiar..." Akina said now, studying Skall.

"He looks like Jorigsveer, remember him?"

"Oh Jor? Yeah I remember...maybe this might be his brother, the one's he talked about."

"More the reason to kill him," Mark said as he took out and arrow from his quiver on his belt.

"Ready," Akina said. The command went down the line as each soldier readied themselves.

"Move," she said, and they slowly approached the tree line, bows at full draw.

"Such a fine day for conquest, is it not Roger?" Skall said to his advisor.

"Yes sir," he said, annoyance evidence in his voice.

"So, first it is Fel hall, then to Fen Hall, and the other army shall take Fox Hall, correct?"

"Yes sir."

"Good, the more blood on me the better my name."

"Fire," Akina said, putting her hand down.

An arrow slammed into Roger's neck, and he fell over in the saddle.

Skall quickly shrugged his shield from over his shoulder in time to block a coming shot bound for his chest.

Ten halberdiers went down nearly one after the other, and the nearby heavy cavalry began to wheel around.

"Fall back!" Skall shouted.

"Spear Wall!" someone shouted.

Skall turned to see a line of Fox soldiers leap from the forests and instantly set up a spear wall, skewering any cavalry that attempted to retreat.

A force of Fen warriors now surged out the trees, cutting down the disoriented Deneaux army.

Skall, seeing he had no chance now, turned and ran for the tree line.

Akina walked through the remains of the offensive force. She nodded, seeing the destruction.

"No casualties, not bad for a third ambush," she said.

"Was there any doubt?" Will said as he dug his spear into the ground.

"Kullskash, get the bodies burned and collect any loot, leave their swords in place though, I don't want us to look like savages or thieves. Any wounded men are not our enemies or allies, treat them and send them to the capitol."

"Yes Chief," she said as she turned to get the other soldiers.

"What?! How the hell is this possible!" Albain shouted. "Why are they beating my armies? These are the great Men of Deneaux! I sent heavy cavalry, halberdiers, my best Generals! By the Divines I even sent Soul Knights and Paladins! How did they die?! Those savages of Den Hall do not have knowledge of Soul!"

"Well it seems now they do," Caroline said, looking at herself in the mirror of the dressing room.

"How could they have learned?"

"Well you did make several Soul Knights and Paladins desert the army. It wouldn't be too unlikely if some decided to help your enemies..."

"Hm...In retrospect, it seems that Meso could have been useful for covertly killing those Souls down in Den Hall, but now he's dead."

"You could get Fenalph or Titus to do it," Caroline suggested.

"Fenalph is too busy being drunk and collecting women. Titus fears that he may get killed by the same fluke that killed Toxotes. Meso as we know is dead, and I can't think of anymore Divines to help us."

"The Ayan Saudi have almost conquered Zeran you know. By now they control nearly all the South."

"So that means that Sahra'a is free..."

"But I doubt he'll get off his lazy butt to help us."

"Then we'll get one of his sisters!"

"Ema is a crazy sadist and not likely to give a damn about what you say, Haima is only interested in gold. Sahra'a is way too lazy and I've lost contact with Toxotes' girl."

"Ugh, why am I already out of resources?"

"You could go down there yourself you know."

"And get a fluke shot through my heart with obsidian, no thank you."

"Exactly why you're not getting things done. If you want it done now, do it yourself."

"What I need is my own private mission force..."

"The Pantheon Castle warriors are your private mission forces," Caroline corrected.

"I want a *better* private mission force."

"Then hire the strongest of the strong," a voice said from behind.

"A man of Meso approaches," Albain said, his back still turned.

Caroline had already pulled out her belt dagger, wondering who was there.

Kinsei appeared out of the shadows, his scimitar strapped across his back.

"At your service, King of Deneaux, what is it that wish must be done?"

"I need to have a particular target in Fel Hall killed…"

"Is it that Jane Pagos girl?" he asked angrily.

Albain turned to Caroline now, confused.

"She's the one that was filed with Jorigsveer Great-Blade."

"And the one that killed my Keelia…"

"Well I need you on the Den Front," Albain said

"She'll take the Den Front," Kinsei said, pointing to the door.

Albain turned to see Dasimay standing before him.

"I'll take the Den Front," she said. "I have a score to settle there."

"Alright then, you'll take the Den Front and Kinsei…you take out Jane, Jor and anyone else who's with him. You damn freelancers do what you want, don't you?"

"It seems they do," Caroline replied. "Well be gone then, go do what you've been told."

The two of them stood in a black circle, and disappeared.

"Back to the war then," Albain said as he turned to leave.

"Don't you want to get a break for once?"

"Kings don't take breaks, especially when they want to conquer the world."

CHAPTER 60

The Khan

"How is this possible?!" shouted the new Khan of Zeran. He sat high on mighty on his throne in the large throne room of Castle Zeran.

He was dressed in decorated red linens, and had a black beard and hair that fell to the back of his neck.

"The people of Zeran are calling this the work of the Divines! I am their Khan, I have power! They see me as their Divine!"

"Well the people don't seem to see it that way anymore my Khan," his advisor said.

"Who is responsible for this? Who?!"

"Zen Zeran of Zeran," a voice said as the door swung open. The Khan covered his eyes as the bright morning light filled the room.

Zen and Amec walked in to face the Khan.

"Good day Khan. I hear you are displeased with our actions," Zen said.

"Yes, we defended your city from complete annihilation, yet you are still displeased?" Amec added.

"An Ayan Saudi? Guards!" the Khan cried.

The doors at each end of the hall opened, and the guards fell to the ground, all knocked out.

"Here they are," Amec laughed.

The Khan got up and ran for the door, But Jor stopped him. He turned to the next door, and Alda stopped him.

"What do you want?" he cried now.

"I want you to make a peace agreement with the Ayan Saudi," Zen said.

"A-A-A," the Khan and his advisor stuttered in complete awe and surprise.

"Please friend, run that by me again," the Khan said.

"Make...A...Peace...Agreement...with the...Ayan....Saudi....," Amec outlined slowly.

"But the ancient ways..."

"Are full of crap," Zen finished.

"B-But who are you to even demand this?!" the Khan said, attempting to regain his dignity.

"I am the rightful heir, as you are just a bastard pretender. But I have no need for the crown. I am content to live a normal life, but I do not wish for my country to fall. I do not wish ill of even the Ayan Saudi."

"So then what do you feel would be the best plan of action?" the Khan challenged.

"We do as the Ayan Saudi, we use tricks. We do not have the strength to face them directly, and dying honorably makes no sense if it's in vain," Zen said. "We'll attack in the mornings before dawn, we'll poison there food stores, we'll steal their weapons. We'll destroy their morale and destroy their ability to wage war."

"But they have the weapons of Deneaux!"

"The weapons of Deneaux will have little impact on us. The last good King is dead, and so there link to the good Divines is broken. We are with the good Divines, and with them, we shall achieve victory! From this day, the men of Zeran are invincible!"

Zen walked through the castle court yard, with Amec at his side. To their left, you could see many beautiful gardens, with servants attending to them, looking up to see the two invaders.

"Beautiful gardens, aren't they?" Zen asked.

"Yes, they are," Amec agreed. He turned to see Alda was approaching.

"One of your friends," he said to Zen.

"Hey, you busy?" Alda asked.

"Not really, why?" Zen asked.

"I just wanted to talk."

"Then speak."

"Privately Zen."

"Oh, well I'll take my leave then," Amec said as he went off.

"So, what did you want to talk about?" Zen asked now as they both continued walking.

"Well, I was wondering, when this is all over..."

"Yes?"

"If you would..."

"Yes...?"

Alda stopped, a bit frozen.

"Don't scold me if I'm wrong, but you would want to possibly go out with me when everything is done with?"

Alda's face lit up bright red.

"Was I that obvious?"

"No, because I was planning on asking the same thing," he said humorously. "I was just scared you would say no."

"I-I was thinking the same thing," Alda said.

"But," Zen said, his mood changing. "First I must protect the city. Then we must defeat the potentially strongest Divine of the Deserts. Will you fight with me Alda?"

"You know I would fight with you any day Zen."

He sighed deeply. "I don't think I want you out in the deserts with me, it may be too dangerous considering Ema's strength."

"Oh come on, you know there's more to me than meets the eye."

Zen smiled. "I'll bring you along then, now let's see if we can meet the garrison."

"The garrison? Won't they find it odd talking to some outsider?"

"Alda, look at these gardens."

"They're pretty, so what?"

"I grew up among servants. My mother was also a servant here, so I worked these gardens myself, and I wouldn't mind doing it again."

"So what does that have to do with the garrison?"

"I've grown up with many of those guys, and I'm sure news of our unit hit hard when we went missing. Seeing me will be like seeing a ghost."

Zen and Turner stood before a group of assembled captains outside the gate house.

"So you're telling me you're in charge of the defense?" Turner said to Zen.

"We're in charge of the defense," Zen corrected.

"And who suddenly put you in charge?" one captain asked.

"The Khan," Zen answered. "I've fought the Ayan Saudi many times. I know there tricks."

"Oh really now, who was in your unit?" another captain challenged.

"You don't remember Zen, Jamaal?"

"Zen, but you're dead! Your unit disappeared in the desert!"

"I know he looked familiar!" another captain shouted.

"I'm the only living member, everyone else is dead. Now I'm here to repay them by defending their home. If we survive at the time of the siege, we may be on the path to history."

The captains muttered among themselves, wondering what he meant.

"We'll push for peace with the Ayan Saudi," Zen said blankly. "Saying this over is getting exhausting."

The Captains stood with wide eyes and dropped jaws, unable to comprehend the idea of peace with the Ayan Saudi.

"This is going to be hard to explain to the commoners," Zen said to Turner.

"Yes it shall be," Turner nodded, seeing that the captains were still frozen up to now.

CHAPTER 61

Holding the Field

"Charge!" Mark shouted, putting up his machete in the air.

The Fen warriors behind him resounded a grizzly and loud battle cry and charged in on the Deneauxmen forming a shield wall.

The wall held for only a few seconds as the Fen cut apart the men piece by piece.

Mark blocked a lunge from a pikeman, and swung, knocking the man's kettle helm off.

Another Fen came from behind and lunged their machete through his back.

Mark dug his machete in the ground and shrugged his bow off his shoulder. He released a string of shots, putting down a force of charging pikemen.

He took up the machete and spun with it, then tossed it. A commander leading a flanking cavalry charge came in, but only had time enough to see the large blade coming. It went through his chest, and the cavalry charge stopped near instantly.

Several Fen warriors threw spears at the cavalry as they tried to escape, taking most of them down.

"Keep it up!" Mark shouted. "They're falling back."

The Fen gave another brawny war cry, and charged the retreating Deneauxmen. They desperately fought off the Fen charge, moving back but losing men at the same time.

Suddenly, several Deneaux crossbowmen leapt from nearby ditches and trenches, shooting down many Fen warriors.

"They're reloading, fall back!" Mark shouted. "Archers, forward!"

A unit of Fox crossbowmen and Fen archers came forward, firing on the trenches. Three men could have been seen falling down, but that was not enough.

"Soul warriors!" Mark shouted.

Two Fen stepped forward, putting their claws in the dirt.

"Geo Ekriksi!" they both shouted, sending stone shooting up in the air. They kept going until they hit the trenches, sending several more men flying into the air.

"Geo Katastrofi!" Mark commanded. The stone went up in an explosion, destroying the entrenched position.

"Fire!" Mark shouted. The men that were running from the trenches fell from the rain of projectiles.

"Keep it up, we can hold the field," Mark shouted to his men. "After them!"

"They're heading into the tree line!" one Fen shouted.

"Bad mistake on their part," Mark said to himself. "We know these woods."

The Fen warriors moved slowly between the trees, staying low in the underbrush. If one had just happened to come by, they would have believed them to be real wolves.

"Deneauxic men in the trees," a Fen said.

"Aim and hit him," Mark commanded quietly.

The Fen readied his bow, but a bolt struck him before he could fire. The shot went off into the bush, and a crossbowman fell out.

"Ambush!" Mark shouted, and the Fen rose up to meet the challenge, firing in the bushes.

Several men fell from the bushes, hit by the barrage of arrows. Several Fen fell in turn, taken down by the powerful crossbows of Deneaux.

"Fall back!" Mark shouted, and the Fen retreated into the woods.

"Sergeant!" Mark called.

"He fell after the ambush," another Fen replied.

"You've been temporarily promoted then. Grab some men and head over there," Mark said, pointing to an area with light growth.

"But sir, there is little cover there."

He pointed to the trees. "They'll never see it coming."

The Deneauxmen moved slowly through the forests, watching for the Fen, waiting for an ambush.

"Look commander, an area of thick overgrowth," one soldier said.

"I see it, and we'll avoid it. Head to the lighter brush, it won't be as bad..."

"Ambush!" another soldier shouted, seeing the Fen leap from the thick bushes. They fired a volley, taking down a few soldiers before running off.

"Follow those Fen!" the commander shouted.

"Keep going, we're near the takeoff point," Mark shouted to his retreating soldiers.

"The savages really are dumb, heading for the light brush," the commander laughed.

"Line!" Mark shouted, and the Fen formed a defensive perimeter.

"They have no shields or armor, open fire!" the commander shouted.

"Open fire!" Mark shouted

A hail of arrows fell on the soldiers, and many of them fell in the lightning quick ambush.

"Retreat!" one shouted, and the others, unable to get a hold of themselves, fearfully ran off.

The commander and several of his men stood before many drawn bows.

"Don't run you cowards, they're just jungle savages!"

"The jungle savages that have just outsmarted you," Mark said. "Open fire."

The commander and his men went down in a hail or arrows, but as he hit the ground, he realized they were minor, but painful wounds.

Mark walked forward and took the man up with one arm.

"You'll make a fine prize," he laughed.

"Don't sacrifice me to your pagan gods, please!" he begged.

"We won't, but an interrogation will be in order. Pick up his men, we're leaving."

"But the routers?" his sergeant asked.

"They won't make it far, too many patrols. They'll be in chains by sun down. Now let's get back to base."

CHAPTER 62

Before the Storm

Adele walked the streets of Zeran alone, looking very sullen. Many of the townspeople nearby would give him concerned looks.

"You guys should be happy," he told them. "An Ayan Saudi has just finished a speech in Zeran without dying, and inspired your hearts at the same time. You should be glad for peace."

"Adele!" Kilan called from away several minutes later.

"Hm?" he turned to her now.

"Why are you looking so...down?"

"The siege Kilan, it's just getting to me."

"Why should it? You're a Great Hero, the Dark Champion! You defended Harmony with your life!"

"I'm not a hero Kilan, I'm a little kid that didn't want to die!"

"But you faced Mortha! That took a hero's courage!"

"It took a boy's rage and anger at losing all that he held dear. I didn't challenge Mortha expecting to win. I challenged Mortha because I no longer wanted to live, and taking her with me was the only way I knew I would find peace."

"Well you can't just give up now."

"I know, but I just don't feel like I'll see the end of this siege. I never saw the end of the Fall of Harmony either."

"Just relax Adele, you'll be fine..."

"I won't be fine!" he cried. "We'll all fall one by one, and the Raiders, bloody axes and spears, bodies of arrows! Wading through blood!"

He had his hands clenched tight on his head, bending over as if in pain.

"Adele," Kilan said, trying to calm him.

"Sir Revaran, don't leave me!" he shouted. "Knights, warriors, they're getting catapults!"

"Adele, relax please!" Kilan begged.

Adele finally opened his eyes to see Kilan holding his face fearfully.

"I'm in Zeran," he said, a bit relieved.

"What happened to you?"

"It's just the memories of the war. The Fall of Harmony was worse than anyone could remember. It still haunts me, but I've always never said anything."

"You can talk to me about it," Kilan said. "Let's go back to the tavern."

Out in the desert later that evening, the Ayan Saudi were greeted by a Soul user far more powerful than any they have ever heard.

"So what do you plan to contribute to our cause, foreigner?" the General of the Ayan Saudi army asked.

"Powerful men are with the Zeran, men with the power of Divines, and men who have killed Divines," Kinsei replied. "I am one of the few who can defeat them."

The General turned to see his fellows, and they nodded.

"Alright then...Kinsei, we'll let you join in on the siege, but we're not liable for your death if anything happens."

"I assure you, I will be fine, I may have to hold back though, don't want to destroy the city."

"No sir, that is the idea," the General laughed.

"Oh ok. This is my kind of job..."

C H A P T E R 63

Akina vs. Dasimay

Will and Mark exited the interrogation room inside of Fel Hall. Both of them had been questioning several prisoners from a battle not too long ago.

"All this fighting is killing me," Mark said.

"Speak for yourself, I still have to go out and train more crossbowmen, then meet up with Roseanne to get her to create a force of Soul warriors in Fox Hall."

"Well, better be off then," Mark said, patting him on the back.

He turned now to see Akina approaching.

"Good, now that we've taken those supply caravans, we can get to... oh Mark," she said, speaking earlier with Illeth.

"Things are going in our favor," Mark said.

"True, maybe Albain might give up soon enough," Akina joked.

Mark ran his hand through her hair.

"Then maybe we could take a private vacation."

"I wish, maybe one day I suppose."

"Akina, Akina!" someone shouted from away.

She turned to see a servant approaching, looking a bit beat up.

"Your sister my Great Chief, your sister is here."

"Why is she here? Did she bring an army?"

"No, she's outside the gate waiting for a challenge!"

Akina's eyes widened at that now. She turned to Mark, who had a troubled look on his face, then at Illeth, who looked even more concerned.

"I don't think you should do this Akina," Illeth said boldly.

"Yeah, it could mean your death," Mark added.

Akina watched both of them hard, then made her decision.

"Mark, get me my bow and your best obsidian arrows."

"You can't really be going to fight her," Mark exclaimed.

"Listen, Dasimay has a weakness that I know I can take advantage of, and if I do it successfully, I should walk back here in the correct amount of pieces. Just wish me luck…"

Dasimay stood alone in a large field over a mile away from Fel Hall. She realized it was getting dark now, but it didn't matter. All she wanted was her final battle with Akina.

"A little late for a walk is it not sister?" Akina asked as she approached. She had her obsidian bow strapped across her back and carried two bone daggers.

"It is Akina. I may have to give the place some light," Dasimay said as she put up her hands.

Flames went up around them, forming a ring that lit up the area.

"A little dramatic maybe?" Akina joked. "I'm not even sure if I'll be able to walk past it when I'm done."

"You're not walking away from this Akina," Dasimay said, drawing an arrow.

"We'll see," Akina said, doing the same.

"Toxotes Barrage!" Dasimay commanded, sending many arrows of energy as Akina. She rolled to the side and ran around the ring, avoiding the arrows as they slammed into the ground behind her.

She slid to a stop and released an arrow at that instant. Dasimay knocked it aside and fired back.

Akina caught it.

"You're far more skilled than I remember sister," Dasimay said.

"And you're still the same," Akina replied.

"Damn you, Toxotes Katastrofi Barrage!"

Akina fired an arrow at Dasimay and ran directly at her.

The arrows slammed into the ground behind her, exploding on contact with the ground.

Dasimay quickly drew and fired at the arrow Akina fired. The two hit and stopped each other.

Akina charged at Dasimay, swinging her bow at her. Dasimay ducked and kicked at Akina, but she leapt up and got behind her.

"Katastrofi!" Akina commanded after placing her hand on Dasimay's back.

Dasimay came flying out of the smoke from the explosion and slid several meters.

"Soul...how on Edafos...?"

"I've been practicing," Akina said.

"You've forced my hand then," Dasimay said, rising up. "Pyras Barrage!"

"Ekriksi Barrage!"

The fire and neutral energy slammed into each other, nulling both attacks slightly.

Akina made a move to rush Dasimay again, but she looked up at the last second, only to be struck by a fireball.

She rolled back, her clothes slightly on fire. "Pertusus!" she commanded quickly.

Dasimay side-stepped the thin beam of energy easily.

Akina got up and fired several arrows at Dasimay, but she only deflected them in return.

"You're tired Akina," Dasimay laughed. "You're not so strong after all."

"We'll see about that!" Akina shouted. "Ekriksi Barrage!"

Dasimay deflected several shots, but the rest completely missed their mark.

"This is actually kind of funny," Dasimay said. "I suppose I could play with you some more."

"Shut up, shut up, shut up!" Akina screamed. Throwing down her bow and charging at her with her bone daggers.

Akina swung at her over and over, but Dasimay simply either dodged the attacks or blocked them with her bow.

"Tahitita!" Akina commanded, her speed increasing.

Dasimay simply continued her pattern of dodging. Her change of speed was useless.

Dasimay kicked Akina in the chest, sending her into the air. She leapt into the air and put her hand on Akina's chest.

"Katastrofi!"

Akina flew from the smoke of the explosion and slammed into the ground so hard she made a crater.

"Apo Pano Ekriksi!" Dasimay shouted, firing a large mass of energy at Akina at point blank range.

"Still alive I see, most mortals cannot live through such things," Dasimay said.

Akina choked up a mouthful of blood, and struggled to breath.

"Oh, did I shatter a rib?" Dasimay asked as she got down next to Akina.

"No, but I broke your heart," Akina replied with a weak smile. She screamed as Dasimay steeped on her chest, shifting all her weight to crushing her.

"This is how it feels to be down, and now, your beloved Mark is not here to save you!"

"Neither is your beloved Toxotes, Katastrofi!" Akina commanded.

Dasimay turned to see the barrage that Akina had fired earlier but missed come back at her.

The area lit up with several explosions, filling the area with smoke.

"This is not good, what if she gets hurt out there?" Will asked fearfully, seeing the smoke rise into the air.

"Akina has this. She won't simply die and leave Fel Hall without a chief," Mark reassured.

"Yeah, Akina could take on anyone. She beat Toxotes didn't she?" Kullskash said.

"It's just a matter of faith," Illeth added.

Dasimay stood with her hand up, fully blocking the attack.

"Seems your little trick failed," Dasimay laughed.

"It seems so," Akina said. "You may have won this time."

"I have, and now, Fel Hall will fall, with all your little friends."

"You're willing to kill your own sisters and all their hopes and dreams, just for what?"

"Revenge for what you did, you took the throne, you took my influence, you took my Toxotes!"

"And you're about to start another trail of revenge. After I die, Mark will hunt you down…"

"Not after I kill him!"

"Me maybe, but once Mark's angry, no physical blow will end him…." Akina coughed, breathing becoming more difficult.

"We'll see about that," Dasimay said as she took out an obsidian dagger.

"I'm sure we could have had fun together if only you stayed home with us," Akina said sadly.

Dasimay stopped for a second, but recovered.

"And what could we play? Catch?"

"A fourth player would have been great," Akina said with a serene smile, imagining how life could be.

"Well you had no fourth player, only three."

"It will be one now, and you can't play catch by yourself."

"You killed Toxotes! I'm alone now!"

"You have your sisters, or at least now, you had your sisters…"

"Damn you Akina!" Dasimay shouted, her dagger rising for a final blow.

"I always wished you could stay instead of running off. Father missed you…"

"Shut up!"

"Toxotes would have never played catch with you, you know? Father would have, but you left early, and he left right after. He said he would have to give up on you since he had to keep up with his duties as chief, but I knew he never forgot…"

"Shut the hell up Akina, shut up!" Dasimay cried, tears rolling down her face.

"I want my voice to be forever with you Dasimay, but not to torment you. You'll soon be alone in the world, and all you'll have are memories. I hope you know though..."

"Know what?"

"I always loved you. We all always loved you. No matter how many of our people you killed, no matter what trouble you caused, we always loved you. I want you to know, even in the other world, I will forgive you for this, and I will love you..."

Akina's eyes went blank, and she remained unmoving.

"Akina," Dasimay said slowly. "Akina!"

She fell to her knees and shook Akina's body, but she remained still, a peaceful smile on her face.

"Akina, Akina, Akina!" she screamed, tears rushing down her face. "I'm sorry, I didn't mean for this, I didn't want you to die!"

The body remained silent, the peaceful look on her face.

"You didn't finish your job as chief! You didn't get to be with Mark, you didn't accomplish anything! Get up!"

"This is what you wanted, wasn't it?" a voice asked.

Dasimay turned to see Eros standing before her.

"You've killed your own sister. You've sent her to her grave, why do such a thing?"

"I didn't kill her!"

"Look at her bloody, mangled body right there in front of you dammit! Does she look alive?"

"I didn't intend..."

"You wanted to get revenge, look where it got you. Go now, go kill your other two sisters, and the rest of Fel Hall. Families, friends, everyone gone. I'm not stopping you."

"I-I."

"Hey, they'll all love you still, just like Akina, so go right ahead."

"You're all messing with my head!" Dasimay shouted angrily. "You're trying to make me feel sorry for them all!"

"Not was not the intended plan," another voice said.

Dasimay turned now to see Akina standing before her.

"It's your heart that's defeating you, not I."

"You're supposed to be dead!"

Akina put up the necklace Eros gave her.

"Saved me twice in a row, though I'm still pretty injured."

Dasimay saw that Eros had now disappeared, and the two of them stood alone in the flaming arena.

"I'll kill you for this!" Dasimay screamed as she charged.

The two exchanged the swings of a knife.

Akina ducked and swung fast, but Dasimay deflected, swinging low in return.

She deflected and swung up. The bone dagger cut a line up Dasimay's face, and she staggered back.

"Pyras!" Dasimay shouted as her two daggers were engulfed in flames.

She jabbed at Akina with lightning speed, but Akina dodged blow after blow.

She slammed her knee into Dasimay's chest, and extended it with a kick, sending Dasimay sliding on her feet.

"Ekriksi Barrage!" Dasimay shouted.

Akina ran, avoiding the shots of energy that landed around her.

"Apo Pano Pyras Ekriksi Katastrofi Barrage!"

Akina stood in the face of a sky filled fireballs.

"So be it Dasimay, we shall dance one last time!" she shouted as the fireballs landed around her, destroying the ground.

Out of the corner of her eye, Dasimay saw Akina coming. She sidestepped the attack, going off balance. She felt Akina's leg rocket into her chest, and she flew into the smoke.

"Kapnizo Katastrofi," Akina commanded.

The smoke retracted into a small ball above Dasimay, and erupted into an even larger explosion.

It slowly cleared, showing Dasimay standing at the center, badly injured.

"I'll drag you to hell!" she shouted as she charged. Akina did the same.

Akina swung high, cutting Dasimay's cheek. Dasimay swung angrily, but Akina duked under it and drove a bone dagger into Dasimay's leg.

She screamed in pain, but slammed her other knee into Akina's mouth. She staggered back, but Dasimay grabbed her and threw her up.

"Katastrofi!"

Akina stopped the attack with her hands, but the explosion sent her flying either way.

She hit the ground, still sliding.

Dasimay approached now, the obsidian dagger in her hand.

Akina took up her bow, aiming directly at Dasimay with an obsidian arrow.

"Do you know what this is Dasimay, this is the arrow that killed our father!"

"It will never end me!"

Akina closed her eyes and released the shot. It flew through the air. And hit its mark.

Dasimay stood before her, the arrow stuck deep in her chest, going straight through her heart.

Black blood began to pour out of her mouth as she weakly staggered around.

"You are now at peace Dasimay, the soul of revenge." Akina said.

Dasimay fell to her knees, and then to the ground. Her body faded soon after.

Akina's father appeared before her now, with a spiritual Dasimay next to him.

"I've...fallen," she said, not believing it.

"Not yet Dasimay, you have a chance to redeem yourself, if you take it," Akin said.

"Father...but how, I've done so much wrong already."

"So what? I've done as much wrong as you, but I learned from my mistakes and turned myself around."

"But it's too late for me..."

"Not yet, a great battle is coming, and we may need as much help as we can get."

Dasimay's eyes filled with tears and she dropped to her father's knees.

"I'm so sorry for everything, I just didn't have a choice, I was so angry!"

"So was I Dasimay, except I was both stupid, and angry," he said with a weak smile. "And for you Akina, I expect more good work from you, no slacking as chief for now!"

"I shall abide by your rules," Akina said tiredly.

Akin faded, but Dasimay could be partially seen.

"I hope you do well too," Dasimay said with a small smile. "And I hope you stay with Mark. He's a good guy, much better than Toxotes could ever be. I'll see you when the time arrives, for now though, I'll learn how a good life should be lived. I'll be watching over you. Farewell..."

Akina watched as Dasimay faded, and finally, she closed her own eyes.

"At least now I'll get a break, Mark better get here...soon..."

CHAPTER 64

Battle for Zeran

Amec and Zen stood atop the walls of Zeran, several thousand defenders standing with them.

"This'll be good," Amec said, looking at the sky.

"Zerani dust, don't worry," Turner said as he approached.

"Nope, sandstorm," Zen corrected.

"Wait, you expect me to fight in a sandstorm?!"

Zen handed him a turban. "Wear it or expect to eat, see and smell a hell of a lot of sand.

"I'll follow you advice..."

"And put on some robes or something over that chainmail, sand has a habit to go where you don't want it to."

"So that's why everyone is wearing all these desert robes?"

"You thought it was for style? Put them on and hurry," said a soldier.

Zen was surprised to see it was a woman. Moreover they looked familiar.

"Bayara was it? Friend of Jor?" Zen asked.

"I told him we'd see each other again. He told me I'd be a great archer, and sieges are where the most archers are needed."

Zen nodded to her. "Everyone soldier is welcome to aid us on this day."

Adele was shaking to the point that you could see it outside his robes.

"You should relax Adele, you'll be fine," Kilan said, her voice muffled though the turban that covered everything besides their eyes."

"I can't, I can hear the voices, the voices of Harmony on that damned day."

"You'll make it through this, I'm telling you."

"I don't think I will…"

"Take off the face mask for a second," Kilan said, pulling hers down.

"Okay, why?" Adele asked, lowering his.

Kilan kissed him on the lips, and his face lit up red instantly, and his shaking stopped.

"Now you have a reason, no, conviction to live. You have to live for me."

"I-I have to live for you," he repeated, still frozen up.

"And yourself."

"I will," Adele said, gripping his staff tightly.

"We've come a long way," Jor said, gazing out in the hazy desert.

"From Denhoec to Harmony," Jane said.

"From Harmony to Deneaux," Jor said.

"From Deneaux to Keels," Lyra said.

"From Keels to Crill," Alda said.

"And now we're here, standing up for those who cannot help themselves," Jor said. "I guess this is what I was born to do."

"Don't forget you're only human. You can't save lives forever," Lyra said, winking at him.

"I'll eventually die, yes, but right after I break a few skulls here."

"Hell yeah, bring on the pain!" Alda shouted.

"Typical Raider," Amec said, watching her from afar.

"Yeah, but she's my typical Raider," Zen replied.

"Here they come," Amec said, hearing the cries of thousands of warriors.

"Archers, ready!" Zen shouted.

Over a thousand bows were raised, drawn and ready.

"This is it," Jor said, his bow raised ready.

"Open Fire!" Zen shouted.

A hail of arrows slammed into the Ayan Saudi as they approached, killing hundreds already.

"Draw!" Amec shouted.

"Fire!" Zen shouted.

More arrows rained down on the attackers, and they seemed to be panicking.

"Bugler!" Zen shouted.

The sounds of bugling went off far into the deserts, and as the Ayan Saudi turned, they saw a large cavalry force charge in.

Hundreds of swords flashed, and hundreds of spears rose and fell.

Before they knew it, the cavalry was already retreating around the outside of the city, clear of the attackers. In that time, extra archers had already filled the walls.

"Light," Zen ordered.

The archers' arrows were lit by a soldier passing quickly with a torch.

"Hold," Amec said, letting it hang.

"Trebuchet!" a soldier shouted, followed by the sounds of a crushed wall and men shouting.

Zen turned to see a section of the wall already gone.

"Hold!" he shouted, keeping his men under control.

Another section of the wall went, then another.

"Damn trebuchets," he said slowly. The sand cleared a bit, and he could see the shadows of something.

"Bows up several more degrees!"

The archers followed the slightly abstract command and raised their bows.

"Fire!"

The arrows landed around the siege machines, setting several of them on fire.

The Ayan Saudi continued the charge, and now, ladders were hitting their walls.

Zen heard something whizzing towards them, then they fully understood.

"Down! Duck down now!" he shouted.

Several of the archers had quick reactions and ducked, but many of the others were struck by the crossbow bolts and fell to the ground.

"Damn it," he shouted angrily.

He saw a small ball roll to his archers nearby, who were still on the ground.

One of them picked it up, but then it erupted in a large explosion.

"Explosives?!" Jor shouted as he ran to Zen's position.

"What is it?" he asked.

"Those explosives will decimate us if we stay where we are!"

"I can't give up the walls or we lose the city!"

"We can't give up our men or we lose the walls!"

Several explosions lit up across the walls, but they were significantly larger.

"Soul warrior!" someone shouted fearfully.

Adele stood before Kinsei, his staff in hand.

"Aren't you that man of Meso?" he asked.

"I was, but now I'm a man of the King, sent to kill you all."

"We'll see about that," Adele said.

"Why are you confident? You do realize you're seeing your death?"

"I have too much to lose."

"So be it. Erebus Barrage!"

"Teresa Barrage!"

The two blasts of dark energy hit each other, setting off many explosions as many shots of energy filled the sky.

Several of the shots landed around Kinsei, but he artfully dodged them.

"This won't end like last time," Adele said, holding his staff tightly.

"Oh, but it will," Kinsei laughed.

Kilan and Jane stood alongside him, but Kinsei seemed to not be troubled by this.

"Zen, you know well that we won't have a wall when that fight over there is over," Jor said.

"Okay then Dammit, we'll give up the walls!"

"We shall get them back," Amec said. "But for now, we'll take refuge in the city."

"But the keep…"

"We won't hide in the keep. We'll go where they least expect us to go. I'll be in the streets. I have a trap to set.

"I trust your judgment," Zen said. "Retreat!"

CHAPTER 65

Rematch, Adele and Friends vs. Kinsei

Kinsei swung rapidly at Adele with his scimitar, Adele blocking over and over desperately to hold off the attack. Adele saw the attack cease for a moment and lunged at him, but Kinsei blocked it easily.

He looked up and deflected a flying dagger of obsidian. Kilan caught it right after.

"Not bad," he said. "But what about when Soul is involved?"

"Khthon!" Adele commanded, and a section of the wall went out towards the city. "Come on!"

Kinsei chased after them as the bridge continued to move.

Now was the time.

Kinsei watched as the sides of the bridge shot up in shards and spikes, making it near impossible to escape.

"A platform over this fragile city? What are you thinking?" Kinsei asked.

"I wasn't for once, but now I see that it was a good idea," Adele replied.

"That was a terrible joke," Jane said, punching him on the arm.

"Alright then. Pyras Ekriksi!" Kilan commanded.

Kinsei dodged the fireball, only to see the knife flying towards him. He simply caught it.

"Little girls should not play with knives."

"Little boys should watch what they're holding," she replied. "Makhaira Katastrofi!"

Kinsei realized he was holding a trick dagger too late, and desperately tossed it. It exploded, sending him rolling into the side of the ring.

"Erebus Katastrofi Barrage!" he commanded angrily as he got up.

"Pagos Pertusus Barrage!" Jane commanded right after.

The shards of ice followed a straight path towards Kinsei, while his shots of dark energy arced in the air towards his enemy.

The ground around Adele and his friends went up in smoke as the attacks landed.

Kinsei leapt out of the way of the ice spikes, dodging them as more came.

He finally touched the ground, but he felt a fist rocket into his chest, and he fell back.

"Got you," Adele said, standing over him.

Kinsei saw that Kilan and Jane had made a shield of ice, avoiding damage while Adele ran through the smoke.

Kinsei put his open palm on the ground beside him.

"Geo Ekriksi!"

A shard of stone came up towards Adele, but he stopped it with his hand.

"This is no longer a game Kinsei," he said darkly. "Aduro Ekriksi!"

Kinsei screamed in agony as the ball of light appeared over him and slammed down on him, burning away at him.

He rolled to the side and got to his feet.

"Teresa Ekriksi!"

Adele knocked the attack to the side.

"Khthon Ekriksi!"

A shard of stone shot out at Kinsei, cutting through him. He put his palms on the stone.

"Geo Teresa Katastrofi Barrage!" he shouted angrily.

The stone shattered into a thousand pieces, flying out at Adele and his friends.

"Damn! Geo Hoplon!" Adele commanded, and a wall of stone shot up before him.

Kinsei fell backwards, putting his hand on the wound. He saw it was slowly regenerating, but he knew he would need to win soon. He couldn't keep up with the amount of punishment he was getting.

"This is no longer a game Adele," he said as he stood up. "Hell's Gate: Two."

A black circle appeared under him, and half his face was covered with a black mask, a red eye at its center.

Dark energy shot up as an aura around Adele.

"Let us do battle then."

"Hades Ekriksi!" he commanded, sending a large ball of darkness towards Adele.

He stopped it with his bare hands, redirecting it at the sky.

"Teresa Barrage!" he replied, charging right after.

Kinsei felt like he blocked a thousand rapid strikes from a staff, and he felt like he gave back a thousand.

He leapt back, seeing the darkness crash down around him. He sliced an ice shard in two as it approached.

"Don't forget me," Jane said, a small blizzard beginning to form around her.

"The more the merrier," Kinsei laughed. "Hades Pertusus Barrage!"

"Dammit, move!" Adele shouted, leaping out of the way of the thin beams.

"Pagos Barrage!" Jane shouted as she leapt away from the attack.

Kinsei kept firing the small beams from his finger as he escaped the ice shards, running half the length of the ring.

"Erebus Hoplon!" Kilan commanded, forming a shield of dark energy.

"No, a shield won't work!" Adele shouted as he ran and pushed her away. He shouted as he was hit.

"Adele, you okay?" Kilan asked.

"I'm just fine," he said through gritted teeth. He could feel his slightly burnt flesh, and knew the shot went straight through his shoulder.

"Teresa Barrage!" he shouted again.

"Pagos Barrage!" Jane commanded.

Jane sliced away each mass of dark energy as he approached with his scimitar, laughing as he did.

"This is hilarious, you're getting weak already!"

"No good," Adele said. "Jane has to hold him, I'm no good right now."

"I thought you said you were fine," Kilan said.

"I'm not dead am I?" he replied.

Jane's blizzard grew with each attack now.

"Pagos Barrage, Pagos Pertusus, Pagos Hoplon Ekriksi!" she commanded rapidly.

Kinsei cut apart the ice shards as they came, and side stepped the thinner shards of ice that approached.

He swung down, slicing the approaching ice wall in two.

"Pagos Toxotes Barrage!" Jane commanded.

Kinsei cart-wheeled and spun mid-air, artfully dodging the rain of ice arrows as they came.

"Hades Toxotes Barrage!" he commanded in turn.

"Pagos Sagittarius Katastrofi Barrage!" Jane shouted.

Kinsei, Adele and Kilan watched fearfully as the sky filled with arrows made only with ice.

"We're in for something here," Adele said in awe.

The area filled with frosty mist as arrow after arrow pounded into the platform around Kinsei.

"He's off," Adele shouted. "I can sense he's running."

"So what will you do?" Kilan asked. "It's a long way down...."

Before she finished, Adele was already jumping through the hole made by the powerful attack.

"Kapnizo Anemos!" he commanded mid-air. The smoke from the platform came down a circled about him, creating a cushion before he hit the ground.

He saw Kinsei running and followed him.

"Now where did that monster go?" Jane asked, panting heavily.

"He jumped," Kilan said. "Adele did the same, but not I."

"Come on, I know a way down," Jane said.

Adele ran, holding his injured arm, through the streets, scanning for Kinsei.

A rough kick told him his location.

Adele fell and slid several feet in the streets. He tried to get up, but Kinsei had pinned him down with his foot.

"Not bad little one, but you cannot defeat me," Kinsei said.

"We'll see when I put my staff through that little eye of yours," Adele said, looking at the red eye on the dark side of his mask.

"You better watch what you say, this is Satan's eye you're looking at."

"Like a give a damn, Satan couldn't hurt me if he tired...."

He was stopped short as he felt Kinsei crushing him like a bug.

"True, but I can, physically at least!"

"Gaia Ekriksi!" Adele commanded.

Kinsei looked up, seeing two shards of stone go through both his shoulders, sticking him in place.

Kinsei grabbed the two shards and shattered them. He then pulled the remaining parts from his shoulders, the wounds regenerating near instantly.

"Irrelevant," he laughed, but it was cut short as he ducked quickly.

Jane came skating down on a path made of ice, her ice great sword already swung, cutting through the clay brick buildings around them and nearly taking off Kinsei's head.

Kilan stepped off from the path, shivering, but from fear.

"That was way too high and way too fast," she said.

"Be happy you didn't jump down," Jane said to her.

"Such a long blade is useless against me," Kinsei said.

"We'll see about that!" she shouted as she swung again. Kinsei ducked again, closing the gap between him and Jane.

Before he got within two feet of her, a burst of icy wind blew him away.

He hit a building hard, leaving a bit of a crater, and rolled to the side, avoiding a heavy overhead cut.

"Pyras Katastrofi!" he commanded, sending a fireball towards her.

She reflected it with the ice blade, to Kinsei's complete surprise.

He was struck in his face and staggered back.

"Keep hitting him!" Adele shouted. "Erebus Ekriksi!"

Kinsei deflected the shot, but a dagger made of soul energy slammed into his chest right after.

He pulled it out and tried to toss it, but then he felt something hit him, and he couldn't stand.

Adele had his staff going straight through Kinsei's body. They both slowly went to the ground.

"I win Kinsei," he said weakly.

"No, I am Kinsei! I do not die! Hades Zoe Katastrofi!"

"Adele!" Kilan shouted. "That attack will destroy both of you if you don't move!"

"He'll get away again, and I don't want to risk him coming back and really hurting one of you!"

"I don't care, get out of there!"

Jane grabbed Kilan's hand and pulled her behind a large ice wall.

"We can't save him now, but I can save at least you!"

CHAPTER 66

The Streets of Zeran

Zen and Jor watched the large explosion that went off in the other side of the city as they stood in the streets.

"That doesn't look good at all," Zen said.

"We have to focus," Jor struggled to say.

"What's wrong?" Amec asked.

"I felt Adele's energy disappear," Jor replied.

Turner was at a loss for words, but he shook himself back to what was currently happening.

"We must continue what we are doing," he said. "Now let's clear these streets and take the walls back!"

The Zerani warriors held their sabers high and gave a mighty war cry.

"Today we cut through and take back or walls! Today we kill a thousand men to save our people!" Zen shouted.

"To arms! For Zeran!" Turner shouted, and the men followed in the charge.

The Ayan Saudi watched as the men of Zeran charged through the streets, cutting them down as a hoard. Several more of the attackers barricaded the road with a spear wall, but they would soon learn that it would be useless.

Zen tackled the shields of the spear wall, knocking down one of the men. Two swings cut down two more men, and before he knew it, he was behind of them.

The Ayan Saudi quickly turned, but with their backs turned, they were run down by the Zerani.

"Line!" Amec shouted, and the Zerani drew their bows, forming up ranks.

"Fire!" Zen shouted, and arrows went straight down the street, taking down several Ayan Saudi attackers. The others took it with their shields, but the next volley knocked them down, and the next volley took more down.

"Keep moving!" Jor shouted, both his eyes glowing red at the center.

"More defenders!" Alda shouted as she saw a large shield wall forming.

The two of them looked at each other and nodded. They broke out in a mad charge, smashing down shields.

Alda swung down the line with her battle-ax, sending the warriors flying into the air.

"Katastrofi!" Jor commanded, and the ground lit up before them, leaving a crater where men were.

"Dangerous people," Zen said, watching them demolish the wall.

"I suppose that's one of the reasons I respect him," Lyra said.

"We'll take the other street Zen, we'll flank the shield wall...if it's still there by the time we make it," Amec joked.

"Good, I'll take the other street then," Zen said.

"I'll watch Jor and the others," Lyra said. "Don't want them to get even wilder."

"That'll be fun to watch," Turner joked.

Zen kicked down the last Ayan Saudi soldier that stood in his path. He looked about to see the street covered in bodies.

"Good thing I didn't bring any of my men. Wouldn't want to risk anymore lives today."

Zen turned to see an explosion light up in the distance.

"The fighting's harder than I thought, I'll need to stop talking to myself here and meet up with Amec!"

"Push!" Amec shouted as the Zerani troops pushed down a shield wall of Ayan Saudi, slaughtering their floored enemies.

Amec surged through the wall, hacking down the Ayan Saudi that were now pushing back.

He swung at one, but they blocked it overhead, and another kicked him in the side.

He blocked overhead and twisted his sword down, blocking a swing from another Ayan Saudi.

He stopped the swings from three Ayan Saudi at one time, but his strength was slowly fading to the large group's power.

"Men of Zeran, I wouldn't mind getting aid!" he shouted. He glanced to see his men behind him were being cut down by Ayan Saudi that began pouring through the houses and alleys.

"Haima Barrage!" a voice shouted.

Amec saw how the blood shot straight from the bodies of the Ayan Saudi at the sound of the command.

He turned to see many wounded Zerani in the street, but he also saw Zen standing between.

"I hope you know that attack took a lot out of me, physically and mentally."

"It saved my life but...that's...what Ema used..."

"I know, that's how she killed many of my friends. Now come on, we need to get some help for these wounded..."

"And not take the walls? We have enough men for that already!" Jor exclaimed, walking down the street with many other Zerani soldiers.

"You never cease to amaze me Jor," Zen said. "Now Lyra, you get half of the men here to a safe location to be treated. Jor and the others will come with me to take the walls, but first, we'll wait for word from either Kilan or Jane..."

The sounds of blasts were heard again, and smoke could be seen rising into the sky in several locations.

"I don't want to be outside with that, we'll take to the buildings...no, let's go to the keep!"

"But that's what the Ayan Saudi will want," Amec argued.

"The amount of men we slaughtered will mean they will have little to throw at the keep, and their ace is already in place, might as well wait till we can play ours..."

CHAPTER 67

Kilan and Jane vs. Kinsei

Kilan slowly arose from where she lay in the streets. Her clothes were thorn, and you could see her bleeding by her lip, among other places.

"Damn daimons," she cursed to herself.

She put up her hand and caught Kinsei's lightning fast punch.

"I'm getting real tired of your games," she said angrily.

"But the fun has yet to begin," Kinsei laughed. He slammed his leg into Kilan's torso, and sent her crashing into a nearby building.

"Pagos Ekriksi!" Jane commanded, sending an ice shard towards him. He easily split it, but Jane came towards him quickly, swinging at him with the ice great sword.

He dodged several times, avoiding it easily.

Jane looked up in surprise as she saw he was balancing on her blade with the tip of his finger.

"More practice is what you girls need," he teased.

Jane swung the blade, but he flew into the air and came down with a kick. She quickly stepped to the side, but as Kinsei hit the ground, he was already releasing a barrage of swings with his scimitar. Each hit shattered more and more ice off her blade.

After many blocks, she tiredly staggered back. She looked up to see Kinsei pointing at her sword, which felt like it had gotten lighter. As she saw it, she realized it was now the size of a rapier, shaved and cut to the point of a tooth pick.

"You have to be kidding," she panted.

"It's all a game to you people until someone gets killed, isn't it?" Kinsei shouted. "You killed my Keelia!"

"We were at war Kinsei, it's not like she was planning on keeping me alive for that matter!"

"By why her! Why her!"

"I don't know okay, I'm sorry!"

"Sorry doesn't cut it! Death is your only repentance!"

"I have too much to die for."

"So did Keelia! She had so many things to live for, but you took her life, you took the other half of my life!"

"Yet you want to take my full life and that of my friends?"

Jane began to choke as she felt the vice grip that had suddenly come around her throat. She didn't even see Kinsei move.

"You will all feel the suffering I had to go through! You'll feel all the pain and sadness, you'll feel sorry for her! You'll lament!"

"Get off of her you fool!" Kilan shouted, a ball of light glowing in her hands.

Kinsei smiled as he saw her and threw Jane aside. She choked and grabbed for air as she hit the hard ground.

"Do you want to die first then?" Kinsei asked.

"I want to kill you first," Kilan replied.

"So be it!" Kinsei shouted as he surged forward.

"Go back to hell daimon!" Kilan shouted. She swung high for his torso, but he stopped her hand with his. She tried to strike him with the other hand, but he stopped that one. He kicked her in the chest, and she slid back, staying on her feet.

"Tamashii Dokujutsu!" Kinsei commanded.

Kilan felt like a thousand vipers struck her as Kinsei's lightning fast hands jabbed into her.

She staggered back, her world slowly becoming dark. She shook her head, regaining some bit of consciousness.

"Aduro Ekriksi!" she commanded.

Kinsei dodged the ball of light. She threw another, and another at him, but the majority missed, and those that didn't he easily dodged.

He walked up before her and grabbed her by the hand, holding her up in the air.

"You look tired, don't you think you deserve a rest?" Kinsei said.

"You...you hurt Adele..." she said weakly.

"He's dead according to my book. No one survives that kind of damage."

He realized now that tears were falling from her eyes.

"Now do you acknowledge your doom?"

"I don't care for that, Adele was scared to fight today...he has to be alive!"

"Well he is not," Kinsei said as he tossed her towards a pile of rubble, topped with sharp shards of stone.

"His eyes widened at what he saw."

Kilan slowly opened her eyes to see Adele holding her in his arms.

"How are you even alive!" Kinsei shouted.

"I dunno? Luck?" he replied.

"Don't mock me! Apo Pano Teresa Katastrofi!"

Adele put Kilan down gently and slammed his staff down into the ground right after. The attack hit, but it slowly diminished before the staff.

"Soul Technique: Anti-dark Burst!" he said as light sparked around his hand as he took up the staff.

A burst of light shot out from before him and crashed into Kinsei.

He staggered back weakly, burnt by the light. His mask was broken and his Hell's Gate was interrupted, meaning he had no Soul energy to use for attacks at the moment.

"Damn it, damn it!" he shouted.

"Now I'm going to make you pay for what you did!" Adele said angrily as he approached him slowly.

"Barrage!" a voice roared from above.

Adele and the others looked up to see a black beast comprised of shining dark scales that looked like they were made of...

"Opsianos?" Kilan said as she weakly looked up.

The Black Dragon landed on a building above them.

"Kinsei, you have been deemed worthy of my cause, come with me to the Obsidian Wall!"

The beast picked up Kinsei and flew off to the South-west.

"What was that?!" Adele shouted.

"Opsianos," Kilan coughed. "He's the Divine of the Obsidian Wall down South."

"You know him?"

"Eros, Alice and some other men of Eros went down there to learn about him...but we soon learned he is not the Divine to mess with..."

Adele picked up her up. "We got to get to somewhere safe."

"We may just need to stay in some house somewhere," Jane said as she limped over to them.

CHAPTER 68

The Last Charge

Zen, Amec, Jor and Alda were on their way to the Keep, several Zerani units behind them.

"So this is where the Khan is hiding?" Alda asked.

"Staying, not hiding," Zen said.

"You sure he's not hiding there?" Jor asked.

"I'm sure," Zen said, ending the conversation.

They now stood before the Keep. Zen pushed open the door and entered.

What he saw horrified him.

Many of the servants and attendants of the Keep were lying dead on the floor. Blood covered the floor and walls. Arrows and javelins were lodged in the furniture around the room.

"Who on Edafos would do this?" Zen said, falling to his knees before the body of a young servant.

"The Ayan Saudi, my kinsmen have betrayed me," Amec said sadly.

There was a scream in the nearby room.

"The Khan!" Zen shouted as he rose. "Come on!"

He ran down the halls of the Keep, looking down each way.

"Which way, come on!" he said impatiently through gritted teeth.

"Down that way!" Jor shouted as he ran to one room. He kicked open the door to see two Mamluk staring back at him.

"I'll take them, you go on your way!"

Zen nodded, and they ran down the next Hall.

A Mamluk flew from around the corner, but Alda's battle-axe came flying down after him, lodging itself deep in his head. Alda tore the blade from his body and kept up the charge.

Jor blocked one slash from the first Mamluk and swung at the other with his great sword. They ducked and lunged, and he dropped his sword, leaping back quickly.

"Damn desert robes!" he exclaimed. He pulled a dagger from his sleeves and threw it at a Mamluk. It hit his knee and stopped him for a few seconds. Jor couldn't have the chance to formulate further. A Mamluk lunged with a scimitar at Jor, but he side-stepped it and grabbed his arm. He twisted it and made him drop the sword, but the Mamluk swung back, hitting Jor straight in the face with his fist. He knocked down several tables as he hit the ground.

The Mamluk laughed as he took up his scimitar and approached the boy with the bleeding face.

"Time's up, Raider," he said.

"Makhaira Katastrofi!" Jor commanded.

The Mamluk turned for a second as the dagger in the knee of his comrade exploded, sending him across the room.

Jor quickly got up and ran for his great sword. The Mamluk got to his feet in that second and came behind him. Jor fell to the ground and slid to the other wall, then threw another knife. It hit the Mamluke's helm, but only went that far.

The Mamluke knew what was next for him and panicked, trying to rip the dagger from his helm.

"Makhaira Katastrofi!" Jor commanded again.

Zen and the others ducked down as they heard the blast erupt nearby.

"The last door at the end of the hall!" Amec shouted.

Zen ran down and slammed the door open with his hand.

He charged in, cutting down two Mamluk in an instant.

"Ema Ekriksi!" he commanded as he turned to another Mamluk. Blood shot out from his neck, and he fell.

"Halt Zerani!" an Ayan Saudi shouted. He held a sword to the Khan's neck. On the ground before him, the advisor lay dead.

"Remove that blade!" Zen shouted angrily.

"Or what, you'll blow out my blood? My units have seen that kind of horror, we're used to it."

"Don't do this, we can have a peaceful end to this!"

"Peace, with a Zerani? No thank you!"

"I swear I will kill you where you stand if a drop of blood leaves from the Khan!" Amec shouted.

"So you're the one that attacked my siege camp? You treacherous bastard."

"I did so because I saw a way to end this blasted war once and for all."

"It will end with this man's death."

"Zen, Amec, help me!" the Khan cried.

"I already told you, if only a drop of blood fell from his neck, you would be finished!" Amec shouted.

Zen's heart stopped that instant as he saw blood spray into the air. He saw the Khan's head roll down before him.

"You fool!" Amec shouted as he charged. Zen's hand stopped him.

"This crime demands blood," Zen said, three dots appearing around his pupil in the form of points on a triangle. They were all colored crimson.

The Ayan swung at Zen, but as the blade neared his neck, it turned to dust. Zen grabbed the man by his neck.

"Retribution is attained," he said softly. The Ayan Saudi's eyes rolled back, and he fell onto the ground.

"Zen, are you okay?" Alda asked fearfully.

"I am," he said, his eyes returning to normal. "I'm a little weak, but I can still keep up the fight."

"For Zeran!" Alda and Jor shouted as they hacked down line after line down the street.

Lyra let three knives fly, and they all hit their mark in the bodies of Ayan Saudi warriors.

Turner fired a crossbow into the neck of a Mamluk. They took the shot in a shield and continued to charge.

Zen threw a spear that tore the shield from the Mamluk's hand, and the bolt flew straight into the Mamluk's neck right after.

"Thanks Zen!" Turner shouted.

"Don't let me have to save you again," he said as he took up another spear and tossed it.

Amec looked up and saw that the Ayan Saudi were retreating back towards the wall, and he knew they were going to have a chance.

"They are retreating!" Amec shouted. "The Ayan are retreating!"

"Charge my Kinsmen, charge for Zeran!" Zen shouted.

"For Zeran!" hundreds of voices proclaimed as they charged.

Arrows slammed into the Ayan as they scrambled up the stairs and ladders to the wall. Some ladders were even hauled down by the Zerani, sending the Ayan on a steep fall.

The Zeran forced their way up the wall, killing any of the Ayan who desperately held the stairs and ladders. Soon enough though, the Ayan slowly gave away. They retreated off the walls, scaling down ladders and running off from the siege towers.

The men of Zeran raised their blades high in victory as the Ayan disappeared into the desert, fighting their way through the sandstorm.

Zen watched them go, and as he looked up into the sky, he saw that the sandstorm slowly subsided.

The men turned to Zen, and awaited his order silently.

"Um Zen? I think the men are waiting for you," Amec whispered

"Waiting for what exactly...?"

"You realize we've won the day..."

"You mean, we defended Zeran?"

"We defended Zeran."

He turned to his men on the walls.

He began to laugh, and it soon went from chuckles to hysterical laughter.

"What's so funny?" Amec asked.

"All that I've gone through, yet I end up in the place I love. I've protected my home! We protected our home, is that not something to be happy for?"

Several of the Zerani on the ground turned to each other, not believing they were alive.

"With our blood and our blades, with our tears and our sweat, with our love and our strength, we defended our Zeran as brothers! Today is the day for joy! We have defended our home! For Zeran!"

"For Zeran!" over a hundred voices chorused, accompanied by cheers.

Today, Zeran was free, and tomorrow, it would be up to our heroes to free the deserts. Something big was coming to Edafos, and it as coming soon...

C H A P T E R 69

Twilight

Zen and the others watched as the priests walked up to the funeral pyre and lit it. They moved to the next, and then the next.

The pyres were for the Khan and his assembly who were killed by the Ayan Saudi.

"Zen, I'm sorry about what happened," Amec said solemnly.

"It's alright, there was little we could do anyways," he replied sadly.

"But in the meanwhile, we have a speech to make."

"A speech? Why on Edafos would they make me do another?"

"They people of Zeran are leaderless, and you are the one they currently look up to."

"But I no longer wish to be Khan, isn't there someone else...?"

"No one but you Zen, this is what you must do."

Zen stepped out of the crowd of mourners and stood before the people of Zeran.

"Good day, people of Zeran," he started meekly. "It is a sad day that we lay our Khan to rest, but we must live through it, as we are the men of Zeran, a strong people. I do not wish to speak at such a time as this, but I have been urged to. What, I ask, will you all do after this is over?"

"We kill the Ayan! We siege their Sultanate!" the crowd shouted.

"Revenge! Blood!"

"No, that is not the path we shall take! Blood leads to blood, revenge ends with revenge! That has been to basis of this war for over five hundred

499

years, and yet still, we kill the Ayan for being Ayan, and they kill us for being Zerani! Have you not enough of this killing? It's not like we have a choice of who to be born of!"

"Then what do we do?" someone asked.

"We do our best to rebuild our city, and soon, we shall work for peace!"

"But how, we have no leader!" someone shouted.

"By the Divines, I was hoping they forgot," he said to himself.

"Khan Zeran! Lead us!" someone else shouted.

"What good would I do as your leader?" Zen asked.

"You lead us in defending our home!" a soldier shouted.

"You traveled the land to return here!" another said.

"I'm telling you, I'm no good for this," Zen said. "There are many great Mamluk and political leaders..."

"I'm no good at politics, but they may be right Zen," Alda said as she walked up behind him.

"But, I don't think I have what it takes," Zen said.

"Well they do, and I do," Alda replied.

"B-But."

"Listen Zen, there are thousands of people over in the sands willing to kill you and your people. They need a leader who can repel them, and you clearly showed how capable you are. Now why don't you help the people again and show them how responsible you are."

Zen looked into her eyes, and he saw that she meant what she said. He turned to face the crowd.

"So, you all really wish for me to be your Khan?"

"Yes!" shouted the crowd with a resounding echo.

"Then I shall do so for your sake!" he proclaimed.

There were cheers from the crowd as people ran throughout the city to proclaim their new leader, taking joyously to the streets.

Several days had now passed, and Zeran was slowly getting back to the way it used to be.

Zen walked around the Palace with Amec. Zen was dressed currently in a cloak of fine cloth. It was red with golden patterns as borders, as were his robes. His hair was still in the same ponytail style, but it had gotten a bit longer.

"So how have things been going?" he asked Amec.

"The reconstruction of the wall has been faster than we expected, and our people are prospering, though still mourning those who fell in the siege."

"What about our friends?"

"They're helping to supervise the different projects."

"Hey Zen," a voice called.

Zen turned to see Alda in a red dress with a golden border. His jaw dropped near instantly.

"What, you seeing a ghost?" she asked.

"No, it's just...wow."

"What, never seen me in a dress?"

Zen shook his head.

"You're beautiful Alda, well, you always were, but that dress fits you well," he said, still in awe.

"The tailors made it. They said it was fit for a Queen."

"Oh really," Zen said as he approached her. "You know, you don't look as big without your armor. I never saw you as short."

"Exactly why I wore the armor all the time, so I wouldn't look like some misguided Raider girl."

"I couldn't see you as that either," Zen said with a chuckle.

"You know, I think you just got taller," Alda said.

"Really?"

"Yeah, you've gotten taller, and your shoulders are a little broader as well. Your hair has gotten a little longer too. The siege must have made you a man," Alda laughed.

"It must have!" he said, laughing also.

They both stared into each other's eyes, but Alda looked away.

"Sorry, I'm just not accustomed to looking people in the eyes. The Jarl I severed under would always try that, made me nervous..."

"Do I make you nervous?"

"You just...just put butterflies in my belly, that's all."

"At the rate you go Alda, you put birds in mines."

"See Zen, you're making me act just like Jane and Lyra," she said, blushing.

"Is that a bad thing? You are a girl after all."

"Yeah I guess. I've always been putting on that tough show..."

"I don't blame you for it, but I guess now I can see what you're really like."

"And you can know what I really want."

"And what's that?"

Alda reached up and kissed him on the lips. He slowly put her arms around her.

"I've waited six months for that you know," Alda said.

"You don't even want to know how much months I've waited."

"So Zen, since that's off your list..." Amec said. "We have to go over the peace treaty with the Ayan Saudi."

"Wait a second, please," Zen said.

"Wait for what now?"

Zen and Alda began kissing again. Amec couldn't help smiling.

"It's good he's happy," he thought. "Now my grief can be displaced with something else..."

"What do you mean you failed!" Albain shouted as he flung an apple into the head of a nearby servant.

"We tried our best, but Jor got away!" Joralkar said.

"Well your best wasn't good enough! I want armies to go to Zeran, now!"

"Not our allies in the sands," Caroline said, knocking him behind the head.

"You do realize we don't want the Zeran as our enemies yet!"

"But Jor!"

"We can care less about him, let's focus on taking somewhere else with little power first!"

"Alright then sister, where would you expect us to take?"

"Fool, get me that map," she said, pointing at the table.

Joralkar looked back at the servant. "You heard the girl!"

An apple knocked him in the back of his head.

"Not the servant, you!" Caroline snapped.

He quickly went for the map and stretched it out on the table before them.

"How about the Spires, or maybe Vinlandt?" she asked.

"All the way in the South?"

"Yes all the way in the South. Look, Holmes is already under Raider control, we can just use that as a base to attack the other countries along that path."

"Not a bad idea sis," Albain said. "And maybe when Titus and Fenalph after finished fooling around, they'll aid in my great crusade."

"I'm sure they will. Now Joralkar, take one of our fleets and several legions. I want a defendable landing to setup a base in Holmes."

"Yes Lady Caroline, I'll do my best..."

"Your best? Wasn't it already established that your best was a failure?"

"I'll do better than that, you'll see!" he said as he got up and ran off.

C H A P T E R 70

Battle of Emir's Rift

Zen rode through the streets of Zeran, followed by Jor, Amec and the others as the people threw flowers and cheered. He was dressed in his regular furs as before, carrying his sabers.

They would now be going off to Ayan Saudi to make a peace agreement, and they would need all the luck they could get.

Zen looked behind him. Jor, Lyra, Jane, Adele, Turner and Amec were behind him. Kilan was staying with Alda, who felt she wouldn't be strong compared to Ema, a person they knew they would cross.

They now rode out of the gates, into the endless expanses of the desert.

A day had passed, and they were still riding. It was currently early morning, as they would camp at mid-day.

"Say Jane, you've been quiet lately," Turner said.

"I've just been worrying about Lane..."

"Oh...You beat her the last time, didn't you?"

"I had Dianne with me that time, and even with her, I nearly died," she replied.

"Well don't worry, if we run into her, it'll be well over six versus one."

"We're the six, right?" she asked, still fearful.

"Hey Zen, what's that out there? A cave?" Adele asked.

"Looks like one," Lyra said, squinting to see.

504

Fear gripped Zen as he saw the mound of sand that rose to cover a cave.

"That's the Rift...let's go."

"But what about the mission?" Amec asked.

"The Divine that caused this whole damn war is down there. Even if we manage to make peace, he could just start another war for no reason, making our efforts useless. I say we end him for good."

"Zen, think about this," Jor said. "Divines aren't weak, you should know this better than anyone."

"I know what we're up...In fact I don't know what we're truly up against, but I swear, we shall defeat Sahra'a!"

He and Kenta stormed off, followed by Jor and the others.

They now stood before the Rift. It was dark inside, but Zen could clearly remember the way.

"Well, time to go," he said.

"Nope, not today Khan," Haima said as she appeared from the shadows.

"Divine, what are you doing out of your debts?" Zen asked.

"I wanted to see you with my own eyes before your death."

"At whose hand?"

Lane appeared next to him, and gave Jane a wolfish smile.

"I'll stay at your side," Turner said to Jane.

"No, go with Jor and the others, I can take Lane," she replied darkly.

"Oh, so a good one on one duel? Fair enough. Ema will take care of the rest of you," Haima said as she walked off.

"Let's go," Zen said as they entered the rift.

Jane and Lane stood facing each other in the sands.

"It's been a while Jane," Lane said. "I hope you've learned something to save you today."

"I've learned, the question is, have you learned?"

"Learn? Not with the toys Sahra'a got me!" Lane laughed as she pulled out to black disks. Obsidian plates shot out from the sides of the rings, forming larger, sharper disks.

"These are called obsidian disks. They'll cut through anything faster than you could comprehend."

"We'll see how effective they are," Jane said. "Pagos Hoplite!"

A spear made completely of ice slowly formed in Jane's hands.

"You fool, you realize those will melt right?"

"Shut up Lane, I'm getting really tired of you crap."

"Either way, here we go!" she shouted as she sent a disk flying.

Jane charged forward, figuring the simple disks would miss, but her eye darted to the left and a disk shifted position near instantly.

She turned and leapt out of the way. The disk hit the sand, but cut through it and came back up. Jane tripped and fell back, the disk flying only centimeters above her. The other came flying right behind it, and Jane rolled to avoid it.

"Pagos Ekriksi!" Jane commanded.

Lane stood still as the attack came. Only centimeters from her face, the disk shattered it.

"Damn!" Jane exclaimed.

She side-stepped a disk and charged after Lane.

She swung for her neck, but Lane bent back and got up. Jane stopped a kick with her hand and turned to block a slash by another disk Lane quickly drew.

Jane quickly leapt out of the way of the two flying disks and swung for Lane's waist. Lane danced away from the blow and swung with the disk, but Jane blocked it again.

"Aerio!" Jane commanded as a disk quickly approached. A burst of wind hit it, setting it off path. It wobbled and landed in the sands.

Jane lunged at Lane, but she cartwheeled away and grabbed the fallen disk.

Lane tossed the disk, but Jane dodged it and threw her spear at her feet.

"Pagos Hoplite Katastrofi!" she commanded as the spear erupted into a burst of frost.

"Pyras Anemos!" Lane commanded as she threw a disk with extreme effort. As they disk took to the air, it was cloaked in flames. Lane pointed down, and the disk went down towards Jane. She avoided it, but at a flick of the finger, it was back again.

"That's it!" Jane said to herself. "Pagos Kopis!"

A sword made of ice appeared in her hands, and she blocked the disk. It was still spinning as it struck the sword.

"Pagos Anemos!" Jane commanded as she reflected the disk. It arced up in the air and came back towards Lane, shrouded in frost.

Lane put up a disk and attempted to block the other. Sparks flew as obsidian hit obsidian.

"Pagos Katastrofi!" Jane commanded. The disk erupted in an icy explosion. Out from the frost came the disk, and Jane caught it.

Lane slowly rose to her feet, but fell back in the sand.

"You okay over there Lane?" Jane asked in mock concern.

Lane looked down fearfully to see her leg was frozen over. She hit repeatedly as she desperately tried to save herself.

"It's over Lane," Jane said.

"Not yet dammit! Tamashii Bukijustsu: Air Demon Barrage!"

"Eastern Styles, how?!" Jane said fearfully as she turned to see nearly thirty disks coming at her.

Jane charged at them, yelling as she did. "Pagos Kopis!" she commanded as two ice swords formed in her hands.

She redirected two of them as they came. Then smoothly dodged another.

"Khthon!" she commanded as a wall of sand rose and stopped five of them.

She turned to see more were still approaching behind her.

Lane smashed the ice that encased her leg and turned to Jane.

"Tachista!" they both commanded.

Jane darted towards Lane with her twin blades. In the blink of the eye, fifty swings were made and dodged. Lane surged back in the sands.

"Pyras Barrage!" she commanded.

Jane dodged the fireballs as they came, and lunged as she made it in range of Lane. She deflected the attack with her disk, sending Jane back several feet. Jane looked back a second the see the disks still approaching.

She skated back with lightning speed, stepping on one disk, and leaping to another, catching those she could. Before she knew it, she was looking at Lane from mid-air.

"Anemos Barrage!" she commanded, releasing the disks.

Lane fearfully ran past the disks, but as she stopped and deflected one, another cut across her back. She staggered forward, and another cut her leg.

"Pyras Katastrofi!" she commanded, pointing at the ground. The disk's paths were interrupted by the fiery explosion, sending them into the sand.

Jane landed in the sands and faced Lane, who was panting.

"You look tired," Jane said.

"I'm not," Lane replied. "Pyras Barrage!"

"Aqua Barrage!" Jane commanded in reply.

The water balls and fireballs struck each other, filling the area with steam.

"Pagos Kapnizo!" Jane commanded.

Lane wrapped her arms around her as the steam soon turned to frosty fog.

"Damn it," she said as she looked around.

"Pagos Hoplite Barrage!" Jane commanded.

Lane dodged the spears of ice as they flew at her from every angle. She saw one coming from the corner of her eye and side-stepped it, catching it in the same movement. She knocked away another spear as it came and tossed the one in her hand.

Jane stood outside the frost prison as she saw the spear coming. She put up her hand and stopped it mid-air.

"We'll see about that," she said with a smug grin.

"Tachista!" Lane commanded from inside the frost.

She surged out with lightning speed and was before Jane in an instant, her hand balled in a fist.

"Pagos Ekriksi!" Jane commanded, sending an ice shard crashing into Lane in that instant.

Lane flew back, rolling in the sand. She weakly rose to her feet.

"I'm getting really tired of your crap Jane," she said.

"Now you know how it feels."

"Silence! I'm the superior one here!"

"How is that? I'm the original."

"Every successful experiment has a first draft!"

"As if this was successful?"

"Grr, damn you!"

Jane side-stepped the fast blow made by Lane and caught her hand from behind her back. Jane's left foot went deep in the sand as she turned and tossed Lane. She flew and landed several feet away.

"Regular attacks will get you nowhere; I've learned that from our first battle," Jane said.

"I'll drag you to hell if I have to!"

"You have to touch me first."

"Then you've forced my hand!" Lane shouted as a fiery circle appeared at her feet. "Be ready—to face the form of the Divines themselves!"

Lane burst into flames instantly, and as the flames died away, she had seemingly turned into a flaming ghost.

"Pure Soul: Fire Form? Not bad Lane," Jane said. "But now you'll have to deal with my form."

A blizzard whipped up around Jane, and as it did, her hair flashed white, then turned pure white, growing a bit longer.

"Half Soul Form? That's nothing in compare to Pure Soul!"

"We'll see about that. By Wintella's wrath, today you fall."

Lane charged at Jane and swung with blades of flames. Jane dodged each strike, and in an instant, a spear of frost formed in her hands. She made a full swing, but Lane flipped back and avoided it.

"Hephaestus Ekriksi!" Lane commanded as she fired a large fireball at Jane. Jane in turn skated away from it, ice forming where she moved. As it hit the ground, the sand turned to glass.

Jane blocked several blows from Lane's fire blades, and swung, but Lane leapt over it and came with a double overhead. Jane blocked it and lunged, but Lane deflected it.

"Pagos Barrage!" Jane commanded. Lane hacked away the ice shards as they came, but was first to leap back from Jane's lightning fast thrust.

"Stalemate eh?" Jane said.

"No, I'm winning!"

"Whatever you say I guess."

A flaming circle appeared under Jane.

"Soul Technique: Flaming Prison!" Lane commanded.

Fire blazed out from the circle under Jane, and for a second, Lane thought it was finally over.

"Useless moves will get you nowhere," Jane said through the flames.

"How the hell?"

Jane dismissed the flames. "Simple. I've been practicing to absorb fire Soul, and now that you've basically charged me up, it's time to show you what I can do."

"By the Divines, no!" Lane shouted fearfully.

Jane was shrouded by a fog of frost. It dispersed, damaging Lane as it hit her.

Jane was now covered in white energy from head to toe. Her eyes and mouth were as black gaps and her clothes were not there. She simply looked like a walking soul.

"This is Pure Soul at its best," Jane said.

"We'll see about that!" Hephaestus Ekriksi!"

Jane put up her hand, and the fireball dispersed as it hit her.

"Fire absorb Lane, don't make this too easy for me."

Lane stepped back fearfully. She only knew fire styles, and nothing else.

"Since you've held your turn, I'll make a move," Jane said. "Soul Technique: Ice Tower!" she said, a woman's voice echoing behind hers.

A tower of ice shot out from the frosty fog from earlier, and it rose as high as the cave ceiling next to it.

Lane didn't even realize that Jane shot past her. She turned to see her upon the tower.

"The pinnacle of strength, the tower of ice," she said. "Isn't it wondrous?"

"It's full of crap!" Lane shouted as she ran and leapt into the air.

"Teresa Barrage!" she commanded.

Jane deflected the attacks as they came, and blocked an incoming slash by Lane with her bare hands.

Lane made a barrage of swing, but they all missed completely. Jane appeared behind her and grabbed her hand. Both the fire swords diminished in an instant.

Lane swung at Jane with her free hand, but she dodged it. A fist crashed into Lane's chest, and she went flying to the other end of the tower.

She rolled and got back on her feet in time to block a strike from Jane. She ducked under a kick and swung at Jane. Jane blocked the hit.

"Face it Lane, it is over."

"Never! Teresa Psyche Katastrofi!"

Jane realized the attack and quickly leapt back but a burst of darkness sent her flying off the tower.

She hit the ground hard. The energy around her slowly faded, and she was back to normal.

Lane landed on the ground before her, still in her fiery form.

"Are you tired Jane?" she mocked.

"I'm just fine," Jane replied as she weakly rose to her feet. She threw off her hat.

"You can't beat me in your current state."

"That's what you think," Jane said as she put up her hand. A spear grazed Lane's neck as it flew to Jane's hand. She swung, tripping Lane where she stood.

Jane ran over to the tower and put her hand on it.

"Where did that spear come from?" Lane asked as she angrily rose.

"The tower. You thought this was for style?" Jane asked.

"I'm going to destroy that damned thing!" Lane said angrily. "Hephaestus Barrage!"

"All that energy wasted," Jane said with a smirk.

The tower faded as Jane absorbed it. A blizzard kicked up around her in an instant. The fireballs crashed down around her, and for the first time in the battle, the place was quiet.

Lane fell to her knees, panting tiredly.

"You're dead Lane," a voice said.

She turned to see Jane standing behind her.

"You don't know how to die, do you?" Lane asked.

"Do I look like I've ever done it in the first place?"

"Just shut up and die!" Lane shouted as she jabbed at Jane. Jane side-stepped the attack and grabbed Lane's arm. She twisted it, and tossed Lane.

The fiery aura around Lane disappeared, and she herself returned to normal.

She rose to her feet and faced Jane.

"Pyras Hoplite!" she commanded as fiery spears flew towards Jane.

"Pagos Hoplite!" she commanded in reply. The two sets of spears collided, shrouding the area in steam again.

"Not this time, Kapnizo Katastrofi!" Lane commanded. The steam imploded, sending a blast of air around them.

Before the steam even cleared, an obsidian dagger came flying through.

It thudded into Lane's chest.

She staggered back, holding the blade. She fell to her knees.

Jane approached her now.

"Why would you kill me? What have I done to you?" Lane asked.

"Why would you want to kill me?"

"Because you deserved it, I was the perfect copy!"

"You only copied my looks and my powers, but now, there will only be one Jane Pagos, now return to me."

Jane held the dagger in Lane's chest. Black streaks of lightning sparked around Lane and Jane. The energy was transferred, and Lane slowly faded away.

Jane stood up, the dagger still in hand. "Strange...It's like I'm...whole again...I better see what I can do for Zen and the others."

Zen and the others ran through the caves. He turned to see Haima standing before them again.

"I can hear the combat taking place outside, it seems that girl that was with you won't be seeing you again," she said with a smug grin.

"Yeah right, Jane has probably frozen Lane into a block of ice by now," Turner said.

"Whatever, either way, I'm giving you the chance to turn back now. Ema doesn't give mercy to anyone, except for our friend the Khan here. She's been expecting you."

"What about Sahra'a?" Zen asked.

"He could care less for you."

"We'll see about that, move out of my way."

"Or what?"

"Or Adele will put and obsidian staff through your chest," Jor said.

"The boy? He has the look of someone who has seen...many trials," Haima said, reviewing Adele.

"I was at the siege of Harmony, and I defeated Mortha," he said.

"Oh, the dark champion? I'm a fan," Haima said humorously.

"Get going you guys, I'll take care of this one," Adele said, spinning his staff.

Zen nodded, and they continued on their way.

"They'll never make it past the sandmen," Haima said.

"We've come too far to be beaten by some half-pint desert princess, her wretched older sister and some fat wad of gold the people call Sahra'a," Adele replied.

"What did you say about big brother?!" Haima shouted.

"Oh, so he really is your BIG brother!"

"Haima Ekriksi!" She commanded, seething with rage.

"Erebus Barrage!" Adele commanded in reply. There was an explosion mid-air, but the rest of the shots struck Haima.

"Teresa Psyche Barrage!" Adele commanded.

As the smoke cleared, Haima's eyes widened.

Nearly twenty Adele's stood before her.

"What kind of evil...?" she said.

"Teresa Pertusus Barrage!" the Adele's all commanded.

Haima watched as over ten beams of dark energy shot through her body repeatedly. She staggered back as black blood poured from each wound.

"Haima Barrage!" she commanded.

Blood splattered from the necks of several of the Adele copies, but they turned back into energy after.

"Attack!" they all shouted. Haima leapt back, dodging several swings. Behind her was another clone.

"Teresa Katastrofi!" they commanded. Haima was rocketed to the other wall of the cave by the blast.

"You're wrecking my clothes!" she exclaimed.

"Let me guess, big brother got them?" one Adele asked.

"Be silenced! Haima Ekriksi!" she commanded as the clone burst into energy.

"You're not getting ahead in this fight," another Adele said. "You first need to fine the right clone, but you don't seem able to do that."

Haima looked around the room. Each Adele looked the same...

Except for the one in the back holding a staff and snickering to himself.

"Now I got you!" she shouted as she pulled an obsidian knife from her side.

She grabbed him and stabbed the knife right in his chest.

"It seems you were a little smarter than I thought," Adele said weakly. He shouted in agony as Haima forced the blade in deeper.

The clones around him turned back into energy.

"You thought you could outsmart Haima of the deserts, didn't you?" she said.

"Yes...and I was...right."

"What?"

"Teresa Psyche Katastrofi!" Adele commanded as he erupted in an explosion of dark energy.

Haima flew across the room, but as she got back up, a hand came from behind her. The obsidian staff fell into the hand and pressed on her neck.

"Game over Haima," the real Adele said, holding the staff to her throat.

"Please, do not kill me!" she begged.

"But if I let you go, there will be a knife through my gullet."

"P-Please," she said, holding back tears. "I don't want to die!"

"Neither did I, but you showed no mercy!"

"I'm sorry Dark Champion, I'm sorry!"

Adele, fed up of her whining, let her go.

"You-you let me go?" she asked him.

"Yes, but you'll be dead if you try anything."

She tried to face him, straight faced, but she couldn't stop herself.

"I'm sorry, so sorry! I'll never do it again!" she cried.

Adele started to feel a bit bad about wanting to kill her.

"Must you be such a cry baby?" he asked.

She stopped for several seconds, but continued again.

"I-I'm sorry...I was just so scared."

"Scared of what?"

"Death. I don't want to meet the cold reaches of darkness by which no man returns."

"I've been dead every day for hundreds of years, now quit whining and act your age!"

"I-I am acting my age," she replied.

"But you're a grown woman."

Haima transformed into a child, a few years younger than Adele.

"You Divines...I'll never understand you..." Adele said, scratching his head.

Zen stopped the group before a spiral pathway down into a hole.

"What's the problem Zen?" Turner asked.

"Sandmen," he replied.

Behind them, mounds of living sand rose up.

"Amec and I will take these guys," Turner said, drawing his sword.

"You wouldn't mind me staying back with these guys, would you Jor?" Lyra asked.

"Compared to what may be coming up, you'll be safer fighting those things," Zen said. "Be careful."

Jor held her hand tight. "Be safe Lyra, Zen and I will be back soon."

"I will, give those guys a thrashing," Lyra said.

Jor and Zen ran down the pathway into the debts of the Rift.

"This should be tricky," Amec said. "I think these things have some control over soul."

"I've fought things worse than this," Turner said.

"Like the Manticore?" Lyra asked.

"Yeah!"

"You do realize it was only one Manticore, and Jor was with you, and you came back with a broken arm..."

"I know, I know," Turner said. "But that's beside the point..."

"Khthon Ekriksi!" several dry voices commanded.

Turner dodged the sharp shard of stone as it shot out the ground before him. Amec did the same.

Lyra ran and as a shard shot out the ground, she flipped, balancing on its tip. She pushed herself back in the air, dropping a barrage of knives on the sandmen.

"Makhaira Katastrofi!" she commanded. They all went up in small explosions.

"Watch out Lyra, behind you!" Amec shouted.

Turner loaded his wrist mounted crossbow and fired in an instant. It struck the sandman, and they fell.

"I didn't need help!" Lyra joked.

"Get your boyfriend to stay around more often then!" he replied.

Amec hacked down a line of sandmen as they came. Turner was alongside him, cutting them down.

A barrage of knives came from Lyra as she threw knife after knife at her enemies.

"Don't you run out of those things?" Amec asked.

"Yeah," she replied, jabbing her knife into a sandman. "I just carry a ton of em'."

Turner ducked as he saw a shard of iron shoot out of one sandman. He blocked another shard and leapt back.

"What is with these things?" he asked.

"They have problems, that's what!" Amec replied.

Lyra blocked a jab behind the back and turned to toss a knife into a sandman's skull. Turner's sword went through another nearby. Amec rushed past them and cut the last sandman in two.

"Finally over," Turner said, sheathing his sword.

"Um Turner, you may have just jinxed us," Lyra said.

The cave began to rumble, and out of the wall came a man made not of sand, but of stone.

"We're in trouble," Amec said.

The golem swung at them with its hefty stone club. The three of them scrambled away in time, but as it hit the ground, the cave shook violently.

Turner got behind it and swung at its leg, but it had no effect. The golem turned and readied an overhead crush.

"Watch it!" Amec shouted as he pushed Turner aside. They both fell into a pile of sand left back by the sandmen.

The giant stopped and turned to face them.

Turner desperately grabbed a shard of iron from the remains of the sand men and jabbed at the golem. It struck it in the joint between its upper and lower leg, stopping it in its tracks.

"That's it," Lyra said as she got a running start. She leapt up in the air and landed on the giants shoulders. She stuck a knife in its shoulder joints, then its forearm joints. She landed on the ground behind it and put two more daggers in the joints by its leg.

"Makhaira Katastrofi!" she commanded. Each dagger exploded at the same time, shattering the golem into useless pieces.

"Whoa Lyra," Turner said as he ran to her. "Not bad."

"So now we need to get to Zen and Jor?" Amec asked.

"I'm going to check on Jane, Lyra, I may need you help just in case," Turner said.

"I guess you may have to come with us," she said to Amec.

"No, I'm going to get Zen and Jor, you catch up with your friends," he said as he ran down the path.

Jor and Zen were walking down the path to Sahra'a's sanctuary.

"All the memories," Zen said. "I can see the fight playing over and over in my mind. I'm still not used to it."

Jor put his hand on his shoulder.

"Don't worry, we'll be the ones to live this time."

"I fear I may not."

"Do not fear that you'll die, that's exactly how you die!"

"Let me guess, you'll tell me not to think about it?"

"No, I'm saying that you won't let yourself die. You have Alda and an entire Kingdom to get back to."

"Having all that won't stop someone's death."

"Listen, when Joralkar came after me I was wounded and battered from crashing the ship, but did I give in to hunger and pain? No, I kept on going. When bandits were attacking Xegel, did they defeat me? When Turner and I were shot down during the battle for Keels, did we die? Men and far stronger than the Divines you know. Hell, we're probably even stronger than we realize."

"Hm, I see why everyone calls you the Leader," Zen said.

"They do? I always thought that was Turner's job."

"Nope, they all look up to you, and you know, I look up to you."

"Wow, I never thought the Khan of Zeran would look up to me," Jor said, blushing a bit in embarrassment.

"Look, the sanctuary is just ahead," Zen said.

"We should have brought along some more Divines," Jor joked.

"Like we have any to call on."

"I just realized a fatal flaw in our plan," Jor said as he stopped.

"What is it?"

"We have no obsidian weapons."

"Oh damn."

The sanctuary doors flung open. Jor was blinded for a second as he saw the room filled with shimmering gold.

"Come in, take a seat," Ema said. She was sitting on a throne of pure gold.

"I'm back Ema!" Zen spat as he drew his sabre.

"Oh you are? Metallos," Ema commanded.

Zen's blade turned to dust.

"Now what may I help you with?" Ema asked.

"I'm here to defeat you," Zen said.

"Oh, that's good to know. Who's that handsome one behind you?"

"He's not important," Zen said.

"Oh, I was just saying. He looks like something I would want. He may even be a good partner for a quick go, if he wants..."

"I've already made a promise to another girl, no way I'm going with another," Jor said.

"My bedroom is right there, I mean, it's not like she'll know what you've been doing."

"No Ema," Jor said firmly.

"Then I guess I'll just destroy you."

"I want Sahra'a first!" Zen said.

"He's not here."

"That coward is too scared to face me? Sahra'a, stop hiding behind your sisters and face me!"

"What did you say about brother?" Ema asked as she rose angrily.

"I said he is a coward."

"Good, now I'll start this fight at full power. I no longer feel the need to see you."

The three dots now reappeared in Zen's eyes.

"I guess I have no need for these," Jor said as he threw aside his weapons.

"Ema Ekriksi!" she commanded.

"Ema Ekriksi!" Zen commanded.

There was a blast of pressure that knocked Jor back a bit.

"Damn, that wasn't a weak attack," he said to himself.

Ema kicked at him, but he ducked under it. He rose up for an upper cut, but Ema caught his hand half-way.

"You are now facing the strongest of the Divines!"

Zen shouted out in pain as he felt his hand being slowly crushed by Ema's grip.

"Ekriksi!" Jor commanded. The blast of energy hit Ema, but had little effect.

"Apo Pano Hermes Ekriksi!" she commanded in turn.

Jor went up in an explosion as the attack hit him faster than he could see.

"Jorigsveer!" Zen cried.

Ema lifted him up and tossed him into the wall.

"Khthon!" she commanded. A fist of stone shot out from the wall and sent him flying back to her. A large scimitar made of bloody iron formed in her hands. She took it with two hands and readied for an overhead slice.

She was slammed aside by Jor, whose eyes were red and blue.

Zen crashed into a pile of gold nearby, but rose up as if he had taken no damage.

"You'll pay for that one!" Ema shouted as she got up and charged.

"Metallos!" Jor commanded, and as he did, his sword flew back into his hands.

He blocked a strike by Ema's blade, and swung at her. She blocked it and slid her sword across his. She spun, and with that came a stronger attack.

Jor blocked it, but he felt it lock his joints. He dropped his sword, but saw the incoming blow.

"Tachista!" he commanded, being within centimeters of the blade before escaping its reach and ending up several feet away from her.

"Ema Ekriksi!" Zen commanded.

She had momentarily forgotten about him and put up her blade. There was a blast of pressure that went around the cave as she blocked the invisible energy.

Zen charged at her, dodging several swings from her scimitar.

He held the hilt of the blade, and the two struggled for the weapon. Jor charged in with his great sword, forcing Ema to release the blade and retreat back.

"You're forcing my hand," Ema said angrily as she walked to the top of a large mound of gold. "Now I'm going to show you one of the horrors of the desert."

Out from the gold came a long blade of obsidian. It was larger than Ema, and had a nasty, serrated edge that was curved. One the small hilt, you could see three red dots, like those in Zen's eyes. Those were the sign of blood.

She took the weapon by the hilt and pointed it with one hand at Zen and Jor.

"If a swordfight is what you wish, then a swordfight is what you'll get!"

She charged down the mound of gold and swung at Jor. He blocked it, but it came back in a lightning fast arc. Jor was expecting it to come to him, but she spun on her heel the last second and swung at Zen. He blocked the hit, but slid back a few feet.

She cartwheeled, and half way through the motion, she pushed herself in the air with one hand and came down with an overhead chop. Zen barely dodged the attack, which left a gash on the ground.

"Ekriksi!" Jor commanded.

"Ema Ekriksi!" she replied. There was another burst of pressure, but Jor was braced for it.

"Ema Ekriksi!" Zen commanded.

Ema swung her blade, redirecting the invisible attack in Jor's direction. He rolled out of the way, but as he got to his feet, Ema was already upon him.

"Ema Tachista Ekriksi!" Zen commanded.

Ema was struck in the back by the attack, and black blood shot from the large wound.

She fell on the ground, unmoving.

"Is she...?" Jor asked.

"I hope she is," Zen said.

She slowly rose to her feet.

"I hope you enjoyed that, because that is the last hit you'll get on me!" she said, tears welling in her eyes.

"Are you really crying from such a little scratch!?" Jor shouted, both eyes turning red. "I was expecting a better match!"

"I'm not crying! Exochos Ema Barrage!"

"We can't dodge that!" Zen shouted.

Blood shot out from his leg and arm and he staggered back. Jor blocked one, but the pressure sent him flying across the room. He tried to reach for his great sword, which fell next to him, but blood shot from his hand before he could reach it.

"Ema Ekriksi!" she commanded, her open palm facing Zen.

He closed his eyes, awaiting the coming blow.

There was a blast of pressure, but no pain. He opened his eyes to see something furry in front of him.

"Hey, I heard you're a friend of Eros," he said.

"Pay attention Kinigos," Eros said.

Zen stepped back to see many old friends.

Eros, Kinigos, Alcino and Dodecagon stood before Ema now.

"W-What are you all doing here?" Ema asked fearfully.

"We've come to finally put you down Ema," Alcino said.

"Yeah, you've been a pain in the rear end for long enough!" Eros added.

Jor walked over to where Zen was standing, holding his injured hand.

"Seems the gangs all here...where's Efiia?" he asked.

The old Divine appeared late in a flash of light.

"Sorry, Soul Travel is not what it used to be," he said. "Oh, Jorigsveer? Khan? I'm so sorry for not realizing you were here sooner."

"Pay attention gramps!" Kinigos shouted.

"Oh, how rude!" he exclaimed.

"Ichor!" Ema commanded.

Black blood shot out from Kinigos' shoulder in nearly an instant.

"You dirty, bloody whore!" Eros shouted angrily. "Hephaestus Barrage!"

"Shut up you damn stray! Ichor Barrage!"

"Exochos Aegis!" Kinigos commanded as he put up a giant wall made of energy.

Zen and Jor covered their eyes as many fiery explosions lit up the sanctuary.

As the first few attacks subsided, clapping could be heard from away.

"Oh, so it truly seems that the stage is set," Sahra'a said from a balcony higher up.

He was now in the form of an Ayan Saudi man, and wore Mamluk armor. Over his face was a mask made of gold. It had the look of an angry monster with horns on it, with three dots on its head.

"I was told you would come, and now, the trap is successful!" he laughed.

"What trap?" Alcino asked.

Sahra'a threw his hands in the air.

"Arise, Tower of the Great Emir!" he commanded.

There was a low rumbling, then it became loud and the cave shook violently.

"Jor, Zen, get over here!" Eros shouted.

Jor took a step forward, but was nearly crushed by a falling stone.

"The place is caving in, come on Zen!" he shouted.

Zen limped over. "I'm going as fast as I can."

Jor took Zen and threw his arm over his shoulder. He slowly hauled him over to the shield.

"Damn Zen, what have you been eating, you don't look that heavy."

"Palace food Jor, it does that to you," Zen said with a hint of humor.

The two of them finally made it to the shield, and Kinigos closed it.

Ema banged on the shield fearfully.

"Let me in, I don't want to get buried!"

"No," Alcino stubbornly replied.

Adele, Turner, Lyra and Adele were outside of the cave with Haima. They had only barely escaped the cave in.

"What's going on in there?" Lyra asked.

"It's happening," Haima said. She was still in her child form. "The trap that was meant for the 'good' Divines of Edafos, it would capture them all and drain them of their energy."

"But isn't your sister still in there?" Adele asked.

"She can't be. Big brother would never let her get hurt...wouldn't he?"

A tower made of gold shot out from under the sands. It rose high into the afternoon sky.

"That's it!" Haima exclaimed.

The tower shined in the desert sun, and it had a long pathway that wound around it from top to bottom. The top was pointed and had a balcony that overlooked the area.

It finally stood upright in the sands, hundreds of feet tall.

"Jeeze," Turner said scratching his head. "Imagine how much that costs."

"Our friends could be dead in a pile of rubble and you're worried about the gold?" Jane asked.

"Jor and Zen are alright, I'm telling you," Adele said.

"Stupid, damn...idiot," Ema said as she slowly rose to her feet. "And my clothes are a wreck...Sahra'a!"

"Keep your voice down Ema," Kinigos said as he appeared before her, sitting cross-legged.

"And why should I?!"

"Well, we're trying to formulate a plan, and you making noise won't solve anything."

"How about I just kill you all?"

"Nope, not today little Ema," Dodecagon said.

"What are you doing here, dragon-kin?" she asked.

"I'm helping Eros and Alcino," he replied brightly.

"So what do you plan to do? Fight me? I've put down enough of you damned lizards."

"Those were the stupid dragons," Dodecagon said, his smile growing wolfish. "You'll find me a much more dangerous opponent. I'm Dodecagon, twelfth child of the House of Polygon."

"Like I even feared Polygon while he was alive," Ema said. "People like him deserved to die during the War."

"Well let me show you a fraction of his power then."

"Khthon!" Ema commanded, and a side of the tower opened up.

"Well let's go then, I doubt this tower will be enough to hold us."

The two of them neared the hole in the wall.

"Ladies first," Dodecagon said. He could have sworn he saw her blush, but paid it no mind.

"Good, now that she's taken care of," Eros said.

"Well, I'm not sure of it," Alcino said nervously. "Dodecagon is powerful, but he's not a Divine."

"Hm, well if you of all people are worried about him, then we really and truly should be a bit concerned," Efiia said.

"We have no time to worry, we have to beat Sahra'a before..." Eros stopped before she could finish the sentence.

Zen and Jor ran to her side, but as they did, they could see the other Divines falling to the ground.

"What's going on?" Jor asked.

"We fell for Sahra'a's trap, that's what," Alcino said angrily.

"He's draining our energy so he can make himself stronger," Kinigos said. "If we don't take him out soon, we may just end up being a pile of obsidian bones."

"If I fall, could I be a sword then?" Efiia joked.

"No one is making weapons from anyone's bones today," Zen said. "Let's go Jor, we have a Divine to defeat."

The two of them charged up the side of the tower, moving up the high path.

"You're pretty for a crazed murderer you know?" Dodecagon said.

"You're pretty stupid for a Dragon from a High House," Ema replied.

"You're bent on hurting my feelings, huh?"

"I'm bent on hurting you! Ema Barrage!"

"Teresa Barrage!"

The two attacks collided, and there were several bursts of pressure. Despite their strength, neither was fazed by the bursts.

"Hephaestus Barrage!" Ema commanded. Giant fireballs took the skies and circled around them.

"Pyras Barrage!" she commanded again as smaller fireballs surrounded her.

"You know, I think I like you, so I'll let you go," Ema said.

"*Now* you're nice. Well sorry Ms. Ema, but I'm beyond that now."

"Did you just call me Ms.?"

"Yeah, it's for respect."

Ema hesitated for a second, but threw the giant fireballs at him.

"Hermes!" Dodecagon commanded.

He dodged the fireballs that came with lightning speed. Around him, everything seemed to be moving in slow motion. For a second, he stopped navigating the falling fireballs.

"Where is Ema?" he asked.

Out of the corner of his eye, a fist sent him sliding through the sand. He rolled out of the way as a fireball slowly crashed down into the sands.

"What? You didn't hear my command?" she asked.

"I couldn't hear over the sound of impending death," he replied.

She gently put her hand forward, and the fireballs went flying at him. He leapt back, then as he began to skid in the sand, he changed paths. He stopped for a second, and quickly redirected three fireballs that approached.

"Teresa Ekriksi!" he commanded. The attack hit a coming fireball, dispersing it.

A giant fireball slowly came down, blocking the two's view of each other.

"Damn it," Ema said softly. The giant fireballs around her fell to the ground, shaking the area as they hit.

When the smoke finally cleared, she looked up to see the large black dragon above her.

"Oh no," she said fearfully.

"Hades Pertusus!" he commanded as a cloud of darkness was spewed on Ema.

She exited the attack, and as she skated back, she could see the dragon coming from behind. A slap from his tale sent her through the sands.

Dodecagon went back to human form and put up his hands.

"Khthon Barrage!" he commanded. The sand in the air went back down onto the ground with a hard drop.

"Come on Ema, you're not dead yet," he said.

"Will you guys leave my clothes alone!" Ema shouted as she rose to her feet, covering in small wounds that poured black blood.

"If you stopped wearing clothes from the last century, they would probably hold together."

"Leave me alone!" she shouted as she charged.

Dodecagon was caught off-guard by the sudden dash, and a fist slammed into his face sending him barreling through the sand.

He rolled back and got back on his feet, still sliding back. He put up his hand, catching Ema's fist. He threw her up.

"Teresa Katastrofi!" he commanded.

Ema gained balance mid-air and put her hands together.

"Aduro Katastrofi Barrage!"

A plume of sand shot up in the air from the explosion they caused.

As the sand cleared, Dodecagon lay in a crater.

"Damn...it..." he said weakly.

"I was expecting you to have a little more fight in you," Ema said.

Dodecagon rose up again, shaking off sand as he did.

"I can keep going!" he shouted.

"That's what I like to hear," she laughed.

The two of them charged at each other, their fists clashing, sending a burst of energy through the deserts.

The held in place, trying to gain the upper hand, but in the end, they leapt back.

"Teresa Ekriksi!" Dodecagon commanded.

"Pyras Ekriksi!" Ema commanded.

As the sand began to kick up again from the collision, Dodecagon charged into the cloud after Ema.

He was struck in the shoulder, but as he turned and swung, he was struck in the back.

"Stop playing with me!" he shouted.

"Ema Ekriksi!" she commanded.

Dodecagon tried to dodge, but blood shot out from his shoulder.

"Ema Barrage!" she commanded again.

"Hades Barrage!" Dodecagon commanded in a panic.

The deserts were lit up with large explosions of dark energy.

Bursts of air sent the sands in many different directions, making it seem like a small sandstorm kicked up.

Dodecagon slowly staggered back, holding his injured shoulder. He couldn't see anything but sand, and it was getting harder to breath by the second.

"Only so far can a mortal go," he said to himself.

"Found you!" Ema shouted.

Dodecagon faced forward as he was sent flying by a single punch from Ema.

He went sliding through the sand, and then stopped as he hit a dune.

Ema now approached the dune and tore him out by his leg. She tossed him aside carelessly.

"Do you give up, dragon?" she asked.

"Y-You got me," he said as he weakly sat upright.

"Good, now I can divert much needed strength towards helping big brother. "See you next time."

A black circle appeared under her, and she disappeared.

Sahra'a laughed as he looked out into the deserts.

"Keeping Ema around was the best idea ever, a living weapon is more than enough to aid in my conquest."

"Sahra'a!" Zen shouted as he ran up the last of the path and stood at the large balcony of the tower.

"Zen Zeran? So strange meeting you again," he replied.

"I'm back Sahra'a, and I've come to avenge my friends and save my people."

"So you actually came back here in attempts to defeat me? Where are your obsidian weapons? Where is your Divine strength?"

Zen pounded his chest.

"Right here Sahra'a."

"Oh really? I hope you know I could rip your heart straight from your body right now."

"Try it."

"Ichor!" Sahra'a commanded.

The three dots appeared in Zen's right eye, and he deflected the attack with his bare hands.

"Now Jor!" he shouted.

Ema's obsidian scimitar came spinning overhead and it dug itself into the floor before Sahra'a. Jor came leaping over Zen with his great sword, nearly cutting Sahra'a down the middle had he not moved.

Zen took up the scimitar and swung an uppercut at Sahra'a. He dodged and drew two sabers. Zen swung, but Sahra'a blocked it with both blades. He lunged, but Sahra'a danced around it and came for a blow for the neck.

Jor got in the way just in time to block him.

Zen ran to a safer position as the two locked blades.

"Ema Ekriksi!" Zen commanded.

Sahra'a swung and deflected the attack, a burst of air knocking Jor back. He went sliding off the edge.

"Dammit, Jor!" Zen shouted as he ran to get him.

Sahra'a went in the way and they both locked blades.

"Seems your friend will be taking quite the fall."

"Jor will be fine, you're the one who should be worried."

Both of them took a step back, and locked again.

"You'll never be able to kill me you know," Sahra'a taunted.

"I would rather have you beaten and alive," Zen replied with a smirk.

"I don't think so."

Sahra'a head-butted Zen with his hard helmet, making him stagger back, dropping his blade.

He kicked it away, leaving Zen standing unarmed with a bloody forehead.

"A cheap shot from a Divine. You really actually are scared of me," Zen laughed.

"Do not take me so lightly mortal, I am the most powerful Divine of the deserts!"

"That title adorns your little sister."

"I'm telling you, she is just a weapon!"

"So that's how you see it? You are even worse than I thought."

"Enough!" Sahra'a shouted. Gold plates began pushing out from the side of the tower, making an even larger space.

Sahra'a swung at Zen, but he danced between the blades, dodging attack after attack.

He swung high, but Zen ducked. He kicked, but Zen propelled himself back quickly.

He lunged powerfully, but Zen gently put his hand over the blade and moved out of its path. In the same motion, he struck Sahra'a's helm.

"The real fight begins now Sahra'a," Zen said.

"What!?" he shouted angrily.

A blade went straight through his chest before he could finish the sentence. He felt the presence of obsidian and moved forward, the blade moving painfully out of his body.

Jor and Amec stood behind him, armed and ready.

"Took you guys long enough," Zen laughed.

"Sorry, I just had to save Jor from eminent death," Amec joked.

Sahra'a slowly rose to his feet, his head down.

"Ready for more Sahra'a?" Zen challenged.

A low laughter rose from him then.

"What's so funny?" Jor asked.

"Look," he said.

A black circle appeared, and with it, Ema.

"Am I late?" she asked.

"Yes, you are extremely late," Sahra'a said, holding his chest.

"By the Divines, are you okay big brother?"

"I'm fine, just kill them!"

"Anything for you big...oh..."

Ema smiled as she laid eyes on Amec.

"I remember you from that Ayan Saudi village...you're the father of our new brother!"

"New brother?" Amec asked.

A black circle appeared next to Ema, and out of it came Ichor, still shrouded in dark energy.

"Aman!" he shouted. "Snap out of this, you are not who you really are!"

"Aman is dead Amec, do you not understand this?" Ema asked. "He's my baby brother now!"

"Baby brother? He is nothing but a slave to your bidding, a soul without will! He has no love for you!" Jor shouted.

"Shut up!" Ema cried, sending such a powerful burst that it knocked down even Sahra'a.

"Big sister loves me, little brother loves me and big brother loves me! Everyone loves me!" Ema snapped.

"I'll show you the error of your ways," Jor said as he readied his blade.

The two charged into battle.

Amec threw the obsidian scimitar to Zen, and drew his own sword to face Ichor.

"I will bring you back son! I'll do anything, for you are all I have left in the world."

"So Sahra'a, looks like your help is preoccupied," Zen said.

"Only temporarily, your friends are about to die," Sahra'a said as he got back on his feet.

"Then let us go!" Zen shouted as he charged.

"I have to get up there!" Haima said suddenly.

"Why on Edafos would you do that? Do you want to die?" Lyra asked.

"Sister is in danger!"

"Do you want to die with her?" Jane reiterated.

"I want to live with her..."

"Exactly why you shouldn't head up there," Turner said.

"But Ema may destroy herself in her angry rampage! Do you know what kind of mental state she is in?"

"Mental state? I always assumed she was just nuts," Adele said.

"Listen, ever since mama died in the Divine War, she's wanted love, but no one could give it to her. Sahra'a thinks she's a weapon, and won't hesitate to set her off into creation mode."

"Creation mode?" Lyra asked.

"A form only few Divines can take. Even Efiia has lost such ability. She is capable in rewriting Edafos as we know it in this form, meaning she'll rule creation itself as a weapon. She envisions a time where she'll once again be able to release her anger, and then shall be such a time."

"Then come with me," Adele said.

"I'm going alone Adele, I'm sorry," she said as a black circle appeared under her.

"Dammit, no Haima!" he shouted as he tried to stop her. She faded in a burst of energy.

Jor blocked what felt like a thousand powerful punches per second as he battled with Ema. Each attack hit harder than the last, and he could feel his weapon giving away.

"Ema Ekriksi!" she commanded.

Jor blocked it, sending a burst of energy around.

"Don't you realize? Sahra'a thinks you're his weapon!" Jor shouted as he blocked a heavy punch.

"I'm his favorite little sister!" she shouted as she leapt up into the air.

Jor blocked her powerful kick, but his blade felt weaker.

"You're his favorite weapon! If Sahra'a loved you, would he have let you be crushed by the tower?"

"I wasn't crushed!"

"But you nearly were! And what did big brother do?"

"Shut up!" she shouted as she punched his blade.

"Ema, do you realize now that you are like me, few in the world loved us, but you can change like I did, you can find someone who loves you."

"Metallos Kopis," Ema commanded as a long sword made of iron animated into her hand.

"Big brother loves me enough."

"Well my brothers don't, they killed my mother!"

Jor watched as what seemed like a million bad memories surged through Ema's mind. Her eyes had a distant shine to them.

"Shut up, you're wrecking my mind!" she shrieked.

"Something is being awakened inside you, I can see it!"

"Shut up!" she shrieked as she swung at him. Jor blocked slash after slash desperately.

Amec blocked a lunge from Ichor's deadly sharp arm. He moved his sword up to block an overhead chop.

"Come on Aman, you're somewhere in there!" Amec shouted.

He blocked a quick kick and stepped back.

"Just show me one sign that you're alive!"

He blocked a swing from the left, but kept his ground.

Zen blocked slash after slash from Sahra'a, fighting at a losing end of the battle.

"Come one Zen, the disks only go out seven sets," Sahra'a taunted. "There's nothing stopping you from falling off."

Zen blocked a lunge, but it pushed him back.

"Six," Sahra'a said.

Zen swung an overhead, but Sahra'a blocked it, then attempted to cut across Zen's chest. He stepped back, dodging the attack.

"Five."

"Ema Ekriksi!" Zen commanded.

"Ichor Ekriksi!" Sahra'a commanded in reply.

The shockwaves from that attack alone knocked him back three disks.

"Oh, two now."

Sahra'a slowly approached, his swords ready.

Zen stepped back fearfully, unsure what to do now.

"One."

Sahra'a swung, but Zen ducked. He kicked Sahra'a in the shin, but it didn't move him.

"Oh, I sense your friend Amec's energy getting lower," he said.

Zen looked over to see his friend weakly fighting off Ichor's attacks.

"Aman, please, just speak one word…please," Amec said, tears rolling out his eyes.

"Ichor!" he commanded as his arm ripped through Amec's chest.

"Amec!" Zen shouted. He swung low, cutting off Sahra'a's leg. Sahra'a fell shouting as Zen ran over to Amec.

"No problem Zen, I got this," Amec said as blood ran down the side of his mouth. He slowly lowered his hand to show that his blade had pierced Ichor.

"Little brother!" Ema shouted as she kicked Jor away.

"So Aman, now will you speak?" Amec asked.

"I can speak now father," a voice replied. "Ichor is finally dead."

"So he is, but are you?"

"I am gone father. I was tied to Ichor, and so I fall with him."

"We fall together then," Amec said as he went limp.

Aman slowly faded with the wind, and Amec fell to the ground, a pool of blood welling up under him.

"Amec, stay with me, I need you!" Zen said as he held his hand.

"That doesn't seem very likely Zen," he replied with a soft smile.

"You're my advisor Amec, you have a Kingdom that you need to help me rule!"

"Zen, you must understand, everyone has a time to die, and today is my day…"

"No it is not, you still have a conviction, to help me rule. Remember what Jor said about conviction?"

"I had a conviction to save my son, and I did so, nothing else binds me to this world."

"But the Kingdom!"

"Remember that pretty girl, Alda was it?"

"What about Alda?"

"You have your Queen then, your other half, your greatest advisor."

"But Amec, you were one of my best friends..."

"I know how it feels Zen, but now, we must part ways..."

"Ichor Katastrofi!" Ema commanded.

Zen covered his eyes as a blast erupted before him. He felt someone pull him out the way.

He opened his eyes to see a puddle of blood where Amec lay previously.

"You killed little brother, and now I'll kill you!" Ema shouted, tears rolling from her eyes.

"What little brother, that was Amec's only son dammit, and you corrupted his mind, body and soul! He was your doll!" Zen shouted, tears falling from his eyes. "He was just like you, a toy for death and destruction!"

"Shut up, shut up, shut up! I am no one's weapon, I am Ema!" she shrieked, holding her head.

"Sahra'a only thinks of you as a weapon, can't you take it as it is and suck it up?"

"I am not a weapon!"

"No one loves you Ema, all they see when you pass is a harlot or a weapon. Amec loved Aman with all his heart, and now they are together for all of eternity, away from you!"

"Shut up about eternity! You don't know what it's like!"

"Then how about I show you?" Zen said as he rose to his feet.

"Mama is in eternity, I do not want to see her!"

"Zen, stop it now," Haima said.

"Why should I?! She killed everyone I loved!"

"Well don't do the same, or you'll just keep up the cycle!"

"The cycle ends once the weapon is destroyed..."

"Kill him Ema!" Sahra'a said as his leg slowly regenerated from energy.

"Kill me yourself why don't you," Zen challenged. "Let's go right now!"

Sahra'a got back on his feet and put up his blades.

"So be it!"

Zen charged and lunged, but Sahra'a dodged it and got behind him. He swung, but Zen put the blade behind him and blocked it. He turned and swung, but they locked blades.

"You cannot kill those with conviction," Zen said.

"I have conviction!"

"To your weapon? To your gold?"

"I shall have power!"

"And I shall have life!"

Zen pushed Sahra'a away, and a barrage of swings followed soon after.

Sahra'a struggled to stop each blow, backing up slowly.

"Five!" Zen shouted as he hit him a heavy overhead.

"Four!"

Sahra'a swung low, but Zen jumped, and as he hit the ground, he propelled himself up and tackled Sahra'a.

"Three!"

He blocked a blow from Zen, but as he readied for the next hit, Zen took an unexpected swing, cutting of Sahra'a's right hand. Zen kicked him, and he staggered back.

"One!"

Sahra'a looked down to see he was standing over Amec's pool of blood.

"Ichor Katastrofi!" Zen commanded angrily. The blood erupted into a large explosion, which tore apart Sahra'a's chest plate.

Zen took the opportunity and drove his blade through Sahra'a's chest, dead center.

"You have fallen, Sahra'a, Bane of the Deserts."

Sahra'a stood in awe, and slowly, as the black energy pulsed around his body, he faded, leaving back a pile of obsidian bones which fell to the ground.

"Big...Brother?" Haima said in awe.

"Big Brother? Big Brother!" Ema screamed as she ran to the pile of bones. She frantically rummaged through the bones, hoping for some sign of life.

"Ema," Haima said.

She continued rummaging through the bones.

"Ema."

She couldn't hear her.

"Ema!"

She looked at Haima, and tears welled in both their yes.

"Big Brother is dead Ema. He his dead."

"No...I can't cry again! No!" she screamed, energy pulsing around her.

"Creation mode," Haima said to herself.

She walked over to where Zen stood and took up a spine.

"It was nice knowing you all," she said with a sad smile.

The spine turned into a spear as she walked over to Ema.

Haima threw the spear up in the air and grabbed Ema. "Hoplite!" she commanded.

The spear shredded through both their chests, and black blood fell to the ground.

"No Haima!" Ema babbled hysterically. "I don't want to die!"

"We fall together Ema!" Haima shouted. "Don't you want to see mama?"

"No, she died weak! I don't want to die weak!"

Haima passed out, her energy falling low. Ema tried to remain conscious, but she passed out, and they both fell into a pool of black blood.

Zen tore the spear out of both their bodies.

"No you don't, enough people have died today!" he shouted.

"Are you trying to get us killed?" Jor said as he got up tiredly, wiping blood from his lip.

"Their energy is all gone Jor, they can't harm us."

Ema and Haima slowly degenerated into the form of young children. Zen was relieved to hear them breathing.

He held both of them in his arms.

"Now what?" Jor asked.

"The Divines!" Zen exclaimed. "I just remembered!"

The tower began rumbling terribly, and it shook violently.

"This thing is falling apart!" Jor shouted.

"Then hurry!" Zen shouted as he ran down the path.

As the two of them ran, they dodged falling pieces of gold and stone debris, desperately trying to survive.

As they got near the middle, they saw the Divines weakly lying around, trying to get back up.

"Hurry, the tower's falling!" Zen shouted.

"Standing is a bit of a chore," Alcino said.

"Yeah, he drained us almost to death," Kinigos said.

"You'll all be dead if you don't get up!" Zen shouted.

"We're trying you damn fool!" Eros said angrily as she tried to get up.

"Jor, take the girls," Zen said as he handed them over to Jor.

"What will you do?" he asked.

"I'll stay here and save these guys."

"But..."

"Jor, I have conviction. With that, not even the Divines will defeat me."

"Then do your best," Jor said as he ran off.

"So professor, how do you plan to stop us from all dying?" Alcino asked.

"Efiia, do you remember your Call of Kings ability?" Zen asked.

"What of it?" he asked.

"Soul Technique: Brotherhood Call!" Zen commanded.

The spirits of thousands of men from past to present appeared now at the tower, ready to serve.

"Zen Zeran, a pleasure," Zil said as he approached.

"Zen, you look like a man," the commander laughed.

"It's good to see you all again, I would have loved to have a talk, but this tower is coming down on us, can you help?"

"Sure can!" Zil said. "You think we were just lazing around all these months, or years?"

"I know you weren't," Zen laughed.

"Well let's get to it then!" the commander shouted.

The tower crumpled before the adventurers, causing a cloud of sand to go up around it. Soon after though, it fell in on itself, collapsing into the desert below.

"I hope Jor, Amec and Zen are okay," Turner said.

"Come on, you know Jor," Adele said.

"Hey!" Jor called from away as he ran to them.

"Who are they?" Jane asked, pointing at the children.

"Haima and Ema, drained of their Divinity," he replied.

"Where are Zen and Amec?"

"At the tower," Jor said quickly.

"Don't tell me Zen is…"

"He stayed back to save the rest of the Divines."

"The rest of the Divines?" Lyra asked.

"It's a long story."

Zen walked through the rubble, a proud look to him.

Zil appeared before him.

"So, I hear you'll be the new Khan," Zil said.

"I will be," Zen said. "And as my first act, I'll end this war."

"Then soldiers like us haven't died in vain."

"You died heroes, and will be remembered as such."

The two of them held each other's hand tightly.

"Brothers forever," Zil said.

"Even unto death," Zen finished.

The spirits of the men slowly faded away, leaving Zen and the Divines alone.

"Zen, this will be one amazing story to tell the grandkids," Kinigos said, patting him roughly on the back.

"They'll never believe me," Zen said as tears rolled out his eyes. That minute, he cried like a baby, but a proud, happy, victorious baby.

"Where's Amec?" Turner asked as Zen approached them.

"Dead. Killed in the fight against Ema and Ichor," he replied.

"Oh," Turner said, shook by the news. "Well we can't stop now, we still need to make it to Ayan Saudi."

"And we will," Zen said as he continued on to the horses.

CHAPTER 71

Ayan Saudi

"So where is Amec?" Adele asked, fearful of the answer. They were riding away from the ruins.

"Yeah, where is he?" Jane asked.

"He was killed by Ichor, his son in a corrupted form created by Ema," Zen said. "They fell together at least."

"Oh," Lyra said, a bit sadly.

"But we can't let that stop us, we still have a desert to cross."

By the time the battle had ended, it was already near evening time. The deserts were cooler now, and they continued their march.

"So about these two," Jor said as he rode up next to Zen. Haima and Ema were asleep on the saddle in front of him.

"I don't know. I can't harm them, but they may not do the same. Haima may be on our side, but Ema is a different story."

"So then what do we do?"

"We keep them until they awake. After that, we just hope for the best."

Lyra rode up next to them now.

"It's hard to believe this cute little girl could be so dangerous," she said, touching Ema's cheek.

"She may not be anymore," a voice said.

The group turned to see Efiia following behind them, and obsidian spear as his walking stick.

"Efiia? What are you doing out here?" Turner asked as they all stopped their horses.

"Well, I had acquired this fine walking stick and wondered, 'I should show this to my friends'."

"You realize how much power is in that one staff?" Zen asked. "If you let that out right now, we'll all be killed by what's in it."

"True, this spear contains all the hate and malice that once filled Ema and Haima, and with it, it took both of their Divinity."

"So they're both mortal now?"

"I'm guessing they are, but this spear can't be held in my possession."

"Why not?" Jor asked. "You're entrusting that to mere mortals?"

"Listen Jorigsveer," Efiia said, turning serious. "You all are more than just normal mortals. You have a great power, but you don't realize it. Edafos is in trouble, and you all hold its fate in your hands. Everything you've faced so far has proven to be as a bit of a preparation for what may be ahead. There may be another war just as catastrophic as the 300 Year War, and it may start soon. Deneaux has fallen from grace, and the Divines against us are plotting to take Edafos and use it to take over other realms. This may be all hard to take in, but you need to be prepared. Death awaits in Southern Cardia, and some of you may be those who lay bleeding in its battlefields, left for the crows..."

The adventurers looked at each other grimly.

"But let's not get all dark and gloomy," he laughed. "You still have a super powerful weapon to take care of."

He tossed the spear to Zen, and disappeared as a ring of energy appeared below him and teleported him away.

"We're so screwed," Jor said.

Zen punched him on the arm. "Don't pressure me Jor, I have enough of it on my head," he laughed.

The gates of the great desert kingdom of Ayan Saudi stood before them. They had been traveling for several days, and now, they were finally here.

"Hey, anybody here?" Zen called out.

"Stand down Zerani, what do you expect to find here, besides your death?" shouted a guard from the battlements.

"I am a peace keeper, one who wishes for peace between our homes," Zen said.

"What?! Captain!"

The guard Captain came soon after, dressed in Mamluk armor. He saw Zen and had a stunned look on his face for a second.

"What makes a Zerani so brave to come here?" he asked.

"A peace treaty, we wish to end the war."

The guards whispered and spoke amongst each other, then finally, they opened the gates.

Zen and the others rode into the city, the streets filled with guards and fearful townspeople.

Zen tried to wave, but several crossbows were aimed as he raised his hand.

"The Sultan is up the street," one guard said roughly.

"Okay, okay," Zen said as he continued.

They made their way until they were in the palace courtyard.

"Now who is this? A man of Zeran...?" the Sultan said as he stood on a balcony. He was a well-built man, and had the look of a warrior, but he also seemed like a skilled diplomat. He was a bearded man and seemed well off in his forties. He wore robes that were made of materials that denoted his rank and a patterned turban.

"A Zerani with a Raider, an elf, a boy and a Deneauxman, why are you here?"

"Our countries have fought for no reason for far too long. I shall not leave this city until we have peace."

"Then come in, but leave your friends behind, they'll be severed separately..."

Lyra viciously destroyed a plate of pork that was placed in front of her. It had been days since they ate well, so anything from the royal guest room would do.

"This is fantastic!" she said, her mouth full.

Jor nodded, a turkey leg taking up all the space in his mouth.

"Such pigs," Jane said, eating with the given utensils. "We're better than that, right Adele..."

He mumbled a reply, gorging himself with bread.

"You're alone on this one Jane," Turner said as he reached for a whole bottle of wine.

"No, not that," Jane warned.

"Oh come on, are you my wife or something?"

"I may be soon, and I'm not having a drunkard husband when I could have a Knight."

Turner, caught off guard, put down the bottle of wine.

"So have Ema and Haima woken up?" Lyra asked.

"I'll have to check the guest rooms," Jor said as he got up. He left the room, but came back quickly.

"Don't eat up all the food while I'm gone."

"No promises," Lyra and Adele said.

"What good friends," Jor said sarcastically as he left.

Zen made himself comfortable on one of the cushions laid out on the floor. He and the Sultan were in the throne room.

"So, who are you?" the Sultan asked.

"I am Zen Zeran, Khan of Zeran," he said, bowing slightly.

"Oh really? So what's stopping me from killing you right now?"

"Those people I brought with me can level your palace before the guards can draw their swords. Don't think about making them mad."

"How do I know you are not lying to me?"

"They helped me defeat Sahra'a."

"The Divine of the Deserts? I think not."

"You see that spear by the wall? That's made of obsidian, and carries power that can recreate Edafos...or destroy it."

"Then prove it."

Zen got up and took the spear. He put it up, then slammed the butt of it on the ground.

There was a shockwave that knocked back even the Sultan, and shook the palace.

As Jor checked on the two, he himself felt the shockwave. He almost fell over, but as he regained his balance, Ema began to cry.

He picked her up and tried to rock her to calm down, but nothing would help.

"Oh man, Lyra! Jane!" he called.

"That...that was no trick! How did you acquire such power?"

"It was a hard battle, but me, and many others, stormed his sanctuary, and defeated him and his sisters in battle."

"So what is it that you want?" the Sultan asked, still in shock.

"Peace between our nations."

"But you could destroy us all right now, why have peace?!"

"I've seen my fair share of men die. This war is useless. It is only a way to keep us in chains and slaves to those evil Divines. Once we rise above our differences though, even we as mere mortals have the strength to surpass that of a Divine. I'm asking that we come together and face the true enemy, the Kingdom to the North that wants to conquer us."

"I have heard, yes. Deneaux had attempted to take over Den Hall, but failed."

"They're trying to take over all of Cardia, and we stand as the only barrier between them and the South. We become brothers, and the men of the deserts will be seen as the heroes who saved the South. What do you say?"

Zen extended his hand.

"We shall protect these sands, brother!" the Sultan said proudly as he stood up and shook Zen's hand firmly. "If we to have a common enemy, we are friends to be true!"

"Come on little one, no one's going to hurt you," Lyra said as she gently rocked Ema. She had already calmed a little, and now held on tightly to Lyra.

"You're not too bad at the child care thing Lyra," Jane said. "You sure you never had a child before?"

"No Jane," Lyra said firmly. She heard Ema fuss a bit, and began to rock her again.

"You're a natural," Turner chuckled.

"I guess I am."

"Guess what!" Zen said as he burst into the room.

"Shh!" they all said.

"Sorry but I've done it" he continued in a hush.

"As if we doubted it," Jor said.

"Hey Zen, we finally got her to do something," Lyra said as she handed Ema over to him. "She cried."

Zen took her in his arms. "That's all?"

He looked down at her to see her eyes were open, staring at him.

"Well that's a first," Adele said.

Zen looked down to see Haima tugging at his pants.

"What? Do I look like their father or something?"

"Maybe they want you to be their father," Lyra joked.

Ema grabbed some of Zen's hair and gave it a good pull.

"Ow, maybe so...ow!"

"So what now?" Turner asked.

"We go back to Zeran and spread the good news."

"This is how you act when you've just made history?" Jane asked.

"I guess the reality hasn't set in yet. Either way, let's get going, I want to be back home as soon as possible."

C H A P T E R 72

Victory

Zen and the others waved as the people of Zeran cheered their names, waving banners and smiling.

"This is a good feeling," Zen said to Jor.

"Hey, you deserve it, you're the Khan."

"So what about when you become Jarl?"

"Of what, a mound of dirt? I'm no King."

"You never know."

Zen and the others entered the palace.

"Alda, Kilan, we're here!" he called out.

The two of them rushed down the stairs to see them all by the door way.

Kilan ran and embraced Adele, knocking them both down.

Alda tightly embraced Zen.

"We were worried about you," she said.

"Well don't worry, I'm here to stay."

Several days had passed since they were staying in the city, and things weren't too bad.

Jor unrolled a map of Cardia. He reviewed it carefully.

"So Lyra, where do you want to go?" he asked, taking a seat on his bed next to her.

"I'd like to go to Keels, I haven't seen my parents or Ifadeel in what? Months?"

"Well, you know how Keels is now, so we may have to revise that choice."

"How about Vinlandt, there looks pretty."

"I've heard some bad things about Spire, and we may have to cross there...unless we take the shortcut..."

"What shortcut?"

"Look, the Andras Boreas have a country to the east of Ayan Saudi, only problem is that we can't fly like them..."

"So that's out of the question?"

"No, I'll figure something out, either that or we go through Spire, though I don't like the idea. Perialites can be...a brick wall when they want to..."

"And you know that better than anyone?" she asked, a bit of humor in her voice.

"Yeah..." he seemed to be lost in thought, staring at the map.

Lyra kissed him on the cheek.

"I'll be glad to follow you anywhere."

"To Spire?" he asked. She nodded.

"To Vinlandt?"

She nodded.

"To the shores of Holmes?"

She nodded.

"Even to Sepal and Changquan?"

She nodded again.

He held her and wrestled her flat on the bed.

"Come on Jor, stop it," she laughed as he kissed her on the neck. "What would it look like if someone walked in on us?"

"The door's locked," he said.

"Oh, okay then, you can continue."

"Hey Jor?" Adele said as he opened the door.

Kilan was a bit at a loss for words at what she saw.

"It's not what it looks like," Lyra said quickly.

"Jor on top, Lyra at the bottom? That looks like a lot of things," Kilan said.

"You could have just left the door locked," Adele said.

"I guess that was my folly," Jor said with an embarrassed smile.

"We'll just leave you two then," Kilan said as she pulled Adele. "Name one of the kids after me."

Lyra got up and made sure the door was locked, then turned to look at Jor.

"We have to have our own place when this is all over with," she said. She lay down next to him.

"What kind of house would you want?" Jor asked.

"I dunno, nothing fancy like a castle."

"A cabin in the woods?"

"Not a small cabin, but that would do."

"Really?"

"Yeah, with a cabin, you can say you built it yourself. And if we ever have kids, they'll know all about nature. They'll be free to see it up close and not out of a book."

"Like you?"

"Like me I guess."

The two sat in silence for a moment, imagining how that could be.

"So we never decided on where we were going," Jor said.

"I could have an adventure right here," she said as she kissed him.

"I thought you said..."

She continued to kiss him, cutting him off.

"I don't think I can keep up with all this," Jane said as she sat next to Turner in the Palace's garden.

"What do you mean?" he asked.

"I'm going home, the tower needs me, and I'm sure they're worried sick."

Turner sighed. "I'm sure they are."

"I was hoping, though I would be asking too much, if you would come with me."

"All the way back up past Crill?"

"Yep."

"That's a long way you know, and I don't know what crazy adventure Jor and the others will be on next."

"So you'll stay with them?"

Turner got up, as did she. He looked down into her eyes, and she did the same.

"I love you Jane, I hope you know that."

"I do Turner."

"I'm coming with you, and no matter what you're grumpy fathers says, I'll love you."

"So when do we get ready?"

"We should start now, the earlier the better."

"Such sweet children these two are," Alda said as she watched Ema and Haima play quietly with several little toys.

"Yes, they are," Zen muttered, reading a petition from the people.

"So who'll take care of them full time?"

Zen grunted a reply.

"Well?"

"Oh, we are."

"Take care of these two? But we're just children ourselves," Alda said, a bit fearfully.

"Children don't save countries, fight monsters and protect the lives of the innocent, grown men and women do that."

"But I've never taken care of children before. I only know combat."

"We'll go through this together Alda. Do you promise to be at my side?" Zen asked, putting down the petition.

"You know I do."

Zen reached into his pocket and pulled out a ring.

"The people of Zeran have petitioned for a strong Queen. Can you be that Queen?"

"Yes!" she said as she leapt up and embraced him.

They both turned to see Ema and Haima laughing and clapping.

Zen took up Ema and Alda took up Haima.

"It seems they're happy about this too," Alda said.

"The whole of Zeran is happy about it," Zen laughed.

"Hey Zen," Jor said as he entered.

"Oh Jor, what is it?" he asked.

"It seems we may be splitting up," Turner said.

"Yeah," Kilan added.

They all stood in the lobby next to the throne room.

"I was hoping you all would stay for a little while longer, but I guess that was too much to ask," Zen said with a small smile.

"It was good knowing you Zen," Turner said as he shook his hand. "Amec would have been proud to be your advisor."

"He would have," Jor said as he shook Zen's hand next.

"You were good friends and allies to me," Zen said. "You'll be remembered."

"Now Adele, I expect you to take good care of Kilan," Jane said.

"Like he takes care of me in general," Kilan said, rolling her eyes.

"You'll have your hands full," Turner laughed.

"Damn right," Adele said, and Kilan punched him on the arm.

"So where are you headed?" Jor asked.

"Hm, maybe we'll go to Sepal," he replied.

"We'll get to see Alice, won't we?" Kilan said.

"We've been through a lot, I'll miss you Adele," Jor said as he and Adele shook hands.

"For my brother in arms," Turner said as he shook his hand as well.

"Veterans must stick together," Jor joked.

"I wish. More battles may be ahead. I just wish I could have you at my side." Turner embraced Jor, and he did the same.

"Till we meet again eh?" he said.

"Till we meet again," Jor said.

They all took one last look at each other, and left the palace.

Jor took a good look at Zeran as he and Lyra rode out into the deserts.

"Come on Jor, gawking won't help any," Lyra said.

"I know, I'm coming..."

Several Longboats broke through the fog that surrounded the harbor at Holmes. They went alongside its high cliff side and threw up grappling hooks. The Raiders slowly made their way up.

"Hurry it up," Joralkar said. "We won't take Cardia at this snail's pace..."

The pieces of this puzzle are moving together, on the verge, but yet so far, from solving the enigma that would follow. Cardia will not be the same again in the near future, and soon, the whole of Edafos will all hang in the balance. The stage is set for another war as the Great Deneaux Empire advances upon new lands, but this will shake Edafos to its very bones.

About the Author

Howard Jones grew up in the U.S. Virgin Islands, a place that highly values its youth and will readily push them forward. He had begun writing and drawing at a young age, though mostly as a hobby. This hobby soon became somewhat of an unattainable goal. There can be no master writer, as it is an ever developing art. Howard aims to improve his skill, experimenting in all forms of fiction, be it sci-fi, Asian fantasy and even steampunk. A writer can only get better as he writes, be it to please themselves, or those around them.